SUMMER OF 1984

VICTORIA MAXWELL

Also by Victoria Maxwell

Class of 1983 | Santolsa Saga Book 1

For the big dreamers and hopeless romantics

Prologue

Sister Helena appeared out of a small room at the end of the abbey. The room had been built to hide a magical time traveling portal which the three nuns (who also happened to be witches) had opened in the Nevada desert. They had built the abbey around the portal to protect it, and had called this abbey St. Christopher's, after the patron saint of time travel.

"Where have you been?" Sister Maria scowled at Helena. A new deep wrinkle had formed on her forehead.

Sister Helena had discovered she was exceptionally gifted at time magic, and so while the other two nuns had been busy building the abbey, Helena had travelled three years into the future, hoping the building would be done. Helena was impatient, and spending her days in the desert heat, building the abbey with her bare hands, was more than she could stand.

Helena didn't even really need to use the time portal. She could easily hop from year to year through her intention alone, but there was great power in the room at the end of the abbey, and she felt each time she entered it, her magic became stronger.

With the help of Helena's magical talents, the three witch nuns had moved forward to a better time. Witches were no longer being hunted and killed and living in the desert had been relatively peaceful. Although, Helena had been going out of her mind with boredom and manual labor.

"I was so very tired of waiting for the abbey to be built," Helena said, tucking back a long tendril of her golden blonde hair, that had come loose from her habit. "So, I travelled forward to see if you had finished."

"Helena," admonished Sister Maria. "This is a great misuse of your power. Poor Sister Catherine and I have been breaking our backs to finish this abbey alone. Sister Catherine was worried sick."

"Were you not worried sick, Sister Maria?"

"I knew you would turn up somewhere in time, and it does not surprise me that you used your magic to escape from your chores yet again. But *three years* of chores Helena? Even for you, this is disgraceful."

Helena looked down at her dusty shoes beneath the thick skirt of her habit.

Sister Maria gestured to the simple wooden walls. "As you can see, we are indeed not yet finished, no thanks to you."

The basic structure was complete, but it certainly didn't look comfortable in the way Helena would have liked. She sighed inwardly. She knew she should have journeyed another year or two further along the line of time.

"Perhaps if you had stayed to help us, we would have been able to build it quicker," said Maria, turning back down the hallway and towards the kitchens and sleeping quarters.

Helena was quick on her heels. "Why do I have this magic if I cannot use it?"

"It is time for you to grow up," said Maria sternly.

"I'll be sixteen in June," said Helena. "I'm practically an old maid."

"Don't be so ridiculous, girl," Maria said. She was by far the oldest of the group and wouldn't let them forget it.

When they reached the kitchens, Sister Catherine dropped a spoon into the pot of soup on the stove and came running towards them. "Sister Helena! I am so glad you are back!" She threw her arms around the girl and Helena embraced her in return. Helena liked Catherine. She was a beautiful and sweet lost sheep who would blindly follow Maria off the ends of the earth if Maria went that way, but she had a good heart. Helena suspected perhaps even Maria had a good heart underneath it all, but it seemed shielded with many iron bars and no one was allowed too close.

There was a time when Helena was thought of as a young witch with no power and little intelligence, but Helena had proven them wrong. She was the one to find this place of power, the place where many energy lines met. She'd felt it and used it to create a time portal all on her own, while the others had been walking around the desert like fools. When Helena realized she had developed such powerful time magic, she began to move through time as easily as if she was swimming in a stream. She rarely went too far without the others, just a few years back or forward, but she longed to travel even further ahead than they had already. She wanted to see the world, perhaps a hundred, or two hundred years into the future. She wanted to see a better world, one in which people were no longer persecuted for their beliefs or abilities.

"You must fix this timeline at once, Sister Helena." Sister Maria's face was red with frustration. "We must be careful with time magic. We did not create the time portal to use time magic for personal gain, only to protect ourselves. We must remember that. We keep to ourselves, keep the portal hidden. We must avoid accidents at all costs."

Catherine nodded in agreement.

"Whatever you say, dear Sister Maria," Helena said. "I shall be off then, and will see you again three years ago."

"Oh, Helena," said Catherine. "You must be careful. Do not get lost in time to us."

"I would never get lost in time," Helena laughed.

"Time magic has the potential to create much chaos," Sister Maria said.

Helena rolled her eyes. "It has created no chaos as yet. If anything, my magic and this portal have been a wondrous help to us all."

And with that, she walked back towards the small room at the end of the abbey. She walked into the room, said a simple spell under her breath, and three flashes like lightning later, she was gone again.

ONE

Popcorn

Jack stood staring at the microwave, watching the jalapeno flavored popcorn go around and around. His thoughts began to drift, like they always did when they were left unchecked, to Magz. No, not Magz, *Peggy*. She was Peggy now. His heart ached at the thought of her, whatever her name was now. He thought about her back in time, in what would now be 1984 for her, and what she might be doing right now. Would she be dating Sammy Ruthven? Would she even still be in Santolsa? Jack thought about the key he had been carrying around in his pocket these last few months and the meeting he'd had with Old Peggy at the diner. She'd looked as beautiful as ever, even though she was old enough to be his mom now. She'd passed him the key in a white envelope and told him it was his "destiny". Jack had never really been into the whole destiny idea. He'd always thought you made your own way in the world. You made your own choices and destiny was just something sad girls made up to give them hope that their knight in shining armor would one day appear. But the key in Jack's pocket was burning a destiny shaped hole in his pants. The idea that he was supposed to go back there, to travel through time, maybe to even have some kind of life with Peggy back there, it truly terrified him. Jack was no time traveling hero. He couldn't travel through time - it was insane. If he hadn't seen it with his own eyes - Peggy walking into the book room, the flashes of light, her disappearing, he wouldn't have believed it in a million years. If he hadn't met Sammy Ruthven as an old man who knew exactly who he was…

The microwave beeped and Jack reached in for his steaming bag of popcorn. He slowly opened the top of the packet, cursing as it burned him, and then poured it into a big glass bowl. He added some garlic salt, a dash of cinnamon and chili powder for extra heat. He shook the bowl around, grabbed a can of soda from the fridge and headed up the stairs of his little small-town house to his bedroom.

He sat down on his unmade bed, turned on his laptop and searched through his files until he found the second season of *Quantum Leap*. He double clicked on the episode he was up to and let it play until he fell asleep in his popcorn crumb-filled bed. Tux, Peggy's tuxedo cat that Jack had adopted when she left, curled up by his feet as always.

His phone buzzed at three in the morning and woke him.

"Sup?" it said.

Jayne.

Jack groaned. Like he needed to think about Jayne right now. Jayne was kind of great in so many ways, but he couldn't remember the last time she'd messaged or called him during daylight hours. He was starting to think he was nothing more than a booty call to her. He wasn't sure she even had feelings for him, she most definitely didn't love him. He wasn't even sure he had real feelings for her if he was being honest with himself. She was hot, and they had a lot of fun together, but she wasn't the girl he loved.

But the girl he loved wasn't here, and Jayne was probably finishing up work at the Stables, the biker bar on the edge of town. He threw his phone down. He did not want to be her booty call. He had never wanted that, but what he wanted didn't want him, so what other choice did he have but to drown his sorrows in free tequila and Jayne's attention?

He looked over at the key on his nightstand, glinting in the streetlight.

He closed his eyes and wished it all away. He didn't want to time travel. He just wanted things to be how they were before, when Peggy was still Magz and their lives sucked together, when they had plans to get out of here, *together*. Plans that Jack had not put to any use so far. His dad had gotten him a junior office clerk job at the law firm where he worked. It sucked, but it was a job, and he needed it. He barely had enough money to get the bus home from Salt Valley on the days his dad worked late and couldn't give him a ride. He would have to put in some serious overtime if he was ever going to get to LA.

His phone buzzed again.

"Wanna meet up or what?"

Jack ignored it and closed his eyes, and when he fell asleep, he dreamed of thrift shopping with Magz, strange popcorn flavors and rabid dogs chasing him down dark alleys.

"Mom," Jack said the next morning after he'd cuddled and fed Tux and sat down for bagels and coffee. "I was thinking I might take a trip this summer."

His mom nearly dropped the coffee pot on him. "Where to?" she asked, wiping down some coffee she'd spilled. She put the pot down and sat next to him. She pushed her dark bob behind one ear and looked at him intensely.

Jack shrugged it off. His mom was always acting kind of weird these days. He just thought it was because of the money stuff. They were still trying to dig themselves out of stupid amounts of debt from when his dad had tried and failed to start his own firm.

"I was thinking I might go see Magz at her college," he improvised. "She's just started summer break and she said I should come visit. Her parents aren't home, so she has no reason to come back for the summer." He hated lying, but it's not like he could tell his mom about the time traveling portal in the book room at St. Christopher's High School.

"Are you sure she wants you there?" His mom topped up his still full coffee cup, concern in her dark eyes.

"She told me herself that she wanted me there," he said.

"Let's talk about this tonight, with your dad."

"I know what Dad will say," Jack said, rolling his eyes. "I'm never gonna get time off from work."

His mom gave him an anxious look. "Maybe it's not the best time. Perhaps you can stay a while longer."

"Mom, my life is so boring right now. If I don't do this I may crack. I would really love to do something cool this summer."

It was one thing for Peggy to go time traveling and be missing from the present for weeks at a time, her parents hadn't even noticed she was gone. There was that one whole week when Peggy was in 1983, that they thought she was just in bed sick. Jack's parents would definitely notice if he disappeared into the past and never came back.

Jack bit into a piece of bagel and chewed. His mom started flicking frantically through the calendar on the wall.

TWO

The Stables

_____

Jack parked his bicycle between two Harley Davidsons, changed out of his sweaty blue t-shirt and into a fresh black one from his satchel, and swept his hands through his dark hair.

He'd been thinking all day about his decision. He was scared out of his mind about time traveling, but he had decided he was done with just sitting around thinking about it. About _her_. He had planned to talk to both his parents at dinner about taking off for the summer, but his dad had to stay late at the office again and his mom was still being weird, so as soon as it was late enough for the Stables to be open, Jack got on his bike and rode over there.

The Stables was a total dive. It was frequented by low-lives - bikers, criminals, strippers, but it was still one of the coolest and safest places in town for Jack to hang out. High school was over, but his tormentors still wanted his blood. With Mindy working at the coffee shop, Big Mick working at the gas station and Jim in training to be a local cop, there weren't many places in Santolsa left for him to go.

Even with the expanse of the desert in all directions around their little town, he often felt like a caged bird.

Jack had naively thought after high school everything would change. He thought the bullies would grow up and move on with their lives, but if anything, things were getting even worse. The thought that Jim, the kid who had slammed him up against a locker almost daily for his entire high school career, would be graduating from the police academy to become a police officer on the streets of his town was just too much to handle.

And here was Jack, with a way out in the pocket of his faded black skinny jeans. He put his hand in his pocket and thumbed the key.

"'Sup stranger?"

Jack looked up. He was sitting at the bar with no recollection of how he'd walked in and sat down.

His stomach lurched as he looked up at Jayne. She really was gorgeous. Her long dark hair and dark red lips were enough to drive him wild without the added torment of her low-cut black tank top.

He shook his head. "Sorry, I was somewhere else."

"So, what else is new?" She gave him one of her disappointed looks that he was becoming so familiar with. She flipped the top off a beer bottle and handed it over to him. "You have to pay tonight, the manager is in."

Jack swore under his breath and scrambled in his pocket for some change.

"I'll cover this one," said Jayne, "but that's it."

"That's it?" asked Jack, feeling like this conversation was maybe about something else.

"I can't keep doing this Jack." She rolled her dark sexy eyes.

"What are you talking about?" He took a long swig from the bottle.

"Us," she said. She went to serve a group of bikers while Jack sat and stared at his beer.

"Hey, kid." It was the old guy with the ponytail from the night he and Peggy were last here together. Jonas. The one who tried to kiss her in 1983.

Jack groaned. "What do you want?"

"I just wanted to say hey, see how you were doing."

"Why?"

"Let me buy you a drink."

"Why?" asked Jack again, and then he let Jonas buy him a drink anyway.

Jonas bought him a whiskey and coke, patted him on the shoulder and walked off.

It was one thing to let Jayne pass him a free drink over the bar. It was another thing completely to let some guy who tried to force himself on Peggy buy him a drink. He had one sip and then pushed it away. This was a new low.

"Why are you talking to Jonas?" Jayne asked when she was done serving everyone else.

"Why are you always hassling me?" asked Jack. He knew he was being a jerk, but Jayne had been calling all the shots since they'd hooked up and now, he couldn't even get a free drink out of it.

"Wow, OK, where did that come from?" she asked.

"I don't know. I'm just gonna go. I don't even know why I came here." He waved a hand in her direction and then walked out without looking back.

Jack was always just a little relieved to see his bike still there, and he was just about to get on and ride home when Jayne came running out of the bar.

"Jack!" she called, running up to him.

He just looked at her.

"I'm sorry about tonight." She shook her head.

Jack just kept looking at her.

"I just, I don't think we should keep doing what we're doing." She folded her arms.

Jack said nothing. He had nothing *to* say. She was so beautiful, but he didn't *feel* anything. He felt like he wanted to touch her, but he didn't feel that *thing* you're supposed to feel. He didn't feel that thing he felt for Peggy. But he still hated the idea of not being with Jayne. He hated the idea that she would stop calling, that he wouldn't be able to come here and see her, that he'd never get to see her naked again.

"It's not working Jack. I thought we could make this no-strings thing work, but I don't think you can do no-strings. Even with no-strings I still want you to be present with me."

"Present?"

"You're always thinking about Magz. *Always*. It's so obvious." She looked defeated.

"She calls herself Peggy now," Jack said.

"See?"

"I was only coming here tonight to tell you it was over," he blurted. Jayne had been a beautiful distraction, but she was right. Even when they had been together, his mind was always only ten percent with her. "You're right," he said.

"OK, that's not what I was expecting," she said.

"No, you're right. I've been unfair to you and I'm sorry," Jack frowned. Jayne was amazing and she deserved better.

"Hey," she said, moving in close to him and running a hand down his arm. She put her lips next to his ear. She smelled like dark chocolate cherry lip balm and stale tequila. "Maybe we can say goodbye at my place later?"

It took everything he had to gently push her away. "I can't," he said. "It's been swell."

"It's been swell? We've been hanging out for nearly a year now and all I get is an *it's been swell?*"

"What else do you want from me?"

"I want you to *want* me," she said, throwing her arms in the air.

"I *do* want you… but I don't *love* you and that's what I want. And you deserve someone who loves you, and I do too. I think."

And he got back on his bike and rode down the highway and back into town.

THREE

Dee's

It was nearly midnight, but Dee's was still open, and Jack wasn't ready to go home. He left his bike leaning on a streetlight out the front and grabbed a booth where he could keep an eye on it.

He kind of liked being at Dee's late. There was one sad old looking guy sat at the counter reading the paper and drinking the disgusting bottomless coffee, and one group of couples about his parents' age all laughing and talking loudly as if they'd been out drinking all night for the first time in years.

A smiley middle-aged waitress with frizzy hair with a name tag reading "Amy" came over to take his order. He reached into his pocket and pulled out what little money he had. He ordered a coffee and a stack of onion rings and looked between his phone and his bike while he waited. A cute cat video caught his attention and he was chuckling to himself when the waitress came back with his order.

"Uh, is that your bike out there?" she asked.

Jack looked up still smiling from the video. "Huh?"

The waitress was looking past him to where he had left

his bike. Jack looked out the window to see Jim, Big Mick and a gang of their friends taking turns riding his bike down the street. Jack felt a big ball of fire ignite in his stomach. Big Mick flipped his mid-length curly blonde locks and waved at Jack through the window, blowing him a kiss. They still thought Jack was gay. Most people in town did. It takes a lot to change a rumor like that. In fact, Jack was sure if he stayed in this town it would never change.

Jack was seething, but more than anything, he felt stupid. He knew it was dumb to come into town, but he thought maybe, just this once, he could eat a stack of onion rings in peace. Big Mick began doing some weird rodeo moves on Jack's bike, pretending he was riding a bull, while his friends laughed and pointed through the window at Jack.

Jack couldn't look at Big Mick without thinking about how he'd taken Peggy's virginity, lied to her and treated her like absolute crap, and once again, that was the worst thing of all. That was the thing that made him move.

Jack slapped his hands on the table and stood up.

"What're you gonna do?" asked the waitress, looking worried.

"I can't just sit and watch this." The sick feeling in Jack's stomach demanded a fight or flight response. His legs started walking before his brain could tell him not to, and soon he was standing on the street watching as Jim kicked one of the wheels of his bike out of shape. This guy was joining the police force. There really was no hope for humanity.

"Look who's come out of hiding," Big Mick laughed.

"All right guys, just give me back my bike and I'll go home," said Jack. A pathetic attempt to avoid a beating. He was almost ashamed of himself. But what chance did he really have against this group of thugs? His anger had cooled and turned into a desire to live at any cost.

Jim scoffed. "You think we're gonna just give you back your bike and let you go?"

"High school is over, man," Jack said. "We're grown-ups now, so let's act like it."

"We're grown-ups now," Big Mick mocked. "Hey, where's Magz these days? She was such a werido, but I gotta tell you Jack, it was really fun popping her ch…"

Everything went black and Jack didn't realize he was punching Big Mick in the face until he had done it. He didn't realize he was kneeing Big Mick in the groin until he was doubled over on the ground in pain. And Jack didn't realize he had kicked Big Mick in the stomach until two pairs of hands were pulling him off.

If he thought he had given Big Mick a beating it was nothing compared to what he was about to receive.

Amy came rushing out and started yelling at the boys to stop, but they just ignored her. She grabbed her phone out of her pocket and dialed 911 and prayed someone would come soon.

Jack regained consciousness in a hospital bed later the next day. His whole body ached, and it hurt to open his eyes, so he kept them closed, but he could hear the comforting tones of his parents talking in the corner of his room.

"It's time," said his dad. "We've got to let him go Pat."

"No, I'm not ready, I want more time with him," said his mom.

"We've had our time with him, we need to let him go."

His mom started sobbing.

"Mom?" Jack squeaked, slowly opening his eyes. "Am I dying?"

His mom laughed through her sobs. "No darling, we were just talking about letting you go to see Peggy for a while."

"I don't think…" Jack moaned as he felt a pain in his ribs. It was hard to talk. "I don't think I can stay here," he managed.

Jack's dad pulled a chair up next to the bed. His bald head shining under the fluorescent lights, his thick aviator glasses couldn't hide that he had been crying too.

"Take it easy, Jack," said his dad. "You have a lot of bruising and a couple of cracked ribs. We're going to prosecute. I already spoke to the guys at the firm. This has gone on long enough. Amy at the diner said she's willing to be a witness and there were a few other people there we can call to the stand. We can try to get it pushed through as quick as possible, but it could take a few months, maybe longer."

Jack groaned. "I just want to get out of here," he slurred. He must have been on some heavy drugs. He felt weird. "I think I really… just wanna go to see Peggy… back in 1984…"

And the last thing he remembered was the sounds of his mom crying.

FOUR

The Eights

A searing pain in his upper arm woke Jack. The room was dark, and it took him a second to remember he was in the Salt Valley hospital. The hallway lights illuminated the room just enough for him to see the outlines of two men standing either side of him, one holding a knife, and a woman standing in front of the door.

Just as he was about to let out a cry for help a hand covered his mouth stopping him.

"Don't suffocate him." The woman's voice sounded like deep sweet syrup.

"Jayne?" Jack asked groggily through the hand. The pain killers were still messing with his head. He wondered if he was dreaming, but his heart was beating so fast there was no way this wasn't real.

Jayne rushed over to his side, swapping places with the man and sitting down next to him.

"It's OK, baby," she whispered as she brushed his hair back from his face.

Jack flinched at the pain in his arm again. "What are

you…?" he asked as he started to struggle again, pain searing through his ribs as well as his arm.

Jayne put her own hand over his mouth. "Just shut up and listen," she said. "You're an honorary Eight now."

Jack tried to squirm away from the man with the knife, but the pain wouldn't stop.

"And if you don't stop struggling, you're gonna mess up your tattoo," she said.

Jack started hyperventilating.

"I'll let go if you promise not to scream."

Jack nodded, although he wasn't sure he could promise anything.

Jayne slowly moved her hand away from his mouth and Jack could breathe again, at least until he looked over at his arm where the man was cutting into his flesh.

"Stop, stop it! Get off me!" he yelled.

Jayne put her hand back over his mouth.

"We heard about what happened to you," she said, her dark eyes glistening in the blinking lights of the hospital machines. "And so, I got some friends to go over there and, well, you're not going to have any more problems with those guys, I promise."

Jack glared at her, confusion and anger in his eyes.

"I'm an Eight, Jack," she said bluntly. Like the fact that she was a member of one of the most dangerous biker gangs in the whole country was something normal. Maybe it was to her, but it definitely wasn't to him.

The pain finally stopped, and the man wiped his work down with what smelled like an antiseptic cloth. Jack could see the outline of the shape of an eight cut into his arm. He began hitting his head against the pillow.

"Baby," Jayne said again.

When did she start calling him baby? Jack had never been scared of Jayne. Intimidated by her, definitely. She was an older woman, she was very hot, and way out of his league, but he'd never been scared of her like he was now. She was so strong, and there was something in her eyes that unnerved him.

He looked at the darkened flesh on his arm and wondered how not one member of the hospital staff had realized this was going on. How could he be here getting mutilated while the nurses went about their rounds and coffee breaks?

His fuzzy brain finally made the connection. Of course, Jayne had the same tattoo. A snake in the shape of an eight, the head eating the tail. It wasn't on her arm though, it was on her lower back. If only he'd known what he was getting into.

As his breathing began to slow again, she removed her hand.

He glared at her.

"Jack," she said. "I couldn't just let them do this to you and not do anything."

"You and me, Jayne, we're not even together!"

The man who had tattooed him wiped his arm a few more times and put gauze over it. "It's not perfect, but it'll do," he said.

"You can always get it touched up later at a tattoo studio," the other man said.

"Jonas?" asked Jack, frowning into the darkness.

"Hey, kid," said Jonas.

"What the actual fuck, Jayne?" Jack sat up a little in bed, ignoring the pain in his chest and putting his hand on his arm. It hurt like hell. His whole body hurt like hell.

"I still care about you," she said.

"You had no right to do this to me." A tear formed in his eye. All he had wanted was to go to the bar, get a few drinks, see Jayne, maybe get laid, say goodbye and then go home so he could talk to his mom and dad in the morning about going to see Peggy. And then, after his morning coffee and donuts, he'd time travel back to 1984 and be with her forever.

But now here he was, with a cracked rib, a psychopathic ex-not-even-girlfriend, a guy who'd just cut a snake into his arm, and Jonas.

"It's too late," Jayne shrugged. "You're one of us now."

Jack didn't know what else to do, and so he just cried. Tears fell fast and hot over his face and into his pillow. It was the first time he'd cried in, he didn't even know how long, but once he'd started it was like the Niagara Falls of tears falling out of his eyes.

Jayne just sat there watching him, and the men kept watch by the door.

"Sorry baby." She reached for his hand, but he pulled it away. "But we were just protecting you, and that tatt will keep you safe now."

"I don't want it, and I don't want you, I don't want any of this. I just want to be with Peggy and be away from here!"

Jayne looked hurt and stood up. "We can talk about this later, when you're off the meds and your tatt has healed. But there is no going back. You can't go back Jack, only forward."

"That's what you think." Jack kicked his legs under the blankets.

Jayne gave him a look. "Come on guys, I think Jack needs some rest."

Jack wiped his snotty face on the hospital pillow.

"Jayne, wait!"

She stopped to look back at him. She really was so pretty, and he could see in her eyes that she really did care about him, even if her actions were incredibly misguided, completely illegal and definitely not OK in any world.

"Why didn't you tell me? And why didn't you just ask if I wanted this?"

"Because I didn't want you to say no, and then go get beat up by those jerks again without our protection. We might not be dating anymore, or whatever we were doing, but I want you to be safe Jack, wherever you are, whoever you're with." She gave him a sad smile and walked out of his room, Jonas and the other guy following behind him.

Jack stared at the ceiling and wished this wasn't happening.

He was an Eight now, a Crazy Eight. This was not the life he had wanted for himself.

He wished he could be as far away from here as possible.

He rolled over as much as he could stand with the pain in his ribs, his arm, his face, and he cried himself to sleep.

FIVE

Diamondback

Jack sat up in his hospital bed. It had been three weeks since what everyone was referring to as "the incident" and he was feeling much better physically. His face no longer hurt, although it still didn't look quite back to normal. His ribs were still tender, but he could breathe without being in pain now.

Emotionally though, it was a different story.

He was doing a pretty good job of keeping his tattoo hidden. When he was wearing a t-shirt it only half covered the tattoo, so when his parents were visiting, he put on a sweatshirt and complained about feeling cold, even though he was melting. Everyone just assumed it was from shock, or the pain killers or something.

He found he almost forgot he had a tattoo at times, and then gave himself a shock when he went to take a shower and saw himself shirtless in the mirror. The guy had actually done a surprisingly good job. The knife must have had some kind of black ink attached to it. It looked just like a bad shop tattoo, not something done in the dark with a kitchen knife. The nurses had seen it, of course, but he just told them he got it done the day he'd come in.

Jack thought his parents were cracking. His mom was always tearing up and grabbing his hand and hugging him awkwardly in the bed. His dad had sat and watched whole seasons of *Quantum Leap*, *Family Ties* and *Breaking Bad* on the laptop with him.

Strangely enough, in many ways, it was one of the best times Jack had ever had. There were moments when he still thought he might actually be dying and maybe everyone was just keeping it from him. His mom was still acting like she was never going to see him again, but mostly, it had just been really nice hanging out with them. No work, no school, just watching old TV shows with his dad, his mom falling asleep reading a book on the chair in the corner. He felt safe here. He felt cared for. But he was also missing his bedroom back home, and he missed Tux's little fluffy face.

"I feel fine. Can I go home now?" Jack asked his dad as another episode finished.

"I'm not sure, son." His dad rubbed the stubble on his chin.

"This is going to be costing you and mom a fortune. I'm OK, I'm well enough to go see Peggy." Jack flinched as he tried to lift himself higher in the bed.

His dad looked at him with concern in his grey eyes. "You're still not well, Jack. But maybe we can take care of you back home for a while, before you go see Peggy."

Jack knew this hospital stay would be hemorrhaging them cash. He felt a pang of something - guilt, sadness, maybe it was love, in his chest for his parents. He wanted to get out of this town so bad, but he also wanted to be here to help them.

"Don't worry about us," said his dad as if reading his mind. "We are going to be fine. Me and Patty will get back on our feet soon. I haven't given up my dream yet, Jackson. And you shouldn't give up on yours either."

Jack rolled his eyes at his dad's use of his full name.

His dad patted his leg. "I'll go talk to the nurse and see what we could do for you at home."

Later that evening Jack was back home, dressed in a comfy grey t-shirt and sleep shorts, lying in his bed staring at the ceiling. His mind churned through the events of the last few weeks and eventually, as it always did, landed on Peggy. He thought of that night she had been here with him. She had slept in this bed with him. They hadn't *done* anything, they'd just slept next to each other, but to Jack, it had been so much more intimate than any of the times he'd slept with Jayne. He thought about the way he had reached over and put his arm around her while he was half asleep in the night. It was as if his arm had a mind of its own, as if he was being pulled to her magnetically. He'd woken up early with his arm still around her, and in that moment all he could think was how much he wanted to wake up every morning with her in his arms, just like this. She'd freaked out, but he knew she felt something too, and now something within him had changed. He'd faced death now. Well, kind of, but it had made him really think about life, and now, staying here just wasn't an option. He wanted to be able to leave the house without fear. He wanted to be able to eat onion rings in public without getting his face kicked in. He wanted to wipe his slate clean and start all over.

He was ready to go. He was ready to use the key and he couldn't wait to see what their future held. He wasn't scared anymore. Whatever happened, it would be better than staying here. He coughed and his ribs ached. He wanted to just run to her, to take the key and go. But his body was a mess, and he didn't want her to see him as poor pathetic loser Jack, getting beaten up again. When he saw her next, he would be different. He would be strong and confident, and he would also be an Eight. The thought of having to explain that to Peggy was petrifying. But if she loved him too, she would be OK with it. She wouldn't care, she'd just be glad he was with her.

"My sweet pea," said his mom, startling him. She was standing at the door with a bowl of soup and bread triangles on the side. She looked like she was as in as much pain as he was.

"I'm fine, Mom," Jack said.

"You're my little boy." Her dark eyes glistened in the corners. "I just can't stand to see you like this."

Jack rolled his eyes at her like he was thirteen, not going on nineteen.

She put the soup and bread triangles on the nightstand and then sat down on the bed next to him, something she hadn't done for years, and looked at him with so much love and pain and sadness in her eyes. Jack quickly pulled the blanket up over his arm, but it was too late. She moved the blanket away and pushed up his t-shirt sleeve, and then she started crying. Again.

"Mom, it's not what you think." If she knew what this tattoo meant, and by her tears it seemed likely, she probably thought he joined up himself. "They did it to me, I didn't want it." He reached out to grab her hand.

"It's not that," she said through her tears before

running out of his room, past his dad who was hanging back at the door holding a stack of books.

"Is Mom OK? She seems to be losing it."

His dad walked into the room and put a pile of old paperbacks on the nightstand next to the soup. "She will be. It's just a lot, seeing your kid beaten up." He gave Jack a sad smile. "I know you said you couldn't watch any more TV, so I brought you some of my favorite old westerns." His dad tapped the top of the pile of books.

Jack picked one up. *Diamondback: Dead Man's Hand*. On the tattered cover was a vintage painting of a guy with a cool moustache and a redhead with her clothes half falling off. Jack laughed. "Dad, I can't read these, they are way too embarrassing."

"Diamondback got me through some tough times," his dad said.

Jack shook his head and reached for one of the bread triangles.

"Try it before you think you're too cool for it," his dad winked. "I'll let you get some rest and I'll go check on your mom."

Jack knew it would be awhile before he would be ready to go see Peggy, but the more he rested now, the quicker it would be until she was in his arms, so he grabbed the first book on the stack. They looked hilariously terrible, but when Jack had lost an hour falling right into one of them, he kept reading and hoped that Cord Diamondback's world could hold him until he was ready to find his own world, somewhere, some*when*.

Interlude I

"We need assistance," said Sister Maria over dinner one night. "We three alone cannot protect this portal of great magic."

Sister Helena sighed. They had made some good progress building the abbey, but her hands had begun to look like those of an old woman and her back was aching from carrying timber all day long and sleeping on a hard bed all night. Sister Maria insisted they always wear their nun's habits, although they hadn't seen another person for months. The summer heat was beginning to become unbearable and the nights were so cold Helena often thought she would freeze to death. Maria had said they would rebuild the walls in stone one day, when they had more money and time, but right now, a rickety wooden abbey would be all they could hope for. Helena had laughed so very hard at that. They could get more time in an instant, and she was sure there were ways they could use this time magic to get more money.

"You said if we built the abbey over the circle that it

would be protected," complained Helena, ripping into a loaf of bread.

"The abbey is just one form of protection," said Maria.

"Why did you not speak of this earlier?" Helena frowned down into her bean stew. "We have been slaving away this entire time, for what?"

Sister Catherine gave her a concerned look. "The portal is too strong for us to close now. That means it will be open forever. If we don't find a way to protect it, anyone could travel through time."

"I am tired of this," said Helena, ignoring Catherine's worries. "I am tired of this life of a nun. I want to fall in love and marry and be free of you both." She pulled up her skirts and kicked her feet up on the chair opposite her.

"And what man would have you, when you have been secretly using time magic to avoid chores and to stop yourself from aging?" asked Maria.

Helena gasped. "I have done nothing of the sort," she lied.

"Perhaps we do need some men," began Catherine.

"Out of the question," said Maria.

"Perhaps they could help protect the circle," Catherine suggested.

"And they could help with the heavy lifting," said Helena excitedly.

"We are not safe around men. We all know what men are capable of."

Sister Catherine cleared her throat. "We blame the men, and yet we must not forget about our sisters who pointed their fingers at us. It may have been the men who tried to hang us, but it was our fellow sisters who turned on us."

The women ate in silence for a few moments.

"Perhaps you are right," said Sister Maria eventually, through gritted teeth. "We are not immortal. One day we will be gone, and we will need others to continue to keep the portal safe."

"How shall we proceed, Sister Maria?" asked Catherine.

"We will create an order to protect the circle," Maria decided. "They must never know what they are protecting, for their own safety and the safety of all. They will protect it, forever and always, in all directions of time."

"What will we call this order?" asked Catherine.

"The Order of the Eights," suggested Helena through a mouthful of bread.

Maria looked at her blankly.

"All directions of time, the lemniscate, infinity?" Helena explained, as if Maria was too simple-minded to understand. "The symbol of the Eight is strong, it has no end. The eight will hold the power of forever and always."

"Yes," said Maria with just a touch of bitterness. "That is good, Helena."

"How will we select these guardians?" asked Catherine.

"We will trust God to bring them at the right time," said Maria.

The next morning, two bewildered looking men appeared at the front door of the abbey.

Helena rushed to push the heavy door open and invite them in, before Maria could stop her.

"Welcome strangers," she smiled.

They walked in, looking around in awe at the abbey.

"What brings you this way?" she asked.

They looked at each other.

"We got lost," said the one Helena thought was better

looking. He was dressed in a plain pair of brown trousers and a beige shirt, with tousled blonde hair.

"Where did you travel from?" she asked.

"The mountains," said the other one who was quite gruff, with much darker features. He wore suspenders to hold up his trousers.

"We were on our way to California," the blonde one said.

"To make our fortune," said the other.

"Your fortune?" asked Helena quickly, hearing the other women coming up behind her.

"Yes, there's gold out there waiting to be found, didn't you know?" the blonde one asked excitedly.

Helena squealed. "Gold! Oh my!"

"Thank you, Helena. And who are our guests?" asked Maria.

"I do believe these are the men we asked God for," said Helena.

The men looked at her with wide eyes.

"Were you sent to us by God?" Maria asked.

The men gaped at each other.

The blonde one nodded. "Why, yes, I think perhaps we were. We were praying last night out by the fire that we'd be led to where we needed to be, and then we got lost and there was nothing for miles but this one dwelling."

"Dwelling?" Maria frowned. "*This* is an abbey."

The gruff man made a face. "This don't look like any abbey I've seen before."

"It was the best we could do with what we had," said Catherine, wiping her hands on her apron. "Like everyone out here in these parts."

The men nodded.

"I am Sister Maria, this is Sister Catherine and Sister

Helena. We are nuns, sent to do God's work here in this desert." said Maria, introducing them.

"My name is Frank," said the blonde one.

"They call me John," said the gruff one.

"I'll show you to your quarters," said Maria, and the men began to follow obediently after her.

Helena giggled and nudged Catherine in the ribs. "Perhaps one of these good-looking men will marry me and spirit me away from Maria at last," she whispered.

"Oh, dear God, help us," said Catherine giggling and nudging her back.

SIX

The Bowl

Peggy wondered if she'd ever get used to the smell of borrowed bowling shoes. She took a pair of size tens and put them back in their cubby until the next pair of sweaty feet would be stuffed into them. Peggy's task for the morning was to reorganize them. When it was a busy night here at the Santolsa Bowl, better known as just "the Bowl" all the shoes just got shoved in any old place by the night staff. The morning shift came on and had to sort them all out.

Peggy noticed a pair of nines in where the eights should go. She swapped them back over and wondered how she got here.

It wasn't that long ago she'd been a regular seventeen-year-old living in the year 2016, about to graduate from high school and dreaming about the future.

Now here she was, working at the Santolsa Bowl, a small-town bowling alley in the small desert town of Santolsa in the year 1984.

She spent her days inhaling the scent of other people's sweaty feet, filling up the drink machine, making popcorn which would sit in the warmer for weeks at a time, cleaning toilets and putting greasy bowling balls in order on shelves, only to have people come in and move them around again a few hours later.

It was not where she'd expected to end up, but the bowling alley was so retro and cool that even though the job kind of sucked, it still made Peggy's heart flutter just to be there. The decor was a mishmash of bright emerald green and various shades of seventies browns. Neon signs lit up the lanes, and the uniform was kind of cute - a silky black bowling shirt with "Santolsa Bowl Staff" emblazoned on the back in glittery emerald green, and "Peggy" embroidered in the same bright green on the front. She got to wear whatever she wanted on her legs, and today she was wearing a black mini skirt. Not the best choice, she realized as she bent over to put some other shoes in the correct places. She knew Tricia had been on the night before by just how many shoes were in the wrong places.

"What?" Tricia asked, standing over her dressed in her matching staff bowling shirt and ripped black jeans. She handed Peggy a paper cup filled with bitter filter coffee.

"You always mess up the shoes on night shift," Peggy said huffily, accepting the drink and inhaling the smell. The coffee here was even worse than Dee's, but it kept her going.

Tricia rolled her thickly lined eyes from beneath her messy black bangs. Peggy stood up, pulling on her skirt with her free hand.

"It's not like it's rocket science, Tricia, and it just makes it so much easier and quicker for the morning staff to do their job," Peggy complained as she took a sip of the coffee.

"What, like there are so many people coming for shoes all at once?" Tricia gestured around the bowling alley.

There was a small group of middle-aged men at one lane, a kid and his mom at another and the others were empty.

"There's a tournament tonight," Peggy said.

"Yeah, and when there's a tournament everyone brings their own shoes," Tricia said. "And it's not like it's going to take that long to do, anyway."

Peggy looked down at the piles of shoes she'd made on the floor and sighed.

"What's going on, Peg?" Tricia leaned her arms on the counter. "Is this really about the shoes?"

Peggy shrugged.

"It's not about the shoes, is it?"

Peggy shook her head. "Well, the shoes are annoying, but mostly I'm just…"

"… Still thinking about Sammy?" Tricia finished.

It was still weird to Peggy that Tricia had become one of her closest friends. She remembered when she first met Tricia and how she was kind of scared of her. Well, Tricia still scared her sometimes if she was honest, but she had seen through the tough exterior and knew now that Tricia was actually kind of awesome. Lacey was still her best friend, but Lacey was in LA and it was so hard to keep in touch without text messaging and social media. And after their many shifts together at the Bowl, Peggy and Tricia had actually become friends.

"Yeah," said Peggy.

"You guys will work it out," Tricia said. "You're kind of meant to be together."

Peggy gave her a look. It was weird for Tricia to be so soppy.

"I have a good feeling about you two."

Peggy sighed. "It's been months, and he still keeps saying he needs time. I don't know if he means another few days, months or years, or forever!"

"Sammy Ruthven is…" Tricia started.

Peggy rolled her eyes. "He's what, Tricia?"

"He's not going anywhere." Tricia patted Peggy on the shoulder. "I'm going for a smoke in the break room," she said, leaving Peggy alone with the pile of shoes.

Peggy took another sip of her coffee. All she'd done since she'd decided to stay for good was obsess over Sammy Ruthven, and all he'd done was ignore her. No, that wasn't entirely true. He had given her little dangling carrots every now and then. They'd tried to see a movie together with a group of friends, but it had been so awkward. They'd seen each other at the Fire Station, and he'd almost kissed her one night after a few rum and cokes, but really, he'd barely touched her, talked to her or even made eye contact. He was so hard to read. He kept saying he wanted to be with her, but he just needed more time. She'd already given him thirty-three years, how much more could he need?

Peggy knew what she'd done last year had been majorly shitty. Running away when she thought Sammy was dead was the dumbest thing she'd ever done. In hindsight, she could see now how much hurt she'd caused everyone, and even if it had been Sammy who had died and not Nick, she should have stayed, she should have been there for his family and her friends. She was still trying to make it up to everyone. Lacey had forgiven her, and Tricia was cool. She even had a few friendly exchanges with Rochelle before she'd moved to Salt Valley with Bruce Johnson who'd been the quarterback at St. Christopher's last year. They seemed almost unbearably happy together. Even Rochelle was getting her happy ever after and Peggy was knee deep in stinky shoes.

But Sammy still hadn't forgiven her. She'd tried everything. She'd given him space, she'd given him time, she'd tried calling, she'd tried not calling. She had even written him a really long letter that she'd never sent, but still.

Part of her felt like giving up on him and she occasionally found herself wondering what her life would have been like if she'd stayed in 2016, curled up in Jack's bed with him, his arm around her, that feeling of being so safe and warm and held...

But she wasn't sure she'd ever really be ready to give up on Sammy Ruthven. No matter how much she tried, she could not get him out of her head or her heart.

"Peggy!" came a shout. "Have you even heard a word I've said?" It was her manager, Hayley-Rae, June-Belle's older sister. She was way cooler and nicer than June-Belle, but she was just as bossy.

Peggy looked up and mumbled an apology.

"Can you go clean up a spill on lane four?" Hayley-Rae handed her the mop bucket and tossed her perfect long blonde hair.

Peggy made a face and grabbed the mop bucket, reluctantly trudging over to the lane where the mom and her kid had been. There was soda all over the floor and all over the bowling balls they had been playing with.

Peggy sighed and started mopping.

SEVEN

Jessie

Peggy was nearly finished mopping the floor, and thankfully nearly finished another shift at the Bowl. Her back was dull aching from standing up all day and she desperately needed a shower. She still hadn't found a deodorant that was as good as the ones back in her time and she knew she smelled bad. She sighed and took the mop bucket out the back and poured the grey water into the sink, splashing it all over the wall and all over herself. She tutted at herself. She kind of loved working at the bowl, but this could definitely not be her long-term future. Peggy had spent so much time and energy focused on getting back to the past she hadn't really thought about what she wanted her future to look like. She knew she wanted Sammy in it, and she knew she wanted to be here in the eighties, but other than that, she had no clue. All she knew was that she didn't want to work at the Bowl forever. Janet had been on her back about signing up for community college, but none of the classes really did anything for her. 1984 wasn't the greatest time for women when it came to career options. Santolsa community college offered courses in typing and shorthand, hairdressing and beauty, nail tech, teaching and not much else.

Peggy walked back out to the main desk wiping the sweat that had accumulated on her forehead and was about to complain to Tricia about why she always seemed to get mop bucket duty, when she saw him. He was standing at the desk dressed in dark blue jeans and a plain white tee, his hair falling in his face as he leaned over the desk and laughed at something Tricia had just said.

Seeing him smile like that momentarily erased Peggy's memory of the events of the last year. In her mind she was back in his arms, walking home from prom, floating on the magic of that smile. It had been a long time since she'd even seen him smile. He was still grieving over losing his best friend Nick, they all were, but Sammy had taken it harder than anyone. He couldn't let go of blaming himself for everything that happened. Nick had died while driving Sammy's car. Sammy had given him the keys. Sammy was driving around a total hunk of junk brown Buick these days and Peggy wondered if he would ever drive a hot car again. She shook her head, she knew he would. He would drive a red Mustang in the future, she knew that he'd lend it to Jack to drive to Las Vegas, but that was still decades away.

Her head started pounding. And between that, and the sick, nervous feeling in her stomach, added to the smell of rancid mop water on her clothes she prayed the green and brown diamonds of the carpet might swallow her up.

"There she is," said Tricia.

He turned around and his smile faded into something a little heavier. "Hey," he said.

"Hey," she said.

Tricia raised her eyebrows and slid out from behind the counter. "I'm gonna get going, are you OK to lock up?"

Peggy nodded.

And then they were alone.

Peggy busied herself with some tidying of flyers on the counter. "What brings you out here so late?" she asked, trying to act as if she didn't really care, even though his presence here was the most exciting thing that had happened to her in months.

"I came to ask you a favor."

"Oh?" She continued to fumble with the papers in her hands.

"I know it's last minute. I was going to call your place, but I was driving past anyway, and I didn't want to wake Janet."

"Janet?" Peggy asked.

"Yeah, your aunt." Sammy gave her a look.

Peggy laughed nervously. "I know who Janet is." She organized the flyers into three neat piles before putting them all back into one again.

"I know you're probably busy, but I really need your help."

Peggy finally finished with the flyers and looked up at him. "Is everything OK?"

Sammy rubbed his hand over the back of his neck. "No, not really."

"What's going on?" She wanted nothing more than to leap over the desk and put her arms around him and tell him everything was going to be OK.

"Just some stuff with my mom."

Sammy had shared a lot with her while they had been dating. He'd told her about his mom's drug problems and how she'd been in and out of rehab and hospitals over the years. He still went to see her nearly every weekend, but the rest of his family never went, and Peggy had never been invited along either.

"Are you OK?" she asked.

Sammy nodded. "Yeah, I will be. We will be, but can you come over tomorrow? I'm sorry it's so late to be asking you this, I just didn't know who else to ask." Now it was his turn to be uncomfortable.

"Sure, yes, of course. I have tomorrow off so I can stay as long as you need me."

"You're amazing," he said. "Thank you."

Peggy blushed and looked down at the pile of flyers again. "No problem at all, it's what friends do for each other, right? What time do you want me?"

Do you want me?

She wished she hadn't said it quite like that, but it was too late to take it back. Sammy didn't even seem to notice.

"The earlier, the better. Seven too early?"

"Seven?" She wasn't usually even out of bed by seven.

Something in Sammy's eyes looked so sad, so worried. It aged him. Not in a bad way, just in a way that showed he'd already been through so much no one in their first year out of school should have to be dealing with.

"Seven, sure," she nodded. This was Sammy Ruthven inviting her over to his place. He said he needed her. He had come down to the Bowl just to ask her to come over. Of course she would go. Even if it was at seven.

He reached over the table and put his hand on top of hers. "Thank you, really," he said, his clear blue eyes full of gratitude.

Peggy set her alarm clock for six and curled up into bed with a trashy romance novel. But every time she tried to picture the lead character in her mind - this handsome prince who was pretending to be a regular guy - he morphed into Sammy. And when she got to the scene

43

where he kissed the lowly peasant girl and began to unbutton her shirt, Peggy had to stop reading. She wanted Sammy back more than she'd ever wanted anything in her life and maybe, just maybe, she could allow herself to consider the possibility that he wanted her back too.

But when she got there right at seven, with her hair curled and wearing her new Jordache jeans with a pale pink blouse unbuttoned just low enough to be sexy but not low enough to be slutty, his whole family was there and there was some kind of drama unfolding.

Sammy was wearing a brown suit and his dad was in a dark blue one. Peggy felt like maybe she was missing something.

They ushered her into the kitchen and Sammy poured her a coffee without even looking at her. He was too busy talking and signing to his younger sister Jessie, who appeared to be yelling at him in sign language. She was stamping her feet and signing wildly, her pigtails bouncing around her head angrily.

"Jessie," he said as he signed at the same time back to her. "You can't come."

She stamped her foot again.

"I'm so sorry, Peggy," he said.

Jessie picked a newspaper up off the table and threw it at the wall.

"She can't yell, but she sure can throw things," Sammy said.

Jessie signed something at him, her face like a balloon about to burst.

"I said," he said, signing back to her, "you like to throw things."

She ran out of the room and up the stairs, slamming the door a moment later.

"She also likes to slam doors," Sammy said.

"Hey Peggy," said Sammy's dad. "Sorry about all this."

Peggy shook her head. "It's no problem, family stuff, I get it."

"We're going to court today," said his dad. "So yeah, big family stuff all right."

"Oh?"

"It's gonna be fine," said his dad. "We've got this."

Sammy didn't look so sure as he started to button up the top of his crisp white shirt. "Do you think I should wear the tie, Dad?" He held out a very vintage brown tie and stroked it in his hands nervously.

Peggy wasn't sure she'd ever seen Sammy nervous before. It was kind of adorable.

"A tie shows respect," said his dad, putting on his own blue paisley tie.

Sammy looked to Peggy for confirmation.

"Wear the tie," Peggy nodded. She had no idea what was going on, but it seemed like the kind of situation that called for a tie.

"I'll go check on Jess," his dad said, leaving them alone in the kitchen.

Sammy fumbled with his tie and without even thinking about it, she handed him her coffee mug to hold and reached out to help him. She felt like one of those women in those anti-feminist commercials that were always playing on TV here, the ones where the woman would do the man's tie and then he'd go off to work and she'd stay home with the kids and do the cleaning.

She straightened up his tie and gently pushed it up towards his neck where she could feel his pulse hammering away.

"What's going on?" she asked, as she took a few extra unnecessary moments to continue to work on his tie just so she could be close to him. Being close to him made her feel more like herself than she ever did when she was alone. It was strange how a person who wasn't even part of your family, someone you hardly even ever spoke to anymore could make you feel so at home.

"Mom is trying to get custody," he said.

"What?" asked Peggy, finally putting her hands down and taking back her coffee. "But I thought…?"

Sammy nodded. "She says she's clean and now she wants custody of Jessie. I'm over eighteen now, so she doesn't want me. Just Jessie."

"How can she do this?"

Sammy shook his head. "I don't know, but you know what the courts are like, they always root for the mother." He ran his hand through his hair.

God, he was sexy.

"Do you need me to be a character witness or something?"

"No, we have a few people lined up already. I just really need you to stay here with Jessie."

Jessie.

Oh. That's why she was here. She wasn't his date or even his friend today, she was Jessie's babysitter.

Peggy took a sip of coffee and tried to act normal. She nodded. "Of course," she said, her face flushing with the stupidity of thinking he wanted her by his side today.

"She doesn't want to go with Mom, but we can't risk her coming with us. She hasn't even seen Mom in years. We have no idea how she'll react, or what mom will do. And I hate to say it, but the judge seeing Jessie run into Mom's arms could be really bad for our case."

Peggy nodded again.

"I'm sorry I didn't tell you everything last night, I guess I was just trying to ignore it, pretend it wasn't happening."

"OK, Sammy, are you ready?" His dad grabbed a dark

blue jacket and handed Sammy a brown one that matched his tie.

"Any judge will take one look at you two and know what the right thing is," Peggy said.

"Thanks, Peg," Sammy said, leaning in as if he was about to kiss her on the cheek before stopping himself midway and settling for a pat on her arm.

She was about to call out for him to text her and let her know how it was going, but instead she'd have to wait here until they returned. She'd have to wait here with Jessie. All day.

Peggy had only met Jessie once before. It was the day she'd come back from the present after finding out that Sammy wasn't dead after all. She'd turned up at his house in her pajamas and watched from a distance as he and Rochelle stood at his door looking very friendly. When she'd finally gotten up the nerve to knock, it was Jessie who answered, and then Sammy had come to the door and in no uncertain terms told her to go away. It had broken her. Again.

And now here she was, alone in the house with Jessie. She didn't know sign language, and she had no idea how to communicate with her, let alone entertain her for the entire day. Could Jessie even watch TV? How would they pass the time?

Peggy drank the last of the coffee, which was now cold, and started washing up the mugs and plates left from breakfast. Five minutes had passed already. Maybe she *could* get through this whole day.

When she turned around, Jessie was standing in the corner staring at her and it made Peggy jump. She looked kind of creepy with her deep scowl on her face, her dark blonde hair up in pigtails and dressed in a pair of corduroy overalls.

Peggy gave her a smile.

Jessie walked off and sat down at the dining table where there were stacks of sketch books and markers out. She began scribbling. She held up a notebook and, in her kid, scrawl she had written "I AM ANGRY."

Peggy nodded.

She wrote again - "WHY CAN'T I GO?"

Peggy walked over and sat down opposite her at the table. She'd seen Sammy talk and sign at the same time, but she didn't know if Jessie could understand. Could she read lips? She thought maybe the best thing to do was just ask her.

"What is the best way for us to talk?" Peggy wrote on a discarded piece of paper.

Jessie looked up at her curiously, her expression softening. "SIGNING" she wrote.

Peggy laughed softly and wrote "I can't sign," and drew a sad face.

Jessie rolled her eyes and jumped up from the table. She grabbed a big brick of a dogeared book from the bookcase and threw it down on top of Peggy's paper. It was a Sign Language Dictionary full of words and pictures and huge amounts of text about tenses and sentence structure.

"This is a big book," Peggy wrote.

Jessie got back up again and brought back a second, much smaller book, a *Sesame Street* guide to Sign Language. Jessie gave Peggy a look as if to say, "start with this then, dumbass."

Peggy looked through the book and tried signing a few words and Jessie waved her hands in the air. "Deaf clapping," she wrote, and did it again.

Peggy laughed and sign clapped with her.

Jessie's face went serious again and she held up her note "WHY CAN'T I GO?"

Peggy wrote for a minute and then handed it over to her. "Because your dad and your brother don't want you to have to deal with this really hard thing. They want to protect you and keep you safe because they love you."

Jessie folded her arms but seemed to accept that response.

Why was it so much easier to write this stuff than say it out loud? Peggy wondered.

"I LIKE YOU" Jessie wrote, and then she showed Peggy the sign language.

"I like you," Peggy signed back, saying the words at the same time.

Jessie smiled at her. "BETTER THAN ROCHELLE" she wrote laughing.

"That's kind of mean, but thanks," Peggy wrote back, grinning.

Jessie pointed to the word "thanks" and showed Peggy how to sign it.

When Sammy and his dad got home late that night, they found both girls asleep on the couch surrounded by piles of scrapbooks and notes and sign language books. Sammy didn't want to wake her. She looked so peaceful. He was suddenly taken back to that night he'd put her to bed at Janet's when she'd first arrived. He put his hand gently on her arm and whispered her name.

Peggy opened her eyes slowly. "How did it go?" she asked, reaching out to him. His body wanted to reach back for her in response, but his mind stopped it.

Sammy put his hand on hers. "It went OK," he whispered. "We won't get the final decision for a few weeks, but it went as well as we could have hoped."

"Good," she said groggily. "I'm glad. I hope it all works out."

"Me too," Sammy said, standing up and pulling off his tie. "Thanks so much for today." He unbuttoned his top button and felt like he could breathe again.

"It was really my pleasure. Jessie is great." Peggy peeled herself up off the couch and looked over at Jessie, who had fallen asleep with her head on one of the books.

"Really?" asked Sammy. "She can be a handful."

Peggy held up the "I LIKE YOU" note and grinned.

Sammy let out a breath for what felt like the first time all day. Coming home to Peggy felt like something clicking in place, something right. And the fact that she'd gotten along with Jessie, that was a big deal. Jessie didn't trust easily.

Peggy folded up the piece of paper and put it in the pocket of her jeans. "I should get going."

Sammy walked her to the door, and before he even knew he was doing it, he leaned in towards her and kissed her on the cheek. Too close. That was too close, too close to her and too close to letting her in again. Too close to getting hurt again.

"Thanks again," he said, stepping back from her. He didn't know if he was ready to do this again. He still had so much pain he was working through, he didn't think he could handle any more right now.

She reached out and brushed his shirt sleeve. "Any time, Sammy."

And then she got in her blue bug and puttered off down the road and all he could think of was how much he wanted to fix that damn car for her.

EIGHT

First Day in 1984

It was a Tuesday morning in 1984 when Jack walked out of the book room and into the halls of St. Christopher's High School. He took a deep breath and grinned. He was *here*. His sneakers felt strange on the wooden floorboards beneath his feet, it wasn't the squeaky linoleum he knew so well. The walls looked like they'd just been painted, but the school still smelled the same – like sweaty teenagers, musty old books and orange peel. Jack swung his satchel over his shoulder and began to walk down the empty hallway. It seemed like class was already out for the summer, but there were a few muffled voices coming from some of the class-rooms. He peered into one of the rooms where a girl with a Farrah Fawcett hairstyle was sitting all alone taking a test. There was a notice pinned up next to the door about where to collect your Class of 1984 yearbook.

Jack felt strange, as if he wasn't really in his own body. He felt like he was going to pass out or throw up or something.

It had worked.

It was true.

It was really happening.

Jack felt a heady mix of both pure exhilaration and terror. How was he here? Was it *really* real? Or was he suffering from some kind of group hallucination he was sharing with Peggy?

He put a hand to his pounding head.

A nun appeared out of nowhere and scowled at him. "Are you here for the make-up test?" she asked.

Jack shook his head. "No, I'm…"

"Then what are you doing here?" she asked impatiently.

"I… I really don't know. I guess I'm looking for someone."

"Who?"

"Uh, Mrs. Willis, I mean, Miss Bates, I think," Jack said.

"Miss Bates isn't here," the nun said.

"OK, I guess I'll just go then." Jack began to walk down the hallway to the front door of the school, looking behind him as he went to see if the nun was watching him, but she'd already disappeared.

He pushed open the big wooden door and stepped out into the sunlight. He grabbed his Wayfarers out of his bag and put them on, grinning as he took in the scene before him. The trees were shorter, the whole place was cleaner, and the grass seemed greener. The sun even felt brighter too, if that was possible.

His head was still pounding, and he felt like he was having out-of-body experience, but he was here. The past was finally behind him, and most important of all, *she* was here.

Jack's expectations of 1984 were varied and mostly irrational. He was planning to find Peggy as quick as he could, and he knew as soon as she saw him, she'd throw her arms around him and she'd be so happy he was here. All her doubts would be gone, and she would know for sure that Jack was the guy for her. She no longer had to choose between the eighties and him. She could have both. They'd fall into each other's arms and everything would just make sense.

Jack didn't really have a plan apart from that. He just needed to get to Peggy's house, to *Janet's* house. He'd only been to Janet's house once, but he was pretty sure he could remember the street it was on.

But first, coffee.

Not wanting to spend any time at all back at school, even if it was the eighties, he decided to walk into town and stop at Dee's to re-group. He knew Dee's had been around forever, and the idea of sitting down for some onion rings and a bad coffee without knowing a single soul seemed like paradise.

It had taken Jack ages to walk into town and he was feeling a little sunburned and blistered. He wasn't sure how he was going to keep walking all the way to Peggy's house. He stopped at a general store at the edge of town which was a liquor shop in his time.

"Howdy," said an old guy with a heavy Tom Selleck style moustache who was busy unpacking boxes.

"Hey," said Jack.

"Need any help, son?" the old guy asked.

"I need a hat," said Jack.

The man nodded to a corner of the store where a display of sunglasses and hats stood.

Jack tried on a cowboy hat and looked in the small mirror next to the sunglasses. No, no way. Jack couldn't wear a cowboy hat, not even ironically. He found a navy-blue Miller Light trucker cap and tried it on. He checked himself out in the mirror and figured it would do. The price tag read two dollars. Jack laughed. There wasn't much you could get for two bucks in his time.

Jack grabbed a can of Pepsi, smiling at the retro design and walked towards the counter.

"Nice hat," the man said. "Don't suppose you're looking for a new mode of transport?"

Jack said raised his eyebrows.

"You got eight dollars?" the man asked.

Jack nodded. "Just."

The man reached over to the boxes he was unpacking. "All the kids are riding these nowadays." The man pulled out a skateboard. It was wooden with red wheels and decorated with two black lines and stars on the front.

"I'll take it," Jack said, handing over the cash.

Jack had played around on skateboards as a kid, but he didn't really know what he was doing. He nearly fell off twice on the way from the store to the diner, and almost smacked into a young woman in thick glasses who didn't see him coming. He would have to do some practice before he would look cool riding it. But he was excited to learn, and he liked the idea of having a set of wheels that he could carry around. And he also thought skateboarding had a pretty high cool factor.

Jack put his new wheels under the table and slid into a booth at Dee's. The familiarity of the place was bizarre. Here he was, thirty-three years back in the past, and yet he was sitting at the same table he'd been sitting at just a few weeks ago when he'd been attacked.

Dee's hadn't changed so much over the years. The turquoise was a little brighter and the red a little deeper, but the waitresses still wore the same stressed out and over it expressions, the tables were still sticky, and the windows were still greasy. One difference was the ashtray in the middle of the table. Jack made a face at it and pushed it aside.

"What can I getcha?" asked a middle-aged waitress with blonde bangs.

"Just coffee thanks," said Jack. "Oh, and some onion rings."

"We're outta rings, but we got a special on pie, cherry." She smacked her softly wrinkled bright pink lips together.

"Sure," he shrugged. A piece of pie could go down pretty well. He hadn't realized until she'd said "pie" just how famished he was. Time traveling was hungry work.

"Slice-a-cherry!" she shouted across to the kitchen as she grabbed the coffee pot and a cup for Jack.

As she poured, the smell gave him a little jolt, and he felt like he finally returned to his body. He nodded thanks and held the cup to his nose. He closed his eyes breathing in deeply. 1980s coffee. He opened his eyes and dropped in two teaspoons of sugar. The coffee was unsurprisingly horrible, although weirdly, slightly less horrible than the coffee in the present, but he needed the caffeine. The waitress slapped a plate of pie down next to him and left him to it.

He sat for a long time just looking out the window. Enjoying his anonymity, his freedom. It was quiet here. Much quieter than it was back home. Women dressed in button-up blouses and long skirts, or outfits entirely of spandex, struggled past with way too many bags. Two cowboys in flared jeans strutted through town with supplies for the ranch or to grab an early beer, but little else seemed to be happening.

"How's the pie?" asked the waitress, taking his plate when he was done.

"Really nice," he said, even though it had really only just been OK. The waitress grinned and refilled his cup.

"You gonna be here for a while, sweet pea?" she asked him.

Sweet pea?

Jack thought of his mom and missed her already. But he'd be OK, he wasn't stuck here, he could still go back and see his folks, for now. Peggy had told him that when you time travelled through the book room you couldn't come and go forever. One day you'd have to choose. But he couldn't even begin to start thinking about having to say goodbye to his parents forever, not even for Peggy.

"I'm new in town, just trying to find my bearings I guess," Jack shrugged.

"I can tell you anything you need to know," the waitress said. She sat down opposite him and made herself comfortable.

"I'm looking for someone called Peggy Martin, or Mrs. Will… *Janet.*"

"Janet Bates?" she asked.

"Yeah, that's her."

"I know Janet, she's on my bowling team, real nice lady."

"Do you know where I can find her?"

"I finish in an hour. If you want to wait, I can drive you over to her place."

"Oh," said Jack. He was thinking he would board over when the pain in his feet subsided, but a ride would be even better. "If you're sure it's no problem?"

"None whatsoever." She gave him a kind smile. "I'll grab you some papers and magazines to keep you busy, and I'll getcha another slice of pie, on the house."

"I've got two girls around your age," the waitress said, lighting up a cigarette and starting the engine of her silver Volvo that had seen better days. She exhaled, sending cigarette smoke throughout the car. Jack coughed and wondered if she was a little younger than she looked. He watched as the wrinkles around her mouth grew deeper with every inhale on her cigarette.

"Oh, really?" asked Jack politely.

"Two *great* kids," she added. "One goes to community college in Texas. She finally got herself together after a few tough years. Met a guy out there, she's staying with him and working part time in a Casino while she studies. He seems like a decent guy." Her expression grew dark for a moment and then shifted again. "The other one just finished school with no idea what she's doing."

"Sounds just like me," he said, letting out a little laugh. "I don't know what I'm doing, either."

"What's with you kids today? I started working at thirteen and haven't missed a day yet."

"Times are changing," said Jack. "We want more, we want to be fulfilled."

"Fulfilled!" She laughed. "'Ain't nothing fulfilling about workin' your ass off to pay the bills."

"Have you worked at the diner since you were thirteen?" Jack asked.

"God, no. I worked in entertainment for years before the kids were born, but when their daddy died, he left me with nothing, so I make ends meet by working three jobs."

"Three jobs?"

"Dee's, cleaning at the Motel and I'm also your neighborhood Avon lady, so if you want to purchase some face cream just let me know. All while that girl works hardly any hours in one job and spends the rest of her time thinking about what's going to make her feel *fulfilled*."

"That does sound kind of unfair I guess, when you put it like that." Jack had been doing the exact same thing until his dad got him a job at the firm. Sitting around at home eating jalapeno flavored popcorn and watching old TV shows while his parents went to work every day. It hadn't even occurred to him to feel guilty about it.

She shrugged. "She'll come around, I know she will. She's a good kid. Anger issues, but she's a good girl."

They sat in silence most of the rest of the way. The waitress smoking while Jack stuck his head out his window and did his best not to cough as he watched the landscape he knew so well go by, some the same, some completely changed. His jaw dropped as they drove past his house, well, what would be his house in his time. It was the same cute brick build but looked brand new. A young girl dressed in a flamingo pink swimsuit stood outside watering the tiny trees that would grow much taller than him.

He let out a gasp.

"Something wrong, sweet pea?" She put out her cigarette out.

"No, nothing." Jack's head began to pound as he watched the trails of smoke twist around each other in the ashtray.

"What are you doing here in Santolsa, anyway? We don't get a lot of out-of-town visitors." Her eyebrows folded together as she glanced in the rear-view mirror.

"Just visiting, I guess."

"Visiting Janet?"

"Visiting Peggy. Her niece."

"Oh, right," the woman smiled. "Her niece, she's from Canada, right? You're from Canada too?"

"Uh, yeah," he said, remembering the back-story

Peggy had used when she first arrived. "I got a letter from her, I think she's still staying at Janet's."

Jack felt his pulse rise. What if she wasn't even there? He hadn't thought of that possibility until now. It had been a while since she'd given him the key that day in the diner.

But what if she *was* there? Last time he had seen her she was old, probably as old as the woman from the diner, but she was still sexy, and she'd been wearing a wedding ring. Last time he'd seen Young Peggy was so many months ago, saying their goodbyes outside the book room. He'd never forget that hug, the way her hair smelled - fresh like mint and juniper, her neck warm and sweet-scented. He'd felt her heart beating heavily and wondered if it was because of the embrace, because of her feelings for him, or if it was the knowing that she was leaving for good that time.

"Uh huh, Peggy's still staying there." She nodded as she pulled up in front of the house.

It was a small brick house, and the front porch was covered in pot plants. A silver Escort was in the driveway and parked next to it on the lawn, was a pale blue Volkswagen Beetle. His heart started beating wildly and his head began pounding all over again. Peggy had always talked about her dream car being a VW Beetle.

"I won't come in but tell Janet I'll see her at the Bowl."

"Sure, and thanks so much Mrs... I'm sorry I don't even know your name." Jack shook his head at himself.

"It's Miss, Miss Arnold. But please just call me Tammy."

"Tammy Arnold?" Jack asked, his head feeling as if it was about to split into two.

"And you are...?"

"Jack," he said. "Jack Forrester."

"Nice to meet you Jack, I'm sure I'll see you around if

you're staying in town for a little while. Santolsa isn't much, but it's home. Little gem of the desert they call it, you'll soon see why." She gave him a smile.

"Thanks. I'm sure I will see you again." He scrambled out of the car and gave a little wave.

He stood in the driveway, his mouth hanging open as he watched her drive away.

Jack's grandmother had died of lung cancer long before he'd ever been born. He felt his eyes begin to water. He was so glad he had been able to meet her.

NINE

Janet's House

Jack's head was pounding, his feet still hurt, and he felt like he was going to be sick. This was not the Jack he wanted to be when he knocked on Peggy's front door. He took a few deep breaths and tried to sort out his thoughts, and eventually his legs started carrying him towards the front door. He stepped up to the front porch and knocked hesitantly.

His stomach was a swirling mess of nerves, pie, and the overwhelming fear that she didn't want him like he wanted her.

A hanging plant tickled his ear. He pushed it away and rubbed his temples. He shook out his shoulders and knocked again a little louder.

He could hear a voice coming from inside, the TV or someone talking, he wasn't sure, but someone was definitely home. He took a deep breath, ran his fingers through his sweaty hair and cleared his throat.

The door swung open, and there she was.

She was looking as incredible as ever and his heart nearly exploded at the sight of her. He dropped his new skateboard onto the porch.

She was young again and dressed in a bowling shirt and denim shorts and she looked so relaxed and cool and *beautiful*. He felt sweat begin to run down his back.

Her face went pale and she dropped the Cosmopolitan magazine she'd been holding.

Jack shrugged.

She screamed and threw herself into his arms. She smelled different, like musky strawberries and cheap hairspray and a little bit like cigarettes. Did she smoke now? His heart hammered into her chest and he felt hers do the same.

"I gave you the key," she laughed. "I've been thinking about doing that!" She hugged him again, so tightly he thought his ribs might break again.

He began laughing, too. He'd been so worried about this moment, but suddenly nothing mattered. Nothing at all. They were together again, and it felt so easy, and normal and right.

She pulled back to get a good look at him. "Wow," she said. "You haven't changed a bit."

"You have," he said, looking her up and down. Not only did she smell different, she looked different, too. She was wearing blue mascara, and something was different with her hair. It was bigger somehow, and there was something else he couldn't quite put his finger on.

She shrugged. "I'm trying to assimilate. Actually, it's more like I spent my whole life trying to assimilate and now I don't have to try anymore," she said, bouncing on her toes.

"You look so… *happy*."

"I am," she grinned. "Happier than I was back in our old time, that's for sure."

Jack's heart dropped. She was happy without him. He suddenly had visions of her and Sammy doing eighties things together, going on dates to the mall and seeing old movies the first time around. Peggy would be in heaven.

"Well," she added, squishing up her face, "mostly. But we can talk about that later. Don't just stand there, come in!" She waved him through the front door.

"Who is it?" called a female voice from the kitchen.

"You'll never guess," Peggy called back. She grabbed Jack's hand and began pulling him into the house.

Jack immediately understood what Peggy had meant about feeling right at home here. He instantly felt the same way. The house was full of comfy, homey *stuff*. Wicker and wood furniture in bright colors and piles of magazines and papers and books all over the place. It smelled like stale cigarettes and that musky smell again, but it felt so comfortable. Maybe Peggy's scent hadn't changed, maybe she just smelled like this house now.

"It's Jack!" Peggy shoved him into the kitchen.

A slim woman with dark spiky hair came rushing towards him and hugged him even harder than Peggy had. "It's so nice to meet you," she said to the back of his neck.

"Mrs. Willis?" he asked. His mind was kind of blown seeing his old English teacher standing before him look-ing… attractive.

"Miss Bates," she corrected, pulling back and exam-ining him.

"She's not supposed to know she's going to be Mrs. Willis," Peggy said. "We're not really supposed to tell her anything about the future."

"Oh yeah, right," Jack shook his head. "Sorry."

"Janet will do nicely, thanks. Are you hungry, Jack?"

"I've been eating pie all day at Dee's, but I'm starving for normal food."

"I'll get a pizza on." Janet opened up the fridge freezer and started rummaging around.

"It's like, all she can cook," Peggy said.

"You know I love pizza," said Jack.

"Did you bring a bag or anything?" Peggy asked, looking around.

"No, I just brought a few things. I mean, honestly, I didn't even really expect it to work. I thought to myself this morning, what do you take on a time travel adventure to the eighties? I got out my rucksack and starting throwing things in and then I began to feel really mentally unstable, so I just brought a change of clothes and my toothbrush."

She took his hand and pulled him into the lounge room. "I'll take you to the Mini Mall! You're going to die when you see how cool it is in this time. I'm sure there are some clothes here you can wear for now. Ray's probably left some somewhere."

"Ray?" Jack felt his heart wobble. Who was *Ray*?

"Janet's boyfriend," Peggy explained, and Jack's heart went back to normal.

Peggy lifted the lid on the record player and put the needle down on an old Fleetwood Mac song.

"Ray Willis?" he asked.

"No, Janet doesn't know anyone called Willis yet," Peggy said quietly. "It's best if we don't talk about it. I've managed to go the last few months without any side effects and I really want to keep it that way. The best way to feel normal is just to act normal, almost just pretend like you belong here, eventually you trick your brain into believing it and the headaches go away."

"Speaking of headaches," said Jack rubbing his forehead.

"Is it bad?"

"Splitting."

"Come on." She grabbed his hand again and led him back to the kitchen. Her hand felt soft and warm and small in his. He wanted her to keep holding it forever. It felt so good, so natural, so normal. So how it should be. Hand in hand with her.

She dropped his hand as soon as he thought it. She motioned for him to sit at one of the bar stools at the kitchen counter, while she rummaged through a drawer on the other side.

"Margarita OK?" Janet asked, wiping her hands on a towel.

"Perfect," he said, taking the bottle of pills from Peggy. She poured him a 7-up and he gulped them down.

"You can stay on the couch as long as you like," Janet said.

"Thanks, I don't really know what I'm doing, so a couple days to get my head around things and work out what to do would be great."

"You're not going to stay?" Peggy's face fell.

"I don't know, Peg. I mean, what am I seriously going to do in Santolsa in 1984? It's bad enough in the present." He was hoping she would respond with some romantic gesture, tell him that being together was all that mattered.

Peggy frowned at him. "It's not so bad now. And why did you come if you didn't want to be here?"

"Because you asked me to."

She was silent for a moment. Jack didn't know what this meant. Did she even really *want* him here?

Jack looked at her shirt. "You're working at the bowling alley?" he asked, trying to lighten the mood again.

Peggy nodded. "It's not exactly the dream job, but it's OK… for now. Until I figure things out."

Jack found it hard to imagine Peggy with a customer service job after living off her parent's credit cards for so long. "I think my mom worked there for a while before they tore it down. She always said it was one of the best jobs she ever had."

"What about you?" Peggy asked.

"I've been working with my dad. Filing and photocopying. Not exactly living the dream, either," Jack said.

"Oh, Peggy," said Janet. "Lacey called earlier."

"She's so hard to get hold of," Peggy complained. "Especially now she's in Los Angeles."

"Lacey's in LA?" asked Jack. "Why didn't you go with her? LA in the eighties *would* be a dream come true."

"She's there with a *guy*," Peggy said.

"She's a groupie," said Janet.

Jack raised an eyebrow and took another sip of his 7UP.

"Janet!" Peggy said. "Don't call her that, it's more than that."

"She's a groupie?" asked Jack.

"Not a groupie," Peggy said.

"So, she's out in eighties LA having sex with rock stars and you didn't want to go join her?" Jack asked.

"*A* rock star, but it's not like that. When I talk to her, it sounds like they're totally in love. It's nice, and Lacey's never had that before."

"Sure," said Janet. "But we all know how it's going to turn out."

"How does it turn out?" asked Jack. "And who's the rock star?"

"If it was up to me, I'd go down there and get her and bring her home," Janet said, ignoring Jack's question. Janet was decades younger, but her mannerisms were exactly the same. It kind of unnerved him. He took another pain killer. Janet reached over and took the bottle off him, giving him that mothering look he'd seen many times on her much older face during English class.

"It's just so weird," said Jack. "You're Mrs. Willis, like, exactly, but *young*."

Peggy patted his knee and giggled. "You'll get used to it."

"These things can be addictive," said Janet putting the bottle back in the drawer and shoving it shut with her hip.

"So what? Maybe they aren't going to end up together," Peggy said. "Just because they don't end up together forever doesn't mean they shouldn't be together at all. You're dating Ray even though he's not your Mr. Willis. Or is it one rule for you and one rule for everyone else?"

"That's exactly right, Peggy, and that's why it's best that no one knows too much about the future, which means we have to let Lacey do what Lacey has to do, even if we wish we could prevent her from getting hurt."

"Uh, yeah, that's what I was trying to say," Peggy said, rolling her eyes.

"Now, Jack," Janet said, changing the subject swiftly, "before you get too comfortable, we are going to need to talk to you about the rules of time travel." Janet topped up everyone's sodas.

"Can't this wait?" Peggy grabbed Jack's hand from under the counter and it lit him up from inside. "We have so much to catch up on."

"No," said Janet bluntly. "The rules of time travel are more important than your gossip session."

Peggy made a face at Jack and he laughed. He'd never seen Peggy act this way with her parents before. She'd never been the angsty teen, she'd just been the sad girl with absent parents. It made him happy to see her like this, rolling her eyes, making faces, acting like Janet was a total moron even though it was obvious she loved her like she was family.

When the pizza was ready Janet cut it up and slid it

onto plates. Peggy took her pizza and 7UP and sat down at the dining table, gesturing for Jack to follow and he sat down next to her. It reminded him of home. After a moment he realized that his parents had the exact same table and chairs.

"I'm sure you know a lot already," said Janet. "You know what happened last summer with Sammy and Nick."

Jack nodded with his mouth full. The pizza was kind of horrible, but he was so hungry he didn't care. What he did care about was knowing exactly what was going on with Peggy and Sammy. She hadn't even mentioned him. In fact, he knew more about Lacey's love life than he knew about hers. Did that mean there was nothing to tell? Surely if Peggy and Sammy were together, she would have said something by now. Jack felt a little relieved and quite hopeful.

"Sure, Peggy found out Sammy was going to die, and so she saved," he made air quotes around the word saved, "Sammy, but Nick died instead. But did she really save Sammy? Would Nick have died anyway? Did Peggy change it, or not?" asked Jack. He looked over at Peggy, but she was just staring blankly into her pizza. "Did it change because *you* changed it? Or was the newspaper report wrong from the beginning? Was it always Nick who died? And please can I have more painkillers?"

Janet shook her head. "We've had this conversation many times, haven't we, Peg?"

Peggy nodded and took another bite.

Jack shrugged. "The way I see it, is that we have no way of knowing why Nick died and not Sammy. Maybe it was Nick's destiny, or maybe it was Nick's free will to get drunk, take Sammy's car and drive way too fast. Maybe Nick would have died another way if it wasn't in the car accident. Who knows?"

A tear formed in Peggy's eye.

"You did all you could, Peg," Jack said. "You can't blame yourself for what happened."

"Everyone else still blames me." Peggy dabbed her eyes with a napkin.

"For Nick's death?" Jack asked.

"No, for running away," Peggy said.

Oh, thought Jack. So, Sammy Ruthven was still mad at her. He struggled to feel happy about that though, knowing how much it was upsetting her.

"Give it time," said Janet, rubbing a hand on Peggy's.

Peggy blew her nose on a paper napkin.

"Rules of time travel?" Jack took another bite of pizza.

"You can travel back and forwards for a limited time only," said Peggy through her tissue.

"This sounds like an infomercial," said Jack.

"It's serious," Peggy said.

"Why?" asked Jack. "You tried to explain this to me before, but I don't get it. Why can't I just go back and forth? I'm not like you, Peg. I have a family back home who loves me, I don't really dig the idea of being stuck here forever."

"Eventually you have to choose," said Janet. "You can't live in two times at once. It's not good for the soul. Or for your head."

Jack nodded. He had never experienced a headache like this. "I guess the human body isn't really designed to time travel."

"Exactly," said Janet. "Peggy's only just starting to feel normal now, aren't you Peg?"

Peggy nodded, wiping the blue mascara away from under her eyes. Jack gave her a sympathetic look.

"But how do you know when you're not going to be able to get back?" Jack asked.

"You don't," said Janet. "So, make sure you don't get stuck somewhere you don't really want to be."

"Right," Jack said. That didn't seem very clear at all. "What else?"

"If you want to go back, you have to wait until sunrise, otherwise you end up another thirty-three years in the past," Janet said.

Jack looked at her questioningly and she responded with a look that said, "don't ask."

"And, while you're here, you need to live normally," Janet continued. "Act like you belong here. Don't bring anything back here that shouldn't be here and don't talk about things that haven't happened yet."

Jack thought about his phone in his pocket. He knew he couldn't use his phone here, but surely it wouldn't hurt to use it to listen to music.

Peggy scoffed. "What about your Bryan Adams Greatest Hits record?" she asked.

"That was different. Old me sent that, so she already knew it would be fine."

"Again, with the one rule for you and one for everyone else," Peggy said.

Janet ignored her and went on. "Just try to live how you would live if you weren't a time traveler. Try to just make choices organically, don't think about how your actions are going to affect your future life. When you start analyzing every action you take, every decision you make, you can end up going a little crazy."

"But what if I do something really stupid and erase myself from existence? You know, like stop my parents from meeting or something?" Jack asked.

"What, like if your grandma hit you with her car instead of your dad?" giggled Peggy.

"She drove me here today, my grandmother," he said, looking into his 7UP.

Peggy's eyes widened.

"Tammy, from the diner."

Janet gasped. "Tammy is your grandmother? Then I guess that…" Janet's dark eyebrows pulled together.

"What?" asked Jack.

"That you know how things are likely to play out for her," Janet finished.

"Yeah, and it's not great to be honest, and I guess I can't do anything about that."

Janet shook her head.

"What about my parents?" he asked. "I already met my grandmother and my parents grew up here, am I going to bump into them? Won't that create a paradox?"

"Probably not," said Peggy. "I've done some pretty dumb stuff and we're all still here."

"What are their names?" Janet asked. "I might know them if they went to St. C's."

"Patty Arnold and Hank Forrester."

Janet shook her head, "I can't say I know them."

"Have they always lived in Santolsa? Or did they live in Salt Valley?" asked Peggy.

"Santolsa I think, you know I don't even know. I just know my family has been around here forever."

"Unless you bump into them, don't even think about it," Janet said. "Just act normal."

Jack nodded. Sure. Normal. Don't think about bumping into your teenage parents. Right. Nothing about this was normal.

A honk outside made them all jump.

"Bowling practice!" Janet exclaimed.

"We'll clean up," said Peggy. "Go, go."

Janet jumped up and started running all over the house

grabbing shoes and bags and cardigans before flying out the door with a quick goodbye.

"Have fun!" Peggy called back.

And then it dawned on Jack that they were alone, for the first time in a long time. So much had changed, but here they were. Together, alone.

"We should get this cleaned up," said Peggy as she began stacking plates and taking them over to the sink.

Peggy did seem so much happier than he remembered her, but he couldn't help but feel like something was still up.

Jack followed with the glasses. "So, what's going on?" he asked gently.

Peggy shrugged as she handed him a dish towel and started filling the sink.

"Is it… Sammy?" Jack asked. Even just saying his name tasted sour in his mouth. He didn't want to know, but he *needed* to know.

Peggy nodded.

"Are you… together?" Jack braced himself for the answer.

Peggy shook her head but seemed unwilling to divulge any more information and so he respected that, and they did the dishes in silence. He didn't care. Silence between them was never uncomfortable. In some ways, the silence between them was comforting, easy, peaceful. They could be alone with their thoughts, together.

"Oh, it's nearly time for *Knight Rider*," she said, grabbing at the gold digital watch on her wrist.

"New watch?"

"Yeah, it was a birthday present from Janet. She baked me a cake and took me out to Super Pan for pizza. I'll have to take you there, the pizza is so good and it's so cute inside."

Peggy's parents had forgotten her birthday once and it was the perfect example of how absent they had been in her life. "Sounds like you finally got your family birthday party after all." Jack gave her a gentle smile.

"Yeah, I did," she smiled back. "Oh, but we have to hurry." She handed him a stack of plates and pointed to the cupboard they went into.

"What? Why?"

"TV," she said. "We can't just stream here. If you miss it, you miss it."

"You can tape stuff though, right? You've got a VCR?"

"Well, sure, but you still have to be there to hit record. The timer never works, it always cuts off the start or the end or records the wrong thing."

Jack put the last few dishes away.

"Will you watch it with me?" she asked.

"Sure," he said.

And just a few minutes later they were sitting on the couch, side by side, with fresh glasses of 7UP, watching eighties television, and for a moment he almost forgot where he was. It was just like old times, except the TV was about an eighth of the size and he could still smell cigarettes.

He looked over at Peggy and grinned.

She grinned back, and then her gaze fell to his upper arm. She lifted his t-shirt and gasped. "You got a tattoo?" She put her hand over her mouth.

"Not exactly, well, yeah, obviously, but it wasn't exactly a conscious choice," he started.

"What's it meant to be?" she asked.

"A snake," he said.

"Well yeah, obviously, but why?"

Jack didn't want to tell her. He didn't want to tell her about how he got beat up and how he stayed in hospital and how Jayne and the Eights had held him down and carved into his skin while he was off his head on hospital drugs.

Jack shrugged. "I guess you could say it just kind of happened."

Peggy gave him a look. "It's kind of cool, it makes you look tougher."

"Really?" He puffed out his chest a little.

She nodded.

"So," he said as an ad for chewing gum came on. "Are you ready to tell me what's going on?"

Peggy sighed. "I don't know, Sammy and me, it's complicated."

"How so?"

She shook her head and reached for her drink.

"It's me, Peg. You can talk to me."

She took a deep breath. "He keeps saying he needs time. He's still cut up about Nick, I know. And he has every right to be mad at me for disappearing. You know he went through everything without me. He spoke at the funeral. He spent time with Nick's family. He did it all while I was moping around in that hotel room in Vegas. I'm so selfish." She hit one of the couch cushions.

"Hey," said Jack, gently removing the cushion. "You were hurting too. You didn't know what happened. You thought Sammy had died, and you were a total mess over it."

She nodded. "But even if it was Sammy, I should have stayed, you know?"

"Maybe. But what's done is done. If he's really the guy for you, he will get over it."

"And if he doesn't?"

"Then he's not the guy for you," Jack said.

TEN

Pancakes

———————

Peggy was lying in bed, staring at the streaks of sunlight dancing on the ceiling. She smiled to herself as she thought about Jack being just downstairs. It made her heart so happy to have him back. It was strange, and yet wonderful how easily he'd easily slotted back into place. Having him back felt like the only thing she needed to feel perfectly complete here in the past.

Well, not the only thing. As always, as she lay there, her thoughts found their way back to Sammy. She closed her eyes and thought about the first day she'd seen him walk into class. The night outside Super Pan when he'd told her he could drive her home. The way he smirked at her across the cafeteria table at school. The night of prom when he'd walked her home and kissed her goodnight.

But it was all shadowed in tragedy.

She couldn't think about him leaning on his Firebird without thinking about Nick, and she couldn't think about kissing his lips without thinking about how she should have been here holding his hand after Nick had died. The eighties were easier in so many ways, but harder in others.

She couldn't just text him or check his social media to see where he was. The only way to contact him was to call his house, and calling was such a big deal, and Sammy hardly ever answered.

Peggy wondered if anything had changed between them since she'd babysat for Jessie. The way he was with her that day felt so easy, so right. But she hadn't heard from him since. Not a phone call, not a visit to the Bowl, nothing.

She put her hands over her face and took a deep breath and tried to re-focus on how good it was that Jack was back. It was great having him here, Jack was such a comfort to her, he was like family.

Her mind drifted to that night she'd slept over at his house. She thought about his arm around her, how comfortable it had been, how safe she had felt.

She shook her head. No. She couldn't think about that. Jack wasn't an object of desire, he was just *Jack*.

The smell of pancakes wafted into her room, pulling her from her thoughts at last.

Pancakes? Janet never made pancakes.

She got out of bed and looked in the mirror. Her hair was a big frizzy mess from all the hot rollers and hairspray she'd used the day before, and she looked ridiculous in her penguin PJ pants and thrifted Bruce Springsteen t-shirt. She wondered why she cared. Jack had seen her looking far worse. She tied her hair back with a blue velvet scrunchie and went downstairs.

Janet was sitting at the table with her Bryan Adams mug full of coffee, looking at the newspaper and laughing hysterically at something Jack had just said.

Jack was laughing too. He was already dressed in a clean dark blue t-shirt and the same shorts he had on yesterday. He was wearing a pink apron over his clothes and flipping pancakes.

"What the…?" Peggy rubbed her eyes.

"Jack's making pancakes," said Janet sounding impressed.

"Oh, really?" Jack came over behind her and pulled a chair out for her. He filled up her coffee mug and went back over to the stove.

"What's going on?" she asked sleepily.

"I don't know," said Janet. "But I could get used to this."

A few moments later, Jack brought over a huge stack of pancakes and a jug of syrup and sat down, still wearing the pink apron.

"This looks great Jack," said Janet. "Thank you."

Jack shrugged.

"I didn't know you could cook," said Peggy.

"You never asked."

"But I've known you my whole life." She scooped up some pancakes from the top of the pile.

"You always wanted take out."

"If I'd known you could cook, maybe I would've just let you cook for me."

"Anyway, don't get too excited, it's just pancakes." Jack poured syrup over his own stack.

"These are so delicious," said Peggy through chews. "What's the secret ingredient?"

"Love," he grinned.

Peggy giggled.

"What are you two going to do today?" Janet asked, reaching over for another pancake.

"What is there *to* do?" asked Jack.

"You need some new clothes," said Peggy. "We could go to the Mini Mall!"

"Oh great, just how I want to spend my time in 1984," Jack said. "At the mall."

"I don't know what you think kids do here, Jack," said Janet, "but hanging out at the mall is the coolest thing, like, ever."

"Please don't talk like that," Peggy said, giving Janet a look.

"Just trying to stay hip and bitchin'," said Janet.

Jack laughed. "*I* think you're totally bitchin' Janet."

"See?"

"Whatever." Peggy shook her head and took a sip of coffee.

"Do you need to borrow some money Jack? For some clothes and things?" Janet asked.

"Uh. That would be awesome, thanks Mrs… Janet."

"Can I borrow some money too?" Peggy asked.

"No," Janet said. "It would do you good to learn the value of a buck and to save up for what you want."

Peggy's mouth dropped open a little. "I saved up for the car."

"You saved up for part of it. I still own most of it," Janet said.

"You said I could pay it back whenever."

"And you can, but paying back your debts needs to come before borrowing more money."

Peggy sighed and added more syrup to her plate.

"What else could we do?" Jack asked. "After I get some new threads."

"Maybe we can see what Tricia is doing? Or try to get a free lane at the Bowl." Peggy said.

The phone rang and Jack jumped, putting his hand to his pocket to answer the call. "This is going to take some getting used to," he said shaking it off.

"I know, I still reach into my purse sometimes to send you a text," Peggy said as Janet got up to answer it.

"It's for you," Janet held out the receiver.

Peggy bounded up to the phone, heart thumping wildly, was it him? Was it Sammy?

"Hello?" she answered squeakily.

"Hello, Jell-O!" yelled a familiar voice that sounded a million miles away.

"Oh My God, Lacey!" she yelled back. "It's Lacey," she said to the others. "How are you doing, Lace?"

"I'm fine, just fine…" Lacey sounded like she was trying to be upbeat, but her voice was flat somehow.

"What's wrong?"

Lacey paused. "Nothing. No nothing at all, I just missed you guys for like one brief second and saw a payphone, so I called, just to say hi."

"How's it all going over there?"

"It's great," Lacey said, sounding really not so great.

"Lacey, tell me what's going on."

"Nothing, I'm just so tired from hanging out with the band every night, you know how it is."

"Not really."

"What's new over there?"

"Jack's here," Peggy beamed.

Jack looked up at the mention of his name.

"Jack?" she squealed. "*The* Jack?"

"Yes, *the* Jack."

Jack made a face at her.

"OMG, you should totally bring him out to LA!"

Peggy laughed. "I have work, and how will we even get there?"

"Drive the bug," said Lacey.

"It keeps breaking down."

"Get Sammy to take a look at it," Lacey suggested.

79

"I don't think we're there yet," she said, twisting her fingers into the curly phone cord.

"He loves working on cars, there's nothing he'd love more than to work on your bug."

"Maybe…"

"Or get a bus, I can meet you at the bus station. You could stay with us here, but it's already really crowded. But maybe we could all get a hotel together," her voice suddenly brightened. "Oh, please come!"

Peggy put the receiver to her chest. "Janet, can we go to LA?"

"If it's OK with work, it's OK with me."

"Jack?" she asked. "Do you want to go to LA?" she grinned.

"Uh, heck yes," he said, grinning back at her.

"Have you got a number and an address there?" Peggy asked grabbing a piece of paper and a pen.

"Not really, but I can give you the number of the club, I'm there a lot and they know how to get a hold of me."

Peggy got the number down and said goodbye just as Lacey's last coin dropped.

Before she had time to get too nervous, she took a deep breath and punched in Sammy's number which she knew by heart.

"Hi, Mr. Ruthven?" she asked nervously when the older man's voice answered.

"Rochelle?" he asked.

Daggers stabbed her in the chest, the heart and the throat. "No, it's Peggy."

"Oh, sorry darlin', so sorry."

"No, no, that's OK, I just wondered if Sammy was around, I have a car question." She felt her face burn and looked away from Janet and Jack.

"Sure, hold on."

"Thanks Sam," she said, her heart racing even faster at the knowledge that Sammy would soon be holding the phone up to his ear to listen to her voice.

"Hey." He always sounded so damn sexy on the phone. His voice sounded deeper and kinda gravelly and just so... *argh*.

"Hey," she said.

"What's up?" There was never much time for niceties on these calls, everyone just wanted to get straight to it.

"Sorry, maybe I shouldn't have called..."

"No, it's OK. What's going on?" he asked, sounding a little less guarded.

"Lacey just called."

"Is she OK?"

"She says she is, but she doesn't sound that great. She asked me to come visit." Me, me and Jack, whatever.

"And you want me to come?" he asked.

Peggy felt as if her face burst into flames. She hadn't even thought about inviting him along, but oh god yes, she wanted him to come with her. She wanted to go to LA with him and spend a week in a motel with a pool and hang out with rock stars and then die happy. She looked over at Jack.

"Oh, well, I, uh, I'd love if it you did, but mostly I just wanted to ask you to look at my car so I could go."

"You can't drive to LA in that thing. Especially on your own."

On her own, with Jack, whatever. "I can if you check it out for me first."

"It needs a lot of work, and I don't have time right now."

"Oh," said Peggy, deflating. Not only would they not be going to see Lacey in LA, she wouldn't get to see Sammy or get her car fixed.

"But I can drive you," he said. "If you want. If that's something you want."

Her stomach did somersaults. She looked at Jack who was gesturing wildly to her - nodding or shaking his head, asking if they were going or not going.

"Jack's here," she blurted.

"Jack?"

"He just got here yesterday."

Silence.

"Hello?"

"So, bring him along," Sammy said eventually.

"Really?"

"Sure, we need to make sure Lacey is OK. We have to look out for each other," he added.

"Wow, thanks," said Peggy, not really sure if she was included in the whole looking out for each other thing.

"No problem. I just need a couple days to sort out some stuff here. Uh, maybe could we go early next week?"

"OK, I'll need to check I can get my shifts covered, I'll call you back later."

They said their goodbyes, and she sat back down to finish her cold pancakes.

"When are you going?" Janet asked, clearing away the other empty plates.

"Hopefully next week if I can get a couple of shifts covered. Sammy said he'd drive us."

Janet looked at Jack and then back to Peggy. "Is that a good idea? The three of you riding down there together?"

"Yes," said Peggy, at the exact same time that Jack said "No."

"Well, I need to get to school to supervise some make-up tests. Yay, summer," she said sarcastically. "You two have a good day." Janet jumped up, poured another mug full of coffee, grabbed a pile of papers and her purse and rushed out the door with her mug in hand.

"Is she really going to drink that while driving?" Jack asked.

"You'd think she'd spill it, but she never does," Peggy shrugged.

Jack cleared away the last of the breakfast things and Peggy headed upstairs to get ready for their day at the mall. She hated that she was trying so hard to look nice, but it wasn't a crime to want to look good! She dressed in a pair of denim Bermuda shorts and a light pink tank top. She lined her eyes with blue liner, put on a touch of peach blush and coral lipstick and put half her hair up in a gold scrunchie. She thought she looked very 1984.

"You look cute," said Jack, when she finally came down the stairs.

"Oh, I didn't make much effort," she lied. "Are you ready to go to the mall?"

"There's nothing I'd rather do." He offered her his arm.

She looped her arm through his and she giggled.

After a successful day of shopping, laughs and catching up, Jack and Peggy had crashed out on the couch.

"Did you see that woman in the G-string leotard?" Jack asked. "I still can't work out if it was the sexiest or strangest thing I've ever seen."

"You think she was sexy? She was like, forty!" Peggy laughed.

"So? Older women can be hot," Jack shrugged. "Janet is pretty hot."

"Please god, tell me you do not have a crush on Young Janet!"

"No, god no," Jack said. "But she is hot for an older woman."

"She's not even that old. Actually, I don't even know how old she is." Peggy reached for one of the couch cushions, squishing it between herself and Jack to get comfortable.

"You're hot when you're old," he said, and then quickly wished maybe he hadn't said that.

"What?" she asked, sitting straight up again.

"When you gave me the key, you must have been about fifty. You still had it. Just so you know."

"Still had it?" Peggy asked.

"You looked good, for an old lady," he shrugged.

"Old lady? You better take that back." She grabbed the cushion, playfully threatening him with it.

"An *attractive* old woman," Jack said, bracing himself.

Peggy hit him over the head, the cushion hitting him with full force.

"Stop, I'm sorry," he laughed. "What I meant was that you hadn't even aged a day!" She smacked him with the cushion again. "You looked better than ever?"

"Oh, so you're saying I could look better than I do now?"

"I don't know what to say to make this better!" He laughed as he ducked, and she threw the cushion at his head and missed. "What if I cook you dinner?"

"OK, as long as it's half as good as the pancakes."

Jack grabbed her hand and pulled her off the couch, leading her into the kitchen. He gestured like a waiter to one of the barstools, and she took a seat.

He put Janet's pink apron on again and went about making mac and cheese.

"That smells so good," Peggy said. "I love mac and cheese. It's probably in my top five."

"Yeah, I know," he said. "After Chinese food and fries though, right?"

She nodded. "It's so weird, you being here. It's like my worlds have collided. You know everything about me from the last seventeen years, but you missed the whole last one."

"Then we better catch up," he said, giving her one of his sweet and comforting smiles.

When the mac and cheese was done, he grabbed some slices of bread, melted some butter in a pan and put the mac and cheese in between the slices of bread.

They took their plates and sat on the couch and it was just like old times. Watching old movies and eating greasy food.

"This is the best thing I've ever eaten," she said, through a mouthful of food. "The bread is so crispy, and the mac and cheese is out of this world. "You're a genius."

He grinned at her.

Peggy looked happy again, and Jack felt like everything was going to be OK. Maybe even better than OK.

And when she fell asleep on his shoulder watching *Scarecrow and Mrs. King* and drooled a little onto his t-shirt, he fell in love with her just a little bit more.

ELEVEN

Jobs

Jack was sitting at the dining table drinking his morning coffee, his attention partly on his newspaper and partly on Peggy who was still in her PJ's. Her hair was sticking up all over the place as she rushed around the house getting ready for work.

Jack had woken up early and already been for an early morning skate around the neighborhood. He wasn't very good yet, and he didn't want too many people to see him if he was going to fall on his ass. But he did OK. He was slow, but he didn't fall off. He'd showered and dressed in one of his new mall outfits - a white short-sleeved button-up shirt with turquoise triangles all over it and a pair of black chinos rolled up at the ankles. He felt kind of dressed up, but he liked it.

Jack wondered if this was what it would be like to live with her, to be married to her. He had a sudden vision of their lives twenty years from now. She'd be fussing around complaining she couldn't remember where something was and he'd just be chilling out with a morning coffee and newspaper, smiling at her and telling her where everything was before she even started looking for it.

It was nice reading the newspaper. Jack had never been a huge fan of cell phones, but he'd found them very convenient. He liked reading the news in the morning on his phone in bed, but here he couldn't just wake up, reach over and start reading a newspaper. He had to get up, make coffee and then settle in with the paper. He kind of felt like an old man, but he liked it.

Janet came down the stairs dressed in a yellow pencil skirt and black silk blouse. She really did look bitchin'. If Jack could stop thinking of how she looked like in thirty-three years from now, he might have even had a little crush on Janet. But looking at her was kind of like looking at a really old photo of your mom. You could see that she had been young and smokin', but she was still your mom.

Janet handed Peggy a pair of blue stonewash jeans. "These were hanging over the banister," she said.

"What? Why were they hanging there?" Peggy made a groaning noise, grabbed the jeans and stormed back upstairs to get dressed.

Janet poured herself a coffee and gave Jack a top up even though he didn't ask for one. He smiled and thanked her.

"So, Jack," she said, sitting down opposite him at the table.

He looked up. This sounded very teacher-ish.

"Have you thought about what you're going to do here?"

"What I'm going to do here?" he repeated.

"Yeah, like how are you going to spend your time? And how are you going to make money?"

Jack laughed. "Are you talking about me getting a job?"

Janet nodded. "Yes. I have a job, Peggy has a job, that's how we do things in this house."

"Peggy didn't have to get a job when she was here last year," Jack complained.

"Peggy was at school then."

Jack put down the newspaper.

"Getting a job here would be fun. You'll meet people and really get to know the place, the *time*."

Jack looked up at the ceiling. "I've been here one day, Janet," he moaned.

"Well, you know what they say, it's one day or day one." Janet began collecting up books and bags. "I'm off to work, I'll see you tonight. There's a spare key by the door if you want to go out job hunting." She gave him a wink, put her mug in the sink and rushed out the door yelling goodbye to Peggy.

Jack rolled his eyes behind her as she left and went back to reading the news.

By the time he'd gotten to the sports pages, which he wasn't that interested in, Peggy was back in the kitchen, dressed in a bowling shirt and a pair of pale blue jeans. Her hair was curled and up in a high ponytail held in place with an emerald green scrunchie, and she was wearing bright pink lipstick. She looked incredible. Jack had missed her so much, and now she was here, right in front of him. He had to force himself to stop staring at her. Hell, he had to force himself not to just jump up and take her in his arms.

Peggy slumped down in front of him. She grabbed his coffee mug and started drinking from it. It was such an intimate gesture, and it made him feel warm and fuzzy inside.

"What's on today?" he asked her.

"Work," she said.

Jack made a sad face.

"This sucks," she pouted. "You just got here, and I want to hang out and show you around and I can't."

"Adulting sucks," Jack said. "Janet is already on my back to get a job."

"What? You've only been here one day!"

"Yeah, but I also don't have any money." Jack hated the idea of getting a job here, but he also knew his job back home wasn't going to wait for him. If he was going to have any chance with Peggy, he needed to prove to her he could make his own way. All he'd done these last few years was let her use her parent's credit cards to pay for stuff for him.

"Want a ride into town?" she asked, passing his nearly finished coffee back over to him.

"Sure." He'd be better off out in town than sitting around here all day. "Maybe I could hang out with you at work?"

"I think the boss is in today, but maybe another time."

"It might be nice to go see Tammy at Dee's anyway."

"I can pick you up later, or you can always walk down to the Bowl to meet me," Peggy said as she stopped the car outside Dee's.

"Where's the Bowl?"

"It's on the other side of the mall."

"Where Sears is?"

"Yeah, in our time it's Sears."

"That's so cool that they made Sears into a bowling alley."

Peggy gave him a look. "No Jack, they make the Bowl into Sears."

Jack rolled his eyes at himself. "Oh, right, yeah that sucks."

"So, do you want me to come get you later? Or will you meet me?" she asked. "You can't just text me or call me, so I need to know now."

Jack didn't like the urgency of this. "Uh, yeah sure, I'll come down. When do you finish?"

"I'll be done at four."

"Cool, so I'll skate over there round four." Jack grabbed his skateboard and got out of the car.

"OK, I gotta go, or I'll be late," she said.

Jack waved as she drove off down the street in the bug, which was making weird chugging noises.

"Hey stranger," Tammy greeted him as he pushed through the door of the diner and walked in.

His *grandmother*.

"Hey," he said. Now that he knew who she was he suddenly felt weird around her, like he had to impress her or something.

"Take a seat, honey." She ushered him into his regular booth. "What can I getcha?"

"Just a coffee, thanks."

Tammy brought it over to him with a slice of pie he didn't even ask for and gave him a newspaper to read.

"Back again, huh?" she mused as she folded her arms and gave him a good look.

"Peggy and Janet are both at work, so I thought I'd come hang out in here a while. I'm supposed to be looking for a job," he added as he searched the paper for the jobs section.

"You can start after you've finished your coffee."

"What?"

"We're looking for a server, you're looking for a job. Funny how life works out sometimes. It's four bucks an hour, and the tips are good."

"Four bucks an hour?" Jack laughed.

"That's a good wage for around here. You won't find better, and the boss is decent too."

"Who's the boss?" Jack asked.

Tammy raised her eyebrow and put a thumb to her chest.

"You're the boss?" he guessed.

"And are you my new server or what?"

"Well, yeah, I guess," he said. "But can I get next week off?"

Tammy laughed. "Kids today, Jeez Louise," she said. "Sure, work a couple shifts this week, and if you're OK, you can come back week after next."

The money was dismal, but it would get Janet off his back and he really liked the idea of getting to know his grandmother. Tammy threw him an apron and an order book and that was pretty much his induction.

Jack had worked at the coffee shop in town in his time for just one week. He had been good at making coffee, but customer service was never his strong point. He was always friendly to people who were friendly to him, but when he'd had to serve people who acted like he was beneath them, he'd nearly flipped his lid a couple of times. One time he even gave a customer a muffin that he'd dropped on the floor. If he'd stayed longer, he was sure he would have done something way worse.

So here he was, dressed in a white apron, filling up coffee cups, emptying ashtrays and taking orders from cowboys and housewives who were meeting up to swap local gossip. Some preppy guys started snapping their fingers at him when he didn't get to their table straight away and he could feel his anger rising in his chest. But they were decent enough when he went over, and they gave him a good tip. He could feel himself already turning into Jack, the diner server.

After the lunch rush, Tammy told him to go take a break. He sat back at his booth sipping on a shake she'd made especially for him and chowing down on a grilled cheese. She came over to sit opposite him. She lit a cigarette and Jack quickly lost his appetite, but he kept eating anyway. He didn't want to be rude.

"How are enjoying your first day?" she asked.

"It's better than I was expecting," he said with a shrug.

"Wait until I get you out in the kitchen with Carlos."

"Please don't make me go back there." He couldn't imagine anything worse than cooking greasy diner food all day. Serving it was almost bearable, but flipping burgers? No way.

"What do you want to do with your life, kid?"

Jack sighed. "I had this dream," he began.

Tammy laughed. "All young boys have a big dream."

"I want to move out to LA and get a job in computers."

"What do you know about computers?" she asked.

"A bit," he said. "Enough? Not much really. I dunno, the plan was never really that clear after the point where I got to LA and got a good paying job."

"A good paying job, or a job you love?"

Jack looked around him. "Is this a good paying job or a job you love?"

She gave him a sad smile. "This is a *job*," she said. "I'm too old to have a dream, but you're not."

"You're never too old to have a dream," he said.

"You should work for a bumper sticker company," she laughed.

"If that was a job, I'd take it," he said, taking another slurp of the melted ice-cream in the bottom of his shake.

"Let me give you some free advice, Jack," she said, reaching over and patting his hand. "A job you love is worth more than any money in the world, even if it means you have to go without sometimes."

"What did you do before you worked here?"

"I used to be a dancer," she said.

"Wow, really?"

"Yeah, you wouldn't know it now, but I used to dance on Broadway." She got up and did a little spin and for a second Jack could totally see it. There was something in the way she moved that was different to regular people.

"What happened?" He felt weird asking her. She didn't know he was her grandson, but she seemed to like talking about the old days, and he wanted to know all he could about her.

"Life," she said as she patted his shoulder. "Live your dream while you can, but just make sure you give me two weeks' notice." She disappeared to go serve a table that had just walked in.

By four in the afternoon Jack had been so busy working and talking to Tammy about all the shows she was in on Broadway that he totally forgot he was meant to meet Peggy at the Bowl. He asked Tammy if he could go, but she said she needed him until the dinner staff came on at six. He looked through the phone book for the number and gave the Bowl a call, but the woman who answered said Peggy had already left. With no way to contact her he started getting worried. What if she thought he'd bailed on her?

He didn't need to worry though. At four-fifteen Peggy and another girl who looked kind of punk with messy jet-black hair, short black skirt and biker boots dressed in the same staff bowling shirt at Peggy's walked through the door of the diner.

"Jack," Peggy called out to him. "Look at you!" She started laughing as she looked him up and down. The other girl slipped past them into a booth. "What happened to you?"

He made a waiter pose and then felt stupid. "Well, Janet told me to get a job."

"When do you finish?" Peggy asked.

"Not until six," he sighed.

"Far out, when are we going to get some time together?"

"I'll see if I can take ten and come hang for a quick break." Jack went out the back to check with Tammy and she said it was OK as long as it didn't get too much busier.

He grabbed some sodas and took them to the table.

"Jack, this is Tricia," Peggy said. "Tricia, this is Jack, my best friend from back home."

Jack looked at Tricia.

Tricia looked back at Jack. "What are you staring at bonehead?" she asked him angrily.

Jack just kept staring.

"This dude is weird." Tricia slipped out of the booth and headed towards the cigarette machine.

"Jack," Peggy said elbowing him in the ribs. It hurt, bad. "What's with you?"

"Tricia," said Jack.

"What about her?" asked Peggy.

"She's my mom."

TWELVE

The Fire Station

A couple of days later, Jack and Peggy's days off had synced. Jack was excited to finally get a chance to cut loose. He'd been working every day since he'd arrived, and even though it was really cool to be a time traveler and get to know his grandmother and everything, he was getting restless. He knew he had LA to look forward to, but a night out, a few drinks and maybe getting to meet some of Peggy's other friends sounded like fun. He hadn't really talked to anyone except Peggy, Janet, his grandmother, Carlos who flipped the burgers and brief exchanges with the customers.

Jack and Peggy told Janet they were just going out for dinner with Tricia, and that she would give them a ride. That made Jack feel super weird. He'd only met her that once, but she'd been so mean and there was nothing about her he'd liked. He felt bad thinking that. In the present he loved his mom. Even though he got annoyed with her sometimes - when she asked too many questions or came into his room when he was busy, she was always so nice, and he loved her a lot. Tricia was nothing like his mom and it gave him a searing headache to see her like this. She was all angsty and hard edged and she wore so much eye make-up.

"I don't want to go with Tricia," Jack said to Janet who was tidying in the kitchen. Jack was already dressed in a pair of jeans and a black shirt with yellow hearts on it, another one of his new mall buys, and he was just waiting for Peggy to be ready so they could go.

"Why not?" asked Janet as she picked up a stack of magazines from the counter.

"She's my mom," Jack said.

"I know," said Janet.

"What?"

"When you said your grandmother was Tammy, I knew your mom had to be Tricia."

"Why didn't you tell me?" Jack asked.

Janet put the magazines in a new pile on the other side of the room. "I didn't think it was my place. I thought it was something you should probably find out on your own."

"She's so different here."

"She's intense, that's for sure."

"And I can't stop thinking about it, but my parents met at school so my dad must be around here somewhere, too."

"You said your dad's name was Hank, but I don't know any kids called Hank from school." Janet looked thoughtful.

Jack shrugged.

Peggy looked stunning when she came downstairs. She was dressed in a sixties style pink skirt with a white blouse and her curled hair was piled up on top of her head. She looked like she'd fallen out of the book room in 1963 not 1983.

"Well, look at you," said Janet, making a whistling sound.

Peggy did a twirl and Jack's mouth nearly dropped onto the floor.

They heard a honk outside, and Peggy ran to the door and put on a pair of black flats. Jack slipped on his Vans and they were out the door.

Peggy rode shotgun and Jack sat like a little kid in the backseat. His mom had driven him around so many times like this, but not like *this*.

"Have you got any painkillers, Peg?" he asked. She threw him her black fringed purse and he found the bottle. He took two straight without water.

Tricia scowled at him in the rear-view mirror.

"Sorry I was so weird the other day, Tricia," he said.

Her face softened just slightly.

"He's still settling in," said Peggy. "It's hard to move to a new place. Remember how weird I was when I first arrived?"

"You were majorly weird," said Tricia. "You're still weird."

When they got to town it was too early to go straight to the Fire Station, so they decided to see if they could get a free lane at the Bowl and maybe even a free beer or two. When they got there Abigail, a middle-aged woman who had been working at the Bowl for decades was working and there was no sign of Hayley-Rae, so they got their free lane and a couple of beers too.

Peggy kept getting total fluke strikes and Jack only ever got that one pin on the end. Tricia didn't want to bowl, she just sat there with a soda, flicking her nails and moaning about how lame the Bowl was, and making comments about how bad Peggy and Jack were at bowling.

"Why don't you loosen up a little and have some fun?" Jack asked her, eventually starting to get bored with her whole miserable teenager thing. He held a bowling ball and wiggled his hips at her. He dropped the ball and it nearly landed on his toes. Tricia laughed for the first time since he'd met her. She looked so much more like his mom when she laughed.

"Come on, Tricia," he said. "Have a go."

"No."

"Are you too cool to bowl?" he asked as Peggy lined up her shot. "Or is it just that you are so bad at bowling it's embarrassing for you?"

"It's that I'm not lame enough to bowl."

"But you work here," Jack said.

"Duh," she said.

"So how do you work at a bowling alley if you hate bowling?"

"It was either this or working with my mom at Dee's, and screw that. I get enough drama with her at home."

Jack sat down next to Tricia while Peggy went for her second turn.

"Tammy seems cool," Jack said. "I like her."

"Oh sure, she seems cool if you know her for eight seconds. Try living with her."

"Maybe you should try to make the most of having your mom around. She won't always be here, you know."

Tricia looked at him darkly.

"Jack," interrupted Peggy. "Your turn." She gave him a look. "And maybe you should leave Tricia alone."

"Yeah," said Tricia, taking a gulp of soda. "Leave Tricia alone."

By the time they finally headed over to the Fire Station, Jack and Peggy were kind of tipsy.

"This is the Fire Station," Peggy yelled over the music, waving her arms around in the dingy bar.

"I figured," said Jack, looking around at the bar. It was a total dive. The music was too loud, and the speakers were too scratchy, the lights were dim, his Vans were sticking to the floor and the smell of stale beer filled his nostrils. Jack loved it.

"I love it," he said.

"I see someone I know," said Tricia, and she disappeared into a dark corner at the back.

Peggy dragged Jack towards the bar, and a vaguely familiar looking guy with long greasy hair and a bandana looked Jack up and down. The guy reached over the bar and held his wrist, Jack didn't know what was going on, but it seemed like an almost friendly gesture, so he held the guy's wrist back. The guy shook it up and down twice and then let go and fist bumped Jack.

"Nice to meet a fellow Eight," the guy said.

"Oh," said Jack, understanding now. The tattoo. He looked over at Peggy, but she wasn't paying any attention. She was just bopping up and down to the music, looking around the bar. Probably for Sammy Ruthven. Urgh. Jack didn't know what he would do if Sammy Ruthven turned up.

The bar guy poured them two strong screwdrivers and passed them over.

"Where are you from, Eight?" the guy asked.

"Canada," said Jack.

"We have Eights in Canada? Cool." The guy seemed surprised, but kind of impressed.

Jack pointed to his tattoo. "I guess so," he shrugged.

"Well, anything you need man, anytime. Eights are Eights," the guy said.

"Eights are Eights," repeated Jack, hoping it was the right thing to say.

"I mean it. You get into any trouble here, you just let me know."

Jack nodded. He really hoped he wasn't going to get

into any trouble here, but it was always good to know someone had your back, even if it was just some random guy who just happened to have the same tattoo as you.

"You two together?" He pointed at Peggy who had her back to them both.

"Yes," Jack said, before his brain could stop him.

The guy passed the drinks over without asking for any money. Jack gave him a thumbs up and passed Peggy her drink.

Peggy looked over at the bar guy and then back at Jack. She pulled him in close. God, she smelled good. Like that musky smell but also something else, some kind of perfume that made Jack think of candy and talcum powder. She whispered something directly into his ear.

"What?" asked Jack, not quite hearing her.

Peggy pulled him away from the bar. "That's Jonas, the guy who kissed me last year. The guy you punched, or should I say, *tried* to punch, at the Stables."

"*Jonas*," said Jack, feeling his stomach sink. Of course, that's why he looked familiar.

Peggy nodded.

"OK, so I should definitely pay for drinks next time."

"He gave you free drinks?"

Jack nodded

"Weird," she said.

Jack shrugged. He wasn't ready to tell her he was an Eight. She would flip out, and he wanted to have a good time tonight.

Peggy sipped her drink. "Maybe we shouldn't have come here."

"No, this is fun," said Jack. "Let's drink these and then go dance."

And they did dance, and he was right, it was fun.

He twirled Peggy around on the dance floor and she

laughed and grabbed his shirt and then held onto his waist to hold herself up. Her hands on him like this felt so right. He took her in his arms and slow danced with her, even though the music was fast and furious and blaring so loud.

"Oh, I feel like I'm at prom again," she said, smiling. And then her face fell.

"Hey," he said, holding her face in his hands. "Everything is OK now, I'm here."

Her body relaxed and she fell into his arms, and he couldn't tell if she was crying or laughing or singing.

"I'm glad you're here," she mumbled into his neck. It would have been the perfect moment if Tricia hadn't chosen that exact second to come storming over, telling them it was time to go, before running out of the bar.

They looked at each other and sobered up a little as they started to follow her out.

"Tricia," Jack said as they were walking to her car. "What's wrong? Why are you so angry?"

Tricia shot him a look. "I'm angry because I've had to look after drunk people all night."

"You've hardly had to look after us, you just left us," he said. "Why did you leave us?"

"I was hanging out with some other friends, and I thought you and Peggy would want some time to yourselves, anyway."

"Oh, so you are nice, really," said Jack, sliding into the back seat of the car and realizing just how much of a buzz he had on.

"She is nice," Peggy said. "You just have to get to know her."

"I'd like to get to know you, Tricia," Jack said. "Not like, in a romantic way or anything, let's get that clear straight away."

"Jack, you can stop talking now," said Peggy.

"Jack, shut up," said Tricia.

"Can we be friends?" Jack asked her.

"No," she said.

"Tricia," Peggy began, "you can tell us, what's going on?"

"Nothing, I'm just done with boys."

"You can't be done with boys," Jack said. "There's a guy out there who you're going to marry and be together with forever and it will be a beautiful thing."

"Jack," said Peggy, "that's enough now, you're drunk."

Jack ignored her. "I feel like I've known you my whole life Tricia, kind of like you're my sister or my cousin or something."

Tricia turned to look at him. "Shoshone?" she asked.

"Yes!" said Jack.

"I felt it too."

"Felt what too?" Peggy asked.

"How far back?" Tricia asked.

"My great grandfather on my mom's side," he said.

"My grandfather on my dad's side," she said.

"Oh, cool," said Peggy, giggling. "So, you guys could be related?"

"Not everyone in the same tribe is related, you airhead," said Tricia. "That's so offensive."

"Sorry, I didn't mean to be offensive, but like, you *could* be right? Just like I could be related to the other Martins who came over on the Mayflower."

"It's so far from being the same thing." Tricia started the car and shook her head.

"Yeah, Peggy, so not the same thing," Jack said, waving her away with his hand.

"Great, so now you guys are friends and I'm the odd one out," Peggy pouted.

"Wow Peggy," said Tricia. "You can be like, so ignorant

sometimes. If you think you're the one being left out, why don't you go spend some time with the native people of this land for five minutes and really learn what it's like to be on the outside?"

Peggy's mouth dropped open.

"She has a point," said Jack. "Check your privilege, Peggy."

Peggy sat in silence.

"Peggy comes from money," Jack whispered to Tricia.

"I can hear you." Peggy folded her arms.

"Just try to be a bit more thoughtful in the future," Tricia said, rubbing Peggy's shoulder very un-maternally.

When they got home, Peggy and Jack tried to be quiet sneaking in. The last thing they needed was Janet coming down and finding they had been drinking. But when they got in, they saw she'd left a note in the kitchen saying that she was staying overnight at Ray's.

"Ooooh," said Peggy. "It must be getting serious with Ray!"

"I seriously can't even begin to imagine Mrs. Willis having a sleepover with a man. It's all kinds of messed up," Jack said.

"Do you want a pizza? I can do a Hawaiian?"

"Do you have a margarita?"

"Uh, let me check." She ran into the kitchen. "Yep," she called back.

"Perfect," said Jack.

They ate the pizza on the couch, giggling about Tricia and Janet and time traveling. They talked about destiny and dreams until minutes turned into hours.

Peggy yawned, her soft hazel eyes began to look sleepy. She rested her head on his shoulder. It was so nice and normal and right to be here with her like this he almost didn't think about it when he put his arm around her. She nuzzled a little deeper into his chest and made a purring sound. His heart started to beat louder, and he hoped she couldn't tell. She sat up and looked at him bleary-eyed. She was so beautiful in that moment. Her mascara was smudged, she still had tomato sauce on her cheek from the pizza and her hair was a mess, but to him, she was perfect. He reached out and brushed a piece of stray hair out of her face. She closed her eyes as if she enjoyed the feeling of it. And when she didn't flinch or move away, he ran his fingers through her hair, and when she made that purring noise again, he leaned in closer to her. And when she still didn't move away, he very gently, very slowly moved his lips towards hers, and when she didn't move away, he kissed her.

Peggy felt so safe here with Jack that when he kissed her, it took a moment for her to realize what was happening. In her sleepy half-drunk haze, she found herself kissing him back, and it was... nice. His lips were soft and gentle and easy to kiss. But when Sammy's face flashed into her mind she pulled away, putting her hand to her mouth as if she was trying to erase the imprint of his lips on hers.

"I'm sorry." He pulled back and looked kind of horri-fied. He shook his head. "I don't think I should have done that."

"I don't think I should have done that back," she said through her hand.

"Maybe we should talk about it," said Jack.

"Or maybe we should just forget that it ever happened and never talk about it again." Peggy bolted up off the couch and rushed upstairs.

THIRTEEN

Science Fiction

It was after midnight and Jack was doing dishes out back on the graveyard shift at the diner. Nobody had been in for hours. The dinner crowd had long gone home, and Jack was enjoying the lull before the bars closed and all the hungry drunks came in. It'd be dead again after that until the early risers started coming in. He didn't even know why they bothered to stay open 24 hours. They had to pay him more to be here than they ever made on food. But even though he didn't make much in tips, Jack kind of liked the late shift. He liked being alone with his thoughts and it was usually just him and Carlos on the late shift. Carlos was cool. He was probably pushing fifty and way out of shape, but he made Jack laugh with his bad jokes and terrible advice about girls. Carlos was a lifelong bachelor and Jack suspected he'd probably been a real lady's man back in his day.

"Never get tied down to a woman," Carlos said as he handed Jack another pile of dirty plates. "Marriage is a prison."

"Have you ever been married, Carlos?" Jack asked.

"Nope, never even had a long-term girlfriend."

"So then how do you know?"

"I've seen too many of my friends go from fun loving guys to prisoners in their own homes." Carlos shook his head.

"I can't imagine living my life without someone by my side." Jack stacked some more plates in the dishwasher.

"You're still young, you'll learn. Girls only want one thing, and it's not your dick."

Jack laughed. "What is it then, oh wise sage?"

"Money. Women only want your money." He tapped Jack on the head with what he hoped was a clean spoon.

"So, is that the real reason you don't have a woman, because you're broke?" Jack asked playfully.

Carlos chased him with a dish towel and Jack ran back out into the front of the diner, still laughing.

A guy about Jack's age had walked in. He had thick frizzy dark blonde hair and wore thick aviator glasses, and something about him was very familiar. The guy took a seat at the back of the diner and pulled out a book.

"I know that book," said Jack, as he walked over with the coffee pot. He pulled a cloth out from his apron and wiped down the table before pouring a cup for the guy.

"Seriously?" the guy asked. "I don't think I've ever met anyone else who likes these."

"I love Diamondback." Jack slid into the seat opposite him and put the coffee pot down on the table. "Those books got me through some hard times." Jack felt a pang in his chest as he thought about his folks back home. He really missed them already. He was planning to go back and see them after the LA trip. He wasn't like Peggy, he couldn't just never see his parents again. Jack had no idea how to navigate the whole making your choice thing. He loved Peggy, and he didn't want to leave her, but he didn't want to lose his mom and dad either.

"I can't wait for number three to come out," the guy said.

"I already read it," Jack said. "I think it's my favorite so far."

The guy gave him a confused look. "But it hasn't been written yet."

Jack wrung the cloth in his hand. "Oh, yeah, I'm getting confused, I meant the second one."

"This *is* the second one." He held the book up.

"Late shift, it's been a long day." Jack rubbed his eyes for extra effect.

"Oh, sure." The guy looked back down at his book.

Jack continued on anyway. "I never met anyone who read them before either, except my dad. He got me into them."

"You're lucky. My dad thinks any kind of fiction will open a door to the gates of hell." The guy shrugged.

"Woah," said Jack.

"Or something," the guy said. "I don't know why I just told you that. It's late I guess." He ran his hand through his hair in a way that gave Jack Deja-Vu.

What was it about this guy that Jack couldn't quite put his finger on?

"You OK?" the guy asked. "You're kinda staring at me."

Jack looked down at the coffee pot. "Sorry. Yeah. Hey, what did you say your name was again?"

"I didn't," he said. "It's Horace."

"Horace? Are you sure?" Jack frowned.

Horace laughed. "Yeah, I'm sure. I wouldn't make up a name like Horace. It's the worst name in the history of the world."

"It's not so bad," Jack said. "I'm Jack, it's short for Jackson but pretty much no one calls me that."

"Jackson is a really great name."

Jack rolled his eyes. "I guess it's OK."

"I wish I had a name like Cord, or Chase or Hank."

"*Hank.*" Jack felt the blood run out of his face.

"Yeah, it's way cooler than Horace."

"Maybe you could just get people to call you Hank," Jack said, staring at him again.

"You're staring again," Horace said.

"Sorry. I know I'm acting weird. It's night shift, it melts your brain."

Horace laughed awkwardly.

"What are you doing here so late, anyway?" Jack asked.

"Just waiting for someone."

"Can I get you anything?"

"Maybe just a slice of pie?"

Jack stood up and brushed his apron down. "Coming right up."

Jack stood behind the counter and lifted the lid off the cherry pie as he continued to stare at the guy from across the diner.

"What's up with you?" asked Carlos, bringing out a stack of clean plates and nudging Jack in the ribs.

Jack grabbed a plate off him for the slice of pie. "You wouldn't believe me if I told you."

"You're a weird kid," said Carlos. "I like you, but you're weird."

Jack nodded. "Yeah, and I think I'm getting weirder by the day."

And Jack cut an extra-large slice of pie for the awkward teenage boy across the diner, who would one day become Jack's dad.

FOURTEEN

Road Trip from Hell

Peggy's clock radio turned on at five and began blaring Kenny Rogers' voice. "*I know it's late, I know you're weary,*" he sang. Peggy groaned. It was early, but he was right, she was weary. It was still dark outside, so she flipped on the bedside light, hiding under the covers until her eyes got used to the light.

"That was Kenny's big hit from last year," said the radio DJ. Peggy grinned to herself. She'd been here for nearly a year now, but the novelty still hadn't worn off yet. She wondered if it ever would. She guessed when she got older and caught up with herself in time, things would be different. Eventually she would be in 2016 again, but for now, it was 1984. Kenny Rogers was still a big deal and Sammy Ruthven was on his way to her house. But he was coming to pick her and Jack up in an hour and she wasn't ready. She dragged herself out of bed and into the shower, and then dressed in a knee-length spaghetti strapped pale blue dress. She'd be comfortable enough in the car all day and she was showing just enough cleavage for Sammy to notice, but not so much Jack would get the wrong idea.

Jack.

Peggy looked at herself in the mirror and wondered for a moment what kind of person she was. She was in love with Sammy, but she'd kissed *Jack.* Well, he had kissed her first, but she had definitely kissed him back. Her stomach churned, and she didn't know if it was guilt or hunger or both. She applied some blue eyeshadow to her eyelids, a bit of black mascara and a dash of blush. She grabbed her favorite frosted peach lipstick and took a deep breath and headed downstairs. Maybe if she just acted like it never happened, everything would be OK.

"Hey," said Jack brightly. He was sitting at the counter drinking a coffee and eating a slice of toast. He was already dressed, and Peggy felt weird when she thought he looked kind of cute in his short-sleeved shirt with the sleeves rolled up. There was something about his tattoo that made him almost... sexy.

"Want some coffee?" he asked.

"I'll get it." She moved her gaze from his arm to the coffee pot.

"About last night," he began.

"Nothing happened." Peggy turned her back to him, as she poured coffee and put some bread in the toaster for herself.

"But something *did* happen."

Peggy pulled the lever down on the toaster and turned to face him. "I think we should just forget about it. It was nothing."

Jack's face fell. "But it wasn't nothing, not to me Peggy. I just thought maybe we should talk about it. Clear the air. Like, these feelings I have for you..."

"Jack." She held up a hand. "Please stop."

"A lot has happened since you left. I've even had a girl-friend, kind of."

"A girlfriend?" Peggy asked, folding her arms. Jack had a *girlfriend*? She wasn't sure why the thought of that made her feel hot and uncomfortable.

"Do you have any feelings for me at all?" he asked, his big brown eyes pleading with her to say yes.

But she couldn't say yes, and she couldn't honestly say no, either. It wouldn't have been so bad if the kiss had been horrible, but it had been kind of nice. She didn't know what that meant. All she knew was that Sammy would be here in a few minutes, and the feelings she had for *him* were a definite yes, and she felt sick.

"I guess, if it's what you really want, we can just try to act like it didn't happen."

Peggy nodded. "I think that's for the best." She took a sip of her coffee.

"Even though it did happen," Jack added.

"Starting from now, we never, ever talk about this again. Deal?"

Jack shrugged, and then gave a noncommittal nod.

"Never talk about what again?" asked Janet, walking into the kitchen dressed in her Japanese robe.

"Nothing," they both said at the same time.

Janet gave them both a look. "I wanted to come down and say goodbye before you left," she said. "You'll be back next Saturday, right?"

Peggy nodded. "Uh huh."

"That was good of the Bowl to give you all that time off in the middle of Summer," said Janet, making her way to the coffee pot.

"They gave me four days off, but I switched a bunch of shifts to cover the week," Peggy said.

"And Dee's was OK about you taking off, Jack?"

Jack shrugged. "Tammy said she can call in some favors, but that I'd owe her."

Peggy's toast popped, and she'd just started buttering it when there was a knock at the door. She felt her stomach lurch and suddenly she wasn't even hungry at all.

"Want me to get it?" asked Janet.

Peggy shook her head and rushed to the door, and there he was. Sammy Ruthven, sexy as ever, dressed in faded blue jeans and a plain white t-shirt. His sandy blonde hair was a mess, and she wondered if he'd even bothered to comb it this morning. She'd spent an hour trying to look pretty for him, and he'd just rolled out of bed and looked like a God.

"Hey." The corners of his mouth moved just ever so slightly upward.

"Hey." She tried to fight the urge to beam at him or throw herself into his arms.

"Hey," said Jack, suddenly appearing behind Peggy.

"Hey," said Sammy, the corners of his mouth going back to normal again.

Sammy and Jack looked each other up and down in the silence.

"So," said Peggy.

"Are you ready?" Sammy asked.

Peggy nodded. Their bags were already stacked waiting by the door and there was no reason for them to be standing there staring at each other.

Janet came over and handed Peggy her toast in a brown paper bag and gave her a hug. "Be good," she said. She gave Jack a hug too. "You too, Jack. And drive safe," she said to Sammy.

Sammy's mouth twitched. "Always." He took Peggy's bag and walked towards the brown Buick in the driveway.

Peggy always half expected the Firebird to be there, and every time it wasn't, it was another reminder of Nick, and everything Sammy had lost while Peggy had been back in her present, thinking she'd lost him forever.

Sammy put her bag in the trunk and Jack threw his in after it and slid into the backseat.

"You can sit in the front, if you want," said Peggy.

"No thanks," said Jack, closing the door on her.

Peggy took the passenger seat and looked back at him, but he just looked out the window.

Sammy got in and started the car, and Peggy's heart began to race along with the engine. Here she was again, in the front seat of Sammy Ruthven's car. Close enough to smell his cologne and for some strange reason, it kind of made her want to cry, or scream or something. He was so close, she could just reach out and grab him, but she couldn't, because even though there was no distance at all between them, he felt so far away.

The Buick felt so much bigger and safer than the Firebird ever had, and Sammy only drove at or below the speed limit. When he changed gears, she couldn't help but glance at his arm. She was taken back to that first time they took a ride in his car together. He'd driven her up to Salt Mountain and held her hand for the first time. Suddenly everything she thought she had felt for Jack just melted away out of her mind. This was it, Sammy was it for her and nothing else would ever come close.

Sammy put a cigarette in between his lips and offered the pack towards Jack.

"I don't smoke."

Sammy put the packet on the dash, reaching across Peggy to open up the glove compartment, gently brushing her arm as he did. He began hunting around with one hand while he held the wheel with the other.

"Let me," she said. He brought his hand back to the wheel but said nothing. She found his matches, lit one and held it up to his cigarette. He leaned into her to light it and the smell of him, all cigarettes and oil changes and woody cologne, so familiar it made her heart ache.

Peggy put the matches on the dash next to the cigarette packet although she had the thought to keep hold of them, so he'd have to be that close every time he wanted one. And it was a long drive, so there'd probably be many. She really didn't like Sammy's smoking, she never had, but she'd use any excuse to get that close to his lips right now.

Jack let out a little cough and wound down his window. "Are you not aware of the health risks of smoking?" he asked.

Sammy laughed.

"There's nothing funny about lung cancer," said Jack.

Peggy thought of Jack's grandmother who was going to die from exactly that. Because she smoked. Peggy wound down her window too.

"You might not care about your health," said Jack. "But what about the people who care about you?"

"They all smoke too," Sammy said as he inhaled.

"Peggy doesn't, and even if she did, would that make it OK?" asked Jack. "Someone really close to me died from smoking. And it sucked, and it didn't have to happen."

"Sorry to hear that." Sammy flicked ash into the ashtray but took another drag anyway.

Jack reached over to wind down the window on the other side.

No one said anything for a good few miles and the tension became as thick as the smoke Sammy was exhaling out his window.

"Do you guys want some music?" Sammy asked eventually.

"Please," said Peggy.

"Can you grab an eight track, Peg?" A tone of ease

and familiarity entering Sammy's voice. It was such a simple request, but one he'd asked her so many times before it had a sort of magic to it.

"Sure, what do you want?" She opened the glove box again.

"You choose."

She rummaged through the tapes and eventually settled on Kiss' Dynasty album.

"*Tonight, I want to give it all to you,*" sang the speakers. She rolled her eyes at herself. Why didn't she pick something less sexy? She turned the volume up so loud that no one could talk over it.

When they stopped for gas in the middle of nowhere a few hours later, Jack excused himself and went off to find the toilet. And when he did, he wished he'd just found a tree instead, it was dirty and smelled disgusting. He had to hold his breath and try not to wretch while he did what he needed to do. He washed his hands and splashed water onto his face. The reflection looking back at him in the streaky mirror surprised him. He looked dark and brooding. He thought he'd been doing a good job of being cool in such an awkward situation, but his reflection told him otherwise. He had been frowning so hard he'd almost given himself a wrinkle. He gagged as he was forced to take another breath. He didn't want to stay in here with the smell of other people's feces, but it wasn't that much worse than having to sit in a car with Sammy Ruthven.

Peggy and Sammy were still obviously still into each other. Sammy clearly had some issues about expressing that, and Jack guessed he probably still hadn't forgiven her for running off last summer. But the way he looked at her, Jack knew that look. He was beginning to feel like he was a little kid in the back seat on a road trip with his parents. Even though they had hardly said a word to each other, Jack could tell. The way he leaned into her when she lit his cigarettes, even though he could totally light one on his own. The way he asked for a new tape, eight track, whatever that thing was, and let her choose it. They'd only been driving a few hours and weren't due to get to LA until sometime later that night. He wasn't sure he was going to make it. Maybe he could get a bus back to Santolsa, or hitch his own ride to LA. He could go missing at this gas station. Maybe he could even walk through the desert to get there. Even that would be preferable to staying on this road trip from hell.

Eventually he gave up on his stupid ideas, gave in and made the bold decision to come out of the toilet. Sammy was leaning against the hood of the car smoking another cigarette and looking like the coolest guy on the planet.

"Hey," said Sammy.

"Hey," said Jack, leaning against the car door trying to act casual.

"Peggy's gone to find the restroom."

"It stinks."

"They usually do."

"It's so hot I think I'm melting. Do you want a drink or anything?" Jack wiped the sweat from his brow. He wasn't really asking to be nice, but just to get Sammy out of his face for as long as possible.

Sammy's eyes flicked over to him. "Sure."

"What do you want?" Jack asked gruffly.

"Pepsi."

"You don't want a Coke?"

"I don't care, whatever." Sammy flicked his butt on the ground.

"I'm just trying to be nice," Jack said. He wished he'd

never asked and that he'd just gotten himself and Peggy a couple of 7UPs. Screw this guy.

"Why?" Sammy gave him a questioning look.

"Because Peggy's my friend."

Sammy just stared at him and pulled out another cigarette.

Jack thought of his grandmother smoking away her days in front of him. "You really shouldn't smoke," he said.

"Like you care about my health."

"I don't, but you're important to Peggy."

"Am I?" Sammy asked, like it was the first time he'd heard this information.

"Yeah. You know, *I* was the one who was there picking up the pieces when she thought you were dead. I don't have the energy to do that again."

"I'm not dead, but my best friend is," Sammy said bluntly as he lit a match and lit his cigarette.

"I guess if you think about how you felt about losing your best friend, then you have some idea of how she felt when she thought she'd lost you."

Sammy's gut felt heavy as he put the key into the ignition. This was the road trip from hell. He still didn't know how he felt about Peggy. She was beautiful, and she made him feel things that no other girl ever had. And she looked amazing in that blue dress, her bare shoulders were driving him crazy and just keeping his eyes on the road was a full-time job. The truth was, he thought he probably still even loved her. But he was still grieving for Nick and he was still so angry all the time, and he couldn't think about anything making him happy when Nick wasn't even here anymore.

And now Jack was here.

Jack.

Sammy couldn't stop thinking about that night he'd taken her home and carried her into Janet's house. He'd kissed her on the forehead, and she'd said *his* name. The way Peggy had talked about him had made him sound like a big nerd, so he'd never thought much more about it. But in real life, Jack was different. He was actually kind of good looking, *and* he was an Eight. Something Peggy had conveniently forgotten to mention. And the way he looked at Peggy. It made all the anger inside him start to crackle and he wanted to punch this guy's lights out.

Peggy was laughing at something Jack had said as they both got back in the car and Sammy felt the fire ignite.

Jack handed him a Coke and Sammy took it without even saying thanks.

FIFTEEN

L.A.

They'd made good time and arrived into downtown Los Angeles by the early evening. The trip had been so awkward and uncomfortable and yet, Peggy wished it would have lasted forever. It had been so long since she had been this close to Sammy, and after a few hours they had both relaxed a little and gotten into a routine. Whenever he reached for his cigarettes, she'd grab the matches and get ready to light one for him. She'd lean over and he'd lean into her for the flame. She'd been playing DJ, flipping between local radio stations and eight tracks. Jack, though, had hardly said a word, only to complain when he was hungry and make coughing noises whenever Sammy lit another cigarette. He didn't seem to be enjoying it so much.

But here they were, driving down the Sunset Strip, and it was everything she ever imagined it to be. She felt like she was in an eighties movie and she wished the car had a sunroof so she could stick her arms out of it. She stuck her head out of the window instead and whooped out into the warm air that smelled like exhaust fumes, hot metal and just a little like vomit as the palm trees gently waved welcome from the vibrant blue sky above them. She closed her eyes and smiled. She was in LA. It was 1984, and she was about to meet up with Lacey and her rock star friends. So what if Sammy and Jack were being jerks? Life didn't get much better than this.

"What's the name of the club?" Sammy asked.

"Uh, The Illusion, I think, something like that." Peggy rummaged through her purse to find the piece of paper she'd written the details down on. It was one thing she missed from the present - her phone.

"Why didn't you save it on your phone?" Jack asked.

Peggy turned to him and gave him a look. "Yeah, I saved it on the notepad *near* the phone, you're right Jack," she said warningly. "But I brought it on a different piece of paper."

Jack shook his head and mouthed a sheepish sorry.

"Illusions?" Sammy asked.

"Yeah, that's it, how did you know?"

"I know it."

"How do you know it?" asked Peggy.

"I've spent some time in West Hollywood."

"How have you spent time in West Hollywood? You're always in Santolsa or Salt Valley," Peggy asked, half sad that there was still so much she didn't know about him, and half pissed that he always seemed to know everything. "You know all the hotels in Vegas, all the clubs in LA. Who are you Sammy Ruthven?"

"I'm an open book. All you have to do is ask," he said. And she thought she saw a bit of the smirk returning to the face that had been so void of feeling these last few months.

"I'm scared to ask," she said. Sammy looked like he was trying to hide a laugh as he turned off onto a side street and parked the car.

"It's not far from here," he said.

It felt so good to stretch her legs, and the balmy summer evening air felt heavenly on her skin after being stuck in the car all day long.

Peggy let Sammy lead the way. She was useless at directions and it always amazed her how he just knew where stuff was. Even if she'd been here a hundred times, she still would have needed the maps on her phone to get her to a specific point of interest. But Sammy had some kind of internal GPS and it made her feel safe, like he always knew where they were, even if she had no idea.

As they began to walk back down the street, Peggy felt kind of uncomfortable. West Hollywood seemed kind of scary. It wasn't how she thought it was in her time. It wasn't all palm trees and women who looked like Malibu Barbies. There was trash and graffiti all over, and so many people who looked homeless. A young girl with sores all over her face came up to them and asked for some money. She was so skinny, and Peggy had to force herself not to look away. Sammy just gave her five bucks and kept walking.

"I guess we're not in Santolsa anymore," said Jack, trying to make a joke of it. He was clearly a little overwhelmed by it too.

"Hollywood not what you were expecting Jack?" Sammy asked smugly.

"Nah, it's just, it's different in Canada," Jack said.

"Really? I've heard Canada has a serious homelessness problem."

"Yeah it does," said Jack. "But not where we come from."

"And where is that?" Sammy questioned him.

"You wouldn't know it," Jack said.

"How far is the club?" Peggy asked, trying to move the

conversation in a direction that didn't involve her having to lie to Sammy again. She'd told him the truth when they'd been dating. She'd told him that she was a time traveler, but he hadn't believed her. She didn't blame him, really. It wasn't very believable. But it felt like this big secret was always spreading out between them. He didn't believe her about the time travel, which meant he'd always thought she'd been keeping something else from him.

"Just on that corner." Sammy pointed across the road.

Peggy took a step across the road and an old Chevy came screeching out of nowhere, heading straight for her. Sammy reached out and grabbed her, pulling her by the waist, and yanked her back into him just in time. Peggy's heart felt like it was going to burst out of her ribs. She was shaking so hard. She put her hands to her face and turned into Sammy's chest.

"It's OK, you're safe," Sammy breathed as he held her tighter.

Her heart started beating even harder as he held her. She was thankful she could pass it off as adrenaline.

"Oh my god, are you OK?"

Peggy looked up. She'd almost forgotten Jack was even still there. She nodded and lifted her head. She was still shaking.

"It's still early and doesn't look like the club's even open yet," Sammy said as he gently nudged Peggy off him. She reluctantly let go of his shirt where she had been clutching it.

Jack gently put his arm around her. "OK?" he asked, concern filling his dark eyes. It was the first time all day he looked like the Jack she knew.

She nodded.

"It's just after five." Sammy looked at the silver digital

watch on his wrist. "Why don't we go find a room and come back later tonight?"

"Where will we stay?" Peggy asked. She hated not being able to book a hotel online. It stressed her out to think they hadn't booked somewhere already.

"There's a motel just a few blocks down," said Sammy. "They should have a room and we can just walk over to the club from there."

They stood in the reception of the California Comfort Motel, which had definitely seen better days and didn't seem all that comfortable either. The paint was peeling off the walls, and the carpet was stained with decades of Peggy didn't even want to know what, but it felt kind of homey in that tobacco stained you're not the only person that's ever been here kind of way that Peggy had always liked.

Sammy was talking to a beautiful dark-haired receptionist, telling her he wanted a smoking room while she made a big deal out of how they only had one room left and it was non-smoking. Peggy was leaning up against the side of a vending machine, trying not to notice how much the receptionist was flirting with him. Jack was trying to work out how to get the candy out. He kept putting in his quarters, but the machine wouldn't accept them.

Sammy came back with a key in his hand. "I got us a room." And for the first time it dawned on the three of them they would be sharing a room for the week.

Jack took his coins out of the vending machine, giving up. Sammy hit the machine with his fist and two Butterfingers, and a packet of candy cigarettes dropped down.

SIXTEEN

Illusions

It could not have been worse, Jack thought as he assessed the motel room in front of him. There were cracks in the wall, almost see-through yellow curtains and a dead fly on the bed. *The* bed. The room contained just one double bed covered in a floral bedspread and a small brown corduroy couch. Jack had been in pain all day watching Sammy and Peggy pretending not to be into each other and then be creepily in sync with each other's thoughts. And then when Sammy saved her from that truck, well, that was just so typical of Sammy Ruthven. The idea of having to spend a week in a stuffy, cramped motel room with them both was enough to make him want to go straight back to 2017.

"How's this going to work?" Jack asked, looking over at Sammy and Peggy who were both staring at the double bed.

"I'll take the couch," said Sammy, without hesitation.

Jack looked over at Peggy who gave him an uncomfortable look. Last time he had shared a bed with her he'd woken up with his chest pressed into her back and his arm draped over her. "No, I'll take the couch," Jack said. He couldn't sleep next to her. Not with Sammy in the room. Not after that kiss, which now felt like years ago, but was somehow still lingering on his lips. He wasn't sure what might happen if he was in a bed with her.

"This is stupid," Peggy said. "I'll take the couch, it's too small for either of you to sleep on, anyway."

Jack looked at Sammy. Sammy shrugged and threw his bag onto one side of the double bed. Jack threw himself on the other side and kicked off his Vans. He was dying for a nap.

It was dark when Jack woke up. He felt around for his iPhone to check the time. It took him a moment to remember where he was. His fingers found a switch. He switched on the bedside lamp and he was blinded by a light in a dive of a motel room in Los Angeles in 1984. He smoothed down his hair and sat up as he groggily looked around. No Peggy, no Sammy. He was pissed that they'd left him behind, but he couldn't say he wasn't glad that Sammy wasn't there. But then, he didn't like the idea of the two of them out somewhere, either. At least it wasn't the two of them in here alone together though. He couldn't find a clock anywhere, so he called reception for the time, who told him in a rather short tone that it was nine forty-three. It was only after he hung up that he saw an alarm clock with flippy numbers sitting on a table across the room. There was a scrawled note next to it.

Gone to get some food, meet you at the club when you wake up? Peggy, x.

It was like a text, but on paper. Weird, but pretty cool.

Jack took a shower and it was awful. The water was lukewarm, dripped down the back of the tiles rather than onto his body and the motel soap made his skin feel like scales. He dried his hair on what felt like a cardboard towel, and then dressed in his faded black jeans and one of his new shirts which was white with silver corners on the collar. He buttoned it right up to the top, turned up his sleeves to show off most of his tattoo and shoved his feet into his black lace-up shoes. He'd spiked his hair using some of Peggy's hairspray and he liked how he looked. It may have been 1984, but Jack thought he was channeling a young Elvis, or Johnny Cash, or maybe it was more like John Cusack or Jon Cryer. Whatever, he knew he looked good, and he was pretty sure Peggy would think so, too. Maybe he could get the attention of some hot eighties girls out tonight and make *her* jealous for once.

Walking out of the motel and onto the strip, he felt in his pocket for his phone, but he realized he'd left it in the room. Not that having it would do any good. He had no GPS here so maps wouldn't help. But he couldn't even remember which direction the club was in from here.

"Excuse me," he asked a group of pretty girls in short skirts, boob-tubes in sparkly bright colors, big blonde hair and way too much make-up. They looked like they'd fallen out of some old school disco porno.

"Can we like, help you?" asked a blonde with short teased-up hair. She pulled away from the group and stood just a little too close to him. She was one of those girls who looked incredible from a distance but was kind of a mess close up. She had nice breasts though. Jack had to work really hard not to look at them.

"Can you tell me how to get to Illusions?" he asked her.

The girl laughed. "Totally! We can like, even walk with you, that's where we're going." She linked her arm into his. "I'm Crystal."

"Jack."

"Nice bod, Jack," said a girl with long frizzy blonde hair, who linked her arm on his other side. "I'm Becky."

"Thanks," he said, feeling kind of cool but a bit scared to have this much attention from a group of hot girls.

"I guess you're like, going for the Rats?" asked the other blonde girl. She had dead straight hair and was probably the prettiest of the three.

Jack shrugged. "Is that the band that's on tonight? I just know I'm meant to go there to meet some friends."

"Oh my god, how do you not know the Rats? Do you like, live under a rock or something?" asked the girl with straight hair.

"Missy don't be such a total bitch, maybe he's not a local," said Becky, smacking gum.

"I'm definitely not local," he said.

"Duh," said Becky. "See, Missy?"

"Whatever," said Missy, dismissing them.

"The Rats are trippin'dicular," said Crystal. "Totally bitchin'. You're gonna, like, totally love them."

Jack gave her a look and she giggled hysterically.

"I guess you're not from the Valley either." Becky laughed.

"I'm not even from this decade," said Jack.

"Obviously." Crystal looked him up and down. "You look like you just stepped out of, like, a Johnny Cash album cover."

Jack grinned.

Missy shoved Becky out of the way and linked arms with him, Becky made a noise but then linked her arm with Missy's on her other side.

Jack couldn't help but grin. In that moment, as he walked down Sunset Strip with this gaggle of Valley girls fighting over who would get to link his arm, he felt like a God, or even better, a rock star. The girls kept giggling and asking him stupid questions about Canada and he made up stupid answers as they giggled and flirted all the way to the club.

The girls led him right past the long line, waving at the bouncer and calling him by name and pointing at Jack. Crystal said he was "theirs." The bouncer gave Jack a pitying look.

The club was smaller than Jack expected. It was and dark and crowded. It was heavy with the smell of warm bodies and sexual tension and it seemed like everyone was either drunk or high, and the cigarette smoke in here was out of control. He could hardly breathe. A band was already on stage, rocking out with distorted guitars and a lot of hair swinging. They were pretty good, but most people were just talking over them, getting drinks and waiting for the headliners, the Rats, Jack guessed. The Valley girls led him to a table at the back and he sat with them while he looked around for Peggy. He had no idea how long they'd be at dinner, but it was getting late. Jack's stomach rumbled. Maybe he should've found some food too.

"What do you drink?" asked Crystal, lighting a cigarette and holding out the packet for the girls, who all took one.

"Beer," he said, coughing as she exhaled. He wasn't sure he'd be able to spend that long in here without being sick. He started thinking about the effects of passive smoking and then told himself not to be so square, to not think about it and just try to have a good time.

"It's on me," Crystal said. "Since you so kindly escorted us through one of the most dangerous parts of West Hollywood and all." She giggled and patted his arm.

He swallowed. He'd noticed it was a bit rough out there, but he'd forgotten for a moment how rough some parts of LA were in the eighties. He could get mugged or shot at or stabbed or anything. He probably needed to be a bit more cautious here.

Crystal returned with a beer for him and a tray of pink drinks for her friends and sat down squishing herself next to him. She rested her hand on his leg while she attempted to do a Canadian accent. Jack smiled at her and flirted back without even thinking about what he was doing. He had never had this kind of attention from girls before. Jayne was different, she was just a hot friend with benefits. These girls seemed to just want the benefits. It was all a little intoxicating, and he was feeling giddy.

At least, until he felt a hand on his shoulder.

"Jack?" It was Peggy. She looked confused but beautiful in a bright pink blouse and tight black jeans. Her hair teased up a little at the top but then falling softly around her shoulders. His thoughts moved back up from his pants and into his heart.

"Hey," he said, putting his hand gently on top of hers.

"Having fun, Jack?" Sammy asked, appearing out of nowhere.

"Yeah," Jack said. "The most fun I've had in ages."

"Oh my God, are you guys like, from Canada, too?" asked Becky as she put a hand on Jack's other leg.

"I am, he's not," said Peggy, giving the girls a dark look and gesturing to Sammy.

"Why don't you guys sit down?" Jack asked.

"I think we're going to go back," said Peggy.

"Go? But we just got here," said Jack. "And don't you wanna see the Rats? Whoever they are."

"You *know* who the Rats are, Jack," Peggy said.

Jack shook his head and stared at her blankly. Until... of course. He was such a doofus. The Rats was the first name of one of his favorite bands in the history of forever. "Wait a second, are you telling me that tonight I'm going to see the Kings of Spades play live?" Jack's mouth nearly dropped to the floor. "Here? In this tiny club? Like, *this* close?" He pointed at the stage.

Peggy shrugged. "I guess so."

"You have to stay," Jack pleaded, grabbing Peggy's hand. "Please stay, this will be the most amazing thing that's ever happened to me!"

Peggy shook her head. "I just wanted to find Lacey. I'm kind of worried. No one here has seen her around for over a week."

"Don't worry, we'll find her, just stay tonight, Please Peggy." He was having so much fun with these girls, but it was nothing compared to being with Peggy and seeing the Kings of Spades before they got super famous. He would even be OK with putting up with Sammy being there if he had to.

"I'm so tired," Peggy said. "Come back with us?"

Jack looked at the scene in front of him. Three sexy blonde girls were all over him and pouring alcohol down his throat. The music was good, and it was about to get even better. How could he say no to this? To his favorite band *ever* being right *there*? Crystal creeped her hand up a little higher towards his crotch. He felt dizzy.

"Why don't you just come back when you're ready?" suggested Sammy.

"Maybe I should stay out all night, I wouldn't want to be interrupting anything," Jack said with venom in his voice. He didn't mean for it to come out like that, he just didn't like the idea of them being alone in that motel room.

"Trust me, you won't be," Peggy said.

"You have my word," said Sammy. And for some

reason Jack believed him, even though he kind of hated his guts.

"OK, fine, I'm going to stay out."

Becky whooped and Missy handed Jack a bourbon and Coke.

"Fine," said Peggy. "See you later, I guess."

They began walking away but Jack was sure he saw Sammy look back and give him a victorious look.

Jack slumped into his seat.

"What's the story with the hottie? Do you like that girl he's with? Because she seems pretty boring," said Becky.

"Yeah, what's the story?" asked Missy.

"Oh, nothing," Jack said.

"Nothing always means something." Crystal raised an eyebrow and the other girls nodded and yepped in agreement.

Jack looked up at her. She was getting more attractive by the sip. "It's a long story."

"Do you love her?" Crystal asked.

"Is it that obvious?"

"Wanna tell me about it?" She ran her bright blue nails down his arm, circling the eight of his tattoo.

Another couple of drinks later he'd told them all the whole story, well, apart from the bit about being a time traveler.

"It's a sad story," Crystal said when he'd finished. "Maybe I can help take your mind off it." She held out her hand and pulled him up, and he followed without thinking.

She took him onto the dance floor, which was getting a little more crowded as people squished in to get as close to the Rats as they could. She pressed her body up against his and began moving her hips in time with the electric guitar blaring from the stage. He couldn't help but feel turned on.

She was damn sexy, and she'd listened to his story, like really listened, and she hadn't looked at another guy all night, and she was *there*. And Peggy wasn't. And so, when she ran her arms up his back and into his hair, and leaned in to kiss him, he let her. She tasted like cigarettes and fake strawberry flavoring and something kind of onion-y, but Jack didn't care. He kissed her back, pushing his body into hers while they moved in time with the music. She took his hand and led him through the other sweating gyrating bodies on the dance floor towards the back of the bar. She pushed him into one of the toilets and pulled the door closed behind them. She pressed herself up against him, pushing her breasts into his chest and thrusting her tongue into his mouth. He thought he could hear the Rats starting, the guitar riff from one of the songs he knew so well. But he was helpless to resist this woman. He began to lift up her top from the hem and ran his fingers across her skin. She unbuttoned his shirt, undid his belt and then unbuttoned the top of his jeans.

He pulled back. He had thought he wanted to go along with this. Sex in a West Hollywood club toilet in the early eighties would certainly give him cred on the sexual experience scale, but the truth was, when he got there, all he could think about was Peggy. He'd spent quite a few nights having sex in toilets or the stockrooms of the Stables, and although it had made him feel a little better at the time, it was hardly fulfilling. He wanted more than that. He didn't want to be this guy. He wasn't this guy.

"I'm sorry," he said, gently pushing her away and doing up his pants. "I'm not this guy."

"You *can* be this guy," she said, taking her top off and showing him everything.

He blushed and looked away. She did have a really great body. Maybe it wouldn't make any difference to anyone if he had sex with her. Maybe it would make him feel better. But then he'd walk back to the motel and Peggy would be there, and how could he do this to her after that kiss they'd shared?

"I don't *want* to be this guy." He fumbled to get his buttons done back up and then he turned and walked out, leaving her standing there half naked. "I'm not that guy, I'm not that guy," he whispered to himself. He tried to slow his breathing and get through the crowds of people who were all watching the Rats, who were now on stage.

He stopped and stood, watching them in awe. This was one of his favorite bands of all time and they were *here*, sounding so raw and so *good*. But his head was a mess, and the smoke was choking him, and there were way too many people in here for it to be safe. He began to push through the crowd to the exit.

When he finally felt the outside air in his lungs, he sobered up slightly. "I'm not that guy," he whispered to himself again as he shoved his hands in his pockets and took some deep breaths. The smoggy LA eighties air was like a mountain breeze after being in that club. The urge to turn around and go right back in there was strong, to see more of the band, to find Crystal. But his urge to breathe and get back to the motel to stop Peggy and Sammy being alone together was stronger. He began to pick up speed as he walked through the scariest part of West Hollywood on his own.

But then, in an instant, everything was different.

When he saw her, he was changed, and he knew nothing would ever be the same again.

She was the most stunning girl he'd ever seen. She was breathtakingly *stunning*. Like movie star beautiful. She was kicking a trash can out the front of a dilapidated building. She was kicking the crap out of it, her short leather skirt not covering much of her long pale legs. Her red hair was flying around her like a cyclone. She screamed and kicked it again before folding into a heap beside it. He ran straight towards her before he even knew what he was doing.

"Hey." He crouched down next to her. "Are you OK?"

She looked up at him, her gorgeous face covered in mascara tears and smudged red lipstick.

Jack never thought he would have one of those love at first sight moments, but he was having one. This girl was *it*.

Jack's heart was racing, and his head was spinning.

"No," she said. "I'm not OK, not even close."

"What can I do?" He reached out to put his hand on her shoulder, but thought better of it, and sat down next to her instead.

"Nothing." She wiped her face with the back of her hand.

"It's a guy, isn't it?"

"Is it that obvious?" She ran her hands through the ends of her long red hair, accidentally brushing his arm. Jack swore he could feel sparks fly between them.

"I've never seen a girl this messed up over anything else," he said. He thought of Peggy when she was mourning Sammy. Peggy never kicked things, but she sure cried a lot.

"He told me he loved me, but... I think he's in love with someone else. I *know* he's been seeing someone else," she said. "In my head, I know he's no good for me, but in my heart, I just... I can't let go."

"If he's making you feel like this, well, maybe he's not the right guy."

She looked up at him, her hazel eyes searching his in the streetlight. He'd never felt anything like it. His heart felt full to bursting, and he was pretty sure, whatever this was, she felt it too. They held each other's gaze and right at that moment a car drove past, REO Speedwagon blaring from the speakers in what felt like a moment the universe had orchestrated just for them. It was as if nothing and no one else existed.

"*You should have seen by the look in my eyes, baby, there was something missin'*," sang the car radio. "*You should have known by the tone in my voice, maybe, but you didn't listen,*" it continued.

The girl shook her head and looked away, breaking the spell that the car radio had cast on them.

"You deserve someone who's going to give you the world," Jack said.

"Everyone always says that crap, but you know what? Maybe there just isn't that kind of love out there for everyone."

Jack shook his head. "I'm sure it's out there for you... and for me. I *know* it."

"*And I meant every word I said, when I said that I love you I meant that I love you forever,*" the car radio sang, before turning the corner and driving off. Jack knew he could never hear that song again without thinking of her, of this moment, sitting on a corner in West Hollywood in 1984, with the most beautiful girl in the world.

"Maybe it's just not in my cards," she said, a tear escaping down her cheek. "I can live with that. But it doesn't mean that this doesn't hurt like hell." She knocked her head against the wall behind them.

"Hey," said Jack reaching out and placing his hand gently on top of hers. "Who says it's not going to happen for you?"

She looked down at his hand for a moment before pulling away. "I think I'm just going to go home, or go somewhere." The girl struggled to her feet. Jack put out a hand to help her, but she didn't take it. She straightened herself up, wobbled on her heels, and then she turned and started to walk away.

What was he doing? He couldn't never see this girl again. He couldn't just stand here and do nothing.

"Can I see you again?" Jack called out after her.

"You don't want to see me again, trust me," she called back. "I'm bad news."

He jogged to catch up with her. "At least let me walk you home."

"I can't walk home from here." She looked around as if she was just realizing where she was.

"How are you going to get home?"

"I don't know, I might go stay with a friend tonight."

"I'd invite you back to my place, but there's not much space," he said. "Not for like, anything like that... but just to help you out."

"You're sweet." She put a hand to his face and searched his eyes. What was she searching for? Why was she looking at him like that? "I don't deserve it," she finally said.

"Deserve what?"

"Anything good."

"I'm not that good," he blurted. "I'm a real bad boy."

She sort of laughed. "You have no idea what a bad boy is."

"I could learn."

"I don't want you to be a bad boy." She shook her head. "There are enough bad boys in this world."

"I can be whatever you want, anything you want."

"You've been an angel to me tonight. I don't know how long I would have been sitting there if you hadn't come along. So, thanks." She put her hands on his shoulders, got on her tiptoes and leaned in towards him. Jack stopped breathing. She kissed him on the cheek, and he felt something he'd never felt before in that kiss. Not with Jayne, not with that girl in the toilet, not even with Peggy. What the hell was that? It was like finding the missing piece to some puzzle he didn't even know he was doing.

"I can't let you go," he said, gently reaching out to hold her hands. Big mistake. She became frantic and began to pull and squeal. Jack let go straight away, and she ran. Too fast. Too far. But mostly she just ran like she didn't want him coming after her, so he just stood there and let her go, but he knew he'd never be the same again.

SEVENTEEN

Jack's Night

Jack had never really known where he stood on the whole destiny, soulmates, falling in love at first sight thing, until it had happened to him.

It was like that moment was playing on repeat in his head. That moment he'd looked into her eyes and felt like something had unlocked in his heart. And now, even though he knew it would've been way too stalkerish to follow her when she'd already been freaked, he just wished he'd done *something*.

But he just stood there, watching her walk out of his life until she disappeared into the darkness, and only when he was totally sure it wouldn't seem like he was following her did he begin to walk in the same direction she'd been going in. Maybe he would catch up with her somewhere, maybe she'd be sitting outside her house, or he'd see her face in a window. Or maybe, if the Gods were on his side for once, maybe she'd be thinking the same thing he was, and she'd turn back around and start walking right back towards him.

It was not a good part of town and even though he had

his tattoo, he still felt more than a little anxious, jumping at loud noises, crossing to the other side of the street when he saw some sketchy looking dude coming his way. If he could get the crap kicked out of him outside Dee's in Santolsa little Gem of the Desert, he really didn't want to think about what could happen to him here.

Arriving in 1980s Los Angeles had been such a trip. There were so many cool things about this time - the scantily clad women on billboards, the hilarious, if questionable, cigarette ads, the neon lights, the girls in spandex and boys in short shorts. 1984 was a lot of fun, but it was not without its problems. This part of LA seemed rampant with junkies, prostitutes and homeless people. There was trash all over and the pollution was high, *very* high.

He heard someone screaming in the distance and began to pick up his pace, walking with his head down, his sleeves rolled up, so his tattoo was on show. He knew his tattoo offered some kind of protection, even here, but he also suspected that if a rival gang member saw it, he'd be screwed and maybe even in worse trouble. But no one bothered him except for a couple of old drunk guys asking for change. Jack handed them a couple of bucks and kept walking.

His brain told him to give up hope, he wasn't going to be able to find her, she could be anywhere by now, but his heart told him to keep the faith. If she really was his soulmate, they'd find each other again. It happened once, it could happen again.

Jack kept walking through the night, and eventually the drunks and drug addicts and prostitutes began to thin out. The trash seemed to disappear, the buildings became cleaner and whiter and bigger and he soon found himself walking through Beverly Hills. The coolest cars he'd ever seen drove past him, Cadillacs, Limos, Mustangs - like the one old Sammy had let him drive when he'd gone to rescue Peggy from Las Vegas last year. He laughed to himself at the thought of it. If he'd known then that he'd end up here, back in 1984 with both Peggy *and* Sammy, in some kind of weird love triangle… he shook his head. He'd been walking for hours and it was the first time he'd even thought about them.

A group of girls in a red convertible waved over at him.

"Wanna come party with us?" one of them giggled, as she beckoned to him with her glossy red talons.

"Come on hot stuff, what are you doing out alone at this hour?" another asked, pouting her orangey lips at him.

Jack shrugged but couldn't hide his smile at getting called "hot stuff".

"We've got cocaine for days!" one of them called out.

Jack laughed and shook his head. They honked, still squealing and giggling and drove off.

A few hours ago, Jack was being pulled into a club by a group of girls nowhere near as hot as the rich girls in the convertible and their attention had made his night, and he'd nearly even had sex with one of them. Now the glamourous girls of Beverley Hills were asking him to come party, and he'd said *no*. What was wrong with him?

But his head was full of thoughts of the girl with the red hair and there was no room for anyone or anything else.

The sun was just beginning to creep up to sunrise when he saw what he thought was water off in the distance.

The Beach.

Jack had never seen the ocean before. He'd hardly ever really been out of Santolsa, unless you count a family vacation to Utah and a couple of summers at Lone Pine Camp in New Mexico when he was a kid.

His feet were aching, but he somehow managed to pick

up speed as the water came closer into view. The sunrise behind him lit up the buildings and the palm trees between him and the ocean, guiding his way.

When he reached the boardwalk at the edge of the sand, he took his shoes and socks off, rolled up his jeans, and he ran as fast as he could towards the water. He ran past the lifeguard towers and past a middle aged lady with her dog and a couple of other people jogging in the other direction, and when he reached the water, he ran straight into it, kicking his legs and splashing around like a kid as laughter exploded out of him. He reached down and ran his hands through the cold water, joy bubbling up from his entire being, tears escaping from his eyes.

Jack's life was certainly not perfect. His dream girl had gotten away, he was sleeping on his teacher's couch, he had no career prospects or money, *yet*, but Jack had never felt as at home, complete and totally himself as he did in that moment.

When the sun had risen a little higher in the sky and the buzz of the night had worn off, the exhaustion finally hit. Jack put his socks and shoes onto his wet and sandy feet and went in search of a bus to take him back up to the motel. Without his phone to check maps he had to resort to asking strangers about buses and bus times, but in a way, he found he liked it. He talked to a woman who was heading to her waitressing job and they bonded over how the diner grease always stuck in your hair no matter how much you washed it. He chatted to an older man who was spending his twilight years taking the bus through every single state. Without his phone to tell him where to go, he had to rely on the kindness of strangers, and he was surprised to find it warmed his heart more than he could've imagined. He felt *connected*. Not just to the internet, but to real *people*.

The bus dropped him off outside the diner down the street from the motel. He got a whiff of coffee and the craving hit. As he pushed the door and walked in, he heard cheers erupting from a table of girls. He looked over to see what they were cheering at and realized it was him.

"Hey Canada!" shouted Missy.

"Well, of all the diners in all the world," said Crystal. It was hard to believe he'd nearly had sex with her in a club toilet. It felt like a lifetime ago to him now. "And you gotta walk into mine," she finished.

"Hey ladies," he said politely.

"Join us," said Missy.

"Yes, join us Jackie boy!" shouted Becky, who looked very much worse for wear. Her make-up was smudged all over her face and her dress was all crinkled.

"If I believed in destiny, I'd totally think this was it," Crystal said, giving him a look.

"Lucky for you, I don't believe in it either," he lied. It clearly wasn't destiny that he'd met them here, they obviously hadn't gone far after the gig last night.

"My treat," said Crystal, pulling out a chair and looking at him seductively. "Order whatever you want."

If he'd had more money, he would've said no thanks and gotten his own table, but instead he shrugged and took a seat and ordered a double pancake stack and a coffee.

EIGHTEEN

Saving Lacey

Peggy woke up groggily. She reached to the nightstand for her phone to check the time, but her nightstand wasn't there. She opened her eyes and looked up at a tobacco-stained ceiling. It took her a moment to remember where she was, *when* she was. Peggy often had dreams that she was back in 2016, and sometimes the absolute absurdity of her life made her wonder if it really all *was* just a dream. Maybe one day she would wake up in her bed in her empty house back in her future. The everyday stuff had become almost normal, but her dream life was still a mess of numbers on calendars, clocks ticking and the book room. She always dreamed about the book room.

But with eyes wide open, here she was, lying on a brown corduroy couch in a motel room in Los Angeles in the year 1984, sunlight coming in bright through the yellow curtains. She shook her head. It never got any easier to understand how she got here, or *why* she was here, but she was absolutely certain beyond a doubt it was her destiny to be here.

She sat up and looked over at the double bed where

Sammy Ruthven was sleeping. In all the time she'd known him, she'd never seen him sleeping. The only time they had slept in the same bed was on their trip to Las Vegas last year, and she'd fallen asleep first and he'd woken up before her. She felt her heart expand, almost to the point of being painful to watch him like this. He looked so different, so calm and peaceful, as if all the weight of the world was off him. There was no bravado, no coolest guy in school, just the gentle rise and fall of his chest under the sheets. A longing moved through her. She longed to be lying there next to him, cuddled up close to him, or even just lying next to him, inches away, feeling his breath on the back of her neck. There was no sign of Jack and the thought that she could have been sleeping in the bed with Sammy this whole time annoyed her, but it wasn't like she could just go over there and get in bed with him. No matter how much she wished for it, she could not get closer than this. She silent screamed into the couch cushion. They were so close, she could almost reach out and touch him, and yet they were still so far apart.

Peggy lay there watching him for a few minutes more before she felt like she was being a creep. She quietly grabbed her make-up bag and went into the bathroom. When she was done in the shower her stomach sank as she remembered she'd left her clothes on the couch. She pulled the tiny scratchy towel around her body and unlocked the door. Sammy was probably still asleep, and he wasn't going to be interested in looking at her, anyway. If he wanted to look at her, he could already. She had made it abundantly clear that she was available for him to look at any time he liked.

She walked out of the bathroom on tip toes and grabbed her bag.

Sammy made a noise.

She turned around to see him looking at her with a sleepy smirk on his face, and she was suddenly very aware of just how small the towel was. She was showing more of her flesh than he'd seen before.

"Hey," he said, looking up at her with the same smoldering look he used to give her when they first got together.

"Hey," she said, clutching her clothes and her towel before rushing back into the bathroom.

She decided on a white sundress covered in pink and yellow flowers and spent some extra time doing her makeup. She was all queasy from the way Sammy had looked at her, and while part of her wanted him to look at her like that again, she was also worried she'd just imagined the whole thing, or that it didn't mean what she wanted it to mean.

When she finally emerged from the bathroom, Sammy was sitting on the desk smoking out of the window, dressed only in a pair of jeans and no shirt. It had been a while since she'd seen him without his shirt on and it made her feel warm, so warm she could feel sweat begin to gather on her upper lip. She patted it away with her finger. She was torn between staring at him for as long as possible to try to make this moment last or looking away because it was just way too much.

"Hey," he said.

"Hey," she said, turning around to organize her clothes and make-up.

"I guess Jack had a good time last night," he said, exhaling smoke out the window as the sounds of sirens and trucks floated into the room.

Peggy looked around. She knew Jack hadn't come back yet, but she hadn't really thought about why until now. Her stomach knotted and took her by surprise. It wasn't that she wanted Jack for herself, but she was taken aback by just how much she didn't like the idea of him being with anyone else either, especially some slutty Valley Girl. She had tried not to think about their kiss, but the more she tried not to think about it, the more she thought about it.

"So, are you and Jack…?" Sammy asked casually, like he didn't even really need an answer.

"No," Peggy blurted, shaking her head. "It's just… complicated."

"Oh, how so?" Sammy flicked ash down onto the street below, not even making eye contact.

Peggy made a face and passed him an empty soda can. His finger gently brushed hers as he took it. She felt her pulse quicken. Sammy took another drag, blowing the smoke out to the street below and tapped his ash into the soda can.

"Jack's, well… Jack was," Peggy began.

Sammy raised an eyebrow.

"He was my best friend all through high school, until I came to… Santolsa. We grew up together, and he helped me through some hard times. But it's not like *that*. It's not like *us*, I mean, how *we* were." She wanted to look away, but his gaze was intense, as if he was holding her there, holding her eyes in place, locked, stopping her from looking away or leaving.

Eventually he spoke. "Sure, like me and Rochelle."

Peggy's stomach lurched at the mention of her name. "Yeah, but you and Rochelle were…"

"Yeah, we were, but it wasn't like *us*, how *we* were."

And they stayed there for a moment, just like that. Her in her pink and yellow sun dress standing in the middle of the motel room, him half naked, soda can in one hand, the other holding his cigarette out the window burning down slowly, and they just looked at each other. Peggy could have stayed like that forever, but eventually Sammy's cigarette burned to the end and he dropped the butt into the can.

"Do you... is this OK with me smoking in here?" he asked.

Peggy picked up the laminate non-smoking sign on the desk and waved it at him.

"You know there really aren't any non-smoking rooms, right?"

"The sign says non-smoking," she said.

He pointed to the stains on the ceiling. "The bedspread smells like stale smoke."

"The couch, too." She wrinkled her nose.

"Maybe it's time to quit," he shrugged.

Peggy raised her eyebrows.

"I've actually been thinking about quitting for a while. I like smoking, but I don't like the idea that I'm... addicted to it, you know?"

Peggy nodded. "Like, how your mom is addicted to stuff?"

Sammy nodded, jumped off the desk and flopped back down on the bed.

The urge to lie down next to him was so strong and she wondered what he would do if she did. Would he push her away? Would he ignore her? Would he scoop her up into his arms?

He looked up at her. "You look nice," he said.

"Thanks." She brushed off the compliment, even though it meant more to her than he'd ever know. "I thought I'd get an early start, find some food and then see what I can find out about Lacey, try her numbers again. Do you want to come?"

Sammy looked at the time on the clock radio. "Nah, it's still early. I think I'll stay here a while and get some more sleep, I'm still pretty beat from the drive." He closed his eyes.

She was glad he couldn't see her face drop in disappointment.

Peggy was amazed at how many people were still out on the street from the night before. There were drunk people all over the place and she had men cat calling her all the way from the motel to the diner on the corner. She didn't feel safe at all and she wished she'd just flat out asked Sammy to come with her, or waited for him to be ready, or worn a longer dress. But by the time she was settled in a booth in the diner, watching the people of LA pass by from behind the safety of the window, she felt a lot better.

She ordered coffee and a pancake stack, and when they arrived, she picked up the mini jug of maple syrup and found herself having a sudden flashback to that day when Mindy had poured maple syrup in her locker and all over her. At the time it had seemed like the worst thing that could ever happen. She was humiliated beyond belief. But now here she was, in LA, in 1984. The pain and humiliation of that moment felt like nothing more but a dream now – it was just a distant memory. Peggy had always heard adults say that high school wasn't everything, that when you left school things changed. She felt like maybe she finally understood that now. Things *had* changed, *she* had changed.

A noisy table behind her interrupted her thoughts. A group of loud girls giggling and saying "like" every two words, and a familiar male voice occasionally getting a word in. The girls were kind of hilarious and Peggy laughed when she heard one of them say "this coffee is so grody, like, gag me with a spoon!"

"Pass me a spoon!" the male voice said.

"Oh, Jack, you crack me up!" squealed one of the girls.

Peggy turned around to see Jack sandwiched in between two blonde girls, another opposite him. The look on his face said it all. He was loving every minute of it.

She got up and walked over, arms crossed, staring at him.

"Peggy!" he exclaimed. He tried to get up to greet her, but the girls were blocking him.

"Hey Jack," she said. "Did you forget why we are here?"

"I'm just here for breakfast."

Peggy gave him a look.

One of the girls went "Woooooo," and another said "Ooooooh."

"Looks like you're in trouble, Jackie," said the blonde next to him.

"Jack, I can't even with you." Peggy stormed off back to her breakfast, but it had already been cleared up by the waitress. She flapped her arms in defeat, threw some money on the table and walked out.

She was halfway down the block when she wondered if she'd overreacted. Jack didn't know Lacey, he had no reason to be here except to hang out with her. But that was exactly it, he was meant to be hanging out with *her*. She hated how jealous she was feeling, but seeing him there with those girls sent her mind reeling. Had he been with them all night? Surely, he couldn't spend a whole night with those girls without anything happening. He must have kissed one of them for sure. She shook her head. She had to forget about Jack and those Valley girls, and she had to forget about Sammy without his shirt on. She would find Lacey before the day was out and that was that.

NINETEEN

Burritos

_____

After he'd finished his breakfast, Jack left the Valley girls and headed back to the motel hoping to find Peggy so he could explain to her what had happened last night. But when he walked into the room, the only person there was Sammy.

"Good night?" asked Sammy, rolling over in the bed to look at him. His dirty blonde hair was splayed out on the pillow and he wasn't wearing a shirt. This was too weird. It was almost as if this was some kind of stupid cosmic joke. You pretend to be gay for long enough and Sammy Ruthven appears naked in your bed.

"Urgh," Jack said.

Sammy rolled onto his back and pushed the sheet down exposing his naked torso.

"Dude!" Jack couldn't look away quick enough.

"What? It's hot." Sammy stretched his arms out above him. His back made a cracking noise as he breathed out a heavy sigh.

"I hope you've got boxers on," Jack said, grabbing a towel and some fresh clothes.

"Wanna see?" Sammy asked, pulling the sheet off him.

"No!"

"Peggy's gone out to find Lacey."

"You didn't go with her?"

"She's independent, she doesn't need me going everywhere with her."

"Why, really?"

Sammy shrugged. "I don't know what she's told you about us, but just so you and I are clear, me and Peggy, we're not exactly together, and hanging out like this, all day and night, is getting heavy."

"So, you let her walk around 1980s West Hollywood all alone?"

Sammy gave him a questioning look. Jack forgot for a second that Sammy didn't buy the time travel thing, at least not yet. What a moron. They were very obviously not Canadians. "It's scary out there," Jack went on.

"She'll be fine."

"How do you know?"

"I just do," he said.

"I'm going to take a shower."

"Enjoy yourself."

"I won't, this shower is total crap. The soap is turning me into a lizard."

"I left some soap in there. You can use it if you want."

Jack's eyes turned to slits. "What are we, sharing soap now?"

"Jesus," said Sammy, closing his eyes. "Do whatever you want, Jack, but if you could stop being such a dick for five minutes, it would make this whole thing easier on both of us."

"A dick?" Jack gasped. Sammy Ruthven was calling *him* a dick?

"I've been really trying to be nice to you, so if you could just try too, even just a tiny bit, that would be great."

"Me? You're the one who isn't trying, you're so… maudlin," said Jack.

Sammy laughed. "Maudlin?"

"Do you need me to explain to you what that means?"

"I know what it means." Sammy scowled. "Do you think this trip hasn't been hard for me too? Imagine going on a road trip with your ex and her best friend who's so obviously into her."

"I'm not into her," Jack said.

"Sure, whatever." Sammy sat up and reached for the packet of cigarettes on the nightstand.

"No seriously, I met someone last night."

"Yeah?" Sammy tapped a cigarette against the side of the box.

"Yeah, she was beautiful, way prettier than Peggy."

"I doubt that," Sammy said.

"Peggy is pretty for sure. But she's like Sears catalogue pretty. This girl was like Miss America pretty."

"Never, ever let Peggy hear you say that." Sammy flipped the cigarette packet open and closed a few times before throwing it back on the nightstand.

"I didn't mean it like that. I just meant that, well, with Peggy it's not just about her being pretty, though right? I like her because of who she is, not what she looks like."

"It's never *really* about what they look like," Sammy said. "I made that mistake more than once. I mean, you have to have some physical attraction, right? But it's nothing if that's all it is."

"Jayne was like that," Jack said. "She was like, stripper pretty, so hot."

Sammy snorted. "Does stripper rate higher than Sears catalogue pretty?"

"Not higher, just different. Me and Jayne, we never really just hung out and talked, or watched some crappy TV show together, it was always just about the physical stuff."

"That's meant to be the dream, right?" Sammy asked.

"I want that physical stuff, but I want the other stuff too. This girl last night, she was the full package. I wanted to kiss her so bad, but I also wanted to just feed her nachos and make her feel happy when she's sad."

Sammy let out a long sigh. "Can we just start over?"

Jack paused. "Sure. Thanks for the soap." So, Jack went and took a shower using Sammy Ruthven's soap which smelled like pine forests and still left his skin drier than his shower gel back home, but it was a big improvement over the motel soap.

When Jack was done, Sammy was sitting upright, dressed in a black t-shirt and jeans, and the bed was made.

"I don't know how long Peg's going to be. Do you want to go for some food?" Sammy asked, throwing the motel info on the bedside table.

"You and me?" Jack asked. "Out for food?"

"I'm dying for a burrito, and I know the best place."

Jack shrugged. He was still full of pancakes, but he could always make room for a burrito.

A couple hours later, and Sammy found himself a little drunk on tequila and full of Mexican food, sitting opposite Jack, who was more than a little drunk, in a bar dripping with Day of the Dead décor.

"We *are* time travelers," Jack slurred into a beer that had just arrived. "This beer reminds me of this girl I knew once."

"An ex?" Sammy asked, totally ignoring Jack's rants and raving about time travel. The guy was wasted.

"Just one, I just have one ex," he said. "Jayne."

"Did Jayne and Peggy get along?" Sammy asked.

"Peggy doesn't know about Jayne."

"Oh, really?" Sammy's eyes lit up with interest.

"Shhhhhhhh!" Jack spat over the table. "It was just a thing, a thing I did when she left me for you. I mean, when she left Canada." He made air quotes around the word *Canada*. "I was hurting you know?" He slammed his fist into his chest and made a pained expression. "It didn't mean anything, and that was the worst part. I wish it had meant something. I wish I could have loved her. Maybe in some way I did. I don't know. But it wasn't the same."

"You can't choose who you fall in love with." Sammy threw back another tequila shot, chasing it with a gulp of beer.

"God damn, that's the truth."

"Girls are going to give you nothing but trouble."

"Ha," said Jack.

"Have you ever been in love? Like really in love?" asked Sammy.

"Yes," said Jack immediately. But he didn't think of Peggy in that moment. He thought of the girl on the street kicking the crap out of a trash can. "And I only spoke a few words to her before she walked out of my life forever."

Sammy laughed.

"But you and Peggy," Jack said seriously. "You guys are the real deal, the whole forever thing."

Sammy looked down into his empty shot glass and he wondered if Peggy thought the same thing.

"I'm going to dance." Jack jumped up out of his seat and began to dance some kind of Irish jig to the Latin music playing over the sound system.

Sammy didn't want to like him. He wanted to hate this guy, the guy who had spent years hanging out with Peggy, pretending to be gay but secretly in love with her. It was such a dick move, and when Peggy had told him the story, Sammy had just written Jack off as some total jerk who had some issues and couldn't get a girl in the normal way. But even though he seemed like he was working through some stuff, Jack actually seemed like kind of a cool guy.

"OK," said Jack, sitting back down at the table, all sweaty from his dancing. "I can prove it to you."

"Prove what?"

"That we are time travelers."

Sammy shook his head. "You're drunk out of your mind, man."

Jack pulled something out of his pocket. "I'm not meant to have this here, but there are these whale sounds that really help me sleep and…"

Sammy frowned as Jack started waving around a thin black plastic object.

"Here." Jack taped it with his finger and brought the object to life. Bright lights and images danced across it. He tapped and slid his fingers around until a grid of pictures appeared. "This is us, this is us in the future," he said, handing the object over.

Sammy reached out to take it. He didn't know what to think. Sammy wasn't stupid. Peggy's story about time travel had always seemed like some elaborate make-believe thing she had going on inside her head, but he knew she wasn't really from Canada. He'd just put it down to some kind of trauma, or witness protection or something that she wasn't really allowed to talk about. But this, this was *strange*. He was looking at a picture of the two of them smiling, both dressed in St. Christopher's uniforms. Behind them was St. Christopher's High School, but it looked different. The trees were taller, and the school looked different somehow. The uniform looked slightly different too. But it would be a pretty crazy prank to take these.

"You can just…" Jack reached over and dragged his finger across, changing the image to one of Peggy standing on the main street of Santolsa, but it was… *different*.

"What…?" Sammy shook his head. "What is this?"

"This is my phone," said Jack. "It's what cell phones look like in the future. I know you guys think we're going to have flying cars and hoverboards, but mostly we just have smaller computers we carry everywhere with us."

"Be serious," Sammy said.

"OK, you want serious?" Jack took the thing back. "I'll show you something that will blow your freaking mind." And when Jack handed the phone back over, he was looking at a picture of Jack as a kid, maybe about ten or eleven years old, standing in front of a mountain, and next to him were two people who looked kind of familiar, but not quite.

"Mom and Dad."

"Wait, what?" asked Sammy, trying to place the faces.

"Tricia is my mom and Horace is my dad."

Sammy's face dropped and then he started laughing. "You are nuts man." He handed it back, waving Jack away.

"You're just going to pretend you didn't just see that?" Jack asked.

"Honestly, I don't know what to think. It's all pretty far-fetched you have to admit."

Jack nodded. "When Peggy first went back to 1983 and came back again, I didn't believe her either. So, you know what she did? She brought me Twinkies with an '83 expiration date and guess what? They were fine. I ate them all."

Sammy reached for another shot of tequila. "When she went back? You mean when she said she was in Canada she was..."

Jack nodded. "That's why she didn't call you, not because she didn't want to, not because she wasn't head over heels for you, but because she *couldn't*. And that's how she knew you were supposed to die in that accident. And *that's* why when she thought you died, she disappeared. She came back to 2016, and she didn't get out of this one pair of PJs for a week."

Sammy ran his hands through the back of his hair. "This is too crazy."

Jack shrugged. "When one person tells a crazy story it's easy to think they're a little loopy. When two people have the same story, and the photos to back it up, not so easy, huh?"

Sammy grabbed a cigarette but didn't light it. He was going to see how long he could go without one. He wasn't that worried about his health or whatever Jack had said, but he wanted to prove to himself he really could quit, that he wasn't an addict. But not lighting up *right now*, that was really hard.

"And if that's not enough for you, I'll bring you something from the future to prove it."

"Oh, yeah?" Sammy asked.

"Who's your favorite band?"

"The E Street Band."

"Who?"

Sammy gave him a look. "Bruce Springsteen and the E Street Band."

Jack nodded. "Sure."

Sammy shook his head. "This is just... I can't believe it. How can I? It's completely insane."

"Let me tell you something, Sammy Ruthven," Jack slurred. "That girl, she's crazy about you, nuts about you. You are probably going to be the love of her entire life. Don't screw it up because you can't see what's right in front of you." Jack waved his phone around and put it safely back in his pocket.

TWENTY

Comic Books

───────────

On the way back to the motel, Jack began to realize just how drunk he was when he found his arm around Sammy's shoulder and his mouth saying, "You're OK, Sammy Ruthven."

Sammy laughed. "You're not so terrible yourself."

"Oooooh," Jack cooed, coming to a sudden stop. Sammy put an arm out to steady him. "Comic books." Jack stared into the comic book store window like a kid outside a candy store.

Sammy laughed. "Really?"

"Yeah." Jack put his nose to the glass. "I love comics. They have the best stories, and you never get bored because of the pictures. It's like one of the few socially acceptable ways you can still be a kid forever. You have to get rid of so many kid things, but you never have to get rid of your comic books. Adults who like comics are cool."

"Not sure I agree with that."

Jack pushed open the door and the bell chimed, letting the balding salesclerk know they were there.

"See?" said Jack. "That guy must be like fifty and he still likes comics. He's even made a job out of it."

"I'm not sure he's very cool," Sammy said, under his breath.

The man looked up at them with an empty stare.

"How long are we going to be in here?" Sammy asked.

"Not long. Why don't you have a look around," Jack suggested. "You might find something you like."

Sammy gave him a look that said, "never in a million years," but started looking through the stacks anyway.

"Can I help you with anything?" the clerk asked in a low drone, appearing at Jack's side out of nowhere.

Jack shook his head. "Just having a look today, I'm kinda broke."

The balding man made a noise like a balloon deflating and walked off.

"You're not really supposed to tell them you're broke."

Jack shrugged and started flipping through the latest releases. His eyes lit up when he found a few comics he knew were worth at least fifty bucks in his time and he wondered if this was the answer to all his problems. He could cough up thirty cents now and get fifty bucks back. This was the kind of job he could get behind. Jack started picking out a bunch of titles he knew had some value and he checked his pocket to see how much cash he had left. All he had was a few dollars.

Sammy started laughing.

"What's so hysterical, Ruthven?"

"Some of these titles are just so ridiculous," Sammy said. "Like what the hell kind of superhero is a Gobbledygook?"

Jack's stomach lurched, and he rushed over to where Sammy was standing in the rare section.

"What number is it? What number?" He shoved Sammy out of the way to have a look.

"Woah, relax, man," said Sammy, handing it over.

"We have number one and number two," said the clerk, who was suddenly standing behind them.

"Twenty bucks for a comic?" asked Sammy. "Sounds steep man, it's not even colored in."

"They are very desired," said the clerk in his monotone. "I can do both for thirty."

"Sammy, can I borrow thirty bucks?" Jack pleaded.

"What? Are you crazy? You're broke and you want to borrow money off me for comic books?"

"I'll pay you back double, *triple*," he asked desperately. His blood was rushing so fast throughout his body and he felt suddenly sober. He had to walk out of this shop with these comics no matter what.

"Jeez, if it means that much to you, sure." Sammy pulled the thirty bucks out of his wallet and put it in Jack's shaking hands.

Jack handed it over to the cashier who wrapped the comics in extra cardboard, put them in a brown paper bag with "Don's Comics" written on the front, and handed them over.

Jack didn't know exactly how much he would get for the comics back in 2017 but he knew it would be enough to get him out of Santolsa once and for all.

TWENTY-ONE

Finding Lacey

Peggy had only showered a few hours ago, but she already felt sticky and dirty as she stood on a corner in West Hollywood. The pollution here was disgusting. Old cars were spewing out black smog and she couldn't walk three feet without someone blowing cigarette smoke in her face. And even when she got some space, the air never felt fresh. She loved the idea of LA in the eighties, but in reality, now that she was here, the clean air of Santolsa wasn't looking so bad at all.

She checked in her purse for the piece of paper with Lacey's last known address and phone number and headed towards a phone booth on the other side of the street. She felt around the bottom of her purse for some change as she dodged traffic, honks, and a bunch of old drunks leering at her to get to the other side.

Peggy lifted the receiver, wiping it on her dress before putting it near her ear. She put the coins in the slot and dialed the number. Peggy felt the corners of her mouth move up. A couple months ago using a payphone was a totally foreign concept to her, now it was almost second nature. As she stood there, in the phone booth in West Hollywood in 1984, she felt a wave of pride move through her. She had really changed so much since she'd left her time. A girl finally answered, and for a second she thought it was Lacey.

"Lacey?" Peggy asked.

"Huh?" asked the girl.

"Oh, I'm looking for Lacey."

"Lacey?"

"She gave me this number. She's dating Rex?"

Silence.

"Hello?" Peggy asked.

"Rex!" the girl yelled. "Who the fuck is Lacey?"

OK, this wasn't good.

"I might be wrong," said Peggy, in a too late attempt to fix her mistake. But the girl wasn't listening, she'd already put the phone down and was screaming and swearing and Peggy heard something smash.

Peggy hung up and cringed. It seemed like things probably weren't so great for Lacey here after all. She just hoped she hadn't made things worse. Peggy didn't want to admit that Janet was right, but it seemed like maybe Lacey really was just a groupie, and Rex's girlfriend, or whoever *that* was, wasn't happy about it. She knew it wouldn't be a good idea to go over there now, and if Rex's girlfriend *was* there, Lacey sure wouldn't be. She picked the receiver up again, dropped in some more coins and dialed Ben's number.

"Ben, it's Peggy, do you have any idea where Lacey might be?" she asked quickly. Dimes ran out so fast in these payphones, there was no time for small talk.

"She's usually at the club or hanging out with the band somewhere," he said. "And how are you Peg? It's been way too long."

Peggy gave him a quick rundown of what happened, and he made a whistling noise.

"This isn't good," he said. "Rex has a reputation for being an asshole, but from what Lacey told me it sounded like it was for real."

"Whatever is going on, it doesn't sound like she's still there. Do you have any idea where else she might be?" Peggy tapped the side of the phone booth with her shoe.

"I have a couple ideas, but they'd be long shots."

"I'm fine with long shots."

"I don't have any classes until later. Why don't I come with you?"

"Really? Are you sure?" She couldn't help feeling like Sammy and Jack had let her and Lacey down today, but knowing that Ben was coming to her rescue, well, coming with a car, was such a huge relief.

They arranged to meet outside the diner on the corner, and Peggy waited on the street dodging cigarette clouds and cat calls until Ben drove by in an off-white Oldsmobile. He pulled to a stop, holding up traffic and getting honked at while Peggy slid into the passenger seat. The car smelled like old cigarette ash and some way too musky cologne.

"Peggy!" Ben beamed, leaning over to kiss her on the cheek.

"Ben, wow," Peggy said, taking him in. Ben looked *good*. He was dressed in a red and white striped t-shirt and he wore a UCLA baseball backwards. He had lost some weight and his jaw was more defined. He just looked so grown up. Peggy thought he actually kinda looked hot.

"They work us hard at UCLA," he said, shrugging. He put the car into gear and waved out the window to the cars he'd held up. "You look good, too." He grinned over at her.

Peggy rolled her eyes.

"Take a compliment, Peg, you're gorgeous. It's like you're growing into yourself."

Peggy laughed. "*Is* that a compliment?"

"Yep."

She shrugged. "OK, then, thanks. But look at you, college guy, and you even have your own car."

"It's not my car. I borrowed it off... a friend."

"Oh, a friend, huh?" Peggy nudged him in the side noticing how hard his lats were.

"It's nothing too serious. But we've been hanging out a lot." He grinned sheepishly.

"Oooh, what's the deal?" Peggy asked as Ben took a left turn off Sunset.

"He works at the club."

"Well, I guess you've got a type, then," Peggy joked. "What happened with you and Greg?"

"I gotta admit Peg, I'm still kinda hooked on Greg." He rubbed the dark stubble on his cheek. "He was my first love. But he's in Santolsa, and I'm here. We talked about it and decided to see other people, but honestly, I miss him like crazy."

"It sucks when you can't be with the person you want," she said, watching the city go by in a stream of palm trees and graffiti.

"So, I'm guessing you and Sammy still haven't gotten it together?"

"You know Ben, I don't know if we will ever get it together. If it hasn't happened by now, maybe it's not going to."

"I know Sammy better than anyone. And I've never seen him as nuts for a girl as he was about you. Give him time. He's not as tough as he seems, you know."

Peggy looked out the window at the cars and apartment blocks and the people walking by. A couple in knee socks, short shorts and roller-skates who looked like they were headed for Venice Beach. A guy with a handlebar moustache so wide he looked like a Muppet. A group of women who looked like they were on a break from the office all dressed in silk shirts with pussy bows and pencil skirts. They stopped at a red light, and a guy who was naked, except for a pair of tiny denim shorts, walked past with a Ghetto blaster blaring Billy Idol. Peggy smiled at him and he waved.

"So," Ben said, changing the subject. "Lacey, huh?"

"You should have heard this girl screaming. Whatever is going on, it doesn't sound good."

"I didn't want to freak you out," said Ben. "And there was nothing you could have done so I didn't say anything, but when she first got here, I went over to her place and it was totally grody."

"What?"

"Grody? Gross? Dirty?"

"Gotcha," she said.

"There was like a whole bunch of old mattresses all over the floor, some without sheets, and a lot of people were sleeping there."

"Oh my god," said Peggy. "Why would she stay *there*?"

"I wasn't that worried, she seemed fine. Better than fine, really, she seemed really happy. She said it was just until her and Rex got on their feet with some cash. She said everyone was really nice and looking out for her."

"Ben, it sounds like it was some kind of drug den. How could you let her stay there?" Peggy couldn't imagine Lacey staying somewhere like that.

"I've never been to a drug den." Ben turned down a side street. "How am I supposed to know what one looks like? But she seemed OK, and Rex was sweet to her, and the other people there kinda did seem normal."

Peggy sighed. "Whatever, let's just find her and get her out of here."

"She's really into this Rex guy, I don't know if she's going to leave willingly."

"From what I heard on the phone this morning she might not have a choice."

After a few more minutes, Ben pulled up to a shabby apartment block that looked like an old motel. The paint was chipped, and the balconies were rusty, but it still looked better than what Ben was describing about where she'd been living before.

"I dropped her off after the club here one night," Ben said. "She said she was visiting her cousin."

"I didn't know she had a cousin here."

"I don't know if it's even true." Ben took off his cap, running his hand through his dark hair and putting it back on again.

"You think she's been lying to us?" Peggy asked. "I can't imagine her doing that."

"There's a lot you probably don't know about Lacey," Ben said.

"I'm starting to realize that. But she's meant to be my best friend."

"That doesn't mean you know everything about her, she's pretty good at putting on a game face."

Ben led her up some stairs littered with broken kids' toys and cigarette butts. He knocked on a door at the top and a young girl with long dark hair opened the door. Peggy thought they looked about the same age, but she had a baby crying on her hip. She was bouncing up and down, trying to get it to stop.

"What do you want?" the girl frowned. The frown aged her by about six years. She gave Peggy a dark look but brightened slightly when she got a look at Ben.

"We're looking for Lacey. We heard she was staying here," said Ben.

"Lacey? That skank."

Peggy's mouth dropped open and Ben tensed.

"I haven't seen her," the girl said. "Not for a while."

"Do you know where she might be?" Peggy asked.

The girl gave her a look as if to say that she knew, but she didn't want to tell them.

"We think she might be in trouble. We just want to help her," Ben added, leaning sexily on the door frame.

The girl's gaze lingered on Ben and she sighed. "You could try a couple places. Maybe Illusions or she might be at Rex's place, but his girlfriend is usually there on the weekends, so probably not." The baby started screaming, and the girl started bouncing again.

"They haven't seen her at the club for a while. Any other ideas?" Ben asked.

The girl eyed Ben up and down flirtatiously while the baby kept crying. "Maybe the Margarita bar on Sunset and Detroit? And if she's not there, come back here, *alone*," she looked at Peggy, "And I'll see if I can think of anything else."

"Thanks so much," said Ben, taking Peggy's arm.

"And if you do catch up with that piece of work," spat the girl, "tell her I haven't forgotten about the twenty bucks she stole from me."

Peggy reached into her purse and pulled out a twenty and handed it to her.

The girl stared at it.

"Take it," said Peggy. "Lacey can owe me."

The girl slowly reached out, and then snatched it quickly as if it would disappear.

"I guess it's the margarita bar," said Ben, putting the

car into gear and going too fast around a corner. "It's not far from here."

Peggy looked out the window and thought about the girl in the apartment. She wasn't so different from Peggy, but her life seemed tough. She wondered where that girl would be thirty-three years from now, and where that little baby would be. It didn't seem like a great start to life. And then a wave of sadness hit her as she thought about her own parents. Sure, they weren't going to win any parent of the year awards, but maybe they hadn't done such a bad job really. She felt tears stinging behind her eyes as she felt the grief of knowing she was never going to see them again. Not as she was now. And what was she going to do? Turn up in 2016 looking as old as them and say she's their daughter? If she ever saw them again, it would only ever be from a distance.

"You OK Peg?"

She nodded and wiped under her eyes. "Just thinking about home."

"Do you miss it? Canada?" Ben asked.

"I didn't think I would, but you know what, sometimes I do," she said. "I mean, I love it here, but…"

"It's OK to miss things even if you don't want them anymore."

Peggy nodded. "Thanks Ben. You know, I've really missed you."

"You can call me anytime, Peg. Or come visit. I'm avoiding Santolsa for a while though. I can't handle my dad right now, and seeing Greg just hurts too much."

"I get it."

"Hey, you could write me." Ben grinned at her. "I've never had a pen-pal."

"Ben, no offense, but you'd be the worst pen-pal ever! Would you ever write me back?"

"I could try. I could promise to try."

"OK, Ben, you've got yourself a pen-pal," Peggy laughed. "I've never had a pen-pal before either, so I'm relying on you, you know, to at least try."

"Sure thing, Peg," he said, smiling out at the traffic ahead of them.

When they arrived, Ben parked behind the bar which was little more than a brown shack with a neon bar sign for Budweiser. Peggy wondered if this was even the right place. It didn't look like somewhere future rock stars and groupies would hang out, but then again, maybe it looked exactly like that.

As soon as they walked in, they saw her. She was sitting on a bar stool in a short black skirt, cowboy boots and a black band t-shirt tied at the back to make it fitted. She was sipping a margarita, laughing and flirting with the bar guy. She looked as gorgeous as ever and Ben was right, she did seem absolutely fine.

"O.M.G!" Lacey exclaimed. "You made it!" She jumped up and gave Peggy a warm hug and then turned to Ben. "Ben! You're here, too!" She gave him a hug too. Lacey seemed totally fine. Peggy and Ben exchanged looks.

"Lacey," Peggy said. "What's going on?"

"I have so much to tell you about LA and Rex and everything that's been happening here," she gushed. "I'm having the time of my life, I really am." She reached for her margarita and took a sip. "You guys want a drink?"

"I should probably get back to school," said Ben, looking a little pissed.

"Benny, nooo!" Lacey drunkenly grabbed his arm. "Skip class and stay out, it's gonna be a totally rad night at the club later!"

Ben pulled away. "I can't just *ditch*, Lace. I'm on a scholarship and school is important to me now."

Lacey pouted. "Peggy, you'll have a drink, right?" She leaned over the bar, giggling at the guy and ordering another two margaritas, even though hers was still half full.

Peggy looked at Ben. "I guess I'll call you?" She gave him a defeated look. All their worry now seemed like a huge waste of everyone's time.

"Sure, call me." Ben gave a half-hearted wave and walked off before they could even say goodbye.

"What's up his butt?" Lacey asked as she handed a drink to Peggy.

"We've been running all over LA looking for you."

"Well, that's dumb," Lacey said. "I'm so easy to find, I'm always at the club, or here," she shrugged. Lacey picked up her other drink and carried one in each hand, leading Peggy to a table tucked away in the corner. It was dark in the bar and it felt like the middle of the night, not the middle of the afternoon.

Peggy took a sip of the drink and made a face. It was strong. She stabbed the ice with her straw to try to get it to melt and make the drink a little weaker.

"What's going on, Lacey?" she asked. "I mean, *really*."

"What?" laughed Lacey. "Everything is great. I love my LA life."

"We came all this way and then we spent days looking for you." Peggy folded her arms over her chest.

"Oh, Peggy, don't be a Joanie."

"A what?"

"A Joanie, a square?"

Peggy ignored her. "I called your number this morning, and some girl answered, and she was way pissed."

Lacey's face fell slightly.

"And then we went to the other address Ben had, and I had to give some girl with a baby twenty bucks."

Lacey rolled her eyes at the ceiling. "You didn't have to do that. Grace is always trying to rip people off."

"Well, maybe I didn't have to, but I did."

Lacey looked into her drink. "I'll pay you back, I'm good for it."

"Lacey, I know you're not OK."

"Everything is totally awesome here, really."

Peggy almost believed her, but there was an edge to her voice that said something different. Peggy reached out and took Lacey's hand in hers. "You can tell me. We used to tell each other everything, remember? You know everything about me. *Everything.*"

Lacey nodded, but said nothing. She just slurped up the end of one margarita and reached for the next one.

"Sammy still doesn't want me," Peggy said. "Working at the Bowl kind of sucks, but me and Tricia have finally become friends. I think. Oh, and Jack's here. He came through the portal in the book room a couple weeks ago and now he works at Dee's with his grandmother. Oh yeah, and Tricia is his mom."

Lacey started laughing hysterically. "That's absolutely ludicrous!"

"And yet, totally true. So now you're caught up on my life, tell me what's happening with you."

Lacey took another sip and began her story. "It's been great," she started. "But OK, kind of hard too, I guess. I stayed with my cousins in Beverly Hills for a few weeks, but they were so straight edge," she said, rolling her eyes.

"Wait a second, I thought your cousin was that girl we just met today, Grace?"

"Oh, yeah, that's a scandal. The straight edge cousins? They kicked her out when she got pregnant the first time."

"Woah. That's not her first kid?"

"Her third. She was fifteen when she had her first one."

"I think I was still playing with Barbies at fifteen," said Peggy.

Lacey made a slurping sound. "You were lucky then, I guess. Some of us have to grow up way too fast."

Peggy looked into her margarita and at the ice that was finally starting to melt a little.

"So, I was staying in Beverly Hills," Lacey continued. "And I wasn't allowed out at night, but like, it's LA, what was I supposed to do? I sneaked out one night. I found a bar and met some guys and they seemed cool and they gave me a ride to West Hollywood. That was where I met Rex. When I met him, I just knew, you know?"

Peggy nodded. She knew. She took another sip of her drink feeling the buzz start to hit her.

"It was like we just totally clicked, like he so got me."

Peggy nodded again.

"He was about to go on stage and asked me to watch, so I did, and he was *amazing*. I've never seen anything like it. He lit up the stage, he lit up the whole club, he set it on fire!" she gushed. "Everyone just stopped what they were doing and watched him. He's really incredible. He's got something, some kind of thing that normal people don't have." She stopped talking to mash up the ice in her own drink.

"And then?" asked Peggy, getting swept up in the romance of it all.

"And then we went back to his place."

"That one big room where everyone slept?"

Just then one of the bartenders walked over to ask if they needed anything. "A couple cigarettes would be nice."

Lacey gave him her best smile. He took a pack out of his shirt pocket and handed them to her.

She put one in her mouth. "Lighter?"

He nodded and leaned over to light it for her. Peggy would never know how to get guys to do this stuff for her.

When the guy left, Lacey took a long inhale of the cigarette. "Ben told you, huh? Yeah. OK, so it sounds gross, but it was actually kinda rad. It was like we were all friends straight away, everyone gave each other space and when me and Rex wanted to be alone, the others would go out for a while, so it was great, really. But then Rex got his own place, and everything was even better."

"What about this other girl?"

"What other girl?" Lacey asked.

"When I called your number a girl answered, and she had no idea who you were, and then she started yelling."

Lacey looked thoughtful for a moment. "That could have been the new girl, I haven't met her yet."

"Don't bullshit me," Peggy said, surprised at her own confidence to call Lacey out.

"OK, fine," said Lacey, not even trying to keep up the pretense. "Rex has this other girlfriend, fiancée actually, who always comes to see him on the weekends and so I crashed with Grace or one of the other girls those nights."

"OK, Lace, I have to stop you there, what do you mean he has a fiancée?"

"He's engaged." She said it like it was just a fact.

"And you're still into this guy?" She couldn't believe what she was hearing. Lacey was one of the most beautiful, smart and kind people she knew. How could she let this be happening?

"I love him," Lacey said. "And he keeps telling me that he's going to leave her. She's crazy, she's always yelling at him and accusing him of cheating and…"

"He *is* cheating," Peggy said.

"Technically, but we're in love. Is it really cheating if you're in love?"

"Lacey, this isn't love."

"Oh, sure, and what would you know about love?" Lacey asked. "You're the one that ran off when you thought Sammy had died. If you really loved him, you would have stayed and been with his friends and family, but you just left."

"Wow, OK." Peggy took a breath. "So yeah, I did do that, and it was really dumb." Peggy was so tired of having this conversation. "And I've said sorry a million times, and I'm trying to be a better person."

Lacey looked into the bottom of her margarita glass. "More margaritas?" she asked, giving Peggy one of her diamond bright smiles.

Peggy shook her head. "Maybe it's time to come home, Lace."

"I can't, I need to be here for Rex. His career is just starting, and he said he needs me. I'm his lucky charm. He always has a good gig when I'm there. I'm great at bringing people into the club, too."

"So, you're basically working for him? For free?"

"No, I'm helping him to get seen, and he deserves to be seen. I think he's going to be really famous one day."

"Come and stay with us tonight," Peggy said. "Me, Jack and Sammy are staying at the California Comfort."

"There's another gig tonight," Lacey said, ignoring her. "You should come. If you meet him and see us together, you'll understand everything."

Peggy doubted it, but she said OK and ordered another margarita.

TWENTY-TWO

The Gig

Lacey flopped down on the double bed and kicked off her cowboy boots. "This is nice," she said.

A few too many margaritas later and Peggy and Lacey were back at the motel so they could meet up with Sammy and Jack and chill out for a while before the gig.

"Seriously?" Peggy asked, taking a seat on the couch.

Lacey shrugged. "It's pretty nice for this part of town." She grabbed a packet of cigarettes out of her purse. "Always sucks to have to smoke your own cigarettes though." She put one between her lips.

Peggy pointed to the non-smoking sign and Lacey groaned but put the cigarette back in the packet. "Square." She made a face.

"I'd rather be square than dead.".

"Wow, that's dramatic."

"Jack's grandmother is going to die from it. Smoking." Peggy said. "Tammy, who works at the diner?"

"Sure, I know her."

"Jack thinks she's only got a few years left, she wasn't alive when he was born."

Lacey shook her head. "I'd almost gotten used to normal conversations. It's been a while."

"Yeah, it has. I've missed you, Lace," Peggy said.

"I missed you too," Lacey said, her eyelids fluttering closed.

"What do you want to do while we wait for the club to open? Should we go get some food or something?"

Lacey made a moaning sound.

"Lacey?"

Lacey began snoring.

Peggy sighed. She had no idea what to do with herself. Before she'd travelled back in time she would have probably just disappeared into her phone until Lacey woke up. But she had no phone, and she didn't much feel like going out on the streets of West Hollywood on her own again. She grabbed the paperback that was lying on the floor next to Jack's side of the bed and started reading.

It was dark by the time Lacey woke up. Peggy had finished the first book already and was a few chapters into another one she found in Jack's bag. She hoped he wouldn't mind, but she really wanted to find out what happened to Cord Diamondback.

"What? Where?" asked Lacey groggily.

"You're at the California Comfort Motel, Lace."

"What time is it?" Lacey asked, sitting up and looking around.

"After nine," Peggy said. "And I'm starving."

"And I'm sober." Lacey swung her legs off the bed and grabbed her purse. She pulled out a mini hotel sized bottle of vodka and took a swig before handing it to Peggy who reluctantly took a small sip.

"Are you going to get ready to go to the club?" Lacey asked.

"I am ready."

Lacey looked Peggy up and down. "You look like you're going to join the Amish, not go see a rock band."

"I love this dress."

"It's not right for the club."

"I went there last night looking for you and I think my outfit was OK," Peggy said.

"Did you see the band last night?" Lacey asked excitedly.

"No, we left when we couldn't find you. I don't know if you quite realize this Lace, but we've all been kind of stressing out looking for you these last couple of days."

Lacey took another drink. "Well, you found me," she grinned, passing the bottle over.

"I'm serious, we've been worried sick about you." Peggy took another small sip. It was disgusting. And why was Lacey drinking straight vodka anyway?

"Worry less about me, and more about what you're wearing," said Lacey, making a face. "Now, what else do you have in your bag?"

After a few minutes of rummaging through Peggy's stuff. Lacey picked out an outfit for her - a short jean skirt and one of Jack's shirts she'd spotted strewn over the back of a chair. It was white with black polka dots. Lacey rolled the sleeves up to Peggy's shoulders and tied it at her waist. Peggy buttoned it all the way to the top, but Lacey unbuttoned it again.

"Jack isn't going to like this." Peggy frowned down at her cleavage.

"Tell him it was my idea. Look, I'll write him a note." She grabbed the pen and notepad and wrote in capital letters: *Jack, I made Peggy wear your shirt. Don't be annoyed, just tell her how hot she looks in it. Love, Lacey.*

"You can't write that," said Peggy.

"Too late." Lacey put the note on the desk next to the phone. "Maybe it will teach Sammy a lesson to have Jack looking at your boobies under his shirt all night."

Peggy blushed and nearly told Lacey about the kiss she'd shared with Jack but decided against it. Lacey had enough of her own drama right now, and anyway, it was probably better to just keep trying to pretend it never happened.

"Come on, let's do each other's make-up!" Lacey dragged Peggy and her bottle of vodka into the bathroom.

"But you're so much better at make-up than me," said Peggy.

"You can do my hair." Lacey took the last sip of vodka and then started lining Peggy's eyes with dark blue liner. She packed her cheeks with apricot blush and grabbed a red lipstick out of her own purse for Peggy's lips. Lacey ran her hands through the water from the tap and got Peggy to flip her head upside down. She tousled it and hairsprayed it and when she was done, even Peggy had to admit she looked almost as much like a groupie as Lacey did.

Lacey did her own make-up exactly the same, and when she was done Peggy got Lacey to sit down on the bed and braided her hair in a long French plait down the back of her head. Lacey brought the end of the braid over her shoulder and grinned. "That was fun," she said.

"It was. I wish you were around so we could do it again soon."

"Peg," said Lacey. "I've got stuff going on here. I have Rex and my new friends and everything."

"Well, we think you should come home." Peggy grabbed the pen, writing a quick note for the boys to say she'd found Lacey and they would meet them at the club. Maybe they were already there.

"I'm glad you came to visit, but I can't go back to Santolsa," Lacey said. "Come on, let's get to the club and you can meet Rex and you'll see what I mean." Lacey shoved her feet back into her boots, put the empty bottle in the waste-paper basket and dragged Peggy out of the room.

Walking down to the club felt just like old times. They giggled all the way there.

When they arrived, the bouncer waved them straight in past the line, and when they walked in, the atmosphere in the club was buzzing. It was busier than it had been the night before and the dance floor was already heaving.

"I wanna go backstage, but I can't if Kyra is there." Lacey tapped her foot nervously. "Let's just get a spot near the front of the stage and I'll see if I can spot her from there."

"Who's Kyra?" asked Peggy.

"Rex's fiancée."

Peggy had a bad feeling. "Maybe we should get a table a bit further back?" she suggested.

Lacey laughed. "You do *not* want to be at a table for this gig."

They spent the next few hours squished up against the stage. They took turns to go to the bar and the toilet and although Peggy wanted to talk to Lacey about everything - about Rex and Jack and everything that was happening in their lives, they could barely hear each other over the music. Peggy had no idea if Sammy and Jack had seen her note or if they would even be coming, but she found herself looking around for them the whole time, and she sometimes didn't know who she wanted to see more. She wanted to see Sammy of course, but there was something about Jack seeing her dressed up in his shirt like this that made her belly do somersaults.

Lacey kept looking around for Kyra, but the more drinks she had, the less nervous she seemed to be, and when Rex and his band came onto the stage Lacey lost all inhibitions. She started screaming his name and jumping up and down.

He caught Lacey's eye and stuck his tongue out at her, but then he pretty much ignored her for the rest of the gig.

Peggy had to admit she was excited to be here. She knew this band was going to end up mega famous. And even if she had never really been into them, being here with them now was pretty cool. And being here with her best friend who was sleeping with the lead singer, well, even though he sounded like a bit of a jerk in the boyfriend department, it was definitely a night to remember. For one small moment she wished that Mindy and Jim could see her now, here at one of the coolest clubs in Hollywood watching this incredible band, best friends with Rex's girl-friend, groupie, whatever.

Lacey had been right. Rex was incredible on stage. He mesmerized everyone, even Peggy. His long dark hair was flying all over the place as he banged his head in time with the music, his steely grey eyes felt like they were looking right at you, even when he was looking in another direc-tion. He drew you in and made you feel special. He made you feel like you were the only one in the crowd, even though you were just one in hundreds.

Some sweat flew onto Lacey and she screamed out, "I love you Rex!"

Although it was all very cool, Peggy started to get really annoyed with Rex. Lacey was so close, and he hadn't looked at her all night. He'd made eyes at so many other girls and even dedicated one song to "the woman I love", but when he said it, he was looking up the back of the crowd. Lacey yelled, "I love you too baby," but so did about twenty other girls.

The further through their set they got, the more Peggy thought Janet was probably right. Lacey really was just a groupie, and for all she knew there were at least another hand full of girls here who were also sleeping with Rex. It made Peggy seethe. She wanted so much better than this for Lacey. The idea of being a groupie for some band on the edge of stardom seemed exciting, until you were close enough to see the truth of what that really meant.

After the band left the stage, Lacey grabbed Peggy's hand and started dragging her through the crowd. "Come on, I'll take you backstage."

But when they got to the door that led backstage, a bouncer stopped them. "Kyra's here," he said shaking his head. "Go home, Lacey."

Lacey tossed her braid over her other shoulder. "I can hang with Damon," she said.

"No," said the bouncer. "Strict instructions from the band not to let you through tonight."

Lacey's face went red. "How come?"

"You're not on the list anymore."

"What? As of when? We just walked right in tonight," Lacey said.

"As of now," said a short girl with high cheekbones and a dark pixie cut. She gave Lacey a smug look from behind the bouncer.

Lacey's mouth dropped.

"Hi, Lacey," the girl said, shoving past the bouncer and squaring up to Lacey even though she was a good head shorter.

"Oh, hi, Kyra," Lacey said, acting like everything was fine. "I'm just here to hang with Damon tonight."

"I don't think so," Kyra said.

"We were just leaving anyway," said Peggy, looking around for Sammy, Jack, Ben, *anyone*.

Kyra grabbed Lacey by the arm and looked her straight in the eye. "If you ever come near Rex again, I'll fucking kill you."

Lacey gasped and then laughed. "Oh, babe, I am so not into Rex. You're like, so totally uninformed."

Kyra gave her a look and then slapped her in the face. She was about to do it again, but the bouncer grabbed her hand. "She gets the message Kyra, I'll make sure she's not in here again."

"And you," Kyra said, looking Peggy up and down. "You're the bitch that called my house earlier, right?"

"What?" Peggy laughed nervously. "I have no idea what you're talking about."

Kyra shoved Peggy against a wall, sending pain down her spine and into her chest. "Don't you ever come in here again, either."

"OK," said Peggy. "Sure, whatever you want." It had been a while since Peggy had been shoved up against something, but it was like it brought all the pain of her high school years right back up to the surface in that one moment.

"Come on, Kyra," said the bouncer, pulling Kyra away. "That's enough."

Lacey took her chance and ran past Kyra and the bouncer to the backstage area. Kyra ran after her and Peggy tried to, but the bouncer stopped her. "No way," he said gruffly before his tone softened. "It's best if you just get out of here, I'll handle Lacey." And he went to follow them both backstage.

TWENTY-THREE

After the Gig

Jack and Sammy had been waiting in line for over an hour and hardly moved any closer to getting into the club. Hot girls in skimpy clothes were walking right past them and getting straight in. Only about six other guys had gotten into the club since they'd been there. They were both starting to sober up, and although they had been acting like best friends earlier that afternoon, now they were both a little less buzzed, a lot more tired and had a lot less to say to each other.

"I think I'm just gonna go back," said Sammy. "The band will be almost done now."

Jack had been enjoying listening to the band from out on the street, even though he was desperate to get in and see them live and up close again. He hoped that this Lacey girl could still get him an intro with Rex if they ever found her, and hopefully some tickets to another show at some point. Being out here like this did kind of suck, but it would suck even more to go home and miss any chance he had of seeing them again.

"I think I'll stay a bit longer," Jack said. "Try my luck."

"Sure, I'll catch you later." Sammy turned and walked off down the street.

After Sammy left, a whole bunch of other people in the line started leaving too, and by the time Jack got to the front the bouncer said they weren't letting anyone else in.

"Typical," mumbled Jack. He stuffed his hands in his pockets and began to slowly walk in the direction of the motel. He was tired as hell, but he wasn't in any hurry to get back and hang out with Sammy alone in the motel room.

He stood on the corner and looked around for something to do, somewhere else to go for a while. He thought about waiting until Peggy and Lacey came out of the gig, but that could be ages, especially if they were going backstage.

Backstage.

Maybe he could get in if he said he knew Lacey. Or maybe he could find them hanging around near the back of the club. Or at the very least he could get a glimpse of Rex in the flesh.

He turned down the side street and saw a sign for the stage door. There was no one around so he leaned up against a wall. Maybe someone would come out soon. Not for the first time since arriving in the eighties he wished he had his phone, so he had something to do while he waited.

But he didn't have to wait too long until the door flew open, and there she was, as beautiful as he remembered. She threw her purse against the door as it slammed behind her, and she crumpled into a heap on the ground.

Destiny.

"Hey," he said, walking over to her and extending his hand. "Are you OK?"

She looked up and started laughing through her tears. "You again? Seriously?"

Jack shrugged. "I guess I'm your knight in shining armor, or your guardian angel or something," he joked.

She looked up at him, and again it was like they'd known each other their whole lives. After a moment's hesitation she grabbed his hand, and he gently lifted her off the ground. Her hand fit in his so perfectly, it was like they were made for each other. As the streetlight lit her face, Jack saw she'd been hurt. Her face was red and blotchy as if she'd been slapped or hit.

"What happened?" he asked, resisting the urge to reach out and push her hair away from her eyes.

"Oh, just a crazy girl at the bar tonight," she said, picking up her purse and fumbling around for her packet of cigarettes.

Jack had never felt so protective of anyone in his life as he did over this girl in this moment.

"Why would someone do this to you?" he asked. "Who did it?" Anger rose in his chest.

The girl laughed. "You can't do anything about it."

"Wanna bet?" He pulled up his shirt to show her his Eight tattoo.

She rolled her pretty hazel eyes at him. "The best thing you can do is walk away from me right now."

"Even if I did, I'm sure I'd find you again," he said, inching closer to her.

She lit a cigarette and then exhaled away from him. "Look, you seem like a decent guy. And in some other life maybe we could get married and have two point whatever kids, and live happily ever after, but this isn't it."

"Why not?"

"Because in this life, I'm in love with a guy who's getting married to someone else and who just told me he never wants to see me again."

"So, what about falling in love with the nice guy, who's single by the way, and standing right in front of you?"

"Oh sure, like falling in love with an Eight would be any easier," she scoffed.

Jack puffed out a breath. "Truth is though, I'm not really an Eight. I got this tattoo by mistake."

"No one gets an Eight tattoo by mistake," she said.

"I did."

Lacey felt her mouth move into a smile, a real smile, with no effort or struggle for the first time in a long time. And as she looked into his warm brown eyes something shifted inside of her. When she'd first met him, she'd felt it too, but she'd just put it down to someone being nice to her for the first time in months. She didn't know exactly what this feeling was, but whatever it was, it was something real. The whole time she'd been with Rex it felt like she was living in a movie. She was in LA hanging out with rock stars and groupies, living day to day, dressing up in sexy outfits and flirting with whoever to get free drinks, stealing money to keep up appearances. It had been both wonderful and horrible, but none of it had felt *real*. The truth was, that was exactly what she'd wanted. She'd wanted to be as far away as possible from everything that was real. And yet here she was, having a moment that felt more real than anything ever had before, and it scared her senseless. It scared her more than Kyra or Rex or not knowing where she was going to sleep that night.

And yet, even though it scared her out of her mind, at the same time, she'd never felt safer just being next to him right here.

She leaned up against the wall and took another drag

of her cigarette. "You know, I could fall for someone like you in a heartbeat, if I wasn't so screwed up."

He leaned on the wall next to her and they both looked up at the Marlboro Lights billboard rising above them like the moon.

"I've already fallen for you," he said.

She laughed. "You don't know anything about me, you just think I'm pretty."

"I do think you're pretty, but when I look at you, I don't just see how beautiful you are on the outside, I feel like I can really see you, you know?"

"What do you see?" she asked.

"I see someone who is hurting," he started. "And she's hurting so much because she has such a big heart. I see someone who has been through some hard stuff, and she's still working through it. But I know she has the strength in who she is to come out the other side. I see someone who brings so much love and joy to the world and the people she cares about, but probably has no idea just how much."

Lacey laughed. "Well, you're definitely wrong about one thing."

"Oh yeah, what's that?" he asked.

"I'm not strong at all."

"Maybe you just need someone else to help you see it."

She pushed herself off the wall and started backing away. "I don't need you, or anyone else to help me. I'm fine on my own."

"Maybe you are." Jack shrugged. "But that doesn't mean you have to be."

She shook her head. "We come in alone and we go out alone." She exhaled cigarette smoke at the sky above her.

"Well, technically you come in with your mom."

She smiled and shook her head. "My life is such a mess. You have no, no idea."

"So, tell me."

"I'll tell you what," she said, stomping on her cigarette butt. "If I ever bump into you like this again, I'll tell you everything."

"We've already bumped into each other twice. I think it's pretty destined that we'll see each other again."

"I'm pretty sure that only happened because we like the same music and hang out at the same club. But if we bump into each other again someplace else, not here, nowhere near this club, then maybe I'll accept that it's destiny."

He nodded. "It's a deal."

He put his hand out to shake hers, and when she took his hand in hers, they both felt like they were coming home.

TWENTY-FOUR

Lucky Charms

"Are you still hung up on that girl you met in LA?" Peggy asked, looking over the dining table at Jack. She'd woken up on time for once and she was still in her pajamas. She grabbed the box of Lucky Charms that was sitting next to Jack's bowl and filled up her own.

Jack looked up from the newspaper. "Huh?"

"That girl, the one you met outside the club. You know, the one you couldn't stop talking about the whole car ride home."

Jack shot her a look. "Whatever, it's not like I will ever see her again." He took the box of Lucky Charms back and poured himself a second helping, whacking the box back on the table when he was done.

Jack had been acting weird since the trip. Lacey had decided to stay in LA and there was nothing Peggy or Sammy could do about it. Ben said he would try to see her when he could and let them know how she was doing. Peggy hated leaving her there, and without being able to text or email she had no idea how to get in touch. She didn't know where Lacey was staying or how to contact her at all. She just had to trust that Lacey would call.

"You are still hung up on her," Peggy said. She hadn't realized how Jack's new crush would make her feel. She'd been so used to Jack having a crush on *her*, and now that he had feelings for someone else it was new territory that she didn't quite know how to navigate.

"Are you still hung up on Sammy Ruthven?" asked Jack, before eating another spoonful of cereal.

Peggy rolled her eyes. "You know I am," she sighed.

"You two are ridiculous." He threw down his newspaper and got up to grab the coffee pot. He poured hers first without even asking if she wanted a refill, which she did, and then filled his own cup before sitting back down again.

"Ridiculous?" Peggy asked.

"Anyway," said Jack, ignoring her. "Mostly I'm just really upset we had to come back to Santolsa, I loved LA."

"We can go back again sometime."

Jack shrugged. "I'm thinking I'm going to move there soon, anyway."

"How can you move to LA? You pretty much just got here, and you have no money."

"That might be about to change real soon."

"Oh yeah? How so?"

"I don't want to jinx it, so I can't tell you yet."

"You can't just move to LA for some girl you met once." Peggy stirred a teaspoon of sugar into her coffee.

"Twice," he corrected. "But it's not even about her, it's about the way LA made me feel."

"Dirty and disgusted with consumerism?"

Jack made a face at her. "No, like coming home."

"LA really got me thinking," she said. "About using time travel to change things for the better. Like what if we could help do something to help the environment? Or help the homeless or something?"

"Peg, that's a bit heavy for a Saturday morning don't you think?" He yawned.

"Seriously though, here we are with this chance to really change things. Maybe we could do something to really make a difference."

"Good morning, youngsters," said Janet, appearing at the doorway in her robe, her hair sticking up on one side and last night's mascara smudged under her eyes. "I guess LA had quite an effect on you. It sounds like you're ready to enroll at Berkeley and study Environmentalism and Women's Studies, Peg."

Peggy groaned. "I was just saying, the environment is totally screwed in the future. And I was wondering if we could do anything about it."

"There's a lot you can do." Janet picked up the empty coffee pot and gave them both a disapproving look for leaving it empty, before banging around the kitchen to make a new pot.

"Like what?" asked Peggy.

"You could donate money to Greenpeace, or say no to plastic bags."

"That hardly seems like enough."

"The leaders of the world already know the environment is in trouble, you just have to do what you can."

"But I do want to make some kind of difference," Peggy said. "I've actually been thinking about teaching."

Janet looked up and gave her a proud look. "That's great Peggy. Anything I can do to help, just let me know."

"I want to make a difference, too," said Jack. "A difference to my bank balance."

Peggy rolled her eyes at him. "I just want to do something meaningful."

Jack nodded. "I want to do something meaningful too, but I also want to get paid for it. Teachers don't make that much, do they Janet?"

Janet gave him a look. "Teaching is not about the money."

Jack gave Peggy a look.

"So, you two work out what you want to do with your lives, and let Ronald Reagan get on with his job," Janet said, taking the newspaper from Jack.

"Ronald Reagan," Jack mused, shaking his head.

"It's a trip, isn't it?" asked Janet. "Bill Clinton was president when I got the key, then I went back, and it was Richard Nixon."

Peggy shook her head. "Total trip."

"Do you wanna do something tonight?" Jack asked Peggy. "I'm only working a few hours today."

"Sure, I'll be done by four. We could go to the mall, it's late shopping. Or the diner, or Super Pan, or go bowling. I can try to get us a free lane."

Jack made a face. "This is *exactly* why I need to get back to LA."

"Santolsa is actually pretty great in the eighties. It's so much better than it used to be. Once you get used to it, you won't want to leave."

"Peg, just because it's 1984 that doesn't make it better here. In some ways it's even worse. It's still a total hell hole. There's nothing to do here except eat greasy burgers and go on road trips to cooler places, and honestly, I'm kind of going out of my mind being here. No offense, Janet."

Peggy looked hurt.

Janet put down the newspaper and gave him her teacher look.

"It's been amazing getting to know my grandmother at the diner," he continued, "but I'm always on late shifts now and I hardly ever see her, or you. And I don't see serving burgers in my future. Maybe you're OK with working at the Bowl and eating at Dee's every night, but that was never what I wanted for my life, and it still isn't."

"I'm not *OK* with it," Peggy said angrily. "I do want to do something more than this, but I also don't want to be away from my friends, and Janet really is like family now. Everyone here is." Peggy folded her arms and leaned back in her chair.

"That's great, Peg. I'm happy for you, I really am. I'm so glad you found your place in this world, but this isn't *my* place."

Peggy turned her empty coffee cup over in her hands, noticing how chipped her pale pink polish had become. She and Jack had been best friends most of her life. He had been the one who had understood her when no one else had. He had been the reason it had been so hard to leave the present and stay in 1983. She had agonized over her feelings for him and even watching him now, drinking coffee and reading the paper over a breakfast of Lucky Charms, she still felt so much for him.

"What if the person you loved was here?" she asked, holding his gaze. She wasn't sure if she was talking about Sammy, or about him. Everything was upside down. She was still thinking about the kiss they shared before they went to LA. She was still jealous from hearing all about this mystery woman for the last few days. And the last thing she wanted was for him to move away now.

"I love you, Peg," he said. "But you and me, it's not..."

"That's my cue," said Janet, taking her coffee and the paper upstairs with her.

Peggy's stomach dropped. "It's not what?"

"It's not going to happen, is it?" He said it like a statement, not a question to be answered.

Peggy looked down into her Lucky Charms. She couldn't say no, but she couldn't say yes either. She could feel him staring at the top of her head.

"I... I don't..."

"I don't want to upset you." He reached over the table to grab her hand. "But this life, this isn't what I want for myself. Can you understand that?"

Peggy nodded.

"But I'm here now," he said with a soft smile.

She nodded again.

"So maybe we could just go get a pizza tonight. Just you and me, like old times."

"Sure," she said.

"It's a date," said Jack, and something inside of Peggy was happy he'd called it a date.

TWENTY-FIVE

Pizza

Peggy had spent all that day thinking about her date with Jack.

Date.

She knew it wasn't really a date, and she knew that when he'd said it, he didn't really mean it like that. Or did he?

And she wasn't sure that she really even hated the idea of it being a date. Or *did* she?

Her head was a fuzzy mess and her heart was a Twister game of emotion. She wanted Sammy Ruthven more than anything on this planet, but what was she supposed to do? Just sit around and wait for him to maybe one day be ready to forgive her and pick up from where they left off? She'd already been waiting months. It could be years before he was ready.

He may never be ready.

"I don't know what I'm thinking," Peggy said to Tricia as they mopped lanes and put bowling balls back in order on the racks along the walls. "I just don't know how long I'm supposed to wait."

"Peg," said Tricia as she dropped a bowling ball down on the rack. "You can't mess around with other guys if you want Sammy to forgive you. That's the bottom line of it. He'll never want you back if he finds out you've been screwing around."

Peggy thought about the kiss, which she still hadn't told a soul about, and blushed. "I'm not screwing around."

"Maybe not yet."

"But even if I was, am I meant to sit around keeping myself pure for Sammy Ruthven when I don't even know what he's doing?"

"I didn't think you *were* pure," Tricia said with a smirk.

Peggy threw a beer-soaked cloth at her. "I just, I think I do maybe have some kind of feelings for Jack. God, I never thought I would say that, and I never thought I'd say it to you of all people."

"You can't mess him around either," Tricia said. "I don't know what it is about that Jack kid, but I feel kind of protective over him."

"I'm not. I mean, I think I might actually *like*, like him. That's not messing him around."

"It is if you only *think* you like, like him. The poor guy was in love with you for years. I bet he had your kids' names picked out and everything."

"Maybe you're right." Peggy put the mop back in the bucket.

"You've come too far to screw things up with Sammy. Didn't you say you had a couple of moments in LA?"

"Kinda."

"Give it time."

Peggy groaned. "I'm so sick of everyone saying that to me."

Tricia shrugged. "My mom always tells me, if you can't work out what to do, just do what's right."

———

Peggy changed her outfit six times and spent nearly an hour doing her make-up while her hair was setting in hot rollers. She didn't quite realize until she was putting on her mascara just how much effort she was making. She'd chosen a blue and white striped dress in a 50s style with a tight bodice and full skirt. She'd picked out the pattern and the material and Janet had helped her make it. It accentuated her curves and showed off a bit more of her cleavage than she usually would. She felt awkward, but she liked how she looked in it. Even after Tricia's pep talk, she still wanted Jack to want her. And even though she really didn't want to, she couldn't stop thinking about the possibility that they might kiss again. When the rollers had cooled down, she pulled them out, fluffed out her hair and sprayed it.

When she finally made it downstairs, Jack took one look at her and ran up to go have a shower himself.

Janet was on the couch marking papers. "You look nice," she said, raising an eyebrow.

"Is that a problem?" asked Peggy, sitting down in the armchair next to her. She reached over and grabbed a magazine off the coffee table.

"No," Janet said. "But you know that boy is sweet on you."

Peggy sighed and Janet gave her a motherly look.

"It's not like that."

"Just don't go giving him the wrong idea. Unless you're over Sammy?"

"You know I'm not over Sammy," Peggy sighed.

"You know, I was young once too. I know what it's like to be confused about your feelings. But if my experiences taught me anything…"

"I get it," Peggy cut her off. "I'm not going to do anything stupid."

"OK, I won't say any more, I'll trust you to do the right thing."

Peggy looked back down at her magazine and didn't respond.

When Jack appeared in the doorway, Peggy's heart gave a tiny flutter. He was dressed in black jeans and a white short-sleeved shirt with little red hearts on it. His tattoo was peeking out from under his sleeve and his bicep looked bigger than Peggy had remembered it. Maybe it was all that lifting of big plates of food at the diner. His hair was slicked back, but one piece had come loose and was falling in his eye.

"Ready, Peg?" he asked.

She jumped up off the couch and grinned at him.

"Have a good time, kids," Janet said back without looking up. "Don't do anything I wouldn't do."

Peggy felt a wave of guilt wash over her. Janet was pretty straight edge, and she certainly wouldn't approve of Peggy drinking. But she was so nervous, how could she get through this night without something to take the edge off?

"Can I drive?" asked Jack as they walked out to the driveway.

"Seriously?"

"Yeah, I need the practice, and it seems weird that you're dressed all like that and you have to drive."

"Don't be so sexist."

"It's bad enough you have to pay for your own dinner," Jack said. "Let me have this one thing."

"You know I paid for the gas too, right?" She threw him the keys and slid into the passenger seat of the bug.

Having him drive made it feel even more like a date. She knew that was sexist and stupid. Girls could definitely drive boys on dates, but she'd never done it before. Sammy had always driven her, and Big Mick had always made her meet him at his house.

Peggy couldn't believe how nervous she was. It was so stupid. It was *Jack*. It was pizza. Why was her stomach flip flopping around like a half empty bottle of soda?

And then, just fifteen minutes of awkwardness later, when they were sitting across from each other at a dimly lit table for two at Super Pan, she *really* felt like they were on a date.

"Sorry I was kind of a jerk this morning," Jack said, tapping the red and white tablecloth with his thumb.

"It's fine." She reached for a breadstick in the center of the table.

"I really do want to stick around in Santolsa for a while, but not forever, you know?"

Peggy nodded.

"Do you want that too? What do you want? Because you were always so sure you wanted to get out of here too." Jack was talking fast and seemed just as nervous as she was.

They'd been out for food plenty of times, but this was... different. Jack looked... nice, and the lighting and the cigarette smoke was making it all feel a little hazy and strange.

Peggy nibbled on a breadstick and accidentally brushed his leg with hers under the table. "I don't know. I don't know what I want right now."

"You must have some idea." Jack poured her a glass of the cheap Italian house wine they had ordered because they thought it was more grown up than drinking vodka with pizza. Although, vodka had been exactly what Peggy really wanted. Maybe she really did know what she wanted but was just too afraid to admit it. Jack said he'd only have half a glass and the rest would be for her. It seemed like a stupid amount of wine considering she'd have to drink most of it. A few sips had already made her face feel flushed. She was going to have to eat a lot of pizza.

"I don't know, I thought I wanted to do something with vintage clothing," she started. "But after hanging out with Jessie, I've been thinking about learning sign language and maybe even becoming a Special Education teacher."

"Jessie?"

"Sammy's little sister." Peggy felt her face flush at the mention of his name.

Jack cleared his throat. "Do you want to do that here in Santolsa, though?" He pulled on a breadstick and snapped it in two.

Peggy shrugged.

"I know you think you love Santolsa now. But in thirty years it's going to be the Santolsa that you hated."

Peggy looked down at the crumbs already accumulating on the tablecloth in front of her. "I hadn't really thought about it like that before. But *I'll* be different, so maybe Santolsa will be different too."

"Maybe, maybe not," Jack said as the waiter came over with two pizzas and a garlic bread.

It smelled so good, and Peggy immediately reached for a slice of the four cheese pizza.

Jack broke off a piece of garlic bread and started eating like he hadn't eaten anything for a week.

"I am so over diner food and frozen pizza," he said. "This is heaven."

As they sat there eating and drinking, Peggy started to feel relaxed from all the wine and happy because her best friend was back, and for the first time since he'd been back it started to finally feel normal again. It was like they had slipped back into who they used to be for each other. They were talking about their plans for the future and how much their jobs sucked. Jack talked about diner grease and rude customers and Peggy talked about smelly shoes and mop buckets. Peggy kind of loved her job, really. She loved going to work every day in one of the most retro places on the planet. But complaining about things had always been the glue that stuck her and Jack together, and so when she rolled her eyes about having to put all the bowling balls back on the shelves only to have a bunch of customers come in and move them all around ten minutes later, she finally felt like things had gone back to normal. And it was almost as if the kiss had been some kind of dream, or weird mishap that didn't really mean anything. Did it?

Jack grabbed the last slice of pizza and Peggy pouted.

"You want it?"

"No, you have it," she said, hoping he would give it to her.

"If you want it, just say you want it."

"I'll have it if you don't want it," she said.

"Share?" He took a small bite and handed it over to her.

She took a bite and handed it back, and they kept going back and forth until it was just a crumb on the end of Jack's finger.

"Don't take the last bite!" she laughed.

Jack put the crumb on his plate and tried to cut it in half with his knife and fork and they were in hysterics.

"Hey," said Sammy, who had appeared brooding over their table, staring at them both.

Peggy was suddenly very aware of how much wine she'd had, and how much this must look like they were on a date.

Was it a date? Oh, God.

"Hey," said Peggy, wiping her mouth where she'd just spat out wine from laughing so hard.

"Hey," said Jack, putting his knife and fork down.

"What are you doing here?" Peggy asked.

"Just picking up a pizza for dinner." His eyes flickered down to Peggy's cleavage.

"Oh." Peggy looked up at him, her heart feeling as if it was about to burst out of her dress.

"What are you two doing here?" he asked coldly.

"Having dinner, obviously," said Jack.

"Why don't you join us." Peggy looked around for a chair to bring over. Jack shot her a look.

"No, thanks."

"You don't need to be so rude," said Jack.

"Me? Rude?"

"Yeah, what's your beef, man?" Jack asked.

"My beef? What's *your* beef?"

"I don't have any beef, I'm a vegetarian."

Peggy laughed. "You're not a vegetarian."

Jack made a weird face at her. "Have you seen me eat any meat since I got here?"

Peggy thought about it, and how he'd only eaten the four cheese pizza and garlic bread at dinner, and all he'd eaten at the diner was pancakes or grilled cheese or fries or onion rings.

"Oh, when did that happen?"

"When you were away, before you gave me the key to the book room and told me you wanted me back," Jack said.

Peggy laughed nervously. "I'm sure that's not exactly what I said..."

"Do you want something, Ruthven?" Jack looked up at him and took the last sip of his wine.

Sammy looked calmly down at Jack and then at Peggy, at Peggy's low-cut dress and then back to Jack again.

"Outside," Sammy said.

"What?" laughed Jack.

"You and me, outside," he said again.

"You're nuts, dude. I'm not going anywhere with you."

"I don't want to do this in front of Peggy."

"Do what?" asked Peggy.

"Punch this guy's lights out," said Sammy.

Peggy laughed nervously. "Sammy, you're acting crazy!"

"OK." Jack scraped his chair back and stood up to face Sammy. "Let's go."

"Guys!" Peggy got up and brushed the crumbs off her dress. "This is stupid!" But Sammy was already marching out of the restaurant, Jack hot on his heels.

Peggy threw enough money on the table to cover the check and raced out to follow them, pushing past the chain smoking cowboys at the bar and holding her breath to avoid too much smoke inhalation. When she made it to the street, Sammy had Jack in a headlock and Jack was trying to bite his arm.

"Stop it!" she yelled.

"Never!" yelled Jack, escaping from the headlock and trying to push Sammy into a streetlight. Sammy just laughed and shoved Jack back before Jack launched himself at Sammy again.

"Let him go!" Peggy shouted, not really sure if she was shouting at Jack or Sammy.

Sammy maneuvered out of Jack's grip and Peggy got in between them. "What are you two doing?" she yelled at them.

"He started it," Jack said, pointing at Sammy.

"*You* started it," Sammy said. "You started it when you turned up here still being in love with my... *Peggy*."

Peggy's stomach lurched. It was the first time since she'd been back that he had even really alluded to still having feelings for her.

"Wait, what?" Peggy turned to face Sammy.

"He told me himself." Sammy pointed at Jack.

"Yeah, and I told you I thought you should stop being a dick and just get back together with her because you're clearly both into each other."

Sammy and Peggy exchanged glances.

"And *you* said you didn't still have feelings for her, but you obviously do, so how can I trust anything that comes out of your mouth?" Sammy lunged for him again.

"I don't," said Jack, as Peggy jumped in-between them both again. "I did OK? I did have feelings for her, I mean look at her, how could you not have feelings for that woman?"

Peggy had one hand on Sammy's chest and one hand on Jack's shoulder and had never felt more confused in her life. Here was Jack, saying these perfect things about her, and Sammy wanting to beat him up because of it.

"Peggy, are you into him?" Sammy asked her, his eyes frantic, searching. She'd never seen him like this. His face was red, and he looked like he was about to explode.

Peggy looked at Sammy and then back at Jack. "I..." she stammered.

"That's what I thought." Sammy stepped away and stormed off towards the parking lot.

And it was in that moment, when she thought she might lose him again, that she knew exactly what she wanted and what she needed to do.

"I have to go after him," Peggy said, running across the road, leaving Jack standing alone in front of the restaurant.

When Peggy caught up to Sammy, he was just about to get in his car. She grabbed his arm and spun him around. His skin felt like it was on fire, he was so hot, and his face was all screwed up.

"All I want is you, Sammy Ruthven," she said.

Sammy let out a breath and smacked his hand on the roof of the Dodge. "I don't know what to do with all these feelings. I've never felt so jealous before." He ran a hand through his hair.

Peggy ran her fingers gently down his arm until she reached his hand, which was balled into a fist. She pushed her fingers into his, her heart beating fast and loud enough for the whole of Santolsa to hear. He pushed his fingers into hers in return and in that moment, the last few months disappeared, and they were right back where they had started, in this parking lot that first night she'd gone to Super Pan and he'd offered her a ride. But this time he was more than a sexy stranger. This time they had history, and she hoped, a future.

He looked down at their hands entwined and then he looked into her eyes, and all the anger he'd been holding softening into something else entirely.

She looked into his eyes and knew she was exactly where she was supposed to be.

And it didn't matter that he'd forgotten his pizza, or that she'd been on a weird pseudo-date with Jack, or that she'd hurt him by leaving or that her heart had broken when she thought he had died in the accident.

All that mattered was that she was back in his arms and that his lips were on hers and that the stars were in the sky looking down on them both.

Interlude II

Helena walked around the back of the abbey to the stables where their horse Elliot was kept. They had employed a stable girl to look after him and the other two horses they had received as gifts from the townspeople of Salt Valley. Helena enjoyed spending her time with the horses. She found it a much-needed respite after Maria's stern rules and Catherine's desire to simply do anything asked of her without a thought in her own mind.

And Helena enjoyed spending time with Kimana, the stable girl. Kimana was kind but clever. She did what she was asked, but she had a mind of her own, and if she felt the horses needed something Maria did not, she would follow her own path and do what she felt was right. The horses were happy and in good spirits and Helena also found herself in good spirits when she visited Kimana.

"Sister Helena." Kimana greeted her with a nod. A strand of her long dark hair, which was braided down her back had come loose. Helena felt her hand reaching up to tuck it back and then stopped herself, clasping her hands together in front of her.

"Kimana," she nodded back.

There was something strange that always happened to Helena when she was with Kimana. She didn't understand it. It was as if she felt ill, and the first time she had felt it, she rushed herself back into the abbey thinking she was to be sick. But she wasn't, and the feeling soon went away.

But whenever she saw Kimana, it returned. It was as if she felt that she was going to be sick, but at the same time, she felt in very high spirits. It certainly was strange.

"It's nice to see you," Kimana said. "Sister Maria was here earlier checking up on me and the horses. She does not always like the way I do things, as you know."

"Sister Maria is my greatest discomfort in life," Helena said.

Kimana laughed. "It must be difficult in that big wooden building to find comfort."

Helena nodded. "It does not soothe my soul to be at the beck and call of two old women."

"Will you ever be free of them?" asked Kimana as she began to gently brush Elliot.

Helena shook her head as she reached out to stroke Elliot's mane. "I fear I shall be stuck with them all my days."

"You are a religious woman, and that is the price you pay for the life of a nun, is it not?" Kimana asked.

Helena sighed. "Spiritual," she said. "I may dress like a nun, but I assure you I have some different views on things than many other nuns have."

"Would you like to brush Elliot?" Kimana asked, her dark eyes shining. "I know he likes you very much."

Helena reached out for the brush and when her fingers touched Kimana's, that sick feeling became stronger. Was she a witch, too? Did she have some magical power over her? She looked away and began to brush Elliot, but the feeling kept growing until she could no longer bear it.

"What kind of magic is this?" Helena demanded.

Kimana looked at her strangely. "Magic? I have a gift with animals, but it is not what your people would call magic."

"What is this feeling? When you touch me, I feel it *here*." Helena gestured to her belly.

Kimana laughed. "Oh, Sister Helena," she said. "I feel it too."

"What is it?"

"It's a strong feeling we have for each other. It's a connection of our spirits."

Helena dropped her hand away from Elliot and looked into Kimana's eyes. There it was again, and yes, it did feel like a connection of spirit, that was *exactly* what it felt like. But so painful to not know if the other person feels it too. "What does it mean?" asked Helena.

"I can show you." Kimana reached out and lightly touched Helena's hands as she took the brush away and put it down. She reached out for one of Helena's hands again and entwined her fingers with Helena's.

Helena gasped. It felt so frightening but so wonderful. Kimana moved closer and Helena felt as if lightening was going to explode out of her chest. Kimana put her hand on Helena's beating chest. "Does it feel good?"

Helena nodded. "Yes, so good, but so terrible." She covered her eyes with her hands.

Kimana laughed again. "I do not think we should do more," she said, her breath warming Helena's neck and sending shivers down her entire body. "Is it not part of your religion to abstain from... this?" She removed her hand and stepped back.

"I do not think it could be Godly to abstain from whatever *this* is," said Helena. "It is too wonderful."

Kimana smiled. "Then perhaps I will show you just one more thing."

Helena nodded quickly and Kimana moved closer to her again, this time placing her hands gently on top of Helena's shoulders. Helena felt her heart beating fast and loud. She was sure Kimana would hear it, but she didn't care.

And just when she thought this was as good as she could ever feel, Kimana placed her lips on top of hers, and her whole world was changed forever.

TWENTY-SIX

Lacey's Night

Lacey had seen the posters for the Rats gig all over West Hollywood, and she knew she had to be there. She knew she had to see Rex. She had been totally cut off from him and everyone in the band, as well as all the other girls who hung out with the band. Lacey couldn't say they were her friends, but the other girls were the closest thing she had to friends here in LA. Kyra had done a good job of getting Lacey out of the picture and Lacey had almost given up and gone home more than once. But if she knew one thing, it was that whatever she had with Rex was worth fighting for.

If Rex could just *see* her, she knew he'd remember everything they had together. He'd remember how much he loved her, how much prettier and nicer and more fun she was than Kyra. He'd told her those things himself hundreds of times. He'd told her all about his fights with Kyra, how mean she could be, how she was always pissed at him. He'd said Lacey was so beautiful and easy to be with compared to Kyra. If he could just see her again, he'd remember. And when he did, he would break up with Kyra and they could be together, maybe even forever.

Lacey had been sleeping in her car for the last few weeks, but she wanted to look good when she saw Rex again, so she'd washed her hair in a gas station toilet the night before and put it up in small braids while it was wet. When she took it out on the night of the gig, her hair was huge, and with a ton of black eyeliner, mascara and some red lipstick no one would have any idea that she was basically homeless. She'd dressed in tight dark blue jeans, black heels and a Rats t-shirt she'd cut and made into a crop top. She caught sight of herself in a comic book store window and gave herself an admiring look. She knew she looked good. She knew she could steal Rex back from Kyra. She just had to get past the bouncer. But she had a plan. She knew the bouncer who would be working tonight, and she also knew his weakness.

The line to get into the club was longer than Lacey had ever seen it. The Rats were fast getting a name for themselves and each time they played, more and more people tried to get in to see them. She scanned the line for pretty girls and noticed a group of blondes who were giggling and getting lots of attention from the guys.

"We usually just walk right in here," one of them said to the guys. She tossed her crispy blonde hair over her shoulder.

They'd be perfect.

"Hey girls," Lacey said, trying to be friendly.

"Hey," said one of the blondes looking her up and down.

"Can you girls do me a favor?" Lacey asked.

"Why?" asked another girl smacking gum.

"So you can skip the line and get straight in to see the band." Lacey put her hands on her hips.

The third girl raised her eyebrow. "What do we have to do?"

"All you have to do is go up to the bouncer and start flirting with him. He's a sucker for a blonde, and I'm sure he'll go totally ape over a whole bunch of them."

"Seriously? That's all we have to do?" asked the one with short blonde hair. "And he'll just let us in? What if it doesn't work and we lose our place?"

"I'll save your place," said a hunky guy who looked like a Ken doll in a denim vest standing behind them.

The girls swapped looks.

"Sure, we're in," said the blonde with the gum.

"Great," said Lacey. "But when you do it, just make him look away from the door for like five seconds."

The girls looked at each other and shrugged. And a couple of minutes later, when the bouncer, and everyone else who was in line were staring at three pretty blonde girls asking the bouncer who he thought had the biggest boobs, Lacey was able to slip through and get into the club. It had almost been too easy.

She knew she had to stay under the radar until Rex came on stage, so she hid out in a corner drinking a warm discarded beer she'd found on one of the VIP tables. Lacey hated beer, but she needed something to take the edge off. What if Kyra was here? What if Rex didn't want to see her? Her confidence from earlier started to wane, and she wondered if this had all just been a huge mistake.

But when the band finally came on, her heart lit up, and all her fears were gone. She pushed and shoved through the crowd until she was nearly at the front. She started shouting Rex's name and jumping up and down to get his attention, but he didn't seem to notice her. She kept pushing and shoving people out of the way. Some pushed back but she didn't care, she would do anything to get to him.

When she finally got to the front of the stage, she started screaming his name. He looked down at her, his steely grey eyes curtained by his long dark hair. He held her gaze for just a moment. And she knew, she just *knew* he'd felt everything she'd felt too. She knew he wanted to be with her, and that everything else had been Kyra's doing, not his. He loved her, she knew he did.

"I love you, Rex," she yelled out.

He smiled at her, his grin melting her wax heart, and she yelled it again.

He kept smiling and beckoned for her to come closer. She could tell the other girls in the crowd were jealous, everyone wishing he'd chosen them, but he'd chosen *her*. She stood on her tiptoes and leaned up towards him.

He leaned his lips towards her ear, and she knew without a doubt he was going to say it back. He cupped his hand around her ear so she could hear every word. His touch drove her wild and everything within her was racing. It was as if her whole body was now functioning at warp speed.

"You're a fucking psycho. Get out of here," he said, before jumping back up on stage and grabbing his mic to sing the final line of their final song - "*and when we're done, we're done forever.*"

The crowd cheered and clapped, and the girls screamed.

"Thank you, Illusions, goodnight!" Rex called out as he threw the mic on the floor and left the stage without looking back.

It took Lacey a moment to understand what was happening. Was it just part of the song? Was it a joke? Did Kyra make him say it? Was he just keeping her at a distance because he was trying to keep her safe from Kyra? Her head was reeling, trying to make sense of his words. She moved through the crowd until she reached the bar. Some guy had ordered a bunch of cocktails and the bartender was lining them up on the bar. The guy was hitting on some girl, and as the bartender turned around to get more liquor, Lacey reached in and took one of the drinks. No one even noticed. The drink was blue, and it was strong. It was exactly what she needed. She threw it back into her throat and put the glass back down on the bar.

"Lacey," said a strong voice as a hand landed on her shoulder. She turned around. It was one of the bouncers. She was busted.

Lacey looked up at him with her best puppy dog look. "Hey, Dave," she said, giving him a flirtatious smile. "How are you doing?"

"Rex wants to see you backstage."

Lacey's heart started racing. He *did* want to see her. Maybe she had misunderstood him after all, or it had just been his weird sense of humor.

The bouncer led her backstage and through to the dressing rooms. They were tiny and cramped but it felt magic being back here again with the band.

"Hey, you guys," Lacey beamed out at the band who were all sitting around in one of the cramped rooms. Girls on their laps, drinks in their hands, cigarettes in their mouths.

A couple of the guys murmured a hello back.

Rex's seductive gaze hit her like a bullet. He was looking at her like he wanted her more than anything. "Give us a minute," he said, and the rest of the band cleared out.

Lacey stepped into the room and Rex closed the door

behind her. He pushed her up against the door and began kissing her hard. She gasped. At first, she thought it was everything she wanted, but not like this. He was hurting her. She struggled against him, but he only held her tighter. She tried to move her head away from him.

"Don't you want this?" he asked, gruffly.

"Yes. Yes, I want this more than anything, but you were kind of hurting me."

"Sorry, baby." He loosened his grip and shook his head. "You know I get rough without thinking sometimes, I'm so sorry." He looked down and gently ran his fingers along the neck of her t-shirt. "Nice shirt," he grinned.

Lacey smiling back at him. "It's OK, I know you didn't mean it."

He took her hand and led her over to the velvet couch that had seen better days. "How about here?"

"Much better." She sat down next to him. She couldn't wipe the smile from her face. She was just so glad they were back together again.

He smiled a sexy grin and her pulse quickened. His smile was so infectious, and she couldn't help beaming back at him. He was so beautiful, and after seeing him up on stage tonight, it was as if he was still radiating that glow, that aura of pure magnetism.

He leaned in to kiss her gently, and she felt him begin to lay her down on the couch beneath him. This was it, this was how it should be. His gentle kisses making her moan with pleasure. But he started getting rough again. He was kissing her too hard and holding down her arms. He was strong, much stronger than her.

"Stop," she said, muffled under him.

But he didn't listen, his grip just became harder.

"Stop," she said, a little louder.

He stopped kissing her but didn't release his grip.

"Stop? Now you want me to stop?" His smile was gone. "Isn't this what you wanted? You show up here dressed like *that* and you throw yourself at me in front of hundreds of people. And out of all of them I choose you, and now you don't want it?"

"I do want it," she said, shaking her head, realizing just how much of a big deal this was. He chose her. Out of all the women in the club. He wanted to be with *her*.

He moved in to kiss her again, even harder this time.

"You're hurting me, Rex." Lacey tried to escape his grip. Yes, it was a big deal that he'd chosen her, but that didn't mean he could do whatever he wanted to her.

His face turned dark. "Do you even know what you've done?" His elbow leaned into her chest, making it hard for her to take a full breath.

She shook her head. It wasn't the first time he'd gotten rough with her, but something felt different this time and Lacey felt scared.

"You've caused a lot of shit for me with Kyra. Coming here was stupid. You could've gotten us both in trouble with her, and now you're acting like a little choir girl."

Lacey shook her head. "It's not like that, I didn't come here for... that. I came here for you, I love you."

Rex gave out a loud, low laugh. "You didn't come here for sex? What do you think you are? You're just a groupie." When he said *groupie*, he pushed his fingers even deeper into her arms.

"Ow," she said. "Stop."

"Don't you get it? You're just a groupie, and Kyra is... she's my fiancé, we're getting married."

Lacey shook her head. "But how can you marry someone else when you're in love with me?"

Rex finally let go of her, pushing her back down on the couch. "You're so fucking naïve. You're just a kid, you have no idea about life. Most groupies, they get it. They hang around for a while and when we're done with them, they know it's time to move onto some other band or get a real boyfriend or go to college or something. But you just don't get it, do you?"

Lacey lay still, sensing whatever she did or said would be the wrong thing.

"Let me spell it out for you," he said, leaning over her. "You and me," he gestured wildly through the air between them. "There's nothing here, I don't have any feelings for you, I never had any feelings for you. You were just *there*."

Lacey felt a tear stream down her cheek. "I know it's not true," she said. "I know you love me."

"Love you?" he laughed.

"You said you did. You said you loved me, remember that first night we…?"

"It's just all part of the game." His eyes turned into slits.

Lacey felt like she didn't even know who he was in that moment.

Rex stood up and he ran his fingers madly through his hair. "You're making me crazy."

Lacey stood up and went to him. She put her hands gently on his arms. "Baby, it's OK, we're OK."

"It's not OK." He grabbed her shoulders and shook her. "You are ruining my life, do you know that? You're wrecking everything."

And before she knew what was happening, she felt his hand connect with the side of her face with full force, pushing her to the ground. She couldn't tell if the water falling from her eyes was from the pain or her tears.

"Maybe that will get it through your thick skull."

Lacey was in shock. She didn't know what had just happened, but she knew she couldn't stay in this room with him, not now. Not like this. She shakily pulled herself to her feet and silently walked out of the room, closing the door behind her. She walked back out into the club in a daze. She knew she was probably expected to go out the back door, but she really didn't care what she did right now, or how much trouble she'd be in. She found another discarded drink at a table and picked it up and threw it back before taking a beer out of some guy's hand. He gave her a look but let her take it.

"Hey, girl," said one of the blonde girls from earlier. "Thanks for getting us in so easy before."

"Sure," said Lacey, holding a drink and trying to act like it was hers and like her world wasn't falling apart.

"Are you doing OK? You look like you could use something stronger," said one of the other girls.

Lacey nodded and the girl put a packet of pills into her hand. "What are these?" Lacey asked.

"Just something that will help you stop thinking for a while," said the first girl.

Lacey poured them out into her hand and threw them back, chasing them down with the guy's drink.

"Oh my god," squealed one of the girls. "You're not supposed to take them all at once!"

"I don't care," Lacey said.

"I guess they are already working," said one of them laughing.

"That's not funny, Crystal," said another girl. "We should stay and keep an eye on her."

"No way," said Crystal. "I don't want to get narked out."

"Just go throw up and you'll be OK," said someone, patting Lacey on the back before they pushed their way into the crowd away from her.

But Lacey didn't want to throw up, and right then, she

didn't even care what she'd taken. She didn't want to think, she didn't want to feel, she just wanted to disappear.

As she stood there drinking the guy's drink, she began to feel more and more out of it. Her legs began to feel wobbly, but it didn't just feel like she was drunk. Something else was happening. She needed to just sit down for a second, and so she took herself into the toilet. The walls of the tiny room felt like they were caving in on her, and part of her didn't care, part of her just wanted to let these graffitied walls consume her. Part of her wanted to just escape it all, all the pain and all the hurt. The thought occurred to her that she could stay in this room and never come out again.

She ran the tap and put her face under the water. She wet her hair and her arms. It felt good to have water on her skin. She sat down on the toilet lid and held her head in her hands as everything moved around her. She didn't know how to make it stop. She slid to the floor. It was comfortable down there. She wanted to sleep, but she started to feel cold, very cold. She began shivering and wondered if maybe the boy would come and find her. He found her twice already, maybe he could find her now. Maybe he could save her.

The boy.

All she could see was his face. She didn't even know who he was, but she couldn't stop seeing his face, his sweet dark eyes. She wished he was here to ask her if she was OK, to tell her he'd keep her safe, to put a blanket over her when she fell asleep here on the cold toilet floor. She hated Rex, she hated him for doing this to her, she hated him for not loving her. She hated him for lying, but more than anything she hated herself for falling for his lies.

The boy. His face, his eyes so full of kindness.

Rex, his hands holding her down, his hand connecting with her face. His eyes full of rage.

The boy, his hand reaching down to help her up, the way it was so easy to be with him.

Lacey decided she didn't want to die here, but she knew that this time, she was going to have to save herself. And so even though she could barely move, she managed to pull her hand towards her face and stick her fingers into the back of her throat. She vomited all over the floor in front of her, and then she did it again. And then she passed out.

———

"Harry!" she heard someone yell. "HARRY!" the voice yelled again.

Lacey opened her eyes slowly. She had never felt worse in her whole life.

"Oh, it's OK, she's alive," the voice said as something kicked her in the side. "Come on, you've gotta get out of here." Lacey looked up to see one of the bar girls who she'd thought of as a friend a few weeks ago kicking her in the ribs.

"What the…?" Lacey asked, pulling her head, which felt like a ton of bricks, off the floor.

"No, what *the*?" asked the bar girl. "Lacey this is low, even for you."

"I'm sorry," Lacey said, and she started crying.

"You can cry all you want, but I'm the one that has to clean this up," the girl said, folding her arms.

Lacey peeled herself off the floor. She still felt wobbly and drunk and fuzzy and her head was banging, but she was able to get up and run some water and wash her face. And when she left the toilet and walked back out of the empty club and into the early morning LA haze, she felt a change in the air.

She had a second chance, and she wasn't going to mess it up. She walked back to her car and fell asleep until the sun was back up in the sky, and then, when she felt OK enough to drive, she knew exactly where to go.

TWENTY-SEVEN

Lacey's Return

Peggy was running late for her evening shift when the doorbell rang. Janet was out for dinner and a movie with Ray, and Peggy couldn't find her new frosted pink lipstick anywhere.

The doorbell rang again.

She grabbed her purse, sticking her hand into it to try to locate her lipstick and open the door at the same time.

Lacey was standing on the front porch in a pair of sunglasses. She looked tired as hell. Her lipstick was smudged, her hair was a mess of tangles and there was a smell of vomit and cigarettes emanating from her that made Peggy want to hurl.

Lacey's bottom lip began to quiver.

"Lacey," Peggy gasped.

"Can I stay here for a couple of days?" Lacey's voice wavered.

"Always." Peggy opened the door and ushered her in. "What happened to you?"

"I'm OK." Lacey took off her sunglasses to reveal

crusty old mascara trails down both cheeks and a bruise on the side of her face.

Peggy led her to the couch and Lacey curled up in one corner - Jack's blanket and pillow still neatly stacked at the other end.

"OK, maybe I'm not totally great right now, but I will be," Lacey said. "I just need somewhere to hide out until the swelling goes down. I can't go home like this. Could you imagine my mom?"

"Who did this to you? *Rex?*"

Lacey nodded and tears began to fall down her face.

"Lacey..." Peggy didn't know what else to say. She knew Rex had a reputation, but this was too much.

Lacey put her head in her hands. Her body began to shake, and she cried like she hadn't cried in years. Maybe she hadn't.

"I shouldn't have left you there," Peggy said, putting an arm around her.

"No." Lacey shook her head. "This isn't your fault, it's my fault for being so stupid."

"No, it's no one's fault but Rex's."

Lacey grabbed a tissue from the coffee table and wiped under her eyes.

"I don't want to leave you like this, but I have to go to work," Peggy sighed. "When I get back, we can talk about everything and you can stay here as long as you want."

Lacey nodded. "It's OK, I'm OK, you get to work, don't worry about me." She waved Peggy off.

"Just make yourself at home. Use whatever you want from the bathroom. There are clean towels in the cupboard next to the bathroom, borrow any clothes or anything. There's pizza, coffee, help yourself to anything."

Lacey gave her a look that Peggy had never seen on her face before. It was like all the glamour, all the guard, all the masks had fallen away, and there she was. Heartbroken, scared, grateful.

"Thank you, Peg." She grabbed Peggy's hand. "I mean, really, this is like the only place I feel safe right now."

Peggy nodded. "Janet will be home late and I'm only working a short shift tonight. Jack's hanging out with Tricia in Salt Valley today and then he's working the late shift, so he won't be home for ages."

Lacey just nodded.

"I don't want to, but I have to go."

"It's OK, go, go. I'll take a shower and watch some TV or something, I'll be fine."

"You're safe here, Lacey," Peggy said, and it made a fresh wave of tears fall from Lacey's eyes.

———

When Jack came home from his late shift, there was someone asleep on the couch. *His* couch. He couldn't make out who it was, but he was pretty sure it was a girl. He went into the kitchen to grab a glass of water and wonder where the hell he was supposed to sleep. Peggy had left a note on the table.

Lacey's on the couch, you can crash on the floor in my room x

Great, thought Jack. Like this Lacey person hadn't caused enough drama for everyone, now she was taking his bed.

After their kiss a few weeks ago, Jack really didn't want to sleep in Peggy's room, but he didn't want to sleep on the floor with some weird girl he didn't know, either.

He took his water upstairs and slowly opened the door to Peggy's room. She didn't wake up, but she'd left him a pink fuzzy blanket and a pillow on the floor with one of

225

his t-shirts and a pair of clean boxers. He didn't like the idea of Peggy touching his boxers, but the gesture was nice. He got out of his work clothes and took a quick shower to remove as much of the grease as possible. He put his fresh boxers and shirt on and then went to lie down on the floor in Peggy's room. It was so uncomfortable, not just because of Peggy being mere inches away from him, but the floor was hard under his back and he'd been thinking all night about how good it would be to fall asleep on the comfy couch. But he curled up on his side and found an almost OK position if he just stayed still, and because he was so tired, he fell asleep as soon as his head hit the pillow.

He woke up at 4:12am according to the bright digital numbers on Peggy's desk. He tried to get comfortable again and go back to sleep but nothing worked. He got up, wrapped the pink blanket around him and went downstairs, thinking he would just make a coffee and watch some TV, until he remembered the whole reason he was sleeping on Peggy's floor - someone else was on his couch.

He didn't want to annoy Peggy's friends, but he didn't want to lie on the floor any longer and he needed coffee.

He moved silently through the house and turned on one small light in the kitchen while he made a pot of coffee. He hadn't realized how loud making coffee was until he was trying to do it quietly. The noise from the coffee maker whirring and dripping was bouncing off the walls. "Shhhh," he said to it, but he didn't hear anyone stir. He flipped through a discarded Cosmopolitan magazine while he waited for the coffee to drip through. These magazines were such trash, always telling girls what to wear, what boys were thinking, and the guys featured in these magazines always sounded like total douchebags, but Jack found himself getting sucked in and wondered if he should get a denim jacket like the one the guy was wearing in the Wrangler ad.

When there was enough coffee in the pot, he grabbed a cup and filled it with one hand while still looking at the magazine.

"Can I get a cup?" asked a sleepy voice. Jack froze still staring down at the magazine. Jack knew that voice.

He looked up and there she was. Her red hair a tangled mess, dressed in nothing but an oversized t-shirt, but she looked like an absolute goddess. The mug slid out of his hand and smashed onto the floor, spraying hot coffee all over his legs, but he hardly even noticed.

The glass of water she had been holding slipped out of her hand and smashed onto the floor, spraying water all over her legs, but she hardly even noticed.

"*You?*" she asked.

"*You,*" he said at the same time. "How is this, what is this... who are you?"

"Who am I? I'm Peggy's best friend, who the hell are you?" She folded her arms defensively.

"*I'm* Peggy's best friend," he said, equally defensively.

They just stood and stared at each other for a moment.

"I'm Jack," he said finally.

"You're Jack... *you're* Jack?"

Jack nodded.

"Peggy didn't tell me you were so..." she began, her gaze moving down to his chest then his boxers and bare legs.

Jack's mouth crept up at the corner. "That I was so *what* exactly?" he smirked.

Lacey felt herself blush. She wasn't sure what was happening. She was not the kind of girl to blush. She was the kind of girl who slept with rock stars and made out with the quarterback because she had nothing better to do. She wasn't the kind of girl who dropped things and blushed in the presence of some boy next door type in her best friend's kitchen at four in the morning. But something was happening, and she didn't know how to stop it. She could feel the train leaving the station and it was getting too late to jump off.

"That you were here," she finished.

"I'm sure she did."

"Well, maybe I forgot," she shrugged, her arms still folded in front of her chest.

"And you're Lacey," Jack said, still staring at her.

She gave a nod.

"This is kind of... I dunno, *destined* or something, don't you think?"

Lacey laughed. Destiny, that was something that happened to other people. That was something that happened to Peggy and Sammy, not her.

"Oh, come on," he said. "I don't usually believe in that bullshit either, but this? This is kind of a big coincidence."

"If you think about it, it's not really."

"Oh yeah? How so?"

"Well, you went to LA specifically to look for me, and then you went and hung out at all the places you knew I'd be, so really, it's just surprising that no one else found me first." She gathered up her hair and pulled it over one shoulder.

"What happened to your face?" he frowned.

Lacey's hand reached up and touched the bruise, which was darkening up already. "Oh, that. I walked into a door."

"Was it *Rex*? It was Rex, wasn't it?" he asked, making fists by his sides.

"It's really nothing."

"It's not nothing though, is it?" His voice turned soft again.

Lacey shrugged. "I don't want to talk about it, especially with someone I just met."

"We didn't just meet, this is actually the third time we've met."

She gave him a look.

"Sometimes talking about things with someone you just met is better?"

She didn't respond.

"Do you still want that coffee?" he finally asked.

She nodded.

"I'll get this cleaned up and bring you a cup. How do you take it?"

"Black, two sugars."

"Same as me," he smiled. "Destiny!"

And although she was trying really hard not to, she felt the corners of her mouth move up into a real smile as she smiled back at him.

By the time Jack had finally cleaned up the kitchen and made another pot of coffee, Lacey had fallen back asleep on the couch. He covered her with a blanket and left a cup of coffee next to her in case she woke up, and then he went back to reading Peggy's fashion magazines until he had to get ready for his morning shift at the diner.

TWENTY-EIGHT

Lacey's Life Story

Jack felt like he was floating on clouds of squirty cream all through his shift at the diner the next day. Even the biggest asshole customers couldn't bring him down. When a bunch of high school juniors made fun of him for being a waste-oid, instead of getting angry at them, he just replied, "That may be, but I'm a waste-oid in love." They laughed even harder, but it didn't matter to him at all.

"I'd know that look anywhere," said Tammy. "It's a girl."

"It is a girl," said Jack, grinning at her as he handed orders over to Carlos in the kitchen.

Tammy smiled and shook her head. "You've got it bad."

"Better you than me," said Carlos, wiping his nose on his sleeve before flipping another burger. "Single life is a dream."

Jack laughed. "Oh Carlos, I love you man, but flipping burgers all day and going home to an empty house isn't my idea of a good dream."

Carlos shrugged. "It gives me my freedom, and I love my freedom."

Jack didn't think Carlos really had much freedom at all, but he was glad he thought he did.

Jack didn't want freedom though, Jack wanted Lacey. He wanted to hold her in his arms, he wanted to watch bad eighties cable with her late at night, drinking Pepsi and eating jalapeno-flavored popcorn. He wanted to marry her. He wanted her to be Lacey Forrester. Just thinking about it plastered a grin on his face that even the diner grease and orders piling up couldn't wipe off.

When Horace came in to grab a burger to go during the lunch rush, even he knew something was up. "What's up with you man?" he asked, giving Jack a weird look.

"I'm in love."

"Oh yeah? Who's the lucky girl?"

"Lacey," Jack said.

Horace laughed. "Seriously?"

"So seriously," Jack replied.

"Don't take this the wrong way, but Lacey doesn't really have a reputation for being the falling in love with type."

"What's that supposed to mean?" Jack asked, handing over a paper bag with his order and extra free fries. Jack always gave Horace extra fries.

"I don't think she's ever had a real boyfriend before, but she... well, she kind of has a reputation."

"What? Lacey? No," said Jack, trying to get the image of her and Rex out of his mind.

"She's kind of known as a runner, she just gets what she wants from guys but doesn't stick around. She's pretty for sure, but she's not really girlfriend material."

"Screw you," said Jack. "You don't know her, and who are you to talk when you've been having some kind of sordid midnight love affair with Tricia that no one is supposed to know about? Talk about not girlfriend material."

Horace looked upset. "No, you're right, I don't know Lacey that well, it's just what people say. I've been a total jerk, I'm sorry. I really hope you guys can work it out. I'm just… I'm going through my own relationship dramas. I really wish you both the best of luck."

Jack deflated. "I think I'm gonna need it."

Horace gave him a sorrowful look and patted him on the shoulder. "Thanks for the burger," he said, looking in the bag. "And thanks for the extra fries. Sorry I was a jerk."

Jack shrugged and went back to taking out orders. He kept kind of expecting Horace to be just like his dad, to act like his dad, to know who he was, to look after him and give him some words of advice. But here in 1984, Horace was just a teenage boy with the same problems he had.

He thought about Lacey's "reputation," which he guessed was only enhanced when she went off to become a groupie for the Rats. He had to admit even he had judged her at first. Hell, he'd judged Peggy enough when she'd hooked up with Big Mick. But it wasn't like Jack was totally innocent and pure himself. He'd spent almost a year hooking up with Jayne in the stockroom at the Stables. He shook it off. He didn't really care about Lacey's past, or his own. All he cared about was what kind of future they could have together.

When Jack's shift was over, Tammy gave him a ride home. His heart was thumping hard the whole way. Lacey had been all he could think about since he left for work, but now the thought of walking through the front door and seeing her there was almost too much to handle.

He had to take a few deep breaths before he put the key in the lock.

But when he walked in, it was just Peggy and Janet sitting on the couch watching *Miami Vice*. Jack's heart rate slowed again, and he slumped down between them.

"Hey," said Peggy, without even looking at him.

"Hey Jack," Janet said, her eyes also fixed to the screen. "How was work?"

"Greasy," Jack replied as he tousled his hair.

"You're not joking." Peggy made a face and moved a little further away from him. "You stink!"

"There's something about the grease that just never really ever washes off you." Jack looked at his hand and rubbed his fingers together, feeling the thin layer of grease on his skin. "I think I'll be a hundred years old and still smell a little bit like Dee's Diner."

"Do you want some food?" Janet asked. "Peggy made pasta."

"Did she really?" he asked, giving her a look.

Peggy shrugged. "You might have to pick out the hot dogs."

"You made pasta with hot dogs? That's disgusting for so many reasons. I ate at the diner thankfully."

"You don't have to," said Janet. "There's always food for you here, you know, Jack."

"Actually, I made this great grilled cheese today stuffed with macaroni cheese, jalapenos, onion rings and corn chips. I know it sounds weird, but it was so good, and Tammy was even thinking about adding it to the menu."

"Sounds cool," said Peggy, not really listening to him.

"Mmm," said Janet, her eyes not leaving the TV screen.

"Whatever, I'm gonna go take a shower and wash this meat grease off." He pulled himself back off the couch and headed upstairs.

He grabbed his towel from the back of Peggy's door and shoved the door of the bathroom open.

Lacey screamed.

Jack dropped his towel. "Oh God, I'm so sorry." He scrambled to pick it up.

Lacey was clutching her own towel to cover herself and Jack's heart started racing. He hadn't seen anything, much. But she was still wet from her shower, her long red hair dripping onto the floor, her face totally bare of make-up. She looked perfect, even more beautiful than ever.

"Jack!" she squealed.

"Sorry, sorry!" He turned around and closed the door behind him. "I'm sorry!" he yelled again back through the door.

"It's OK," she called out. "I should have locked it."

"Yeah, there is a lock on this door, you know," he said, chuckling. "It's almost as if you wanted someone to walk in on you."

Lacey made a scoffing noise and Jack heard the lock click.

"Are you going to be long?"

"No, I'm just drying off."

Jack couldn't stop thinking about her in there, *drying off*.

"Are you in a hurry to use the toilet or something?" she called through the door.

The last thing Jack wanted was for Lacey to start imagining him on the toilet. "No, I was just heading in for a shower. I smell like diner food."

"I like diner food," she said, opening the door, now dry and dressed in one of Peggy's old vintage band t-shirts and a pair of black satin sleep shorts which really didn't leave that much to the imagination, and her hair was up in a towel.

"Hi," he said.

It was stupid but all he could think about was them living together and her walking around the house like this all the time. He liked that idea a lot.

"Hey," she smiled.

She stood on her tiptoes and leaned in close, her breath on his neck. Jack felt a quiver go through him as he thought she was going in for a kiss. Without thinking, he leaned into her.

But she just sniffed him. "You smell OK to me," she said.

Jack made a weird noise that sounded like "hablergh."

Lacey squeezed past him and headed down the stairs without looking back.

Jack went into the bathroom, closed the door, locked it and then slumped down on the floor. He'd never felt so hopeless and hopeful all in one moment.

When Jack had showered, he dressed in a pair of pajama pants and a white t-shirt that he wished was tighter and showed off his body a bit more. He'd checked his appearance way too many times and then headed back down to the living room where Peggy, Janet and now Lacey were on the couch watching the opening credits of *Magnum, P.I.*

Jack sat down on the floor in front of the TV to watch it with them.

"Jack," Lacey said, and his heart lurched. "I hope you don't mind me sleeping on the couch. I know it's kind of like your bed."

Jack felt his face and ears heating up. "No, of course not. Sleeping in Peggy's room on the floor is fine," he said, not sounding that believable.

"I shouldn't be here too long. As soon as my bruises go down, I'll go home for a while. I don't like outstaying my welcome, but my mom, well, she has enough on her plate."

"Bruises? Where else are you bruised?" Jack turned around to face her, feeling a blaze of fire rise in his chest. It was bad enough she'd been hurt once, but how many bruises were there?

Lacey shook her head. "Just a couple on my arms, it's nothing."

"It's not nothing," said Janet. "It's abuse, and you really should report him."

"Report him how?" Lacey said. "I don't think it stands up in court to say you are an assaulted groupie. And it will be my word against his."

"Well, it *should* stand up," said Peggy. "That guy is a monster."

"You've been through a lot Lacey, and if you need someone to talk to, you can talk to me anytime, or we can find you someone else to talk to."

"What? Like a therapist?" asked Lacey.

"It could be useful," said Janet.

"I'm fine," said Lacey. "I made some dumb mistakes and I'm paying for them."

"Don't blame yourself," said Jack. "Rex is the one you should be blaming. He's the one I blame for this. Who does he think he is? If I ever see him, I'll give him a piece of my mind. And I'm definitely not listening to any of his music anymore."

"His music?" Lacey asked, her eyes nearly popping out of her head. "You know his music… from the future?"

Jack nodded. "He ends up pretty famous, *really* famous. He doesn't have the greatest reputation when it comes to his romantic life though. There have always been rumors that he hasn't been very nice to his wives and girlfriends, but still, everyone keeps buying his albums. You know I feel so dumb. I did it too." Jack shook his head.

"It's different when it's right in front of you, isn't it?" Janet asked.

Jack nodded.

Lacey shook her head. "That's so crazy. Is he married now? I mean, in your time?" she asked.

"I think he's on what, wife number four now?" Peggy said.

"Something like that," said Jack.

Lacey made a whooshing noise. "Wow. So, even if… he probably wouldn't have…"

"You better not go back to him," said Jack, feeling all protective. "I mean, it's your choice what you do with your life, but you can do so, so much better than that asshole."

"Better than a famous rock star?" Lacey asked.

"Yep," said Jack. "You deserve someone who's going to treat you like the goddess you are." He blushed. He didn't know he was going to say that out loud.

"Yeah," said Peggy. "And you are in no way to blame, Lace. It's not your fault he did those things to you."

"Maybe, but I let him in," said Lacey. "I opened my heart to him, and I was stupid enough to think I was different, that we had something special. And you tried to warn me, Peg, and I just ignored you. I should have listened."

Peggy shook her head. "That doesn't matter, all that matters is that you're safe now."

"And if you do want to talk, to me or anyone, you just let me know," said Janet.

"Thanks, Miss B," said Lacey. "But I think I just want to try to put it all behind me now. I'll try to get out of your hair as quick as I can."

"No rush at all, Lacey. I never really had a family, so it's kind of nice having you all around," Janet said. "I just wish we had a bit more space."

"What happened to your family?" asked Lacey.

"That's a story for another time," Janet said, patting her leg. "I think I'm going to head off to bed. You know where everything is, Lacey?"

"Yeah, thanks, Miss Bates."

"Oh, for goodness sake, Lacey, call me Janet." Janet scooped up some plates and glasses and said her goodnights.

"I might go to bed, too," said Peggy. "I kind of hate watching TV this way, like you're always missing episodes and you never really know what's going on." She waved her hand at the screen. "I can't wait until they invent streaming, but that's so far away."

"What's streaming?" asked Lacey.

"Are we allowed to talk about this?" Jack gave Peggy a look.

"It's just Lacey," Peggy shrugged. "Streaming is where you can just press a button on your TV and pretty much watch any show you want."

"What do you mean?" asked Lacey, her eyes wide. "You can watch from the start of the episode even if you're late?"

"From the start of any episode," said Jack. "Like a box set but on your TV."

"What's a box set?" asked Lacey.

Peggy and Jack started laughing and Lacey frowned.

"Sorry, Lace," said Peggy, still giggling. "A box set is like all the DVDs of all the episodes of a TV show."

"A DVD is like a VHS, but on a disk instead of a tape," Jack explained. "It's what we have before streaming."

"Sure, have your weird time travel secrets about the future," said Lacey, folding her arms.

"Oh Lacey, don't be like that," said Peggy. "They're not really secrets, just stuff you don't know about yet. And we're not even meant to tell you *any* of this."

"It's not because we have secrets," said Jack. "Me and Peggy don't have any secrets." He said the words before he realized they weren't actually strictly true. They *did* have a secret.

Peggy looked at him and blushed. She actually blushed.

Lacey, clearly sensing something was up, raised an eyebrow. "Sure."

"Well," said Peggy, breaking the silence. "Goodnight." She gave Jack a look which he couldn't quite make out. Was this a cue to follow her to bed? But how weird would that be? And what kind of message would that send to Lacey? But if he stayed here with Lacey, what kind of message would that send to Peggy?

"Goodnight, Peg," he said, after a very long pause.

"Try not to be too noisy when you come up," she said, with an edge to her voice.

And then he was alone with Lacey again. He pretended to be transfixed on the TV even though he couldn't care less about what Tom Selleck was doing.

"So," said Lacey. "How was your shower?"

Jack laughed. "Cold."

"Sorry. It's been a while since I've had a decent shower. I mean, it's not that I haven't been showering, I just…"

"It's OK, I knew what you meant," he said, even though he had no idea what she meant or how long it had really been since she'd had access to a decent shower.

Lacey reached over to near where he was sitting, grabbed her purse and pulled out a packet of cigarettes. She offered him one, but he shook his head. "Janet smokes outside," he said.

"Oh sure," Lacey said. "I wondered where all the ashtrays had gone Do you want to come sit outside?"

Jack nodded and followed her out the back door and onto the porch. It was cute out the back. Janet had one of those double chair swings looking out onto a small patch of grass and a few shrubs and cacti that were the garden.

It was a warm night, and the stars were out, lighting up the garden. They were brighter than he'd ever noticed them back in his time. He wondered if it was because of light pollution, or if Lacey just made everything brighter. They sat down on the swing, Lacey tucked one leg up under her and pushed the swing with her other leg. Jack found it hard to look away from her perfect pale leg shining in the starlight.

"I'm pretty sure you owe me your life story," he said.

Lacey ignored him and lit a cigarette. She took a drag and offered it to him.

Jack waved it away. "My grandmother is going to die from lung cancer."

Lacey gave him a look and exhaled away from him. "I'm sorry. How long has she got?"

"I'm not sure exactly, but only a couple of years I think."

"Tammy from the diner, huh?" Lacey took another drag.

"Yeah, which makes Tricia my mom."

Lacey laughed. "It's too much," she said, waving her hand at him to stop.

"It's funny, huh?"

"It's goddamn hilarious. I can't imagine Tricia being a mom, like at all, ever. And trying to imagine her as *your* mom? It's just too far out."

"Yeah, it's weird, like she knits and makes these scrap books and she always wears floral now."

"Stop," she laughed, giving him a shove and nearly sending him flying off the swing.

"She's also really good at making cookies."

"No, please," said Lacey through her laughter, her hand still resting on his bicep from when she shoved him.

"And she still does my laundry for me, and she makes me soup with these little triangles when I'm sick."

Lacey laughed into her hands. "You have to stop now, I can't take it."

"Yeah, I'm not even meant to be talking about the future, so I won't even mention what happens to my dad."

"Wait, who's your dad?"

"Hank. Horace he's called now."

"Horace?" Lacey squealed. "You are frickin' kidding me? Tricia and *Horace*?"

"I wish I was kidding. You should see those two in the future, cuddling up on the floral couch together."

"OK, you seriously have to stop now, it's giving me a headache." She rubbed her temples and got ash on her shirt in the process.

"That's weird, I thought only us time travelers got the headaches, maybe I'm telling you too much."

"It's too hard to wrap my head around. You are *Tricia's* kid. it's too far out." She shook her head. "And it definitely makes it weird that I'm hanging out with you."

"It's no different from Peggy hanging out with Sammy."

"Oh, sure, and look how all that turned out," she said, exhaling smoke out into the night sky.

Jack shrugged. "I hope they make it. They still seem really into each other they just can't seem to tell each other that."

"Hope's a nice thing, I guess."

"So..." Jack gave her a gentle nudge with his shoulder. "Life story."

"Really? You're really going to hold me to that?" She put her cigarette out in the ashtray on the table beside her.

"You don't have to tell me everything. Just the good parts."

Lacey reached for her lighter, but she didn't light another cigarette, she just held it in her hands, flipping it around, as if she needed something to do with them.

"OK," she said. "But you have to tell me yours tomorrow night, deal?"

"Deal," he said, enjoying the warmth in his heart at the knowledge that she wanted to be doing this with him again tomorrow.

"I was born in Salt Valley Hospital on the 12th of June 1966," she began.

Jack laughed. "You're so old!"

Lacey gave him a look. "I'm eighteen! You're the one that hasn't even been born yet. In fact, you're just a sperm swimming around in Horace."

"Ew!" said Jack. "And incorrect, sperm is reborn every couple of months. I guess I'm still an egg inside Tricia's ovaries though."

"Gross!" Lacey laughed and covered her eyes.

"OK, so you were born, then what?"

"My mom was an ex-beauty queen, and from the moment I came out she was living vicariously through me. She entered me in baby beauty pageants, dressed me up real pretty all the time. The woman literally wouldn't stop talking about how pretty I was, like that was all that mattered."

"Woah. Don't take this the wrong way, but you don't seem like the pageant type. I mean, I think you're beautiful, but pageants?" Jack looked away. He hadn't meant to say all that.

"You think I'm what?" she asked playfully, a smile spreading across her face.

"You heard me," he said, looking out at the stars, avoiding her gaze.

"Well, yeah you're right, I'm not the pageant type now. Although I was for a while if you can believe it. I was really into it. When I was a kid, I wanted nothing more than to win Miss USA and make mommy proud."

"What happened?"

"My dad split when I was eight, and things changed." She ran her hand through the ends of her long red locks. "I still entered pageants, I was Miss Teen Santolsa in 1981."

Jack made a whistling noise.

"But it had stopped being fun. Mom was taking it even more seriously, getting angry when I didn't do well, and she was off her face half the time while I was trying to keep my grades up, and enter all these competitions."

"I'm sorry your dad left."

"Don't be, it was one of the best things that happened. He wasn't a good man. But then came a string of pseudo-stepdads, all with just as many problems as the last one. Roger came along a few years ago though, and he's OK, but he hasn't totally got my mom all figured out and he still struggles to handle her sometimes. I've kind of been looking after my mom this whole time. She... well," Lacey shrugged. "She still likes getting high. A lot."

Jack nodded. "That sounds tough."

She nodded and lit the cigarette, taking a pause as she inhaled and exhaled smoke curls into the sky. "She married Roger a couple months ago, and I took it as my cue to get out for a while. It felt like she was relieved, even though I'd looked after her for years. As soon as she got married it was kind of like - get lost Lacey, you know?" She paused to take another drag. "I planned my trip to LA, I'd been saving my allowance for ages. Mom usually found my hiding places and took most of it over the years, but I figured I still had enough to pay for gas and find my cousin and I'd work the rest out from there."

"How did you stay in LA for so long without any money?" Jack asked.

She shrugged. "I made ends meet, I guess. I still owe a few people. Then I met Rex, well, you probably know this bit."

"Not really," he said. Jack was struggling to look away from her leg. It was so close to his and so *bare*. It was taking a lot of strength for him not to just reach out and trace his fingers along her thigh.

"I thought Rex was the most amazing guy in the world when we met. What we had was, I can't even explain it, when it was good it was the best thing I've ever had in my life. When it was bad, it was pretty bad."

"It's OK, you don't have to tell me any more," said Jack. He didn't really want to hear any of the details between her and Rex. "It was just a dumb pact we made, you don't really have to tell me."

"I thought you wanted to know."

"I do, I want to know about *you*, but I don't want to know about you and some other guy. Especially you and Rex."

"I knew they'd make it big," she said, shaking her head. "I guess I just really wanted to be a part of that in some way."

"It sounds like maybe you were." The more he thought about Rex the more he felt anger rising in his chest like some wild beast. "Next time I'm in LA I'm going to smash his face in," Jack said.

Lacey laughed. "You're very sweet."

Sweet? Jack didn't want her to think he was sweet, he

wanted her to think he was strong and confident and could defend her honor.

"I really thought I loved him," she said sadly.

"I guess sometimes it can feel like love when it isn't really."

"What about you and Peggy?" she asked, her mouth twitching ever so slightly giving her away. Was she jealous?

Jack laughed. "There is no me and Peggy."

"Oh, really? Because you could cut that tension with a knife." She made a cutting gesture with her hand.

"The truth is, I used to have a pretty huge crush on her, but things have changed a lot since then."

"Yeah? Like how?"

"Well, she was never really into me anyway, and then she met this guy called Big Mick. She probably told you about him."

"Kinda."

"Well, he was a total jerk, and then she met Sammy."

"Sammy's not a jerk."

"That's debatable."

"If you were over Peggy you wouldn't hate Sammy," Lacey said as she stubbed out her cigarette.

"I still care about her, I'm just not... in love with her."

"She cares about you a lot, too," said Lacey.

"Yeah, well, something else happened that changed how I felt about Peggy."

"Oh yeah? What's that?" she asked.

"I met you."

TWENTY-NINE

Marshmallows

Jack lay awake that night on Peggy's floor, but all he could think about was Lacey. About how her hair had shone in the starlight. About how close her leg had been to his. About how hard things had been for her growing up. All he wanted to do, was take her up in his arms and hold her and tell her everything was going to be OK now.

But then he thought about how she was born in 1966 and it gave him a headache.

Peggy was snoring gently like she usually did. It hadn't bothered him before, but for the first time ever he found it irritating. He got up and walked as quietly as he could downstairs. He didn't want to wake Lacey, but he couldn't just keep lying here, listening to Peggy's snoring and thinking about touching Lacey's leg.

When he got downstairs, he saw Lacey was still awake too. She was sitting up on the couch, the light from the tiny TV lighting up her hair like a halo. It looked like a re-run of *Highway to Heaven* and she looked like an angel.

"Hey," he murmured from the doorway.

She startled and then relaxed when she saw it was him and smiled.

"Hey," she said softly. "Sorry, was the TV too loud? Sometimes I can't sleep."

He shook his head. "No, I couldn't sleep either."

"You wanna join me?" she asked, looking up at him.

There was nothing he wanted more in the world. "Sure, I was going to make hot cocoa. Do you want some?"

"I think you officially just became my dream man," she yawned.

Jack hoped she wasn't joking.

She followed him into the kitchen, and he made quick work of finding a pan and measuring the milk into it by filling a mug twice and adding a bit.

"Why don't you just do it in the microwave?" she asked from behind him. He turned around to face her, one hand on the pan and one on the milk.

She looked so perfect in that moment. She'd put her hair up in a loose braid and soft red tendrils were coming loose near her ear, cascading gently down her neck. She looked sleepy, but her eyes were clear, and even her bruise looked like it was fading a little.

"I think it tastes better done in the pan, more authentic." Jack turned on the stove and began to heat the milk slowly, stirring it with a wooden spoon.

"I think Janet used to have some marshmallows around here somewhere." Lacey stood on her tip toes and reached up into a top cupboard. Her t-shirt rose up exposing her lower back and Jack nearly dropped the spoon into the milk.

"Knew it." She pulled down the marshmallows and opened the bag.

Jack's pulse was hammering, and he tried to focus on

stirring, but it was hard work. She was so beautiful and distracting. When the milk was hot enough, he stirred in the cocoa, poured it into the mugs and Lacey popped the marshmallows on the top.

"Mmmmmmm, this looks so good." That moaning noise she made nearly pushing Jack off the edge of, well, whatever he was on the edge of.

He opened the fridge to put the milk carton away and he could sense the heat of her body as she came up close behind him. He felt her hands on his biceps and he froze. She ran her hands down his arms then gently pressed her body into his back. He was all at once marshmallow in her hands. When she reached up on her toes and kissed him on the back of his neck, it was as if the ground was shaking beneath him. And when she gently turned him around to face her, he knew with all his being that this was it.

She was the one.

And when she leaned in and her lips found his, they didn't care that the milk was all over the floor or that their hot cocoa was going cold. Everything was right and good in his world.

Lacey didn't know what she was doing. A few days ago, she thought she was in love with Rex. But being here with Jack, talking to him like they'd known each other forever, telling him things she hadn't even told Peggy, watching him make hot cocoa, she'd never felt *this* before. No one had ever made her hot cocoa before. Boys had bought her popcorn and vodka, but she'd never watched a boy make anything for her, especially hot cocoa at two in the morning.

As she watched him carefully stir in the cocoa and pour their drinks, she felt her heart begin to crack open, finally letting in the light. It was like all the times she thought she loved someone before was just practice for this. And before she even realized what she was doing her hands were reaching out for him, and then she was turning him around and looking into his dark kind eyes and knowing everything had changed. And before she knew it, she was moving in to kiss him, and when her lips met his, it was like suddenly everything made sense. It didn't matter that the floor was covered in milk or their cocoa was cold. Everything was right and good in her world.

THIRTY

The Phone Call

Lacey woke to the sound of ringing and whispers.

"Lacey," said a soft voice.

She opened her eyes, and it took her a moment to remember where she was, to remember that she was lying on the couch in Janet's house, still wrapped in Jack's arms.

Jack.

"Phone," the voice said.

Lacey sat up, gently and slowly moving Jack's arm to get free. He was sound asleep and didn't even stir.

When her eyes had adjusted to the light, she saw it was Peggy who had been whispering her name. "Peggy?" she asked sleepily.

"Just take the call. It's five in the morning and I want to get back to sleep. You're lucky I answered it before Janet did," she said huffily.

"Oh, sorry, thanks," Lacey said. "But who's calling me here?"

Peggy just gave her a look.

Lacey made her way into the kitchen and picked up the receiver. "Hello?"

"Lacey, baby."

Rex.

"Rex?"

"Thank God I found you," he said. He sounded frantic.

"How did you find me here?"

"I called the only Fitzgerald in Santolsa, but no one answered, and then I remembered you talking about your friend who lives with your teacher and for some stupid reason I remembered her name - Miss Bates. There's only one Bates in Santolsa."

"You remembered…"

"Lacey," he said, his voice thick with emotion. It almost sounded like he'd been crying.

"Yeah?"

"Baby, I'm sorry. I'm so, so sorry. For everything I did. I need you, I miss you, I screwed up. I screwed up everything."

Lacey frowned. "Yeah, you did."

"Kyra and me, it's over, really over this time."

She was suddenly feeling so many things, but anger was the one that rushed to the surface. "Am I meant to care? All I am is some groupie, right?"

"No, no, baby, I was just saying that stuff because Kyra was listening. I had to tell you that stuff, but it's not how I really feel."

"How do you really feel?" Lacey asked, twisting the phone cord around in her fingers.

"I love you," he said.

Lacey's stomach flipped.

"I really love you. I'm sorry I couldn't say it before, I wasn't in my right mind, I was so drunk and messed up on other stuff that night, I didn't mean any of it. I'm so, so sorry babe."

251

And just like that, her life was in chaos again.

THIRTY-ONE

The Note

They had fallen asleep on the couch together, entwined in each other's arms, but when Jack woke up, she was gone.

His heart leapt up into his throat.

She was gone.

No, she couldn't be gone. His whole world had changed last night, she had changed everything. She'd made everything better, brighter and more meaningful and now, just like that, everything was in danger of going back to black and white again.

There was a note on the coffee table. Jack reached for it and felt daggers in his chest when he read it. It was a note for Peggy, saying Lacey would pay her back and thanks for everything, but there was nothing for him, not even a mention.

They had spent all night talking and kissing and laughing and reheating hot cocoa. It had been the best night of his whole entire life, and now she was gone.

Jack felt like he'd been given the most incredible gift, only to have the person who gave it to him take it back and stomp on it a few hours later. He couldn't understand it.

"Hey," said Peggy. She was standing above him, dressed for work in her Santolsa Bowl shirt and a pair of light pink jeans. She handed him a steaming cup of coffee. "I guess you saw the note."

Jack shook his head. "I, I just…"

"What happened last night?" Peggy asked, perching on the chair opposite him and taking a sip from her own coffee cup.

"We… everything, and…"

Peggy gave him a kind of pitying look.

"I thought we had something." He held the mug of coffee so tightly it burned his fingers. He didn't want it. He didn't want anything, he just wanted Lacey to come back. "Where did she go?"

"She probably went back to LA," Peggy shrugged.

"Why would she do that?" Jack asked. "After everything?"

"Rex called here."

"What? When?"

"Last night, well, early this morning."

Jack hated that his first thought was how cool it was that Rex had called here, called this house. He shook his head. No, this was a bad thing. Rex wasn't the rock star idol of his high school years, Rex was a monster.

"What did he say?" Jack demanded.

"He told her he was sorry, and he still loved her."

"And you just let her go back to him? Are you crazy?" Jack smacked his cup on the table sending coffee spraying all over the place.

"It's not like I could stop her," Peggy said.

"Yes, you could have, you could have stopped her. You could've woken me or Janet, or both of us. You saw what he did to her last time."

Peggy folded her arms. "Have you ever tried to stop

254

Lacey once her mind is made up? No, you haven't, because you don't even *know* her. You spent one night together, and you think you know everything about her? I've been her best friend for over a year and I still don't know her."

"You could have done *something*."

"I'm sorry she left, but don't take it out on me, *I'm* still here."

"Oh, that's rich, coming from you."

"What's that supposed to mean?"

"You're the one that just leaves. Maybe she got this idea from you. You left me then you left Sammy. Shit, maybe me and Sammy have more in common after all."

"Wow, I can't believe you just went there."

"Lacey's in trouble, that creep isn't good for her, and you just let her go right back into his arms!" Jack ran his hands through his hair.

"I tried, I told her not to, I told her to think about it, but she just grabbed her car keys and left. I could hardly tailgate her all the way to LA."

"Why not? I would've done it, I would've done it for her, or for you."

"Well, I guess that's it isn't it? You're just a much better person than me. Just say it, that's what you're thinking, that's what you've always been thinking."

"Right now, I just don't know what to think, all I know is that I have to go after her."

"You think you can just go to LA and find her?"

"I found her like three times already, I can find her again," he said.

"Sometimes you just have to let people make their own mistakes. We can't just keep messing with everyone here."

"Helping someone isn't messing with them," he said, getting up and grabbing his bags from the side of the couch.

"Don't you remember what happened with Sammy? I saved him, but Nick died in his place."

"You don't *know* that." Jack zipped up his bag. "Maybe you didn't save him, maybe he was never going to die anyway."

Peggy just stared at him and shook her head.

Jack gave her a look and threw his bag onto one shoulder. "You need to get over it, and I'm going after her," he said.

"And how exactly are you going to do that?"

"I'm taking your car." Jack grabbed her keys and slammed the door behind him.

Peggy followed him and started yelling at him to stop, to come back inside. She even yelled that she would call the police and report her car stolen. But soon she was getting smaller in his rear-view mirror and it wasn't that long until he was hurtling down the desert highway back towards LA.

Interlude III

"Where is Kimana?" Helena demanded. "Why have the men taken over with the horses?" Helena was furious.

She had been to see Kimana that afternoon. Frank had told her Kimana was gone and not coming back. Helena and Kimana had spent many an afternoon these last few months together in the stables. It had been the one true joy of Helena's life and now it had been taken from her.

"Gone," said Sister Maria.

"Gone *where*?" Helena asked through gritted teeth.

"It is for the best, child," said Sister Catherine.

"Child? Don't you dare to call me child," Helena said.

"We know you are no longer a child," said Maria. "And that is exactly why Kimana had to go. The way you two were together," Maria shook her head. "It was unnatural."

"Unnatural?" Helena exclaimed. "We are witches dressed as nuns and we travel through time, and you think my feelings for Kimana are unnatural?"

"Sister, it is for your own protection. You do not know what can happen when a witch shares her powers in this way. It is why we stay celibate," said Catherine.

"As far as I can tell, nothing happens but two people enjoying being alive," Helena spat. "Have either of you seen what our powers will do? No, you have not, no one has, everyone is too scared to try. Well, I am not too scared. I am not too scared to push against the old ways and change them for the better, and the way I feel for Kimana, it is more magical than any spell either of you have ever cast."

"You will understand in time," said Maria. "And one day you will thank Frank for alerting us to what was going on."

The breath went out of Helena's chest. The life felt as if it was being ripped out of her, as if her soul was being wrenched from her heart.

"Frank," she fumed. "I will kill him, I swear it."

Catherine gasped. "Helena, he only did it to protect you, to protect us. That is his job. All these men are our protectors now, and they will soon be tested for their initiation into the Order."

"When was this decided? And without my approval?" Helena demanded, slamming her hand against the table.

"The order is bigger than you, and does not need your approval," said Maria bluntly.

"And you," Helena said, pointing at Maria. "My oath to the coven may keep me tied to you, but I will never, *ever* forgive you for this." Tears began to stream down Helena's face.

"Perhaps it would do you good to take an assignment," said Maria, her voice void of emotion. "We need you to travel to the nearby towns and cities and raise some more funds for us."

"I will not," Helena said. "I will stay here, and I will find Kimana and you will not stop me from seeing her."

Catherine shook her head and placed a hand on Helena's shoulder. "Kimana is gone. Her tribe has been moved on."

"Her whole tribe?" Helena gasped.

"Yes, they have been removed," Maria said. "And it's for the best."

"Removed by who?" Helena asked.

"Removed by the men who are in charge," said Catherine, with just a hint of vinegar to her voice as she looked at Maria.

"No, no!" Helena shouted. She ran out towards the stables. She took Elliot and rode him all the way to where Kimana's tribe had been, but it was like the others had said. They were all gone.

And in her chest, she felt a pain like nothing she had ever felt before. It felt as if her whole body was being snapped in two from inside. She dropped to the ground and sobbed into the earth.

THIRTY-TWO

Death Valley

Jack's rage finally subsided around Death Valley. He was so hot he didn't have the energy to be so angry anymore. Peggy's car was a complete piece of crap with no air conditioning. He was on fire. He'd cranked the windows and been splashing his face with water from a bottle he found in the backseat, but nothing was helping. His biggest concern, however, was showing up like this - drenched in sweat, his hair all stuck to his face and stinking.

He just kept reminding himself that if she really was the girl for him, she wouldn't care about a bit of sweat. OK, a *lot* of sweat. But he had a little bit of money from his paycheck and tips at the diner. He could probably just about afford to get a cheap hotel room so he could take a shower. He was annoyed he hadn't had a chance to get home and cash in his comic books yet. If he had, he'd be able to stay anywhere in LA without worrying about it. He wondered what it would be like to have that much spare cash to play with and all the places he could take Lacey.

He wiped his brow again and blew air up into his face.

He'd definitely buy a car with air conditioning.

There was nowhere to stop for a cold drink for miles and if he got out of the car now, he would probably die. That was a sobering thought. There was a reason they called it Death Valley after all. He wondered if he should have stuck with his original plan to go straight through Las Vegas, but he was here now. He just had to hope and pray this wasn't the time that Peggy's car was going to finally give out. Why didn't she get it looked at? Jack did not like that rattling noise it was making. But he believed in destiny now, and destiny was surely going to take him straight into Lacey's arms.

Destiny had other plans, though.

When Jack finally arrived back in LA later that evening, he checked into the same motel they'd stayed at before, this time alone.

When he was clean and ready and dressed in a pair of denim cut-offs, mint green button-up shirt and his Vans, he winked at himself in the mirror, grabbed the motel key and went out looking for his destiny.

But the magic was missing. He thought it was going to be as easy as it was bumping into her the last few times, but as he stood on the corner of Hollywood Boulevard, he didn't feel much of anything at all. He sighed and started walking. Maybe if he moved, something would happen.

After a few hours of walking in the sweltering heat with no luck at all, Jack found himself back at the diner near the club. He sat down and ordered exactly what he felt like – a bowl of onion rings, a grilled cheese, side of slaw and a strawberry milkshake.

He read the local newspaper while he ate, and it struck him how it was kind of the same as looking on his phone when he thought about it. He caught up on the local gossip, got the news, got advertised to - that seemed to be one thing that never changed.

Jack was munching on an onion ring dipped in slaw when he recognized the voices.

"… I feel bad, maybe it's my fault she overdosed," one of the voices said.

"You can't blame yourself," said another voice.

"Maybe you *should* blame yourself, Crystal. You didn't have to give her so many pills," said the third voice.

"Shut up Becky, you're not helping."

"Why don't *you* shut up, Missy. You're the one who got those pills in the first place."

"And you were the one who was happy enough to take them off my hands."

Jack peered around the edge of his booth and saw them. *The Valley Girls*. He tried to hide, but it was too late.

"Well, lookie who we have here," cooed Crystal, her tone changing from worried to flirtatious.

Jack gave a noncommittal wave.

"What are you doing back in town?" asked Becky, flicking her hair.

"I came to find a friend, maybe you know her," he said.

Crystal raised an eyebrow. "Her?"

"Her name is Lacey. Long red hair, she used to go out with Rex?" Jack said.

The girls all exchanged looks.

"I'm sorry to tell you this," said Becky. "But Lacey is dead."

Jack's heart rate shot up and he shook his head. "What do you mean, *dead*?"

"She died at the club a few days ago," Missy said, with not quite the right amount of sadness to be giving that information.

"A few days ago?" Jack asked. "So, you mean, not since this morning?"

"No, she died at the last Rats gig. They are playing again tonight if you want to come," said Missy.

Jack couldn't believe what was happening. These girls were flirting with him in the same sentence they were telling him Lacey was dead.

"She can't be dead, I just saw her this morning," said Jack.

Crystal let out a breath.

"See?" Becky nudged her. "I told you she was fine. Why do you listen to all the gossip Kyra tells you, anyway?"

"Let me ask again," Jack said. "Have you seen her since about four o'clock this morning?"

The girls shook their heads.

Jack felt his heart rate go back to normal, kind of.

"Come to the club later," Crystal said as she stood up and draped a hand over his shoulder.

It was the last thing he wanted to do, be around those girls back at the club, but if Rex was playing, Lacey might be there.

Jack nodded. "Yeah sure, I'll see you there."

Jack's heart was threatening to beat right out of his chest as he stood outside in the line for the club. It was still so hot, and he was melting in his jeans and black shirt. He had wanted to look extra nice tonight and so he'd taken another shower, changed his clothes and fixed his hair. But it was all for nothing, he was so sweaty already and his hair was all flat and sticky.

But the magic was back. He had a feeling something was going to happen tonight. He knew it was going to be big. It was as if the air was magnetic, drawing her to him. He could almost feel how close she was.

When he got into the club and saw all the girls walking around in their Rats shirts talking about how amazing Rex was, his anger started to burn up in his chest again.

Rex hit Lacey. And god only knows what else he did to her before that. And what he'd done to other girls, maybe even some of the other girls here.

Jack had a beer and kept looking around for her, but she wasn't anywhere to be seen. He kept one eye on the bar and one eye on the door, but she wasn't there. Why would she be here, after what Rex had done to her? Maybe she wasn't even here at all. Maybe she'd never even come back to LA. Jack was such a hothead at times, he probably risked his life in Death Valley for nothing.

Jack had another couple of beers, and by the time Rex came on stage he was full of Dutch courage, *and* he was livid.

No. Jack didn't risk his life in Death Valley for nothing. Lacey might not be here, but there was still something he could do.

It only took three bars of Rex's singing low and seductively into the microphone while staring down at some young girl in the crowd who was very clearly underaged for Jack to lose it.

He smashed his beer bottle down on the bar and stormed up towards the stage, pushing and shoving as he went, ignoring the pushes and shoves he was getting back.

He made his way to the front of the stage and looked up at Rex. All his life he had thought this guy was a real rock star, the coolest guy ever. Jack had all his albums and now felt such a deep sense of shame at ever spending money on supporting this guy. He felt stupid. He felt like he'd been conned into some amazing image of this guy, he'd been tricked by an illusion.

But the worst thing of all was what he did to Lacey. To hurt her, and then tell her he loved her? That was unforgivable. The anger rose even higher and before he really knew what he was doing, his feet found the edge of the stage and Jack launched himself onto it.

The band just ignored him at first, and then Rex started looking at him weirdly.

"We've got a live one," Rex laughed as he gestured over to security.

A few years ago, this would have been a dream come true for Jack. Being here in this club with one of his favorite singers, being on stage, being this close to a band he had always loved. He was so close he could see the little balls of sweat forming on Rex's brow. He could smell him, and he smelled bad. Jack had taken two showers today in case he saw Lacey, and this guy smelled like he hadn't showered in a week.

For some reason that tipped him over the edge.

Jack reached out and grabbed Rex's microphone.

Rex stood back and just laughed, pushing his long dark hair behind one of his ears. Jack pulled back his arm and hit Rex square in the face, sending him crashing into the drum kit as cymbals and drums fell on top of him.

Jack put the microphone to his lips and said, "That's for Lacey, you asshole."

THIRTY-THREE

Nick

———————

Lacey got in her car and began to drive just as the sun was just beginning to become a small sliver of light on the horizon.

She drove through town and out towards the highway.

Her head was a jumbled mess. Thoughts of Rex swam through her mind. Him telling her he loved her, him hurting her, him telling her he loved her. Then there was Jack.

Jack.

It was like her mind couldn't breathe and being in the car, on the road, doing *something*, going somewhere, was the only way to find some relief from all the thoughts that constantly spun around in her head.

Lacey still found it hard to drive past where Nick had been killed. The Joshua tree he'd hit had been badly damaged and so they'd removed it, along with his car, Sammy's car. All that was there now was a small shrub and a cross that Nick's mom had put up. Lacey found it hard to really get her head around it. One minute you are a living, breathing thing, a person making choices, doing things, talking to people, going about your days. And then, just like that, you are nothing but a small shrub and a cross.

She pulled off the highway and stopped. She hit her hands on the steering wheel and tears began to stream down her face. She got out of the car and sat down next to the cross and the shrub. Her tears continued to fall until she was sobbing harder than she had in a long time. She'd cried over Rex, but losing Nick was something else. She let the tears fall until they started to slow down to just a trickle down each cheek.

"I miss you, Nick," she said. "I know I wasn't always the best friend to you, and I'm sorry. I wish I had talked to you more often, I wish I had asked you if you were OK. I wish I had known what was going on with you." She took a deep breath and wiped her face on the sleeve of her sweatshirt. "I wish I knew if it was an accident… or if you did it on purpose."

No one had even mentioned it as being a possibility, they just kept referring to it as "the accident," but Lacey knew Nick hadn't been drinking that night, and if she knew one thing, it was how good people could be at pretending things were OK when they weren't.

"In a weird way," she said, scooping her legs up to get more comfortable, "you and me, we were probably more alike than we knew…. I tried to kill myself, too," she whispered.

Lacey sat there for a long time, watching the sun rise over the Nevada mountains in the distance. She felt like Nick was right there watching the sunrise with her, she felt like he was sitting right next to her. She knew he was.

And by the time the sun was beginning to heat up the ground beneath her, ready for another unbearably hot summer's day in the desert, Lacey had made some decisions.

She got back in the car, turned it around and headed back towards Santolsa.

THIRTY-FOUR

The L.A. Times

Jack pulled up outside Janet's house late the next night. He'd planned on staying as long as it took to find Lacey, but when he called Peggy the morning after the gig to check-in and see if she'd heard anything, she had. Lacey had barely even made it out of town before turning around again. He probably would have driven right past her going the other way. So much for fate! Although, thought Jack, maybe it was fate that he was here, that he'd punched out Rex on stage and that a photographer from the LA Times had been there to catch a picture of him in full swing. Jack grinned as he thought about the moment where his fist had connected with Rex's face. He couldn't wait to give everyone a copy. And even better, the review of their gig was scathing.

As soon as Jack knew Lacey was safe at back in Santolsa, he checked out of the motel and got back in Peggy's car. He just had to make one small detour. He couldn't come all this way without seeing the ocean again. He walked up and down the boardwalk, from Santa Monica Pier to Venice Beach and back, dodging roller-skaters on the boardwalk and stopping for coffee and donuts when he got hungry.

He knew he would come back soon, but first he had to take his comics back to the present and make some real money so he could come back and live his dream life here with Lacey.

Jack walked up to the front door with the bundle of newspapers in his hand was about to knock when Peggy threw open the door. "Why are you still knocking? You live here, come in!"

He grinned as she ushered him into the living room where Janet was grading make-up tests.

"I have news!" He waved the newspapers around.

"Oh?" Janet looked up at him curiously.

He handed them each a copy of the LA times. "Page 23," he instructed.

Peggy gasped.

Janet rubbed her brow thoughtfully.

"This is you." Peggy pointed at the grainy image.

"Yeah, I know. I kind of punched Rex in the face last night, and someone got a picture of it." Jack grinned so hard it felt like his mouth was going to split open. He was so darn proud of himself. All those beatings he'd taken at high school, and how he was punching rock stars in the face. How the tables had turned.

Peggy unfolded the paper to see the whole story. "Crazy Eight attacks Rex from the Rats," she said, reading the headline. "Crazy *Eight?*" She shook her head. "Who's the Crazy Eight? I don't get it." Peggy gave him a confused look.

"Ah, about that," Jack started.

Janet gave him a look but didn't look at all surprised. She'd probably seen Eight tattoos before, she wasn't stupid.

Peggy wasn't stupid either, but it wasn't like she'd ever dated an Eight before. Jack had, and he still didn't even know she'd been an Eight.

"Is this some kind of mistake?" Peggy asked.

"I kind of joined the Eights, Peg."

"Wait, *what*?"

"Before I left. There was… an incident."

Jack told her the whole story. He told her about the onion rings and the waitress and his bike getting smashed out of shape. He told her about the beating and his time in hospital and his midnight tattoo. The only part he left out was what Big Mick had said about her.

Peggy looked thoughtful. "I wish you'd told me. We used to tell each other everything."

"I didn't want to tell you, because I didn't want to be that guy anymore."

"What guy?"

"The guy who couldn't stick up for himself, the total loser that I used to be."

"You were never a loser, Jack. You were my best friend in the world, and I don't know how I would have gotten through high school without you." She reached out and put her hand on his. "I'm so sorry you had to go through that, and that I wasn't there for you." A tear began to well in her eye.

Jack shook his head. "It's OK, Peg." He squeezed her hand.

Janet cleared her throat. "Well, I'm glad you're OK Jack. But you probably need to think about what to do next. That tattoo may offer you protection, but it could also get you in serious trouble." Janet waved the paper around.

Jack shrugged. "I kind of like being an Eight."

"But you're not *really* an Eight," said Peggy.

Janet looked concerned. "If I was you, I'd get that tattoo altered and put this whole thing behind you. I know a thing or two about the Eights, and trust me, it's not a direction you want to take unless you have no other option."

"What do *you* know about the Eights?" Peggy asked her.

"What about the Eights?" asked Lacey, appearing in a fresh pair of pajama shorts and an old grey t-shirt. Her hair was still damp from the shower. Jack's heart did a little flip and he pulled his hand away from Peggy's and grinned at her.

"Let's just say, I know enough about the Eights to know they're trouble," Janet said, taking her papers into the kitchen. Peggy followed after her, still asking to know more about the Eights.

"You're back," Lacey said, smiling at him.

"I'm back." He handed her one of the newspapers.

Lacey grabbed the paper out of his hands, her smile disappearing. "How could you...?"

Jack's face fell. "How could I? I thought you'd be happy."

"What? One black eye for another?" She handed the newspaper back to him and grabbed her purse. She pulled out a cigarette packet and a lighter and headed out the back door.

Jack threw the newspaper down and followed her out.

"Is this our first fight?" he asked, leaning up against the wall of the back porch while Lacey took a seat on the swinging chair.

"No," she said.

"It seems like it."

"It's not like we're even together. We can't be having a fight." She looked up at the sky. The moon was almost full tonight, lighting up the garden brighter than it had been the last time they had sat out here.

"It sure feels like a fight for two people who aren't together," he said softly, sitting down next to her.

"You had no right to do that." She pulled out a cigarette but didn't light it.

"*He* had no right to do that to you."

"It was my problem, and I didn't need you coming in like some zooped up knight in shining armor trying to defend my honor."

"It wasn't really like that. I went there to look for you, and when I saw the way Rex looked at this girl in the crowd... she looked young, like really young, *too* young, something in me just snapped. The idea that he could do that to someone else who loves his band, and someone who isn't as smart as you."

"Oh sure, because *I'm* so smart."

"Yeah, you are. You got into a dumb situation, but that wasn't your fault. He manipulated you. He told you that he loved you, and maybe he even really thought he did, who knows. But that's not love, what he did is not love."

"I know that now," she said, flipping the cigarette packet open and closed.

"Exactly, but there are girls out there who don't know how smart and beautiful and strong they are, and guys like Rex use that to their advantage."

"I can't believe I fell for it, him treating me like that and then telling me that he loved me."

"It's not your fault," Jack said. "But I promise you something. The next guy who tells you he loves you is going to mean it. It'll be the real deal."

She looked over at him.

"True story," he said.

"OK," she said. "Well, then, thanks I guess."

"Thanks?"

"Thanks for doing this," she said. "It was idiotic, and it could cause a lot of problems for you. Rex's bass player is an Eight, and when Eights go against Eights, it's a fight you don't want to be a part of, you're going to want to lay low."

"You know I'm not really an Eight, right? This tattoo really was a mistake."

Lacey laughed. "How did you join the Eights by mistake?"

"I got beat up," he said. He hadn't planned to tell Lacey the truth, but it just started pouring out. "And this girl I was kind of dating, she was an Eight, but I didn't know it at the time."

"You didn't see her tattoo?" asked Lacey.

"I did see her tattoo," he admitted. "But I didn't realize what it was until later. It wasn't on her arm so... *Anyway*, when I got beat up, they sneaked into my hospital room and tattooed me."

"Wow, that must've hurt."

"Yeah, kinda. No, OK, it really hurt a lot."

Lacey laughed.

"I was so angry at them for doing it, but it helped me out with some bullies."

"Bullies?" Lacey asked.

Jack nodded. "There was this group of guys that made my high school years a living hell. I thought when we all left school it would be different, but they attacked me one night, the whole group of them. Cracked some ribs."

Lacey shook her head. "Why did they do that to you?"

"Because they thought I was gay."

"They sound like a bunch of assholes."

"Totally," he said.

"Sometimes I forget that everyone is going through their own stuff," she said. "I have been pretty caught up in my own problems lately, but what you've been going through sounds just as bad. And then everything with your grandmother. I can't imagine losing my nana, she's like the only sane one in our family." Lacey studied the packet of cigarettes in her hand.

"I only just told Peggy about it tonight," he said.

"Peggy didn't know?"

"This will sound dumb, but when I came here, when I... time travelled... Sorry that just sounds so weird to say."

"It sounds weird to hear."

"Well, I still had feelings for her, and I didn't want her to think I was some loser who couldn't take care of himself."

"Is that why you hit Rex?" she asked, tossing the cigarette packet to the side.

"No, I wasn't even thinking about that, I just really hate that guy."

"I'm sorry I got angry with you, I think I get it now," she said. "I just don't need anyone fighting my battles for me, OK?"

"I wasn't trying to fight anything for you, I was trying to fight it *with* you. But you're right, I should have checked with you first. I should have called you and asked if it was OK for me to get up on stage and punch that jerk's face in."

Lacey laughed. "Maybe it wasn't the smartest thing to do, but I appreciate the gesture."

"Hey, Lacey?" Jack said, after a moment.

"Yes, Jack?"

"I need to go back and see my mom and dad. Will you still be here when I get back? I'd really love to take you...

on a date, maybe?" Jack cleared his throat. "Like, maybe we could hang out somewhere else besides this back porch and street corners."

Lacey smiled. "I'm not going anywhere, Jack. And I'd love to go on a date with you."

THIRTY-FIVE

Jack's Back

Jack stood at the back door of St. Christopher's High School and memories of the last year of school came flooding back. Peggy leaving, the bullying, the loneliness. The finals.

But so much had changed since then. *He'd* changed. He wasn't scared of teenage bullies anymore. He'd survived a beating that could have killed him, he'd survived a night being held down and tattooed by the Eights. He'd survived West Hollywood in the eighties. He'd time travelled.

He'd met the love of his life.

He unlocked the door with the key Janet had given him and let himself in. There was no summer school, no security guards. The school was deserted and it kind of gave him the creeps.

Jack walked towards the book room and felt his breathing becoming shallow. Would it even work? Would he be able to get back? Jack missed his parents. Even though they were here, it wasn't the same. His mom was so angsty here, and although they had bonded a little over their shared ancestry, she still kept him at a distance. It seemed like she kept *everyone* at a distance, including his dad. He had no idea how they got from midnight meetings at the diner to getting married and having him. They seemed so happy and in love in the present, but here in the eighties he was a total nerd and she was such a hard-ass. He'd never even seen them together for more than five minutes.

As much as Jack wanted to go home, he was also terrified he might not be able to get back here again. But Peggy had done it, she'd done it plenty of times - surely, he could do it at least once. He had to be able to get back to Lacey.

He stood in front of the door to the book room and took a deep breath. He put the key in the lock and pulled back as it shuddered. He turned the handle, walked in, locked the door behind him and closed his eyes as three flashes of blinding light lit up the room. When the flashing had stopped, he opened his eyes and took his phone out of his pocket. He turned it on and saw that he had a signal. He was back.

He stepped out of the book room to find Summer School very much in session. It was between classes and students were hanging around lockers and looking sorry for themselves that they had to be there when everyone else was out enjoying the summer. No one paid any attention to him at all as he strolled down the hallway. They were all just thinking he was another one of them. Jack was feeling very much like he was *not* just another one of them.

His phone started buzzing in his pocket. He sighed. At first he thought it would be horrible giving up his phone and the Internet, but after the first few days he hadn't missed it at all, and he hadn't realized just how much he'd been OK with not having it until he suddenly had it again. The buzzing in his pocket was like a rope around his neck, demanding his attention be pulled away from whatever he was doing, making him feel like he had to read and respond to everything immediately. He missed the old way of doing things - a note scrawled on paper and left somewhere prominent so it would be read by the person it was for whenever they happened to see it.

His thoughts went to Lacey's note after she'd left that morning and how worried he'd been about her. Maybe he was wrong. Maybe all this buzzing was worth it if it meant you could easily contact the people you loved and know that they were safe.

He finally succumbed and pulled his phone out of his pocket. A bunch of texts from Jayne had come through saying she was worried about him, where was he? Was he ever coming back? And one asking him to come see her at the bar as soon as he could. It sounded desperate. He wasn't sure if he should be worried about her or just ignore it.

Weirdly, there wasn't one single message or missed call from his mom or dad, just one from Uncle Jack, who he hadn't even seen since he was a little kid, telling him not to do anything stupid. Jack brushed it off. Uncle Jack had always been a bit of a weirdo. He came over for dinner sometimes, but always when Jack was out, and he never stayed long. Uncle Jack had probably sent the text to the wrong person.

He messaged Jayne to say he'd been out of town with bad service and asked her if everything was OK, and then he called his mom to come pick him up.

When Jack slid into the passenger seat of his mom's SUV, he was all ready with a reason for being at school, a story about getting off the bus early to pick up a transcript from school.

But his mom didn't ask for a story, she just gave him a big warm hug over the front seats and a kiss on the cheek.

"Mom?" Jack asked, looking over at her as she put the car into drive and drove out the front gates of the school.

"Yes, darling?"

Jack's head started spinning. He had too many thoughts, too many emotions. He was looking at his mom, at *Tricia* thirty-three years in the future. It was too much, and he started to cry.

"It's OK, sweat pea," she said, reaching over to pat his leg. "We know everything."

THIRTY-SIX

Uncle Jack

The next morning, Jack awoke to a loud knock on the front door, followed by his parents' attempts to speak in hushed voices, and one voice that was not so hushed.

Tux, who had been curled up next to Jack all night, gave a soft meow at being woken up.

"Where is he?" the loud voice asked. The voice sounded familiar and took Jack a second to place it.

Uncle Jack.

"I need to see that kid, *now*," Uncle Jack was saying.

"He needs his rest," said his mom. "Let him come down when he's ready."

"Give the kid a break," said his dad. "This whole time traveling thing has been hard enough on him already without *you* showing up like this."

That got his attention. Jack jumped out of bed. Still dressed in his PJ pants and grey tee, his hair sticking up all over the place, he ran downstairs.

"Jack," said his mom, trying to stop him from running straight into the lounge room where he could hear Uncle Jack and his dad talking, arguing even. He pushed past her and two seconds later found himself face to face with Uncle Jack.

It had been a long time since he'd been in the same room as Uncle Jack. Now he realized why Uncle Jack had only ever stopped by when Jack was out.

Jack's jaw dropped, and he felt like he was going to faint.

"Jack," said his dad, putting a hand on Jack's shoulder.

Jack brushed him off. "Uncle Jack," said Jack.

"Jack," said Uncle Jack.

They both nervously ran their fingers through their hair at the same time.

His dad coughed.

His mum made a squawking noise.

"I know it's weird," said Uncle Jack finally.

Jack blinked. *Weird?* He was standing face to face with his future self, this was far beyond weird. Definitely the weirdest thing ever to happen to him, and he was a *time traveler*.

Uncle Jack looked tired, unhappy, unhealthy, *old*. Frankly, Jack thought his future self looked like shit. Jack had overheard his parents talking about Uncle Jack's drinking problem and on and off again attempts at rehab, but Jack didn't expect his future self to look quite so... *broken*.

Jack didn't know exactly what was going to come out of his mouth, but he opened his mouth to speak anyway. Something usually came out when he did that, but instead of something witty or clever the only thing that came out was a torrent of vomit.

His mom handed him a tissue, and he blew his nose.

"Oh, sweet pea," said his mom. "Go clean yourself up."

"I'm not what you expected," Uncle Jack said, once Jack had stopped vomiting, taken a shower and they were all sitting down in the floral arm chairs his mom had picked out years earlier.

His mom handed him a cup of coffee. The smell turned Jack's stomach, but he took a small sip anyway.

"Not exactly," said Jack.

"You're so young and naïve," said Uncle Jack.

Jack scoffed. "And you're so old and crinkly."

"Jack!" said his mom. "Your Uncle Jack has been through a lot in life."

"He's not my Uncle," Jack scowled.

"Well, we weren't sure what else to call him," his dad said. "We can't call you both Jack."

"Call him, old man that ruins my future life," said Jack. Whatever choices this version of him had made clearly sucked, and he was in no way going to make them again.

Uncle Jack laughed. "Oh, I remember being you," he said. "You were such a dick at times."

Jack's mouth dropped open. "*I* was a dick? Look at you." He waved a hand up and down. "From here it looks like *you're* the one messing up *my* future."

"Your attitude right now leads to everything you see here." Uncle Jack gestured at himself.

"Whatever, old man," said Jack.

Jack's mom and dad looked at each other.

"Maybe this was a bad idea," said his mom, wringing her hands.

"What else could we have done?" asked his dad. "It's happening now, anyway."

"We weren't going to let this happen though, were we, Hank?" She looked at Jack. "We had talked about this years ago and we all decided that you and Uncle Jack spending time together was not a good idea. When you turned six, we stopped it."

"And that obviously worked," said Uncle Jack, leaning back on the couch.

"It worked for a while," said his dad.

"No, it's good," said Jack. "I'm glad I've seen this version of myself, so I can make sure I don't end up like that."

"I don't need this." Uncle Jack stood up and brushed himself off like so much dirt was on him from being in their house.

"Jack," said his dad, and they both looked at him. "*Uncle* Jack," he clarified.

"What's the point?" Uncle Jack said. "He's made up his mind. We can't change fate, we can't do anything to stop him."

"Stop him what?" asked Jack.

"He can still change things," said his mom. "He can make things better for himself."

"He's not going to change things, he's right on track to screw it all up, just like I did. I've already had this conversation once and I didn't listen to *my* Uncle Jack, why do we think it will ever be any different? Nothing will ever change, and we will be caught in this vicious loop for eternity."

"What are you talking about?" Jack's head began to throb.

"This," said Uncle Jack. "This conversation. When you're old, you'll come here to try to talk some sense into your younger self, and he still won't listen. You'll think you can get him to change some of his stupid choices in life, but he won't. And *he'll* end up right here, where I'm standing right now."

Jack's head felt like it was going to explode.

"When I was you," Uncle Jack continued, "I didn't listen either. I thought I was king shit. I thought I would rule this world. I thought I could cheat time. I thought I had it all figured out. And in the end, I lost the only thing I ever cared about." His lip began to tremble, but he quickly began speaking again to hide it. "But I've said this all before, damnit, I'm just saying exactly what I said to myself all those years ago and nothing is changing." Uncle Jack ran his hands down his face.

"Do something different," yelled his mom. "Make it different," she said grabbing onto his dad.

His dad just shook his head. "I don't know how…"

"Let's talk, Jack, just the two of us," Uncle Jack said. "My Uncle Jack didn't do this, but maybe we should try."

Jack looked up at him. "Talk about what?"

"It's about Lacey," Uncle Jack said running his hands through his hair. "It's always been about Lacey."

Jack's heart skipped a beat. "What about Lacey?"

And something moved across Uncle Jack's face which looked like deep thirty-three-year-old regret and Jack thought maybe he should listen after all.

Sliding into the front seat of his future self's black Mercedes, Jack had a lot of feelings and a lot of questions. Like, how the hell did he ever make the decision to buy a Mercedes when his dream car was a '68 cabana blue Cadillac convertible? And why was there an empty vodka bottle rolling around by Jack's feet? He picked it up and gave Uncle Jack a look.

"I don't drink and drive," Uncle Jack said. "Never."

Jack raised an eyebrow. "Sure."

"Sometimes I park and drink, down by the beach, and then sleep in my car until I'm sober enough to drive home." Uncle Jack put the car in drive and checked his mirrors before turning back onto the street.

"Wow," said Jack. "That could be the most pathetic thing I've ever heard."

Uncle Jack ignored him. "I know there's a lot you want to ask me, and trust me, there's a lot I want to tell you, but I'm in desperate need of caffeine and no offense to Mom, but I didn't want to stick around there."

The way he said *Mom* as if he was talking about his own mom was too weird, and it also pissed him off. Who was he to talk like that about his mom? "Why not?" Jack asked.

"You'll understand one day."

"Try me today."

Uncle Jack blew a breath out of his teeth as he indicated left. "It brings back too many memories."

"What's wrong with memories?"

"To me, going back to that house is like you going back to St. Christopher's High School. It's weird, awkward. Like, you left already, you got away from all this, and now you have to come back. It makes you think about the person you used to be when you were there. The time travel element just makes it even harder."

"Sure," said Jack as he turned on the radio. It was tuned to an eighties station and their song was playing. Jack felt a smile creep over his face as he thought about the first time he heard it.

"And I'm gonna keep on lovin' you, 'cause it's the only thing I want to do..."

Uncle Jack smashed his hand at the controls. "Turn that off," he said angrily.

"Woah dude, what's your problem?"

"My problem? My problem is that I screwed up the one good thing in my life and I don't want you to make the same mistakes."

———

The last place Jack wanted to be was at Dee's, but here he was, sitting in a booth, his future self sitting across the sticky table staring at him.

"Jack!" The waitress said, as if she was addressing a long-lost cousin.

Jack looked up to see the middle-aged woman with frizzy hair beaming down at his future self. *Amy.* The same waitress who'd tried to help the night of the "incident."

"Amy, oh, sure. I forgot you worked here." Uncle Jack ran his hand through his hair and looked away from her.

"It's so good to see you," she said. "It's been, well gosh," she threw her hands in the air. "It's been years."

"I don't get to Santolsa much these days," he said shortly.

"Well, it's good to see you back, and this is, oh I remember, how are you doing?" Amy gave Jack a motherly look.

"My nephew," said Uncle Jack.

Jack ran his hand through his hair. "Hey, yeah, I'm fine, thanks."

Amy's eyes grew wide. "You look just like… you could be…"

"Same gene pool," Uncle Jack said.

Amy shook her head. "It's incredible, you look just like Jack did when he was younger. We never properly met that night, I'm Amy," she finished.

"I'm Jack."

Amy's face went all screwed up.

"Named after me," said Uncle Jack. "Poor kid."

Amy laughed awkwardly. "What can I get you fellas to eat?"

"Pancakes," they both said at the same time. "And coffee," they both said again.

Jack looked at Uncle Jack and Uncle Jack shrugged at him.

"Sure thing," said Amy, giving them another strange look as she filled their cups and then left them to it.

"I hate this coffee," said Uncle Jack. "I don't know why I always order it."

"Me neither," said Jack, taking a sip and making a face before adding in a few sugars.

"So, do you have any questions?"

Jack looked up at him. "You think I'm going to have breakfast with my future self and not have any questions?"

"Well, do you?"

Jack shrugged.

"Don't do that," said Uncle Jack. "Just ask."

"OK." Jack put his coffee cup down, clanging it on the saucer. "What the hell happened to you?"

Uncle Jack nearly spat out his coffee. "Don't you like what you see?"

"No, not really. I thought we were going to have an awesome life. The car is OK, but it's not a Cadillac and you look like... bad."

"I've made a lot of money." Uncle Jack said, trying to smile. "I made too much money, and I had no one to share it with so I spent a lot of it on... well, things you shouldn't even be thinking about at your age."

"How did you make it all?" Jack asked.

"I sold those comics."

"You got all that money from a couple of comics?"

"No, that was just the start."

"It was such a good idea, what went wrong?" Jack asked.

Uncle Jack stared at him intensely. "Did you ever play a computer game and use the cheats?"

Jack shrugged. "Sure, sometimes."

"Is it as fun as playing without the cheats?"

"Maybe, for a while."

"Exactly," Uncle Jack said. "Winning when you use the cheat codes doesn't feel nearly as good."

"What's this got to do with anything?"

"I used the cheats."

"OK, so is this like some kind of warning not to use the cheats?" Jack made air quotes around the word *cheats*.

"Exactly."

"But if I don't use the cheats how will I win?"

"Maybe you won't, but if you do use the cheats, you lose before you even start playing the game."

"That's deep," said Jack sarcastically as Amy came over with their pancakes.

"I don't want you to use the cheats, I want you to play fair and win, win the only thing that's important."

Jack took a bite of his pancakes and chewed.

"Do you get what I'm saying to you?" Uncle Jack asked.

Jack felt frustration rise in his chest and put his fork down. "What's the point of all of this?"

"Maybe we can change it," said Uncle Jack.

"Oh sure, here we go again, it's like you forgot everything that happened with Peggy and Sammy last year. She agonized over this for months, she still is."

"I think there's another way," said Uncle Jack.

Jack took another bite.

"Timelines," said Uncle Jack.

"Oh, here we go," said Jack between chews.

Uncle Jack ignored him. "I don't think it's exactly about *changing* things, I think it's about skipping into a new timeline. I think that's the way to change it. Technically, you won't change things for *me*. I'll continue to exist as I am, but you can create a new timeline that takes *you* on a different path."

"Timelines?" asked Jack. "Sounds kind of far-fetched."

"You're a time traveler and you're having breakfast with your future self and you think that's far-fetched?"

Jack thought maybe he had a point. "OK, so how does someone change a timeline?"

"You just have to make different choices."

"This is exactly what Peggy was trying to do last year," Jack said, his frustration growing. "Make different choices, blah blah blah, just tell me *how*."

"I think what happened with Nick may have created a change in timelines. I think there were two potential lines – one where Sammy died, and one where Nick died. I like to think there is another timeline that exists right now, where Nick is still alive."

Jack raised his eyebrows.

"Every choice creates a new timeline, a new reality that exists somewhere."

"OK, so if that's true, how do I stop becoming you, and create a new timeline for myself?"

"Don't leave Santolsa," Uncle Jack said.

"No can do, you know I hate it here," Jack said matter-of-factly.

"Don't sell the comic books."

"I already put them on eBay," he said. Not totally true, he'd uploaded everything he just hadn't made them live yet. But nothing was going to stop him going back to 1984 with some cash in his pocket.

"Going to LA, it's not what you think it's going to be. Not without her," said Uncle Jack.

"As soon as I get out of here, I'm never coming back, and I'm going to take Lacey with me."

"I know you have big dreams and you don't want to give them up. You don't want to stay in Santolsa right now, and I get it. You're an eighteen-year-old kid, you don't want to stay in some backwater Hicksville town like this one." A family walked by their table and gave him a disapproving look. "But if you do want to leave, you're gonna have to use hard work to get out."

"Hard work? What, like working here forever?" Jack looked around at the diner. That was just so not his dream.

"No, not forever, just until you have enough money behind you."

"It would take me like two years of working here and saving every penny to have enough money to get myself set up in LA."

"So? Two years hanging out in Santolsa with Lacey and Peggy and your folks wouldn't be the worst thing in the world, would it?"

Jack shrugged. "Feels like it."

"Look." Uncle Jack slid his empty plate off to the side and leaned forward. "This is important. I screwed up. I screwed up big time. I thought having money and success and status was a way to make it all go away. I thought I'd never get bullied again if I had it all, but I also lost the love of my life, and talking to you is the only way I know to make things right."

"Have you ever just tried calling her?" Jack asked.

"Yes, I have, smartass. Lacey's with someone else now. She's married to some guy in Connecticut. No kids. I looked her up on social media. She's miserable too, I know she is, but she won't talk to me. When I tried to message her, she blocked me."

"How do you know she's miserable?" asked Jack.

"Maybe we should just leave her alone? Maybe she's happy?"

"I could see it in her eyes in her profile picture. She never got the life she wanted either, and I think I'm partly to blame for that."

"OK, so what if I do change it but it changes this timeline?" Jack asked. "What if you stop existing? Won't this version of you disappear from existence?"

Uncle Jack shrugged. "Honestly, that's a chance I'm willing to take."

Jack ran his hand through his hair. "This is just…"

"Look kid, I don't know what will happen. I don't know if I'll exist or not, but I feel like *this* is the wrong timeline. It's not like you're going to change things, it's like you'll be putting them *right*. I can't explain it, but it's like I messed up. I messed up the timelines, or I chose a bad one. Don't think of it as changing anything, we're putting it *right*. You and Lacey, it's meant to be."

"The one true pairing…" Jack mused.

Uncle Jack's phone started ringing. "I need to get this, but I just wanted to tell you one last thing."

"What's that?" Jack folded his arms.

"You can do a lot with the cheat codes. You can get rich and have all the stuff you think you've ever wanted. But money won't help you make friends or even like yourself. And you can't win at love using the cheats."

Jack rolled his eyes. "What a cliché."

"And, the most important thing - stay the hell away from Crystal." Uncle Jack stood up, brushed down his suit pants and threw fifty bucks onto the table before answering the call and walking out.

———

Later that night as Jack was putting the comics live on eBay, he thought about what his future self had told him. He thought it was crazy that having money meant that he'd lose Lacey. If anything, surely it would bring them closer together. They could both move out to LA and get a place together. They wouldn't have to work, so they could spend their days doing whatever they wanted. It could be an absolute dream life for them both.

Jack knew he wasn't going to lose Lacey. She was it for him, he knew it, and if he used the cheats, he'd have money behind him, and it would help them both make their dreams come true. He couldn't understand what could be wrong with that. And he really didn't understand what Crystal had to do with anything. He would happily stay away from those crazy Valley girls.

The comics had only been up for a few minutes when bids started coming through, and by the time Jack went to bed they had already reached nine thousand dollars.

Interlude IV

So far, the men had been through two initiations. The first had been simple. Sister Maria had given them the job of standing guard at the portal. They weren't to know what they were protecting. They had just been told that one of them must sit outside the door at all times and not let anyone in the room. If they didn't ask what it was they were protecting, and if they stayed guard for three days and didn't once try to open the door to see what was in the room, they would pass the test. What they didn't know, was that the nuns were also taking turns watching *them*. However, they had all passed. They asked no questions and didn't open the door.

The second initiation was to spend three days traveling into the nearest town to get supplies. They had been given money and horses and trusted to return with the horses, supplies and proof of amounts spent. It was a trying few days for the nuns. They had put protection spells around their money and their horses, but they knew that a man with a strong intention to steal could be just as powerful as any magic. But the men had returned with the horses and the supplies and they had even found some good prices, meaning there was even money left over.

The next initiation would involve the three women traveling ahead in time three years. If the men were still working hard, looking after the vegetables, the horses, and the abbey they would be fully initiated into the order and given leadership of all those who would come after them. Their descendants were expected to follow in their footsteps. They were not to tell their wives, but when their children turned sixteen, they were to automatically become members of the Order of the Eight, and take on the responsibilities of those before them.

"Why can't Helena just go forward on her own?" asked Catherine. "Her magic is strong enough and it would save us all from the headaches."

Catherine had been suffering crippling headaches whenever they travelled through time. Maria also got them, although she managed her pain better. Helena never seemed to even flinch when the portal opened and sent them plummeting through time and space.

"Yes, let me go on my own. I *want* to be on my own." Helena was still grieving the loss of Kimana and was holding so much anger inside of her towards Sister Maria. Many times, she had thought of leaving them, but no matter how angry she was, she was still connected to the coven in a way she couldn't explain. Maria was horrible, but she was still the closest thing to a mother Helena had ever had.

"That would not do," said Maria. "If Helena were to go and leave us two here, of course the men would continue their work. We must see what happens if we leave them to their own devices. One day we will be gone, and we must be sure that this portal will always be protected."

"And what happens if they don't protect it?" asked

Catherine. "What if we travel forward to find that they have left, or the abbey has been taken over? Or burnt to the ground? Or…"

"Catherine," said Helena. "You are not remembering the power of time magic." She rolled her eyes.

Catherine looked confused.

"If we go forward and the men are gone, and the abbey is in strife, then we come back to this moment in time and we don't let that happen."

"We could," said Maria. "But meddling with time magic in that way is dangerous. It would be better for us to just fix any problems with the abbey and the portal in the time we are in."

"Why?" asked Helena. "We have this power, why shouldn't we use it?"

"This power is a gift," said Maria. "We were given it because we needed help from God. When need turns to want God responds differently."

"God sometimes does give us what we want," said Helena.

"Sometimes we are given what we want, and then it causes problems for us," said Catherine. "We wanted to come and join the witches of Salem. We wanted to learn from them, to become more powerful from their knowledge. It wasn't a need, it was a want. We were powerful enough already. And look what happened."

"All happens as it is meant to," said Maria. "If we had not followed our desires to visit Salem we would not be here now."

"No," said Helena. "We'd be back in Europe, in a civilized country, with civilized weather!"

"That's enough now Helena," said Maria. "It's time to let the men know we will be going on our travels."

They told the men that they would be traveling on a

spiritual pilgrimage for three years, that they would be leaving them in charge, and would trust to find all was well on their return. The men were free to eat from the garden and to stay in the abbey, and they had left some money for supplies. They would be given enough to cover their basic needs, no more. The men had to be willing to protect the abbey without promise of reward, the only reward would be the reward it gifted their soul.

In the dead of night, the three nuns crept down to the time portal. Sister Maria unlocked the door, and they stepped into the room. Three flashes like lightning later, and they walked back out. It was three years later, and all seemed well with the abbey, so they simply went back up to their quarters and went to bed.

In the morning the men were surprised to find them back. John at once began to make his special pancakes for them. He looked a little older and all the work he'd been doing in the garden had made him much more muscular than he'd been before.

"Is all well?" asked Catherine over breakfast.

"Yes," Frank replied. He looked older too, some grey hairs were even starting to show around his temples. "We have been working hard and I think you will be impressed with what we've done in the garden. We have also been working on building a fence and gate to keep you safe."

Sister Maria nodded. "I am impressed, you have done well."

That night the men were initiated into the Order of the Eight.

THIRTY-SEVEN

Karate Kid

Jack returned to 1984 a few days later with twenty thousand dollars in his pocket. He hadn't expected the comics to go for so much, and with inflation he expected it was worth a lot more here. Jack was thrilled. It was the first time in his life he'd had money. He couldn't wait to take Lacey out somewhere nice or to buy Peggy a dinner of Chinese food. He owed her enough of them.

He was anxious about carrying that much cash around, but he figured he could get a bank account set up soon. He'd called in a favor with Jayne and the Eights and got fake birth certificates made for himself and one for Peggy. Jack had to hand it to the Eights, they didn't ask too many questions and didn't even raise an eyebrow when Jack asked it show that they were both born in 1966.

Arriving back in 1984, Jack felt a huge wave of relief. He didn't have to worry about Uncle Jack or his parents freaking out and he didn't have to think about Jayne's barrage of annoyed/annoying text messages. There was a freedom he felt in 1984 that he didn't feel in his present. Everything here felt slower and less frantic. The only thing he really missed was decent veggie burgers and late-night talks with his dad.

Jack took a seat at the counter in Janet's kitchen. Peggy was cooking pasta again and Janet was looking through piles of magazines for a student essay she'd misplaced.

"So, I met my future self back in the present," he said, reaching over for an apple and taking a bite.

Peggy and Janet both stared at him in weird frozen facial expressions. Peggy's was like, "I can't understand what you are saying right now," and Janet's was like, "I knew something like this would happen, but not exactly like this."

"Uh, so yeah, that happened."

"What do you mean?" asked Peggy, finally breaking out of her freeze.

"I mean, that me and my future self went out for pancakes," he said. "At Dee's," he added like that was the important part of this information.

"How did that happen?" Janet asked.

"Uncle Jack."

Peggy gasped. "Crazy Uncle Jack is… *you*?"

Jack nodded.

"What was he like?" asked Janet, leaning in like she was getting the local gossip off her girlfriends.

"A total ass, honestly," Jack said. "He has no friends, no wife or even any romantic life at all. He drinks vodka in his car, and he looks like total shit quite frankly."

"Woah," said Peggy. "So that's how you're going to end up?"

"No!" said Jack. "No way in hell."

"But if you've seen it," said Peggy. "If you've seen yourself like that…"

"He was talking about timelines, saying I could create a

new timeline where I could make different choices and not end up like that."

Janet nodded. "That makes sense, I guess. We could well be changing timelines all the time."

Peggy looked confused.

"What did he say to you?" Janet asked. "He wanted you to change something, what was it?"

Jack shrugged. He didn't want to tell them about the money. He certainly wasn't going to tell them about Uncle Jack's warnings about using the cheats. He knew they'd both just agree with him.

"He said he lost Lacey over some dumb decisions he made, so I need to not make them."

"What decisions?" asked Peggy.

"Are you putting hotdogs in that again?" Jack made a face at the macaroni dish she was preparing.

Peggy made a face back. "No, I'm making it plain, for your information."

"It's good with jalapenos, and it sounds weird, but put in a dash of maple syrup at the end."

Peggy raised an eyebrow. "Look at you, Mr. Flavors."

Jack shrugged. "I've kind of always had a thing about flavors, I think being at the diner and getting to make my own meals there has really opened up my culinary creativity. Did you know they are thinking about letting me make a veggie burger?"

"Does anyone in the eighties even eat veggie burgers?" asked Peggy. "It's all pretty meat and grease here and free-range organic isn't exactly a thing yet."

"I dunno," said Jack. "Maybe you're right, maybe it won't take off, maybe it's stupid."

"It's not stupid, it sounds really creative. I'd eat it," Janet said.

301

"Do you want some of this?" Peggy waved a creamy spoon at him.

"Nah, I'll get something at the diner. It's my last shift tonight."

"Your last shift? Why? What happened?" asked Peggy, putting down the spoon and staring at him.

"I thought you were enjoying hanging out with your grandmother?" asked Janet.

Jack shrugged. "I came into a bit of money and so I won't need the job anymore."

"How exactly did you come into some money Jack?" Janet glared at him.

"A long-lost uncle left it to me," Jack said, one corner of his mouth moving involuntarily.

"Yeah, right," said Peggy. "You are the worst liar ever. You always do that thing with your mouth when you're lying."

Jack sighed.

"How did you really get it?" Peggy asked.

"Fine, I sold some comics."

"No good can come from this." Janet folded her arms.

"Except for the good that is spilling out of my wallet right now," said Jack grinning

"Don't forget you're playing with *magic*, Jack. If you use it for your own personal gain it could come back to bite you," Janet warned.

"Maybe it's my destiny for time magic to bite my butt," Jack shrugged.

Janet shook her head at him. "I guess we all have to make our own mistakes."

Peggy went back to stirring the macaroni.

"Do you want to come bowling tonight, Peggy?" Janet asked.

Peggy shook her head. "I'm going out with Sammy tonight. We're going to the movies in Salt Valley."

"Ooooh," said Jack childishly. "Is it a date?"

Peggy blushed. "Shut up, Jack."

"How are things going with you two?" Janet asked.

"Good… I think."

"What movie are you seeing?" asked Jack.

"*Karate Kid,*" said Peggy.

Jack's mouth dropped open. "I want to see *Karate Kid*!"

"You've seen it," Peggy said.

"But not when it's just been released," he gushed. "Not when it's on at the *movies*!"

"Find your own date to go with," Peggy said. "It would be way too weird if you came with us."

Jack rushed over to the phone and flipped open the telephone index. "Where's Lacey's number in here?"

"Under Fitzgerald," said Janet.

"If you really loved her, you'd know her phone number by heart," Peggy teased, waggling the wooden spoon at him.

"Oh yeah? Do you know Sammy's?" Jack said.

"She knew Sammy's by heart before she'd even dialed it," teased Janet.

"Embarrassing but true. It's like a thing girls do here, they memorize boys' phone numbers. I don't know why. I guess it's like an eighties version of stalking your crush on social media," Peggy snorted.

Jack felt nervous. Now that he thought about it, he'd never actually called a girl before. Since he'd been living here in the eighties, he'd only called the diner, and he'd called Peggy a couple of times at the Bowl, but that wasn't the same as calling a girl he had feelings for. His fingers shook as he flipped through the pages to find her number.

And he felt a sick feeling inside as he picked up the receiver and dialed.

When it started ringing, he felt so sick he almost hung up, and just as he was about to, a voice answered.

"Fitzgerald residence," it said.

"Hi, uh, can I talk to Lacey?"

"Yeah, who's this?"

"It's Jack," he said.

"Jack!" the voice said brightly. "It's Lacey!"

Jack didn't know what to say, was he meant to just ask her to the movie? Or was he supposed to do small talk? He had no idea what he was doing.

"Did you call for something?" she asked.

"Yeah, I was wondering what you're doing tonight."

"Oh," she said before pausing.

"I guess that means you're busy?"

"No, well, kinda. Why, what's on?"

"I wanted to ask... if you wanted to double date with Sammy and Peggy and go see *Karate Kid* in Salt Valley?"

"I'd love to," she said. "I just need to check if it's OK with my mom. She's had a tough day."

"OK sure, I need to call work anyway and let them know I won't be in for my shift."

"You're ditching work to take me on a date?" Lacey asked. "Isn't that kind of uncool to let them down? We can just go another time."

Jack didn't want to go another time. He wanted to go on a date to see *Karate Kid* with Lacey *tonight*. "Nah," Jack said. "Tammy will be cool."

But when he called Dee's, Tammy was less than cool. She told him she was disappointed in him, and he had to admit it did feel kind of uncool. When he told her that actually, it wasn't just tonight, it was all the rest of his shifts too she totally flipped. Jack didn't like the heaviness in his stomach making him feel so bad. After all, she didn't have a lot of time left and they'd kind of become friends. But right now, all he could think about was Lacey. He finally had money, for the first time in his life, and he wanted to enjoy it. He wanted to buy Lacey her movie ticket and the biggest popcorn she wanted. Maybe even some nachos.

Jack got in the passenger seat of Peggy's bug, and they drove to pick up Sammy first and then to Lacey's. Jack got out of the car and walked up to her front door. Her house looked fancy. Not huge, but bigger than his house back home. It wasn't like the mess of homely pot plants Janet had at her place. It was one of those houses that was very white and had matching curtains and vases full of flowers in the windows.

Jack knocked on the door, his heart racing. He couldn't wait to see her.

When she opened the door, Jack nearly fell backwards. She looked amazing. She was dressed in skin-tight blue jeans, red heels and a slinky white tank top with skinny straps and she was wearing red lipstick. He could barely catch his breath.

"Hey, Jack," she said, looking him up and down and giving him a dazzling smile.

He was dressed in jeans, Vans and a Hawaiian shirt. He looked like a fool next to her. What did she even see in him?

"You look... *incredible*," he managed.

She slapped his arm flirtatiously and then linked her arm in his. "Thanks, Jack." He loved how she always said his name. It made him feel all full and fuzzy, and her arm in his was nearly driving him over the edge. She smelled amazing, like freesias and vanilla. He led her over to the car, opening the back door for her before going around the other side and sliding in next to her.

Sammy and Peggy were mid-way through a conversation about the latest gossip at the Bowl. Jack wasn't interested in what Hayley-Rae did or didn't do with an old pair of shoes and a popcorn machine, he just couldn't take his eyes away from Lacey. It had been less than two weeks since he first saw her on that street kicking the trash can. A lot can change in two weeks, he thought.

Jack gently reached his hand out and brushed his little finger against hers. She looked up and their eyes locked. Jack felt a rush of heat move through his entire body as she smiled at him and took his hand.

And she didn't let go of his hand all night. They held hands walking to the movie theatre. She held his hand while he paid for everyone's tickets and ordered snacks for them all. She held his hand all through the movie, and in the final fight scene she squished up so close to him he thought he might burst. They held hands as they walked along the street to get ice-cream after the movie. They held hands under the table while they ate their banana splits with hot caramel sauce and peanuts. Jack struggled to eat with his spoon left-handed, but he wasn't going to let her hand go for anything.

The whole night had passed in a blur and Jack had almost forgotten many times that Sammy and Peggy were even there. It was like they were in their own little bubble of love. Nothing else existed but Lacey, Mr. Miyagi and banana splits.

When they drove up to Lacey's house, Jack jumped out and rushed around to her door to open it, and then walked her to her front door.

"Well," she said, fidgeting with her hair.

"Well," he said, leaning up against the door frame.

"I had fun tonight," she said. "And I hope you don't get in too much trouble at work."

Jack laughed. "I'm not even going back. So, I won't get in any trouble."

"What? Where are you going?" She looked worried. "Are you going back to the future again?"

Jack let out a gentle laugh but shook his head. "What I really want, is to get set up in LA."

"LA?"

Jack nodded. "It's always kind of been my dream."

"Even now?" She looked up at him through her thick lashes.

"Even now what?"

"Even now that we…"

"There's a *we*?" he grinned, leaning in closer towards her.

Lacey squished up her nose. "We just spent like four hours holding hands. I don't know about you, but I've never done that with anyone before."

"Me neither."

"So, doesn't that mean something?"

"It means *everything*." He leaned in even closer.

"It sounds like you are about to disappear," she said, taking a step back.

Jack reached for her hands and slowly brought them up to his lips.

"I will never disappear," he said into her hands before kissing them.

"But you're not going to stay in Santolsa?"

"What I really want, is for you to come with me."

"Come with you?"

"Yeah, to LA."

"I've done LA, I'm done *with* LA." Lacey pulled her hands back.

"It would be different with me."

"I know it would, but…"

"I have a bit of money now. I can set us up, get us a place. I can get more money too, if we run out."

Lacey shook her head. "Jack, I don't want your money."

A vision of Uncle Jack with all his money danced through Jack's mind. He pushed it out.

"You can have me *and* have money too." He smiled smugly.

Lacey gave him a look. "I really like you," she said. "I mean, I *really* like you, but this is all so new to me. I can't just run off to LA with you. I'm still working through everything that happened there last time, and my mom seems like she's on the verge of spiraling again, and…"

Jack put a finger to her lips. "It's OK, I'm here, I won't go without you, OK?" he said.

"Would you wait for me?"

"For forever," Jack said. And he held her face in his hands and kissed her goodnight.

THIRTY-EIGHT

Help Wanted

As much as he tried to pretend he didn't, Jack did feel very uncool for just leaving Tammy in the lurch the night before, and so the next afternoon he grabbed his skateboard and headed out to the diner to see her and apologize.

As he skated down the suburban streets, the desert heat making his shirt stick to his back, he could not stop thinking about Lacey's fingers entwined in his. The way her red nail polish made her skin look so milky and perfect, the way he felt inside - all warm and tingly and safe and excited when he looked down and saw their hands interlaced like that. Then there was the way she squeezed his hand in the fight scenes and buried her head into his shoulder when Daniel Larusso got his ass kicked. The way she looked at him nervously as he walked her to the porch, the way her lips tasted like cherries, and how when he got home later he realized he still had some of her cherry lip gloss in the corner of his mouth, and when he licked it, it brought back everything.

He also couldn't stop thinking about the conversation

they'd had about LA. Jack was torn. He didn't want to stay here in Santolsa, but he didn't want to leave Lacey either.

And then there was Uncle Jack and all his weird warnings and desperation. Jack had no intention of ending up anything like that version of himself, but it was kind of terrifying to see himself like that. Rich, but alone and sad. And he couldn't get the vision of Uncle Jack parking the car at the beach and downing a bottle of vodka out of his head.

Jack shook it off as he turned down the main street of Santolsa. He would make better choices. He would do good things with his money. He'd set himself up and then eventually work out what he wanted to do for work. He'd have a career and do something meaningful, not just move around stocks and shares and watch his money grow.

Jack flipped his skateboard into his hand and pushed open the door to the diner.

"Hey," he said as he gave a little wave to Tammy, who was behind the counter slicing pie.

"Well, look what the cat dragged in," she said, putting a hand on her hip and eying Jack up and down.

Jack shrugged.

Tammy shrugged right back at him.

"I'm sorry about last night," he said.

"Sorry doesn't get the dishes cleared and the burgers out." She put a coffee cup down on the bar, filled it with coffee and nudged it in his direction.

Jack sat down at the counter.

Tammy coughed a couple of times and Jack's face fell. He'd been so caught up with his double date with Lacey he'd almost forgotten why he'd stayed at this job in the first place.

"Are you OK?" Jack asked.

She waved her hand. "Fine, I'm fine," she said. "I'd be finer if I didn't have to work twenty hours in a row."

"Wait, you worked my shift as well?"

Tammy nodded. "Help is hard to find in this town."

"Ah, Jeez," Jack said, jumping up and heading into the back room to grab an apron. "Go home, Tammy."

"Are you kiddin' me? You ditch us all night and then turn up here and send me home like some kind of good Samaritan?"

"I'm just trying to do the right thing, most of the time," Jack said. "Sometimes I screw it up. I'm sorry. Go home. I've got the shift covered today."

"What about graveyard tonight?" she asked.

Jack thought about it. "I'll do that, too."

"I could do it," said Horace from his booth in the back.

"Oh, hey, Horace," said Jack.

"You?" Tammy looked over at him. "Who are you?"

"That's Horace," said Jack.

Horace got up, paperback in hand and walked over to them and shrugged. "I'm Horace."

"Don't you have classes or something?" Jack asked him.

He shook his head. "Salt Valley Community College is pretty low on the course content. I'll be fine if I can just work part-time hours, and I could use the money."

"Done," said Tammy. "But I'll need another part-time employee too." She glared at Jack. "And you're responsible for finding me one."

Jack nodded.

Tammy untied her apron and threw it over the counter. "I'm going home. Jack you can get Horace to fill in the employment forms and show him the ropes."

Jack nodded again.

During the dinner rush Jack was trying to keep everything moving, but it was hard. Horace was an OK server, but he was slower than Jack was, and he didn't know where anything went. Jack was trying to get his own tables out and half of Horace's, as well as put everything back where it went. When he saw Horace taking forever at one table of girls, Jack felt the fire of frustration light inside of him. But he couldn't get annoyed with his *dad*. He couldn't tell him to pull his weight, could he? Jack walked over and grabbed some plates from the girls' table. It was passive aggressive, but it worked.

"Sorry, Jack, I just got stuck talking."

"No problem, H, but it's super busy and I'm already serving half your tables." Jack tried to sound chill but wasn't sure it came out that way.

"Sure, sure," said Horace as he started awkwardly piling up some plates.

"Let me do this. Can you get coffee to table three?"

Horace nodded and disappeared while Jack stacked plates and glasses on top.

"You guys seem really busy," said one of the girls. She had frizzy hair and glasses, but her smile was huge, and she seemed genuinely worried about them.

"Yeah, we are kind of short-staffed right now." Jack wiped the sweat off his forehead.

"Really?" the girl asked. "Because I've been looking for some part-time work."

"When can you start?" Jack asked.

"Uh, tomorrow, I guess?" she said.

"Great, come in tomorrow at eight, and ask for Tammy. Tell her Jack sent you."

"Sure," she said. "You're Jack?"

Jack nodded.

"I'm Amy." She smiled that bright smile back at him.

And Jack felt his head start pounding again.

———

"So, what's the story with you and Tricia?" Jack asked later that night when the dinner rush was over. He was teaching Horace how to make a pot of coffee and to make sure there was always one pot being made and one pot full at all times.

Horace shrugged.

"Are you and Tricia, like, together?" Jack asked

"Why are you asking about Tricia?" Horace asked without giving an answer. "Are you into her or something?"

A laugh exploded from Jack's mouth. "Oh, hell no. I mean, no offense, I'm sure she's great but she's... not my type."

Horace seemed to accept that answer as he opened a giant tin of coffee.

"Maybe I can help you out. I'm pretty good with women." Jack cringed as soon as he said it. It couldn't be further from the truth.

It was quiet in the diner, just one table finishing their meals and an older couple eating pie and drinking coffee.

Jack poured two cups of coffee, one for each of them and then leaned back on the counter and folded his arms. "Spill."

"I don't know," said Horace, running his hand through the back of his hair. "I guess we kind of have a thing." A light blush spread on his cheeks.

"What kind of thing?" He wanted to know about how his parents met and got together, but at the same time, he also didn't need any details about it.

"It's pretty casual." Horace picked up his coffee and took a sip. "I don't think she wants anything more right now. I really like her, she's such an incredible girl, but I think all she wants me for is sex."

Jack nearly spit out his coffee.

"And don't get me wrong, the sex is unreal, the best I've ever had, and I've been with a few girls…"

"OK," Jack waved his hand between them. "I don't need details, dude." Jack felt physically sick. He wouldn't in a million years think of his dad, *or* Horace as someone who was having that much sex. Jack shook his head. "So, you want a relationship, and you think she just wants… something physical?"

"Well, yeah. I mean, I'm not going to say no to the physical, but I'm really starting to have some deep feelings for her."

"You could tell her." Jack took a sip of his own coffee.

"Have you met Tricia? I don't think she's really a relationship kind of girl."

"I think she probably is, under all that eyeliner."

Horace sighed. "Maybe."

"She wouldn't be having a thing with you if she didn't like you at least a bit. I mean, look at you."

"What about me?" asked Horace, his eyes wide beneath his thick aviators.

"Well, you read Westerns, for a start."

"So do you."

"This isn't about me." Jack threw a cloth at him. "And you kind of dress like a dork."

"What? No, I don't." Horace looked down at his brown flared trousers.

"And those glasses," said Jack. "Don't take this the wrong way, but you're basically a middle-aged man."

Horace threw the cloth back at him and it landed on Jack's head.

"I'm just kidding. Kind of." Jack removed the cloth and gave it a sniff before replacing it with a fresh one. "But seriously, why would she be with you if she just wanted a casual thing? Wouldn't she be with one of those guys who runs with gangs and rides a motorcycle or something if that was all she was looking for?"

Horace shrugged. "Yeah, I don't even know why she's with me at all."

"You can't help who you fall in love with," Jack shrugged. "And trust me, she's into you, so just tell her."

THIRTY-NINE

Making Plans

Jack and Lacey were in the midst of a whirlwind romance.

Now that Jack wasn't working, he could spend all his free time with her. And because she wasn't working or going to college and still trying to figure out what she wanted to do, they had a lot of time together.

They were spending just as much time at the diner as Jack had when he worked there, but now he was there as a customer, and he could order endless food and drinks for him and Lacey, and sometimes for Peggy and Sammy and Tricia, too. They also spent a lot of time at the Bowl and even though he didn't need it, he still liked it when Peggy hooked them up with a free lane for the afternoon. It was one of their favorite dates, just hanging out at the bowling alley, throwing balls and eating as many fries as they could handle.

At first it had been kind of fun and exciting trying to find places they could be alone. But Lacey's house was pretty much a no-go zone, and every time Peggy walked in on them kissing on the couch at Janet's it was Awkward City - population three.

And Jack was getting tired of sleeping on the couch. He had money, he wanted to use it. He wanted a real bed to sleep in, but he couldn't bring himself to get a place in Santolsa. That felt way too much like putting down roots here, like settling.

"Hey," he said, late one afternoon as they'd been 5% watching reruns of *Starsky and Hutch* and 95% kissing and cuddling on the couch. "I've been thinking." He held her hand, twisting his fingers into hers. God, it felt good.

"What's up?" She smiled up at him.

"Come to LA with me."

"What?" She sat up, her hair all messy on one side where she'd been lying on it.

"Let's just do it. Things with your mom seem to have chilled out a bit and I have enough money to last for ages."

Lacey made a face. "You know how I feel about that."

Jack sat up too. "I know you don't think using time travel for financial gain is ethical or whatever, but it's not like it's hurting anyone. In fact, it's really just helping us. It means we can go to LA and live life the way we really want to."

"Money isn't everything, Jack."

"I thought that too, when I didn't have any."

She gave him a look.

"Sorry, I didn't mean…"

She shook her head. "It's OK, maybe you're right. I've been thinking maybe I should do something. I can't just let Roger keep paying me an allowance. It's starting to feel kind of gross. It's like he's paying me so I'm on call for my mom. So he doesn't have to handle it if she goes down into one of her spirals."

"But she's doing OK, right?"

Lacey shrugged. "I mean, for right now, she's better."

"But, she has Roger now, too?"

"In theory."

"So, come with me." Jack reached out for her hand again.

She took his hand in hers and stroked the top of his thumb. "I want to be with you more than anything," she said. "But does it have to be LA? And right now?"

"I would wait for forever for you, Lacey Fitzgerald, but I'd rather not have to."

"I don't know, Jack…"

"Well, I know for both of us. I'm ready. I'm ready to start my life. I'm ready to start my life with you by my side."

Lacey smiled, and when she smiled, it was like the whole world came alive.

"How about this," Jack suggested. "We go for a couple of weeks, and if it sucks or you feel like you need to, we can just come back? No pressure to stay, at all. But if we do want to stay, we can talk about that too. It could be like a trial run. How about we just plan three weeks and if we want to stay, we can do?"

Lacey sighed. "If I say yes, will you make me a grilled cheese?"

"Yes," he grinned. "I will make you the best grilled cheese you've ever had in your life, and I'll keep making grilled cheese for you for as long as these hands are able."

She nuzzled into his chest. "That sounds kind of nice."

"Just think about it, Lace. You and me in a cute little motel room, walking distance to Santa Monica beach. No more West Hollywood junkie dens, just sun and sand and you and me…"

Lacey smiled. "How can I resist you and your crazy dreams?"

And two weeks later they were in Lacey's red Chevette,

driving back down to LA, and this time it felt like they were both going in the right direction.

FORTY

The Motel on the Beach

When Jack and Lacey arrived at their motel on the beach, which was actually called The Motel on the Beach, it was everything Jack had hoped it would be. Even though it was just a block from the beach, it had its own pool surrounded by palm trees, sunshine and sun loungers. Their room was cozy, the wood paneling and tropical prints on the wall giving it a kind of Tiki vibe, and there was a mini fridge to keep their sodas, beers and chocolate bars cool. And best of all, their room had a view right out to the beach.

Lacey put her bag down on the wicker chair next to the bed, which had a giant shell shaped headboard. She stared at the 1970s style fuzzy chenille bedspread. She took a deep breath and looked around the room.

"Is everything OK?" Jack asked, walking towards her and putting his arms around her waist.

"Yeah, I just, I just realized this is the first time we've been properly alone, like *ever*."

"Oh," said Jack, his eyes growing wide as he realized the same thing.

Lacey looked up at him and bit her lip nervously.

"We don't have to… do anything," Jack said, giving her a kiss on her forehead.

He was a little surprised she was so weirded out. She had been a groupie for his ex-favorite band, and he was sure that meant she was not inexperienced when it came to being alone with boys in hotel rooms. He hated himself for thinking that. He was no saint either. But he hardly expected her to be nervous about being here with *him*.

"Are you…? Have you…?" he began, without even really knowing what he was trying to ask.

Lacey shook her head. "I mean, I have, *obviously*. But just not like this, not with someone like you."

"Like me how?" Jack took his hands off her waist and gestured for them to sit down on the bed.

"I…" she started, taking a seat next to him.

"It's OK, you can tell me." Jack reached out for her hand. He gently pushed his fingers between hers and felt a flutter in his stomach when she pushed her fingers back into his.

"I've only ever been with Rex like that." Her eyes flickered around the room, at anything but him.

"Really?" Jack asked, a bit too surprised.

"Does that surprise you?" Her perfect auburn eyebrows drew together. "I guess you thought someone like me has been doing it all over town?"

"No, I… well, you… no." Jack shook his head.

"And there was another time too, but that wasn't my choice." She looked down at their hands.

"Oh," said Jack. "I'm so sorry, I didn't know…"

Lacey shrugged. "I'm OK, now. It happens to lots of girls."

"It shouldn't." Jack felt anger rising inside him. The idea of someone doing that to Lacey, to *anyone*. He took a deep breath. "I'm so sorry, Lace," he said again, not really knowing what else to say.

Lacey nodded. "Not many people know, I just, I wanted you to know, in case anything weird happened. Sometimes, I remember."

Jack looked up at the ceiling trying not to ask more. He wanted to know who'd done it so he could hurt them. Bad. He wanted to call the Eights on whoever it was. But he also didn't want to know any more, and he definitely didn't want her to have to talk about it if she didn't want to.

"I shouldn't have told you," she whispered. "I'm damaged goods." A tear rolled down her perfect face.

Jack put his arms around her, and they fell back onto the bed, silent tears falling from her eyes onto Jack's shoulder.

"You are so perfect and so amazing, and you are not damaged at all." He gently wrapped a strand of her red hair around his finger.

"I'm just a broken person," she said, crying into his shoulder. "You can't put me together again."

"I'm not here to put you together, I'm here to remind you that you're already whole."

She wiped her eyes on his shirt.

"And," he began, "I love you just the way you are." He gave her a gentle kiss on the top of her head.

"You... you love me?" she asked, looking up at him.

He nodded. "I told you some guy would tell you that, and he'd really mean it. But I think I forgot to mention how incredibly good looking he would be."

Lacey laughed through her tears.

"Everyone has stuff they are dealing with and healing from. I've still got a rib that will never heal straight, do you think I'm damaged goods?"

"No," scoffed Lacey. "I would never think that."

"That right there. That's how I feel about you and everything you've been through."

She pushed herself up, so her face was next to his and kissed him on the nose. "Thank you."

"I'm so sorry that happened to you. I'm so sorry for everything that's happened to you. But I'm glad you told me. I don't want us to have any secrets." He kissed her nose back.

"OK, no secrets."

"And Lacey," he said. "We can do or not do whatever you want. I didn't bring you here for that."

"Why did you bring me here?"

"Because living in LA has been my dream for so long, and I couldn't imagine being here without my dream woman."

Lacey giggled and threw a pillow at him.

"Hey, I nearly forgot." Jack jumped up off the bed and grabbed his bag. He rummaged through it and brought out a box wrapped in bright blue paper with a gold bow.

"It's not my birthday." Lacey gave him a confused look.

"Yeah, I know. This is just a gift for no reason."

"A no reason gift?" Lacey looked at him like he was crazy. "You know, I've kind of gotten used to the idea that you have a bit of money, but I really don't want you to be spending it all on stupid gifts for me…"

He put a finger to her lips and grinned at her. "How about this is an early birthday present? I won't get you anything on your birthday."

Lacey made a face. "I guess I could be OK with that."

"Good, now open it," he said, handing it to her.

"What is it?"

"Open it and see." He was still grinning. "I really hope you like it. If you don't, we can take it back, it's no problem."

Lacey untied the gold ribbon and ran her fingers over it. "This ribbon is really nice," she said as she pulled back her hair and tied a bow in it with the ribbon.

Jack rolled his eyes playfully. "Well, I'm glad you like the ribbon. Come on, open it!"

When she peeled back the layers of paper she gasped. "A Polaroid camera," she whispered, turning around the box in her hands.

"I thought it would be fun to take photos of our trip, or for you to take photos of whatever you want, really."

"This is…" she said, opening up the box.

"In my time we have cameras on our phones and take pictures of anything we want all the time, and it kind of spoils the moment, you know? Someone always has photos of everything, and it's kind of stupid, but I thought this was cool."

"This is the coolest." She beamed up at him.

"Really? You like it?"

"I love it!" she exclaimed. "Now how do I load this film?"

"I think maybe it goes in here." Jack flipped open the bit at the bottom and slotted in the film pack.

Lacey gave Jack another big grin as he handed it back to her, and before he could do anything, she had snapped a picture of him. The photo came out, and she frowned. "Where is it?"

"I think it takes a minute."

They both stared at the blank photo for a few moments until Jack's face began to appear, and Lacey squealed again.

"That's not half bad," Jack said, looking at his photo. In some ways it was like looking at a stranger. There he was, dressed in his eighties shirt, his hair a mess from driving all day, the motel room in the background. But the thing that surprised him the most was the look on his face. He looked *happy*.

Lacey clapped her hands together. "This is the best thing ever. Thank you so much, Jack."

"You are so welcome, I'm glad you love it."

"I do, I really do." She gave him a kiss on the cheek and then started kissing his face all over.

"You know what I want to do more than anything?"

She shook her head.

"Go for a walk on the beach, get some takeout, watch a bad movie and just fall asleep together in an actual bed."

"Sounds perfect. Oh, and Jack?" she asked.

"Yeah, babe?"

"I love you, too."

FORTY-ONE

Girl's Night

"So, I guess Lacey and Jack are in love or whatever," said Peggy, putting the phone receiver back on the hook and swinging herself onto a barstool at the kitchen counter.

Janet was busying herself with frozen spring rolls, pizza and mini quiches. They had a girl's night planned with junk food and *Grease* I and II on VHS ready to go. It had been a while since Peggy and Janet had hung out like this, and she was really looking forward to it.

"Lacey said they are having the time of their lives," Peggy sighed.

Janet put two wine glasses down in between them. "That's a good thing though, right? I mean, you want your friends to be happy, don't you?"

Peggy shrugged. "Yeah, I guess."

Janet gave her a knowing look. She filled a wineglass with 7UP and pushed it towards Peggy and filled the other with Mellow Yellow for herself and took a sip. "It sounds to me like you have a case of the jealousies."

Peggy scoffed. "What? No, I don't."

"Are you sure you don't have some feelings for Jack?"

"Of course not," Peggy blurted, trying not to think of the kiss they had still never talked about. The big fat make-out session that was the elephant in the room. Not that it was a make-out session. It was just a kiss. Just his lips, on her lips, and yes, she had kissed him back, and yes it had been nice. She threw her hands over her face. "No, I don't, I don't have feelings for him. I thought I did, I don't know, I was confused, stuff happened, but I don't want Jack like that. I just don't want him to be with Lacey."

"Are you sure? It's OK to have feelings you know, even if you never act on them."

"What do you mean?"

"Well, it's OK to be deeply in love with Sammy and still have some feelings for Jack. It doesn't make you a horrible person, and it certainly doesn't mean you need to ever act on those feelings."

Peggy felt the heat rising to her face.

"Or act on them again, if you have."

"I don't know what my feelings for him are," Peggy said. "I like Jack, I like him a lot, and we have so much history, and he is kind of cute."

"OK, and what are your feelings for Sammy?" Janet prodded, while she moved around some things in the oven.

"Sammy?" Peggy took a deep breath. "I don't even have words for how I feel about him. I love him."

"You can love Sammy and still think Jack's kind of cute."

"I really think Sammy is it for me," Peggy said. "But I still don't like hearing about my two best friends getting it on," she pouted.

"Why don't you see if you can get some time off from the Bowl before the summer is over, and go join them in LA for a few days? Take Sammy with you. Maybe it'll be good for you all to spend some time together."

"That would be so weird. Sitting around while my two best friends in the world are hooking up?" She sighed. "It's like I'm all alone in the world again." She put her arms on the counter and flopped her head into them.

"But you're not alone," said Janet, getting out the plates. "You have me, and things with Sammy are moving forward, aren't they?"

"Kinda." She swirled her 7UP. "It still feels like we're a million miles away from getting back to where we were."

"These things take time."

"It's just hard seeing them both so happy together. I know it sounds mean, but they are so annoying, like they don't stop talking about each other."

"Are you forgetting what it was like when you and Sammy first started dating? You were terrible."

Peggy laughed. "No, I wasn't!"

"You were utterly unbearable."

"How so?"

"You floated around this house like you were on clouds, and whenever I asked you to do something you said, 'yes Janet, whatever you say Janet' and then you'd forget two seconds later. But the worst part was that you took twice as long in the bathroom."

Peggy giggled. "I did not."

"One time you were in there for two hours before Sammy picked you up."

"It's all this eighties hair and make-up, it takes so long!"

"It was nice," Janet said as she started piling up the plates. "It's been a long time since I felt that excitement of first love." Janet's green eyes glazed over.

"Isn't it like that with Ray?" Peggy asked, sliding off the stool and taking her plate.

Janet grabbed her plate, and they moved into the living room, making themselves comfortable in front of the TV.

"It's nice with Ray, but it's different."

"Nice? Just Nice? Not incredible, wonderful, amazing?" Peggy took a bite of her pizza.

Janet looked thoughtful. "It feels very comforting."

"Oh jeez, don't let Ray hear you say that."

"In a very nice way," Janet added.

"Did you ever have someone like Sammy? Like someone who made you feel the way I feel about him?"

Janet nodded. She put her plate on her lap and picked up her wineglass. "I did."

Peggy waited for her to say more.

"And it was incredible, wonderful, amazing," Janet added.

"What happened?"

"Dale, he… he died." Janet looked down into her plate.

Peggy gasped. "Oh Janet, I'm so sorry." Peggy remembered Mrs. Willis' story about her husband dying that day in class when they had been looking through the year-books. It made Peggy so sad to think Janet would have to go through this again. Yes, she still had getting married to whoever Mr. Willis was to look forward to, but then she would only end up losing him, too.

"It was a long time ago. Many years ago, now."

Peggy shook her head. "All that time when I thought we'd lost Sammy, I had no idea that you'd lost someone."

"It was Vietnam. We lost a lot of young men there. I was distraught, but I wasn't the only one. We were all losing our lovers, brothers, fathers."

Peggy felt a tear fall down her cheek, but Janet just took a bite of a spring roll.

"What was his name?" Peggy asked.

"Dale," said Janet. "Dale Williams. He was gorgeous."

"What did he look like?"

"I have a photo, do you want to see?" Janet asked, her eyes sparkling.

"Of course!"

Janet disappeared upstairs and returned with a small wooden box. She opened it up and handed Peggy an old weathered photo of a young African American man in a US Army uniform. He *was* gorgeous. He was beaming, as if he was so excited about the future ahead of him.

"He's a real hottie, Janet," said Peggy, handing the photo back.

Janet smiled wistfully at it. "He certainly was. We couldn't keep our hands off each other. And at that time, it still turned a lot of heads to see a white girl and a black boy together. Even here in 1984 there are people who have a problem with it."

"Even in my time," said Peggy, shaking her head.

"It gets better though, so much better than what we went through." Janet put the picture back in the box and put it down beside her before returning to her spring roll.

"You still think about him," Peggy said.

Janet nodded. "Every day. And I dream about him all the time."

"How did he…?" Peggy asked.

Janet shrugged. "I think that's the worst part. I don't even know what happened to him. He was missing in action."

Peggy felt the weight of what that meant. "I'm so sorry, Janet." Peggy reached out and touched Janet's hand.

Janet put her other hand on top of Peggy's and nodded. "Thank you, Peggy, now let's watch the movies."

And she got up and pressed play on the VCR.

FORTY-TWO

Road Trip Again

A week later and Sammy found himself driving into the early morning sunrise on the highway out towards LA. Peggy was sitting in the front passenger seat of his car again. Only this time it was different. There was no annoying Jack sitting in the backseat amping up the volume on the awkwardness between him and Peggy. But there was a different kind of awkwardness going on in the back seat this time. When Peggy suggested they go to LA to visit Lacey and Jack, Sammy had mixed feelings. He really wanted things to work out with Peggy, but he wasn't ready to be alone with her for a whole week, so he invited Horace along. He didn't know Horace all that well, they had never really been close friends in high school, but since school finished, they found themselves hanging out in some of the same places. A few drinks together at the Fire Station, and they realized just how much they had in common. They both loved Santolsa, cars and books. And they were both in "complicated" relationships.

Peggy had probably felt the same way, because she'd invited Tricia along, too. So, there they all were, the four of them, sitting in awkward silence at the start of what was going to be a very long road trip.

"Nice hair," said Sammy, giving Horace a look from the rear-view mirror.

"And did you get contacts?" Peggy asked, turning around in her seat.

Horace nodded. "Yeah, and thanks." He ran his hand over his new buzz cut.

Tricia was sitting next to him in silence.

"And nice dress." Sammy raised an eyebrow at Tricia in the mirror.

"Shut up, jerk," said Tricia, who was dressed in a black and red floral sun dress.

Horace let out a short laugh.

"I've never seen you in a dress before," said Peggy.

"It's hot, OK? Jeez." Tricia folded her arms and turned to look out the window at the desert whizzing by.

"Maybe we need some music, Peg," suggested Sammy, trying to hide a smile. He loved that Horace and Tricia were falling for each other. Even though they seemed like a bizarre couple from the outside, they were very alike, really. They both had big hearts and guarded exteriors.

Peggy grabbed an 8-track tape and slipped it into the player on the dash and Bruce Springsteen began to sing about being born in the USA.

"You got the new Springsteen?" Horace asked. "Can I see the box?"

"Yeah, just came out last week," Sammy said. "I love this track."

Peggy started singing along to the chorus and the second time Sammy joined in, and on the third time Horace was singing with them, too.

A few more 8-tracks, snack stops and way too many games of twenty questions later, the mood in the car had shifted. Tricia had never been to the ocean before and Horace had only been once when he was a kid, so as soon as they could see the water out on the horizon, they were both acting like excited little kids in the backseat.

"Oh, my god," said Tricia. "It's so *blue*, I didn't know it would be so blue."

"What color did you think it was going to be?" asked Sammy.

"Shut up, Ruthven," she said, slapping his shoulder.

"It looks incredible, I can't wait to put my feet in the water," said Horace.

———

Sammy returned from the reception desk of the Motel on the Beach with two room keys and raised his eyebrow at Peggy. Her stomach did a cartwheel, and she wondered if she'd ever get used to his smoldering looks.

"Do you want to go girls' rooms and boys' rooms or...?" he said, swinging around the keys.

Not girls and boys, not girls and boys, thought Peggy.

"Don't be stupid," said Tricia. "We're all adults here." She snatched one of the keys out of his hand and gave Horace a look to follow her.

Sammy looked down at the key. "Room seventeen." He threw her duffel bag over his shoulder and picked up his own bag with his other hand.

"Seventeen," Peggy repeated. She picked up her cosmetics case and followed him up the stairs to the room, her stomach flip flopping around a little more with each step closer to *their* room.

Sammy unlocked the door and pushed it open. He walked in and threw their bags onto the double bed.

One bed.

No Jack.

Just them.

Her pulse quickened, and she excused herself to go to the bathroom. The bathroom was small, but clean and the dark green tiles made her feel protected and safe somehow. She looked at herself in the mirror. Her hair was flat, and mascara had melted down underneath her eyes. She wiped it away and splashed some water onto her face. She took a few deep breaths. She didn't even know what she was worried about. They'd never had sex before, and hardly anything had happened between them for months. It wasn't like they would jump from practically nothing to... *that*, would they?

She was nervous as heck, and also kind of excited. What if she was going to have sex with Sammy Ruthven on this trip? What if *this* was going to be the night?

Her heart was fluttering like crazy and she could hardly catch a breath.

"Everything OK in there?" he called.

She didn't want him to think she was sitting on the toilet for that long, so she quickly fluffed up her hair with her hands and went back out into the room.

Sammy was lying on the bed with his shoes kicked off. He was looking at a local map.

He looked perfect. His hair messed up from the heat, his white t-shirt crinkled from the trip. She wanted to just jump on top of him right here and now.

"Helloooo Jell-O?" called a voice from outside the door.

Peggy ran to the door and swung it open. "Lacey!" she exclaimed, and they threw their arms around each other.

Lacey looked good. She'd gotten a bit of color from the sun and some new freckles. She was dressed in a short white dress with black boots and she was positively glowing.

"LA looks good on you," said Peggy.

"Shame I can't say the same thing about you. You two look terrible." Lacey pushed her way into the room and flopped down on the bed next to Sammy.

"We've been driving all day," said Sammy as he reached over to hug her.

"You two get in the shower and get ready to go out!" Lacey instructed.

Peggy couldn't stop the visual of her and Sammy in the shower together from forming in her mind.

"Me and Jack are taking you to our favorite bar in Venice Beach tonight. You're gonna love it."

Something twisted in Peggy's chest. The way Lacey said, "me and Jack," Peggy didn't like it. *Peggy* used to say, "me and Jack." For *years* she said that, and now after just a few weeks it was Lacey who got to say that. It didn't seem fair somehow.

Peggy tried to look happy. "Sounds great," she said. She grabbed her cosmetics case and rushed into the bathroom again before she said something stupid or gave away her true feelings.

And what would Sammy think if he knew she was so cut up about it? Would he understand it had nothing to do with him? That it was really just about her not wanting Jack to be with someone else, not because she had feelings for him? She felt horrible even thinking it. If anyone deserved to be happy it was Lacey, *and* Jack. Why couldn't she just be happy for them? She berated herself about it as she showered and tried to let the feelings go. She tried to remember she was here with Sammy. Finally, the two of them had some time together, some time to really talk and get closer again. She tried to remember there was a time when being alone in a motel room with Sammy Ruthven was all she would have ever wanted, and now here they were.

"I'm happy for them, I'm happy for them," she repeated as she washed her hair.

And by the time she had dried herself she almost felt like she was.

She looked around for her clothes and swore under her breath. Why was she always doing this? She wrapped the towel around her so she was covering up as much of her body as she could, but she was still revealing way more than she would like to. She opened the door and peeked out. Her bag was on the bed, on the far side of Sammy, who was still lying there, but now reading a dogeared copy of *The Grapes of Wrath*.

He looked up and smirked. "I'm starting to wonder if maybe you always forget your clothes on purpose," he said.

Peggy rolled her eyes at him and reached for her bag, but just as she was about to grab it, he moved it away, a smirk spreading across his face.

"Sammy!" She stomped her bare foot on the carpet.

He laughed. "Just come get it."

She reached out and he moved it back again. She playfully slapped his arm.

"Careful with your towel," he grinned.

She held onto her towel with one hand and started attacking him with the other until they were both in fits of giggles on the bed.

Peggy reached for her bag again, which was now behind Sammy's head, and as she grabbed it, they both stopped laughing.

Peggy's breathing became shallow and Sammy's quickly matched it.

"I like this look for you," he said. "You look damn sexy."

Peggy snorted. "Really?"

"Really." He leaned gently towards her.

"I like this look for you."

"What look?"

"This disheveled James Dean look."

Sammy laughed. "Disheveled James Dean?" He pushed her wet hair back from her face and kissed her lightly just above her eyebrow. And then he kissed her on the cheek, and then he found her lips. And as his lips pressed against hers, she felt pure joy move through her veins, and all her worries about Jack and Lacey disappeared. In fact, the deeper Sammy's kisses became, the happier she felt that her friends had finally found something like this too. Something real in this crazy world.

FORTY-THREE

Happy Hour

Lacey grabbed Jack's skateboard from him and took off down the boardwalk, the early evening breeze catching her hair and sending flames of red in her wake. Jack ran after her, but she kept going, laughter exploding out of her lips. "The student has become the master!" she called back to him.

"She's good," said Sammy.

"We've been coming down here most days," Jack said. "She started off renting skates but she's a natural on a board. Way better than me."

"Maybe *you* should get skates?" Peggy suggested, nudging him in the ribs.

He flinched. His ribs were probably never going to be normal again. "Not the ribs Peg," he said, watching as Lacey nearly smashed into a group of girls on roller-skates.

"Are you OK, babe?" he called out.

She flipped the board and waved, yes.

"No fear," Jack said. "That's why she's so good. I have no desire to go back to hospital."

Lacey waved for them to follow her, and soon Jack was

338

standing with his feet in the Pacific Ocean. He closed his eyes. Lacey came up beside him and took his hand. He didn't think he had ever felt this happy, or ever would again. This was the perfect moment. Everything was right with the world. His dream girl here beside him, in his favorite place on the entire planet.

"It's amazing here," said Peggy, stepping into the water. Jack heard splashing and her squealing and Sammy laughing.

"It is really beautiful," said Tricia.

"It sure is," said Horace.

Jack opened his eyes. It was super weird that his mom and dad were here. Tricia and Horace were standing close to each other, not holding hands or splashing around in the water together, but closer than two people who were just friends would stand. And their lingering looks were enough to make Jack want to hurl, or run to them and tell them how beautiful they were together, or something.

It was like some kind of bizarre couples' vacation with the girl he was currently in love with, the one he used to be in love with, his nemesis Sammy Ruthven, and his parents.

OK, so maybe not everything was right with the world, but it was still pretty close.

"The bar is just up there," said Lacey, pointing back up at the boardwalk. "The view is amazing and they never card. They have live bands some nights, but I think it's just the Jukebox tonight, right, babe?"

Jack smiled at her. "Yeah, babe," he said, not really having any idea what she'd said. He'd been too distracted staring at Sammy and Peggy. It seemed like things were back on with them again. Sammy was chasing her around with a piece of seaweed and she was squealing again. Sammy grabbed her and threw her over his shoulder and Jack felt something yank in his stomach as he caught a flash of her light pink underwear from underneath her floral summer dress.

"Let's go, you guys," he said. "We can still make it for happy hour."

"Let's sit outside on top," said Lacey when they arrived at the bar. It was called Shades, and the walls were covered in surfing nostalgia and old license plates and the bar staff all wore Wayfarers. Lacey led them through to the upstairs bar, which was a bit brighter than downstairs with pink geometric wallpaper, an old surfboard hanging off the wall behind the bar and a big open door leading out to the balcony. The outside area was full of pale pink tables and chairs and giant pink flamingos wearing Wayfarers.

"It's the perfect night, and we can watch the sunset," said Lacey, leading the group to one of her and Jack's favorite tables on the balcony that hung over the Venice boardwalk and looked out over the Pacific Ocean.

"We'll get the first drinks," said Horace, and he and Tricia went back to the bar leaving Peggy, Sammy, Lacey and Jack together.

Jack didn't like how it made him feel seeing Peggy and Sammy together. It wasn't that he wasn't madly in love with Lacey, but it was just weird. And for some stupid reason, that night when he'd kissed Peggy entered his mind again. Before she'd arrived, he hadn't thought about it in weeks. Now he couldn't stop thinking about it.

It wasn't that he wanted to kiss her again, but it just kept playing on his mind, like a VHS that kept skipping.

Jack grabbed Lacey's hand under the table. It felt good, safe, right. He looked at Peggy across the table and felt annoyed. He could tell Sammy was holding her hand under the table, too. Sammy and Peggy beamed at each other and Jack felt his face go into a frown.

"You OK, babe?" Lacey asked, giving him a shove.

"Yeah, just feeling a bit tired," he said, running his other hand over his forehead.

"Tired?" Lacey laughed. "It's not like we've been doing anything." She looked over at Peggy and Sammy. "We've been having the best time," she gushed. "We've spent most of our time here just lazing around, sitting in bars, walking on the beach, and... well, you guys know," she giggled.

Jack gave her a look.

"What?" she asked.

Horace and Tricia returned with a tray of Venice Beach Iced Teas, a local version of Long Island Iced Tea, and it didn't take too long before they were all a little tipsy and the sun was setting, creating pink and orange streaks in the sky above the ocean.

Tricia and Horace were sitting with their legs touching and sharing a cigarette. He didn't know his parents ever smoked. She kept leaning into him, and he kept looking like he was about to put his arm around her and then thought better of it. Whatever was going on between them, it looked like it was becoming more than just casual sex, which Jack was happy about.

Peggy and Sammy couldn't keep their eyes off each other, and Lacey was talking really loudly and sharing too many personal stories.

But he was here, and his mom and dad were here, and his best friend was here, and the love of his life was here.

So then why was he feeling so annoyed?

He tried to shake off his bad mood by draining his second iced tea and ordering another one, and he did feel a little better, but not much.

Lacey put her hand on his leg. "What's going on?" she asked quietly.

Jack shook his head. "It's just weird, that's my mom and dad."

"Oh yeah, of course." She ran her fingers through her hair. "I almost forgot, god that must be such a spin out."

Jack nodded. "Totally."

"I'm nearly out of gum again," she said, grabbing her purse. "I swear I've never chewed so much gum since I quit smoking. I'll take those guys with me. Give you a few minutes to feel normal."

He looked at her and mouthed something that could have been either thank you or I love you. It didn't matter which, he felt them both.

"Tricia, H, will you come with me to get some gum?" Lacey asked, jumping up. "We can go past this great bookstore I want to show you, Horace." She looked back at Jack like she was just making it up on the spot and was such a genius for thinking of it.

"You know I can't say no to a bookstore," said Horace, standing up and pulling Tricia up by the hand in the process. They had been holding hands and now that they'd had a few drinks they didn't seem to care that anyone saw.

"I need some cigarettes," Tricia said.

"I'll come too," said Sammy. "I just finished my book and I need a new one."

They all got up to go, and Jack looked over at Peggy. It was just the two of them.

He sighed.

"What's up with you?" she asked, once they were alone. She moved her chair around to sit next to him, so they were both looking out at the view.

Jack shrugged.

"Don't give me that, I know you." She leaned closer towards him. "I know when something is up."

Jack shook his head.

"You used to tell me everything."

"Yeah, well, I guess that's changed."

"Tell me about it."

"Tell *you* about it? You're the one who's so busy being obsessed with Sammy Ruthven you've barely spoken to me since I got here."

"Wait, what? *You're* the one who just disappeared to LA with my best friend."

"I thought *I* was your best friend?"

"I thought so, too," she said. "But I guess things are changing."

Jack just looked out at the ocean. She was right. He couldn't just go on pretending like he would always have Peggy around the way he used to. Things *were* changing.

"You and Lacey, it's great," she said, not looking at him, but still sounding genuinely pleased for him.

The sun had just about set now, but Jack felt a warm feeling move through his body. "Look at us," he said.

"What about us?"

"Look at where we are. Drinking cocktails on the beach in 1984."

Peggy grinned at him and then looked out at the ocean again. "This *is* kind of amazing huh?"

"It really is. Sometimes I think about that day at St. Christopher's, that day you got the book, when Jim and Mindy put that maple syrup in your locker... and I think about how long ago that seems, and how much has happened since then."

"And how much we've matured?" Peggy asked, flicking an ice cube his way.

He stuck his tongue out at her and threw one back.

"I want to talk to you about something, though," he said seriously. He couldn't keep pretending it didn't happen. He had to clear the air, and this may be the only time he had to do it.

"Shoot."

"I want to talk about the kiss."

"What kiss?" She took a sip of her drink.

"The one where you kissed me."

"Oh, I kissed _you_, did I?" she asked.

"Yeah, you kissed me."

"I'm pretty sure you kissed me first."

"Well, whoever kissed who first, the other one definitely kissed back."

Peggy looked down into her drink.

"I think, in some way, you liked it," he said. "And I think at the time, I liked it too, and I just hate how we never talked about it."

"There's nothing to talk about," Peggy said. "It was just a stupid thing that happened. We have so much history, that's all. When you have a history with someone sometimes you mistake it for feelings."

"But you know we've always had feelings for each other," Jack said.

Peggy shook her head. "_You've_ always had feelings for _me_. And I was confused."

"I don't buy it. That night you kissed me like you really wanted me. And what about that other time?"

"What other time?" she frowned.

"When you came over that night and we... we slept together."

Peggy's face went red, and she looked away from him. "Whatever I felt then I don't feel now. It's in the past, OK? And it needs to stay in the past. And if you ever tell Sammy that I kissed you, or about that night we slept together, I'll never forgive you. I love Sammy and I don't want anything to screw that up again. And if I was you, I wouldn't tell Lacey either. It's probably hard enough for her knowing that you had feelings for me."

Jack nodded. "No, you're right, it's in the past, and it's

not going to happen again. But I just wanted you to know, that no matter what happens with you and Sammy or me and Lacey, I'll always love you."

"You still love me?"

"Not like, romantically," he rolled his eyes. "Like as a friend, like a sister."

"I'll always love you like that, too," she said, and she leaned over and gave him a hug and a kiss on the cheek and Jack felt like everything was OK again, and he couldn't wait for Lacey to get back so he could tell her he loved her, too.

But Lacey was already back, and she'd heard the whole thing.

FORTY-FOUR

Running

Lacey ran back out of the bar and down the boardwalk, hot angry tears in her eyes clouding her vision.

She couldn't believe it. All this time she'd thought Jack was this normal nice guy, but he was just like the rest of them. He was a cheater and a liar, and if Jack could be an asshole then what hope was there?

So many feelings were pulsing through her as she ran. She was angry, she felt betrayed, but most of all she felt like such an idiot that she could fall for him, that she could tell him she loved him, that she could buy into this idea that Jack was such a nice, great guy. At least with Rex, she knew he was sleeping with other girls.

And not only did Jack lie to her, the girl who was supposed to be her best friend had lied to her, too. And told him to lie to her! Lacey felt molten lava moving through her veins as she ran, shoving past roller-skaters and skateboarders and flying through crowds of families and tourists.

She'd thought maybe she could stop running now that

she'd found Jack, but no. He was just one more thing to run away from.

She got back to the motel room and threw herself down on the bed and sobbed.

She couldn't understand it. Just a few hours ago he was kissing her on this bed and telling her how much he loved her.

Lies.

Asshole.

She wanted to just cry herself to sleep and never come out of this room, but Jack had a key, and she did not want to be here when he got back. She never wanted to see him again.

She grabbed her bag and started wildly throwing in her things which had been scattered all over the room. She went into the bathroom and cleared the shelf into a plastic bag. She saw her camera on the bedside table and couldn't decide if she should take it or not. She didn't want something *he* had given her, but she loved that camera and didn't want him to have it either, so she grabbed it and put it in her bag.

She was about to run out the door when she thought about leaving a note. There were still things unsaid, things she wanted to say to him. She wanted to tell him how she was feeling, to yell at him, to tell him to never talk to her again. But no, he wasn't worth it. Let him worry about her and wonder where she was, if he even would. He'd probably just go running back into Peggy's arms and forget all about her by tomorrow.

And she walked out and slammed the door behind her.

FORTY-FIVE

Another Note

"Where's Lacey?" asked Sammy, sitting back down at the table with a fresh round of pink cocktails with umbrellas and maraschino cherries stuck in the top.

"She went with you guys, remember?" Jack said.

Sammy looked around the bar. "Yeah, but she came back before us."

Jack shook his head. "What do you mean?"

"What do you think I mean, genius?" Sammy asked. "We were in the bookstore and she said she was worried about you acting weird, so she wanted to go back."

"You lost Lacey?" Jack asked, jumping up from his chair. His stomach suddenly tied up in knots. All the worst-case scenarios immediately jumped into his mind. He thought about her floating out in the ocean, he thought about Rex appearing out of nowhere and stealing her back, he thought about all the gun crime and crime in general here in LA in the eighties.

"We didn't lose her, she was on her way back here," Tricia said. "Don't flip out Jack, she probably just got distracted somewhere."

"Lacey's known to get distracted at times," said Sammy.

"Shut up, Sammy," said Jack, pushing past him and heading towards the door. "I'm going to go find her." Jack paused and stared at them. Sammy, who was being a jerk, Peggy, who didn't seem to care, and his own parents who were just gawking. Weren't they the ones who taught him about stranger danger? "Are you guys coming to help or what?"

"We'll find her," Peggy said, putting a hand on Jack's arm.

Jack looked down at her arm and threw it off him. "How? She could be anywhere, anything could've happened to her. I wish to god we just had cell phones already," he said, running his hands through his hair.

Tricia and Horace both looked at him weirdly.

"Let's split up and go to the places you think she might be," said Sammy calmly. "Where do you think she would go?"

"I don't know," said Jack, clenching his fists. "Nowhere, she wouldn't go anywhere without telling one of us."

"Maybe she just went back to the motel," suggested Horace.

"Yeah, maybe she just went back to get something," said Tricia. "Me and Horace will go back there and check."

Jack nodded, but he knew she would never have done that.

"I'll go back to the bookstore and the store we got the cigarettes and gum from," said Sammy. "You two go to the beach and see if she's there."

"What if we don't find her?" Jack asked. "I don't know what I'll do."

Peggy grabbed his hand. "We *will* find her."

A couple of hours later, after they had combed the beach and asked around in what felt like every single local bar and store, they finally went back to the motel.

They all crowded into Tricia and Horace's room. Jack stood by the door as if he was ready to run right out searching for her again.

"She left a note," Tricia said, handing it to Jack.

"A note? What do you mean, a note? You mean she just *left*?"

Sammy and Horace exchanged looks.

"It says not to tell you," Tricia said. "But…"

"Not to tell *me*? I'm worried sick, I don't care about anything else, I just want to know she's alive."

Tricia handed the piece of motel stationary to Jack.

Tricia,

I'm going back to my mom's, please don't tell Jack or Peggy where I am. I don't want to see them. They will know why.

L x

"Don't tell Jack or Peggy?" Jack read, his brow knotting in confusion. "Why not? What is this?" He gripped the note tightly. It was suddenly all he had left of her.

Peggy shook her head in disbelief.

Jack flapped the note around frantically, looking on the other side to see if there was anything else. "Why has she done this?"

"Lacey is a runner," said Sammy, giving Jack a sympathetic shrug.

"What?" Jack glared back at Sammy.

"She's a runner, she runs. It's tough man, I know, but this is kind of classic Lacey."

"Don't be a jerk, Ruthven," said Tricia.

"Well, it's true, isn't it?" Sammy asked. "She's run

away from everyone who ever got even a bit close to her, and I've never seen her closer than she's been with you, Jack."

Jack just stood staring at the note.

"But why me?" Peggy asked in a small voice.

Jack shook his head. "I don't know."

"Did anything happen today, between you two?" asked Sammy. "Did you have a fight or anything?"

"No, everything has been really great. I was kind of acting like a jerk before you guys went to get cigarettes, but…"

Peggy threw her hand to mouth. "Oh," she whispered.

"What?" Jack asked. "What is it?"

"She heard us."

"Heard us what?"

"In the bar."

Jack froze.

"What happened in the bar?" Tricia asked.

Peggy's eyes darted around them all before settling on Tricia's. "We were talking about something that happened between us… before. Lacey must have heard and thought that… *oh, no.*"

Sammy took a step away from Peggy and glared at Jack. "*What* happened between you?"

"Nothing you need to worry about," said Jack.

"Really?" asked Sammy, squaring up to Jack by the door. "Because if it was enough to send Lacey packing, maybe it's something I need to know about, too."

"Which is it, Ruthven? Is Lacey a runner, or is she right to leave me?"

"Shut up, Jack, and just tell me the truth."

Jack took a deep breath and looked Sammy square in the eye. "I kissed her," he said.

"You *what?*" Sammy leaned in closer.

"Stop it, just stop it, you two. It was nothing, Sammy."
She grabbed the sleeve of his t-shirt.

Sammy's head flipped around to look at Peggy. "He
kissed you and you say it's nothing?"

"Hey," said Jack. "Calm down man, it really was nothing. I kissed her, and she didn't stop me for like a whole two
seconds, and then she did stop me. And before you go
getting all stress-o-rama about it, you two weren't even
together then. You were off pouting and refusing to get
over the fact that she'd run off when she thought you
were dead."

Sammy shoved Jack against the door.

"Woah," said Horace, jumping up to break it up. "Cool
it boys."

"Shut up, *dad*," said Jack.

"Dad?" asked Horace.

"I mean, Horace, whatever, just stay out of this."

Horace took a step back.

"Dad?" Tricia laughed.

"You shut up, too," Jack said, scowling at her. "And
you." Jack poked Sammy in the chest. "You don't even
know a good thing when you have it. I mean, look at this
woman." He nodded his head towards Peggy. "She's beautiful, and she's kind and generous and every day she tries to
be a better person, even if she messes up sometimes. She's
trying really hard."

Sammy scowled at him.

"And if you don't get your act together soon, some
other guy will come along and take her away from you, but
it won't be me. I'm in it with Lacey, until the end. Whatever I felt for Peggy is *nothing* compared to what I feel
for Lacey."

Sammy just kept scowling. He was like a balloon that
had been blown up too far about to burst.

"Sammy, come on, it was really nothing," said Peggy. "You and me, we weren't together, Jack hadn't even met Lacey yet, and *still* nothing happened. It didn't go any further than a dumb kiss on the couch, and the reason it didn't was because of *you*. Because I was still in love with you. Don't you think if anything was going to happen with me and Jack it would have happened by now?"

Sammy let out a breath.

"I think maybe everyone should go to bed," said Horace.

"I can't, I have to go to her." Jack clutched his chest. "I have to tell her she misunderstood, she didn't hear the whole story. She needs to know the whole story," he said frantically.

"There's nothing you can do tonight." Horace reached out and put an arm on Jack's shoulder. "You've had a lot to drink, we all have. Let's just get some rest and call her in the morning. We know where she's going, at least."

Jack nodded. His dad was still a voice of reason, even at eighteen.

"If you still want to go after her, you can take my car in the morning," Sammy said.

———

The next morning, after barely even sleeping at all, Jack took Sammy's Buick, which was definitely not as nice to drive as the Mustang Sammy would have in the future, and he drove all day with the desert heat blazing down on the car's roof. He only stopped once for the toilet, and to buy a bunch of sodas. The whole way all he could do was think about her, about how much she must be hurting, about what she must be thinking about him, about him and Peggy. It was all wrong, and it broke his heart to think that she was in pain over something that wasn't even real.

When he finally got to Lacey's house later that evening, it took him a minute to work up the nerve to get out and knock. He felt horrendous. His clothes were sticking to him with sweat and his nerves were shot. He'd been running on adrenaline all day, and now that he was finally here, it was like his whole system was ready to shut down and go to sleep.

When Lacey answered, she looked like an absolute mess too, but she was still the most beautiful thing he'd ever seen. Her make-up was smudged all under her eyes. It looked like she hadn't taken it off from the night before, the night they had been out at their favorite beach side bar drinking Venice Beach Iced Tea. It felt like a lifetime ago now.

"It's not what you think," he said, jamming his foot in the door so she wouldn't slam it on him.

"Not what I think? You cheated on me and you lied to me," she said, both anger and sadness in her voice.

"Lacey, I…"

"You were the one person in my whole life who made me feel like I was worth something, do you know that? And now you've made me feel like it was all just bullshit."

"It wasn't bullshit. I love you, Lacey."

"Move your foot." A tear rolled down her cheek.

"Please, just let me explain," he pleaded.

"Move. Your. Foot." A tear rolled down her other cheek and Jack felt the tears stinging behind his own eyes. This really did feel like the wrong timeline. This wasn't how it was meant to go. He was here to explain everything to her, to make her see how crazy this was, to bring her back to LA with him so it could all be back to how it was just a few hours ago.

Jack didn't want to move his foot. But she had asked him to, and so he did, and the door slammed in his face.

"I didn't cheat on you, I would never do that. It all happened before we even met," he yelled through the door. "It doesn't mean anything now." He banged on the door with his fists. "I love you!" he called out. "You're my life, Lacey, you're my everything!" Tears of frustration finally beginning to fall from his eyes.

The door opened again, but this time it was her mom. She looked just like an older version of Lacey. Her hair and make-up were immaculate.

"My daughter doesn't want to see you," her mom said, folding her arms in the same way Lacey had.

"I can't go, I won't go, I love her." More tears began to stream down his face. "You don't understand, just let me explain."

"If you don't go, I'll call the police," his mom said. "You wanna try explaining to them?"

Lacey pushed past her mom and looked at Jack. "We are done, Jack. Don't you ever come back here."

FORTY-SIX

Finally

———————

Sammy sat down on the edge of the bed and stared at the painting of the palm tree in front of him. Peggy sat down next to him as close as she dared. She didn't know where he was at right now. Was he still angry about the kiss? He'd offered to let Jack take his car, so he couldn't be too angry. But he was shutting down again, and Peggy didn't know what to do.

"Is everything OK with us?" she asked.

Sammy shook his head. "It pains me so much to say this, but I think Jack was right."

Peggy's stomach dropped. "About what?" She wasn't sure if she was really ready to hear the rest.

Sammy looked up at her, his clear blue eyes beaming right into her soul. "He's right. About the way I was acting, how I pushed you away."

Peggy shook her head. "I was the jerk, not you. You did nothing wrong."

"Yeah, you were a jerk, but I've been a jerk, too." He grabbed her hand. "I've thought about everything so much, over and over, too much, and it always comes back to me being scared, but now I'm scared I'm going to lose you anyway."

"You? Scared?"

Sammy nodded. "I was so scared of losing you again, it was easier to push you away than to face the possibility that you'd run away again. Seeing what Jack's going through right now, I don't want to have to ever feel like that again."

"I'm not going anywhere, Sammy. Santolsa is my home now." And she only realized after she'd said it that it was true. Santolsa really was her home.

"I'm so tired of pushing you away." He pushed back his hair back from his face, only to have it land right back over his eyes again.

"I know I've said it already, and I can probably never say it enough, but I'm sorry."

He shook his head. "You don't need to keep being sorry." He gently rubbed his thumb in circles over the palm of her hand, making her feel all sorts of things in her hand, heart and in other places. "I think the best thing we can do now is to stop agonizing over the past and start looking toward the future. That means you have to stop apologizing and I have to stop needing you to."

Peggy nodded. "I'm ready to look to the future if you are."

"I am." He reached out and pushed a strand of her hair back from her face. "I guess you've already seen the future, but not the one we could have together."

"Wait, what?"

Sammy gave her one of those smoldering smirks and it gave her butterflies. "Jack told me everything."

"But, I told you everything ages ago, and you didn't believe me. You thought I was nuts, but you believe *Jack*?"

"I still think you're nuts."

She gave him a gentle push, and he grinned at her.

"He had all these photos of the two of you. It was hard to see that, and not just because it's so weird, but it was hard seeing all the pictures of you through his eyes. He really loved you."

Peggy nodded. "I think he really did, and I think in some way I loved him, too, but it was never like this." She gestured at the space between them.

Sammy nodded and paused for a moment as if taking in what she'd just said. "And then he brought me a present from your time," he finally said.

"Twinkies?"

"Bruce Springsteen's greatest hits on vinyl. There are songs on it I've never heard, and I've heard all his songs. It says it was printed in 1995. And at first, I still didn't believe it, you know? I thought maybe it was some printing error, or maybe Jack had it doctored or something. But then I started thinking about that day you gave Janet that record, and you said it was Bryan Adams' greatest hits, and all the other little things that just didn't ever quite make sense about you. I realized they all made sense if it was true, and even though I still think it's completely insane, I believe you. I believe in… time travel." He ran a hand through his hair. "I can't believe I just said that out loud."

Peggy didn't know whether to laugh or cry and so a bit of both escaped from her lips and eyes.

"I'm sorry I didn't believe you, but it's just, it's a lot."

Peggy nodded. "You're telling me. It was never a part of my plan to travel back in time and fall in love with the raddest guy in the class of 1983."

Sammy smirked. "Fall in love, huh?"

Peggy blushed and gave a little shrug. "Maybe just a little bit." She smirked back at him.

Sammy leaned into her and took her in his arms, and before she knew it, they had fallen back on the bed together. "Maybe I'm just a little bit in love with you too, Peggy Martin," he said, before his lips found hers.

Her hands found the hem of his t-shirt and worked their way up to the bare skin of his back. His breathing deepened as she pulled his shirt over his head and threw it onto the floor.

He grinned at her. "Are you sure?"

"I've never been as sure about anything as I am about you, Sammy Ruthven," she said, grinning back.

"I just want you to feel sure. I want it to be special, and this is a big deal."

"I am sure. And I think you and me are kind of a big deal."

"The biggest deal," he said. "The biggest, most radical, most forever deal."

"*Forever?*" she asked, raising an eyebrow.

He leaned in toward her and she put a hand on his bare chest. "Yes," he said softly, before placing a gentle kiss on her neck, and then another a little further down.

"Always?" she asked, her whole body tingling with excitement.

"And forever," he said.

FORTY-SEVEN

Gay Night

The next few weeks went by in a long slow blur of tears, heartbreak and frustration for Jack. He'd spent a couple of days on the couch at Janet's house in Santolsa while he tried to get Lacey to hear him out, but when he tried to call, the phone was off the hook, and when he went to her house her mom always answered the door, or no one did. Eventually her mom did call the cops, and Jack had never skateboarded as fast as he had when he saw the cop car appear from around the corner near her house.

The irony was not lost on him. He had always treated Lacey so well, and her mom had called the cops on him. Rex had gotten away with covering her in bruises. The whole situation was making him crazy.

It was Janet who suggested that he go back to LA for a while. "There's no point in staying here right now. Give her time to cool off."

Jack didn't want to leave without Lacey, but he knew Janet was right. There was nothing else he could do. Maybe she just needed time to calm down, and then she would be willing to listen. There was absolutely no point in staying here and crying on Janet's couch any longer.

Jack got back to LA just in time to get Sammy's car back to him so everyone could get back to their lives in Santolsa. He stayed in the motel on the beach for a few more nights, calling Lacey's number over and over again until he eventually heard a message that the number was no longer in service. He never knew a recorded message could make him feel so broken inside.

Eventually, he came around to the idea that he wasn't going to be able to get her back this way, and so he decided to go back to LA. Jack found an apartment in an old art deco block just a few minutes' walk from the beach. It was nice, *really* nice and as soon as he moved in, he felt right at home. It was totally his own space, and he made quick work of decorating it with brightly colored abstract artwork and framed movie posters. He bought a peach-colored sofa set, fluffy rugs, big lampshades, a king-sized bed with a white shell shaped headboard and gold bedside tables. He bought a VCR and a collection of old eighties movies he loved.

It was only after the apartment was done, he realized he'd decorated it for Lacey.

Without a job and with no one to keep him company, Jack had started to go a little stir crazy. He found himself spending his time in the bars, drinking with the locals and drowning his sorrows with middle-aged men who were out of work or had been kicked out of the house by their wives.

Jack's apartment was beautiful, but his life was not even close. Sometimes late at night, when he was drunk and alone, he pictured Uncle Jack - his broken future self. He could see the thread connecting him to that future becoming thicker and stronger with each passing day. He could feel his Uncle Jack, that jaded man, growing stronger inside of him. He hated it, but he felt like there was nothing he could do to stop it.

One night Jack sat down to write Lacey one more time. When he could no longer call her, he started writing. So far, all his letters had come back to him with a return to sender stamp. This time, instead of addressing it directly to Lacey, he would send it to Tricia and hope that Tricia could get Lacey to read it. As he sealed the envelope, he said a prayer to the Gods of destiny, or whoever it was who had orchestrated their first two meetings, and hoped with all he had that she would get this one, that she'd read it, that she'd understand and that she would come back to him.

His Uncle Jack was right. Nothing mattered without her. He was torn apart and alone and he had nothing in his life except for a decent collection of VHS movies and a beach view.

———

On a night when Jack was feeling particularly lonely, he called Ben. Peggy had given Jack his number weeks ago. She'd thought they could get together if Jack needed a friend. It had sounded lame at the time, but Jack felt like he could use a friend now. Ben was more than happy to hear from him. And an hour later Jack was dressed in a pair of jeans and a new light blue button-up shirt and was heading down the stairs to meet a taxi to take him to West Hollywood.

"Jack!" called Ben, waving from the line outside the club.

"Ben!" Jack gave him a strong hug. "I can't believe I'm back here."

"Oh yeah. I heard about what happened with you and Rex. Nice one, man." He gave Jack a fist bump.

"Will they even let me in?" Jack asked.

"It's gay night. As long as you're a dude and you're not causing trouble, it's good. They won't even look at you twice."

"It's gay night?" Jack shifted from one foot to the other.

Ben looked him up and down. "The guys in here will take one look at you and know you're not gay."

Jack raised an eyebrow. "Are you sure?"

"It'll be fun, and there are always a few girls hanging out, but they *will* think you're gay."

"Oh, great."

Ben nudged him in the rib, and he winced. He wasn't sure that rib would ever fully heal. "It's a really fun night, Jack. You'll have a good time, trust me."

They got into the club with no problem. The bouncer was even the same one who pulled Jack off the stage weeks ago, but he didn't look at him twice. There was a drag queen up on stage miming to Diana Ross, and the club was full of buff young men with no shirts on. Jack felt uncomfortable. He didn't want to feel uncomfortable. He wanted to be a good ally, but he'd never been in a gay bar before, and it was kind of a lot to take in all at once.

Ben grabbed the hand of one of the half-naked men and pulled him over. "Jack, this is Diego," Ben said, introducing them.

"Hey, Diego." Jack gave a wave.

Diego greeted them by leaning in and kissing Ben on the cheek and then kissing Jack's cheek too. "Hang on," Diego said, squinting at Jack and putting a hand on his hip. "Are you the guy who pretended to be gay to trick your friend into falling in love with you?"

"Uh, it wasn't exactly like that. People just assumed I

was gay. No one believed me when I said I wasn't, and I just got tired of trying to correct them."

"Shame on you." Diego shook his head.

"Diego," said Ben.

"No, Ben. This is important." Diego waved Ben away and turned to glare at Jack. "Do you know what hell we have to suffer through? Do you know what it's like? This club night is one of the few places we are safe to be ourselves, and even then, we have to be careful when we go home, always going in groups or waiting inside for our rides or going out the back. There are always assholes lurking out there waiting to try to beat one of us up."

"Diego, he's cool, man," said Ben.

"No," continued Diego. "Our friends are dying. Do you know how bad it is? Every month I come in here and there is someone I know who's gone. And you're pretending to be gay to hook up with girls?"

Jack shook his head. It was hard enough to be gay in the present, but here in the eighties HIV was rampant, and so was prejudice. It wasn't great in his time, but it was so much worse here.

"I'm so sorry," Jack said, shaking his head and feeling tears in the backs of his eyes ready to try to escape.

Diego nodded, patted Jack's shoulder and went to the bar to get them some drinks.

"He just lost a close friend," Ben explained.

"I'm sorry," Jack said again, running his hands through his hair. "I hope you're being safe Ben."

Ben rolled his eyes. "I'm not sleeping with *him*. He's like fifty."

Jack laughed. "Well, I hope you're being safe with whoever you're dating."

Ben nodded. "Yeah, there's this guy from college. He's not out, he'd never come to a night like this."

"He's missing out," said Jack, looking around at the heaving dance floor as everyone danced to some disco song Jack didn't know.

"What about you?" asked Ben. "What went down with you and Lacey?"

Diego returned and passed around some beers and then disappeared into the dance floor.

Jack took a swig of his beer. "I don't even know. One minute everything was better than it had ever been before, the next, she was gone."

Ben nodded. "Sounds like love to me."

"If that's love, I'm done with love."

Jack proceeded to get stupidly drunk, and when Ben said they should go home, Jack flat out refused. He was having too much fun dancing to disco and everyone was so friendly, and it was so nice to not have to worry about girls for once. Jack was having the best time he'd had since Lacey had left.

It was only when he found himself later that night, doing cocaine in the toilets with a drag queen that he wondered for a moment if he was on a good path, if he was on the best timeline, but a moment later when the coke hit his brain, he felt sure he was. Everything was awesome. *He* was awesome, and he deserved so much better than a girl who wouldn't even hear him out.

But somewhere deep inside, he knew that he would never again be as happy as he was that summer in 1984 when he was with Lacey.

FORTY-EIGHT

The Letter

Lacey had barely moved off the plush pink couch in her mom's pristine lounge room for the last three weeks.

Her mom was standing over her, arms crossed.

"What?" Lacey asked, not looking up from a copy of Mademoiselle magazine.

"That's enough now, Lacey. It's time to get up and get your life back on track."

"On track? You say that like my life was ever *on* track." Lacey looked up and gave her mother a look. "Anyway, that's rich coming from you. How many times did I pull you off this very couch? You of all people have no right to tell me how to live my life. Leave me alone." Lacey looked back down at the magazine. It wasn't like she was even reading it. She hadn't been able to think clearly since that night she'd found out about Jack and Peggy. All she'd been able to do was pretend to watch daytime TV and flip through old magazines and try to ignore her mother.

"That boy was no good for you, Lacey. You are better off without him, and the sooner you realize that and get off this couch the better it will be for everyone."

"You don't even know anything about him, or what happened." Lacey didn't know why she was defending him after everything.

"I know he upset you, that's all I need to know." The doorbell rang and her mother harrumphed. "I suppose I'll get that."

"It's Tricia," her mother called from the front door.

"Tell her I don't want to see anyone," Lacey called back.

"Hey," said Tricia, slumping into a pink armchair next to Lacey.

"Oh, great. I told Mom I didn't want to see anyone."

"Not even me? You haven't returned any of my calls, I've been getting worried."

"I'm fine," Lacey said, absently flicking through the pages of her magazine.

Tricia grabbed an envelope out of her purse and handed it to Lacey. "I'm supposed to stay until you read it."

Lacey took the envelope and frowned. "Is this from... *him*?"

Tricia nodded.

Lacey handed it back. "I don't want to read it."

"I talked to him. It's not what you think Lacey. You've been here crying over this guy for weeks and it's stupid. He's crazy about you."

"Just get out, Tricia. Mom! Tell Tricia to get out!"

"He never cheated on you. It was all just a big misunderstanding. What happened with him and Peggy – it was before he even met you."

Lacey shook her head. "I don't care. I'm not interested."

"OK, fine," said Tricia, standing up to go. "But I'm going to leave this here, and I really hope you read it before you just throw away everything you could've had with him. You know I nearly messed up everything with Horace, I nearly pushed him away, and I'm so glad I didn't, because this is the best thing that's ever happened to me. Don't make the mistake I nearly made. Don't lose Jack. He's a good guy, everything you think about him right now isn't true. What you had before, what you had all summer, that was the truth." Tricia threw the envelope between the pages of Lacey's magazine. Lacey picked it up, tore it in half and threw it on the ground.

"If you won't read it, you're going to shut up and listen."

Lacey gasped. "You can't talk to me like that in my own house. Mom!"

Her mother appeared at the doorway. "I'm not helping you until you help yourself," she said, jangling her car keys. "I'm going to the mall." Her mother disappeared and Lacey made a groaning noise.

Tricia grabbed the letter and opened it, holding the torn pieces together, and she began reading.

Dearest Lacey,

I know you don't want to hear from me. You probably won't even open this letter. It's not the first one I've sent. I've been writing you every day. I'm not sure if your mom has been intercepting them and returning them, or if you really didn't want to hear what I had to say. But I hope you hear it now. I hope that Tricia is with you and she's making you read this. If anyone could do it, I know it would be Tricia.

What you heard that night, it wasn't what you think.

Me and Peggy have never been more than friends. There was a time when I wanted more, when I really felt like I loved her, and maybe I did love her, in some way, but it was never anything like what

Summer of 1984

I feel for you. It was a confusing time for me. I had no other friends, I didn't know who I was in the world and she was the one person who got what I was going through. We told each other everything, well, nearly. I never actually lied to her about being gay, but I didn't offer up the truth when I should have.

But I'm not that guy anymore, and now I want to offer up the truth to you.

I kissed Peggy twice. Once when she came back to our present, after she thought Sammy had died. That wasn't about any feelings she had for me, it was about her grief. Then once when I first got to 1984. It was when Peggy and Sammy weren't even together, and I hadn't even met you yet. It was a kiss that lasted a whole two seconds and then she stopped me. And that whole thing about us sleeping together? That was us sleeping in a bed together, not sex. The only thing that happened was that I woke up with my arm around her. Again, before I had even time travelled, and way before I had ever met you.

When I met you, my God, Lacey, you changed everything for me. I remember that moment so vividly. You were so sad that night, but you were so beautiful, and there was such a spark of light within you. I wanted to just be as close to you as possible so I could bask in it. That moment I first saw you, it was as if a lightning bolt hit me right in the chest and anything I ever felt for any other girl before you just burned away. I knew in that moment that my past was done, and you were my future.

I walked all night that night. I walked all the way from West Hollywood to the beach, and all I thought of all night, was you. You're all I've thought about since.

When I saw you the second time, I thought the Gods really were smiling down on me, but just as soon as I found you, you were gone again.

But then, there you were again, in Janet's kitchen that night and it was like the stars had aligned. Seeing you standing there in that baggy t-shirt, your hair a mess, your eyes all sleepy, that moment will be imprinted on my soul forever.

You will be imprinted on my soul forever.

And so, in keeping with the theme of this letter - the truth - I do love Peggy. But I love her as a friend. As a sister. I love her like I love my own family.

The way I feel about you, well, I don't even know how to put it into words. It's something I can't explain. It's like trying to explain the first time you see the ocean. It's so much bigger than you thought it would be, it's so big you're not sure you can even comprehend it and being near it makes you feel so excited and yet so calm, and yet kind of terrified, too. It's like you finally found where you belong and you had no idea it could be so beautiful, so perfect, and you can never unsee it. You can never go back to how it was.

I love you, Lacey. If I kept that kiss from you it was only because I didn't think it mattered. All that mattered was you. All that will ever matter to me again is you.

Say the word, and I'm yours. Forever.

I hope you read this. I hope you understand, and I hope more than anything I've ever hoped before, that this isn't the end of our story.

My past is done, and I want you to be my future.

All my love, forever and always,

Jack x

FORTY-NINE

Timelines

Jack woke up to a banging on the front door of his apartment. It was still dark, and he had no idea what time it was or how he'd gotten home, or what had even happened last night. The last thing he remembered was learning the dance moves to The Hustle and doing them on stage in front of the whole club.

The banging was getting louder.

"Urgh, what is that?" asked a female voice.

There was a girl in bed with him. Jack felt panic rise in his chest. He had no memory of coming home with anyone.

His eyes adjusted to the darkness.

Crystal.

"How did you get in here?" he demanded.

"You invited me in." She reached over to touch him.

He jumped out of bed. He was naked.

This was not good.

He grabbed his jeans off the floor and pulled them on.

"I don't remember what happened." He rubbed his temples.

"Remember, at closing time? You saw me outside the club, and you invited me back here."

"Did we…?""

She laughed. "No, you just passed out."

"Why was I naked then?"

"I undressed you," she said. "And I undressed myself, in case you woke up in the night and wanted to." She gave a shrug, like that was a completely normal thing to do.

Jack shook his head. "You have to go. This isn't who I am, this isn't… how did this even happen?" He threw his hands to his face.

"That's not very hospitable of you," she pouted. "How will I get home at this hour?"

The banging on the door got even louder and someone started shouting Jack's name. A man's voice.

Jack shoved a twenty in her hand. "Get dressed, go out the window and get a taxi."

"If I jump from here, I'll like, *die*."

Jack ran his hands through his hair, closed her in the bedroom and looked through the peephole.

Uncle Jack.

He opened the door and Uncle Jack stormed in. He was furious. He began throwing on light switches and looking around frantically.

"What are you doing here?" asked Jack. "Wait, *how* are you even here?"

"I time travelled. I figured it out Jack," he said, still searching the apartment. "I figured out everything."

"What are you talking about?"

"Where is she?" Uncle Jack demanded.

"Where's who?"

"Crystal."

Jack let out a sigh. Of course, he knew.

"In the bedroom."

"Did you…?""

"No, of course not!" Jack said.

"Didn't I tell you to stay away from her?"

"I don't even remember inviting her back here!"

Uncle Jack threw open the door to the bedroom.

Crystal screamed and pulled the sheet around her still naked body.

"Get out," Uncle Jack said.

"Jack, what's your dad doing here?" she shouted. "Tell *him* to get out!"

"Get some clothes on and *get out*," Uncle Jack said.

He opened his wallet and handed her a fifty and she was dressed and out the door in seconds.

"What the hell?" Jack asked, flopping down on to the couch and putting his head in his hands.

"I figured it all out," Uncle Jack said.

"How are you even *here*?" Jack shook his head.

"I time travelled," he said. "I didn't think I would be able to. I thought after all this time the door to the book room wouldn't work for me, but it did, it did work!" He grinned manically.

Jack's head was splitting, and he felt like what little grasp he had on reality was slipping away from him rapidly.

"It wasn't about you," Uncle Jack said. "All this time I was trying to make *you* change your choices, but it was never about you. You couldn't do anything differently. *I* had to do something different."

Jack shook his head. "Huh?"

"*I* had to change it, not you. I'm here to help you, to help *us*."

"I don't know what's happening. How are you here? And why was Crystal here?"

"You'll remember later. You saw her outside the club

last night. She looked like she'd been crying. She told you that she got mugged, that they'd stolen all her money and keys and she couldn't go home. She asked if she could stay on your couch and you, being the chivalrous guy you are, said yes. As soon as you were asleep, she took your clothes off and got into bed with you."

"That's... that's so not OK. Why would she do that?"

"She likes you," Uncle Jack said. "And I don't think she really knows how to express that. But she's trouble."

"I don't feel good." Jack felt like he was going to puke.

"Go back to sleep, we can talk more in the morning." Uncle Jack gave him a fatherly pat on the shoulder.

Jack fell asleep on the couch, and when he woke up to the smell of coffee and pancakes and early morning sunshine streaming in through the blinds, he was part thankful and part felt like he was dying.

"Oh good, you're up." Uncle Jack smiled at him as he handed over a mug of coffee.

Jack had never seen Uncle Jack smile like that before.

"You're here," Jack said. "It wasn't a dream."

"Yeah, I'm here, and I've changed your timeline, so don't act like an asshole and just thank me."

"Wow, OK," said Jack, taking a sip of coffee.

"Last night was the night everything went off course for me, for *you*. You've been on the path for a while, but last night was the turning point." Uncle Jack said. "I worked it all out, and I pinpointed everything to that night, last night. I thought we needed to change it earlier. I thought if you didn't come to LA, we could stop it, but you had to come here, and I guess, in some weird way, you needed to experience all of this. But last night was the point of no return for us."

"What are you talking about?"

"Last night was when you started to go down a spiral that would mess up your whole life."

"I'm listening," said Jack.

"The partying, the drugs, it was all downhill from there, but the worst part was Crystal."

"What about her? Nothing happened, did it?" Jack's face went white at the thought that maybe, actually, something did happen between him and Crystal. He would never forgive himself if it did.

Uncle Jack shook his head. "No, nothing happened between you. But to someone else it sure would have looked like something happened."

"So, what happens now?" Jack asked.

"I don't know," Uncle Jack said. "You're on a new timeline now, and so am I."

"Can I still get back to my present? Did you mess up the portal?"

"That was a risk I needed to take. I hope you understand. I think you will be able to get back, though. After all, it wasn't just *someone* that got in, it was me, *you*. If I went back, you should go forward. In theory."

"Great," said Jack rubbing his temples. This was the worst time travel induced headache yet.

"I made pancakes," said Uncle Jack.

Jack looked up at him. "Wow, really?"

Uncle Jack nodded. "You want some?"

"Yes, please."

And so, he sat there eating pancakes and drinking coffee with his future self, talking about timelines and their parents and all of Uncle Jack's wild ideas about what he might do next. Joining AA, a world cruise, signing up to a video dating service...

When they were done, Uncle Jack did the dishes and said his goodbyes, but they decided to stay in touch, and

Jack thought maybe they could actually end up being really good friends.

When Uncle Jack had left, Jack took a shower, changed his sheets and just as he was about to sit down and watch *E.T.* with a giant glass of soda and a bag of Chex Mix, there was a knock on the door.

FIFTY

The Future

Lacey threw her arms around him. "I'm so sorry!" She gripped the back of his shirt so tightly.

"No, *I'm* sorry," Jack said, holding her tight. He never wanted to let her go.

"I never even got your other letters," she said, shaking her head.

Jack nodded. "I thought as much, your mom really hates me."

Lacey made a face. "Yeah, she kinda does. That's going to take some time to fix."

"There's something I have to tell you," he said, pulling back from her. "No more secrets, right? I never want to have any secrets from you again, ever."

"What? What is it?" Concern flashing through her beautiful hazel eyes.

"I… last night, I…"

She shook her head. "It's OK, I don't need to know."

"No, it's not, OK. I need to tell you. There is this girl who goes to the club. She came over here last night, she'd been mugged, or at least, that's what she said, and I said she could sleep on the couch but she, well, she tried to... but nothing happened, I swear."

Lacey's face fell.

"Nothing happened, nothing at all, but I just wanted you to know." Jack didn't know what Lacey was going to do now. He knew that there was a chance she would run again, or that she wouldn't believe him, or that she'd hate him forever. But he couldn't keep that from her, he couldn't keep thinking about Crystal being here just this morning and not tell her.

Lacey reached out and put her hands on his shoulders. "It's OK, Jack."

"No, no, it's not OK, I should never have let her stay."

"If she told you that she'd been mugged, what were you supposed to do?"

"I don't know, take her to the police station or something?" He ran his hand through his hair.

"You did what you thought was right. Sometimes we do what we think is right, and it turns out not to be what's right after all. You can't blame yourself if you thought your intentions were good."

"I don't know if I'm a good person," Jack said, tears beginning to form in his eyes. "I messed everything up with you, and now this, and I..."

Lacey pulled him closer to her. "You are a beautiful person Jack," she said.

He nodded, choking back the tears. "I messed up, Lace."

"We both messed up. I should have listened to you. I should have let you say what you needed to. I should have let you explain. It would have saved me a lot of tears and heartache. I messed up too, but from now on, if I'm going to mess up, I only want to mess up with you."

Jack grabbed her up in his arms and never wanted to let her go. "I only want to mess up with you too."

She whispered into his ear, "My past is done, and I want you to be my future."

Jack pulled back so he could look at her beautiful beaming face. She'd been crying too, a streak of blue mascara running down her left cheek.

"My past is done, and I want *you* to be my future, too," he said back to her.

"Are you going to let me in or what?" she asked.

And so, Jack opened the door and let her in.

FIFTY-ONE

Goodbyes

"I love you guys," said Jack, wiping his eyes. He was standing outside the door to the book room with a couple of suitcases and Tux meowing unhappily in his carrier. Jack knew it would be years, thirty-three years, until he would see his parents again. Well, he'd see them soon, but not looking like this. His heart was heavy with sadness to be leaving, but so full of gratitude for everything they had done for him.

He knew it had been a risk coming back to see them, but he had to try. The portal had worked, just like Uncle Jack had hoped, and sent him back to the present. There was still a gnawing inside that maybe he wouldn't be able to get back to 1984. But he had to see his folks one more time and tell them goodbye. As much as he loved his new life and Lacey and everything that he had in the past, he loved his parents so much, too.

"We're going to grow up together," said his dad. "I know it seems weird now, trust me, it's weird for us too, but we will never be apart for too long. We will come visit you and Lacey in LA, and you'll see us all the time. We will always be around."

His mom was crying.

"Mom," Jack said, putting an arm around her. "I'll see you in just a few hours."

She just sniffled.

"I'm not going to be like Uncle Jack." Jack shook his head. "I'm going to really make something of myself this time around."

"You have to make your own choices," said his dad. "The best choices you can in each moment."

"I wish you could stay with us," his mom said, tears falling down her softly wrinkled cheeks. "I love you, Jackson. I love you how you are now, and I still love your Uncle Jack, but he's not *you*."

"I know mom, and it's going to be hard for me not having any real parents."

"You'll have Tammy and Janet though, but we'll have no one," his mom cried.

"Patty," his dad said. "This isn't about us, we knew this was going to happen. We've known for a long time."

She nodded. "I know, I'm sorry. It's just after so many years of trying to be strong, sometimes it comes out all in a big rush."

Jack put his arms around his mom. "Mom, I'm always going to be with you."

She nodded.

"And dad, you know we're going to be best friends, right?"

His dad nodded. "I know."

The three of them hugged until his mom stopped crying and his dad started crying, and then they were all crying together.

"It has been an honor to be your dad," said his dad.

381

"It's been the biggest joy of my life to raise you," said his mom.

Jack tried to speak through his tears. "Thank you, thank you for everything. Thank you for all the love, the support, the guidance, the books…"

His dad shook his head. "You're welcome, more than welcome."

Jack picked up his bags and Tux's carrier and pulled the key out of his pocket.

"We love you son, no matter where you are, or *when* you are, we're always with you," his dad said.

Jack dropped his bags, and Tux, and ran one more time towards them, hugging them and holding onto them like he'd never let them go.

"It's time," said his dad, patting his shoulder.

Jack kissed his mom on the cheek, wiped away his tears and put the key into the lock. The door frame shuddered to life and he opened it and stepped through.

And when the door closed behind him, his mom and his dad watched as three flickers of light lit up the bottom of the door, and then all of a sudden stopped, and he was gone.

Interlude V

"There is a problem in time," Sister Helena said frantically as she rushed into the kitchen, still in her nightgown.

"Helena," demanded Sister Maria. "You are in your nightgown. Get dressed at once!"

"I had a dream, a vision!"

Sister Catherine dropped a spoon into the broth she was stirring. "What was it, dear Helena?"

"Well, what was it, child?" asked Maria.

"It's the Order of the Eight."

"What about them?" asked Maria.

"They have time travelled!"

Catherine gasped.

"When?" demanded Maria.

"A long journey forward." Helena clutched at her chest. "I saw a notice on a wall. It said 2, 0, 1, 7."

Sister Maria frowned.

"The distant future!" Catherine had to hold the table, so she didn't fall down.

"What did you see?" asked Maria. "Just tell us, quickly so we can decide if it's important or not."

"Oh, *you* get to decide?" Helena asked. "Do not all three of us get to decide what's important and what is not?"

"Yes, we do. But you have reasons to lie to us, so we must first know if what you tell us is truth or not," Maria said.

Helena felt tears stinging at the backs of her eyes, but she would not cry in front of Maria, never in front of Maria. "I saw a boy. He had the symbol of the Order of the Eight on his arm. He opened the portal and went through."

"How could it be?" asked Catherine. "Have we not enough protections around the portal? Have the Order of the Eights fallen into ruin?"

"If the members of the order are using the portal, then who is protecting it?" Helena put her hand to her forehead.

"We need to fix this at once," said Maria.

"How, Maria?" asked Catherine.

"I will stay here and continue to teach the order. Perhaps there is something we forgot to include in their initiations. You will both travel ahead in time and check on the portal. Catherine, you will go back to some years before this incident and find out where the order is, and if they are protecting the portal. Helena, you go to this time you saw in your dream and find out everything you can."

Helena nodded. She was thrilled at the idea of going so far ahead, but mostly she was glad to finally have some distance from Maria.

Helena had thought Maria would know she was lying. Maria had a special gift for knowing when someone was being dishonest. But Helena had hardly had to lie at all. The dream had been real, she *had* seen a member of the order go into the portal, but she had also seen that his intention had been pure, and that the portal had only opened for him so that he could escape his own persecution in his time.

But Sister Maria didn't have to know that. And now Helena could finally be free of her.

FIFTY-TWO

The Dream

Jack woke up disoriented. He'd had another weird dream about the future, or the past, he couldn't really remember which. He just remembered his dream had felt so real, he almost wasn't sure if it had really happened or not. He tried to hold on to it. His mind grasped at a thread of long red hair, a coffee pot, a pile of books, a flash of light, a sunset. And then, it was gone.

He rubbed his eyes and then flicked them open. It took a moment for his eyes to adjust to the light. The early morning sun was streaming through the spaces between the blinds. He reached over to check his phone for the time and looked down at his hands. His hands were showing signs of age. In his dreams he was always eighteen. It continually came as a shock to him when he woke up and remembered he was much, much older.

He sighed and checked the time. It was only six, so he rolled over to get some more sleep.

"*Jack.*"

"Hmmph?"

"It's time to get up," said a voice.

"Get up for what?"

"For work, you have to go to the diner."

"I don't work at the diner," he said. "That was a dream."

The voice laughed and gentle hands began to nudge him awake.

Jack's eyes flew open and there she was. Older, but just as beautiful, no, even more beautiful, than the day he'd first met her. He grinned. "I must still be dreaming."

She rolled her pretty hazel eyes and put her long red hair into a messy bun. "Come on, stop playing around. You have to get to the diner for the new staff inductions, you always do it."

"I do?"

She pushed his hair back and kissed his forehead. "Yes, it's what makes you a good CEO, and it's why they call you the friendliest man in food."

"Who calls me that?" He opened his eyes wider and looked up at her again. Her beauty never failed to astound him.

She shook her head and gave him a playful grin. "Do you always need me to remind you how wonderful and successful you are?"

"Apparently I do, yes." He grabbed her around the waist and pulled her back into bed.

"You, Jack Forrester, are the incredibly successful CEO of Uncle Jack's plant-based diners in six locations here in California. Oh, and award-winning writer of two cookbooks."

"I am?" he smirked.

"Yes," she said. "Now stop fooling around, you need to get ready."

Jack looked at the large photograph of Santa Monica that was on the bedroom wall. "You're a photographer," he said, the last thirty-three years suddenly flooding back to him.

"Yes, and I've nearly won as many awards for my photography as you have for your food, so don't get smug. But then, I guess I would never have won them if you didn't buy me my first camera all those years ago, so maybe you can share in my success just a little."

"It's all you," he said. "You deserve all the good things in the world." He leaned in and kissed her.

She giggled. "Come on, we don't have time this morning. We have to get ready so we can head straight to Santolsa this afternoon."

"Santolsa?" He climbed out of bed and went to the window. He opened the blinds and found himself looking out over the Pacific Ocean. "That's not Santolsa, that's LA!"

"But we're going back to Santolsa tonight, remember?"

Jack made a groaning sound. "Why on earth would we do that?"

"Because your mom needs you, and you're not just a good CEO, you're also a good son and a good father."

"Father…" Memories of the birth of his two children flooded back. He never thought his heart could grow so big.

She rolled her eyes. "Yes, and Nick and Alexandra are starting school next week at St. Christopher's."

"We made two incredible children," Jack said.

"Yes, and luckily for them, neither of them are quite as crazy as you are."

He took her in his arms and kissed her again. "He fixed the timeline," he said.

She gave him a confused look.

"Everything is fixed!" And he kissed her again.

FIFTY-THREE

The Nuns of Santolsa

"Where do you think you're going, Miss Bates?" asked Mrs. Mitchell, one of the oldest and most evil teachers in the whole school.

Janet rolled her eyes. "Home," she said.

"I don't think so, young lady," said Mrs. Mitchell, spit globules forming in the corner of her mouth.

Gross. "Why not?"

"First of all…"

Oh, here we go, thought Janet.

"Those shoes are not school uniform."

Janet looked down at her thrifted black army boots. "These are all I have."

"And," Mrs. Mitchell continued, ignoring her. "You're wearing too much make-up." She waved a hand at Janet's face.

"It's just a bit of eye-liner. All the girls wear it."

"Not as much as you do."

"Is that all?" Janet knew from experience there was probably going to be more.

"And, there is a rip in your stocking."

Janet sighed. "I can't afford new ones. You *know* that."

"Oh, yes, of course, you're the social services girl."

"Excuse me?" Janet felt the blood rising to her face.

"You can take that tone to detention."

"What? You can't be serious. These are the only clothes I have. You're putting me in detention for being poor?"

"No, I'm putting you in detention for talking back." Mrs. Mitchell passed her a detention slip.

It took everything Janet had not to scream.

"You'll need to hurry if you don't want to be late." The teacher gave her a self-righteous look and walked down the hallway back towards the office.

Janet was about two seconds away from throwing the slip in the trash and just going home anyway when she saw David walking towards her.

"Hey," he said, pushing his floppy dark hair out of his face. "Detention?"

She held up her detention slip and made a face.

"Same." He held up his own detention slip. "What are you in for?"

"Eyeliner and army boots, oh, and a rip in my stocking. Mrs. Mitchell so has it in for me."

"Funny, because those are all the things I like best about you." He gave her a gentle nudge, forcing a smile out of her.

"You?"

"I started a fight in the cafeteria at lunch." He held up his bandaged hand.

Janet winced. "Oh, woah. Are you OK?"

"It sounds cooler than it was. I missed the guy and punched the drinks machine. And yeah, I'm fine. It was just that prick Jefferson again."

"Why do you let him get to you?" Janet asked as they started walking down the hall towards detention.

"He started it."

"You have such a short fuse."

"So do you." He raised an eyebrow at her.

She couldn't disagree with him.

They walked into the English classroom that was always used for detention. Brian Lawrence was sitting looking out the window. He was the only kid who was in trouble more than David. Janet knew him from the trailer park and gave him a wave. And sitting in the front row was the blonde straight edge Julie Jones.

"What's *she* doing in here?" whispered Janet.

"I don't know, but it's nice to have some eye candy in here for once."

"Don't be an asshole," Janet said, punching his arm.

"Just kidding, you know you're the prettiest girl in school, Jan." He gave her a wink.

She shook her head at him and wondered how she could have a crush on such a jerk.

"Take your seats, please," said Sister Catherine's gentle voice from the front of the classroom. Janet and David slid into their usual seats right up the back.

Janet had always liked Sister Catherine. She had her for Religious studies and it was one of the few classes she actually enjoyed. Janet wasn't religious at all, but she liked Sister Catherine. There was something about just being in her presence that made Janet feel like everything was going to be OK.

"We have an hour and forty-five minutes and I thought it might be nice to use the time to build some school spirit. I thought maybe if you learned a bit more about the school, you might be less likely to try to destroy it." She gave Brian a gentle smile and then pulled out a stack of old books. "Did you know this school was originally an abbey built by a group of nuns? Well, they had a bit of help, but mostly those three women built it with their own bare hands."

"Wow," said Brian. "Who cares."

"I wonder, young Brian," Sister Catherine began, "If you would fair very well to put up an entire building in the desert heat?"

"I could totally do it," Brian said. "And I'd make it way better than this stupid school."

"I think it's cool," Janet chimed in. "That a bunch of nuns could put this place up. It's really impressive."

"It is, isn't it, Janet?" Sister Catherine said, giving Janet one of her serene looks that made everything seem just a little bit less terrible.

"I brought some books on the history of Santolsa which I thought you may like to take a look at." Sister Catherine put one of the biggest books on Brian's desk. He ignored it and kept looking out of the window. Sister Catherine gave him a look that was something like pity and sadness and she moved on to place a book on Julie's desk. She opened hers straight away and started reading. She dropped another big book onto David's desk and a much smaller one onto Janet's.

The Nuns of Santolsa

Janet frowned down at the book. Sure, it was cool that nuns had built this school out here in the middle of the desert, but she wasn't sure she wanted to spend her whole afternoon reading all the boring details.

She looked up, but Sister Catherine had pulled up a chair in front of Brian's desk and was talking to him in a hushed whisper.

Janet looked back down at the book and opened it, and there, tucked in behind the book sleeve at the very front of the book, was a key. She looked over at David, who had propped his book up and was hiding behind it while he was trying to engrave something into the desk with his pen.

Janet looked back at her own book and stared at the key blankly. She picked it up and rubbed it between her fingers, and then, not quite sure knowing why, she grabbed it and put it in her pocket.

To be concluded...

Author's Note

I am absolutely amazed, so excited and beyond grateful that you've read *Summer of 1984*. I really hope you enjoyed time traveling with me and that you're excited to read the next and (what I'm *pretty* sure will be) the final instalment!

Writing the Santolsa Saga has been an absolute labor of love. As an indie author, I have no agent, publisher, publicity or marketing team to help get the word out about these books, so if you enjoyed it, it would mean the world to me if you could share a review on Amazon, Goodreads and hey, even go retro 1984 style and tell a friend or lend them your copy!

If you would like to receive occasional love letters and updates from me about books I'm writing and books, movies and music I'm loving, head on over to: www.magicpizza.press and sign up for the newsletter.

If you want to be friends on Instagram you can hang with me at: @victoriamaxwellauthor or drop me a line at: hello@magicpizza.press

Acknowledgments

First up, thank you to everyone who read *Class of 1983* and wrote reviews and/or got in touch to let me know how much you enjoyed it. Your love of this first book was the wind behind the sails of this one. Without you, this book may not exist. You may not think an Instagram comment, DM, email, or a rating on Goodreads means all that much, but it really, truly does, especially for us indie authors.

To my incredible beta readers – you have helped breathe life into this book. Without you, this book would be full of plot holes, bits that only made sense inside my own head, and bizarre grammar. OK, this book still contains some bizarre grammar, but that's kind of just how I write. Thank you so much to Gaby, April, Heather, Amber, Elizabeth, Tammi, Jessica, Louise, Kimmy and Cynthia. Thank you for your time, your helpful feedback, words of encouragement and support, and most of all, thank you for your enthusiasm and love for these stories.

To my magical witchy friends. You are the coven I'm very glad to be stuck with! To Hannah, Lauren, Tamara, Carrie, Vanessa, Emma, Elle, Dot, Gail and everyone else in my Insta-soul-fam community. Thank you for all the readings, healings, magical voice notes and Skype dates. Thank you for helping me to surrender and trust in the universe, and in myself.

To Dad. I wish I could travel back in time and get another thirty-three years with you.

And thank you to my husband, Ian. So much of our own story is in these pages – driving through Death Valley, watching bands at the Viper Room (the inspiration for Illusions), and chasing each other through the sand on Venice Beach on our honeymoon. Thank you for being my biggest fan. You are the Sammy to my Peggy and the Jack to my Lacey. Our love story is my greatest inspiration.

About the Author

Victoria is a YA author, pizza lover and believer in magic.

Her debut YA novel *Class of 1983* hit number one on the Amazon charts and has since gained a cult following.

When she's not scrunchie deep in writing, Victoria can be found watching 80s movies, scouring through thrift stores for vintage treasures, listening to power ballads, going on road trips, and hanging out with rescue cats.

Made in the USA
Middletown, DE
13 December 2019